JIM IS TIRED OF JO'BURG

Jim is Tired of Jo'burg - A Review

I0669541

In this novel, the author revisits and recasts old motifs in a refreshingly unique way. He explores cultural and socio-economic dynamics through the juxtaposition of rural and urban landscapes with remarkable flair of language. He poignantly grapples with the recurring themes of clandestine land deals, rural economy and wealth. It is also a tale of love, deceit and perseverance. At times funny, at times sad, but always captivating, *Jim is Tired of Jo'burg* is an entertaining and edifying read.

Dr Siphiwo Mahala - award-winning author of, among others, the novel "When A Man Cries" ("Yakhal' Indoda"), and the short story collection "African Delights".

Published by:

Write-On Publishing

59 Tom Brown Boulevard
St Francis Bay 6312
Tel: +27(0)422941023
frank@writeonpublishing.co.za
www.writeonpublishing.co.za

Edited by Frank Nunan
Cover Design: Frank Nunan

ISBN: 978-0-6398103-8-6

JIM IS TIRED OF JO'BURG

A NOVEL

BY

MZUVUKILE MAQETUKA

Dedication

*To my loving family -
my wife Hopolang Maqetuka,
my daughter Lindelwa
and grandchild Catina.*

About the author

Mzuvukile Maqetuka was born in 1952 in the town of Graaff Reinet, in the Eastern Cape, a sprawling province of the Republic of South Africa.

He matriculated from Themba Labantu High school in Zwelitsha, near King William's Town, and thereafter enrolled for his BA degree in Accounting and Economics at the University of Fort Hare in Alice.

Owing to involvement in banned student activities in the 1970s, under the auspices of the South African Student Organisation (SASO), he was refused enrolment in his second year and was unable to complete his studies.

Harassed by the apartheid security police and subjected to a string of arrests, detention and a prison sentence served at St Albans Prison in Port Elizabeth, he finally skipped the country after his release from jail in 1979, going into exile. He then underwent military training with Umkhonto weSizwe, the military wing of the African National Congress (ANC) between 1979 and 1990, operating in several countries, including Lesotho, Mozambique, Zambia and Botswana.

In 1990, Mzuvukile left for the United Kingdom, where he enrolled at the University of Westminster, London, for a BA (Hons) Degree in film studies and completed his postgraduate studies in 1994. He came back to South Africa in May of that year, working in various government departments and serving on various company boards until 2012, when he retired.

Mzuvukile is now settled back in his home province of the Eastern Cape, and lives with his wife, daughter and granddaughter.

Other Books by this Author

1. *Impressions of my Hometown Rhafu: A Photographic journey through the Town of Graaff Reinet*, 2012. Xlibris publishers. Re-published in 2019 as *"Impressions of My Hometown"* by Write-On Publishing

2. *Children from Exile and Other Stories: Featuring Oom Asval and His Donkey Cart*, 2015. 1st edition Amazon publishing

3. *The Sahrawis: A photographic book on the Sahrawi refugee camps in Southern Algeria*, 2016. Self-published

4. *I will Write this Story: As short biography of the author's grandparents*, 2016. Self-published

5. *Camdeboo Stories: A collection of short stories on the Camdeboo region of the Karoo*, 2017, first edition: Partridge Publishers; 2nd edition: Self-published

Story Notes

Mythology - a collection of myths, especially those belonging to a particular religious or cultural tradition. In this instance, *Jim is Tired of Jo'burg* could be associated with a cultural, rather than a religious, tradition The myth of a 'Jim comes to Jo'burg' was first explored in the late forties and early fifties. For example, in 1946, renowned South African novelist Peter Abrahams wrote *Mine Boy*, while in 1949, a movie, *African Jim* - dubbed '*Jim Comes to Jo'burg*' - was produced by Donald Swanson and featured Dolly Rathebe in the lead role.

Many times, both recent and past, we have heard of a '*Jim comes to Jo'burg*' mythology in the South African context. The author has deconstructed this myth by reversing it.

"Jim" (Kgabalatsana Monare), who has come to Johannesburg in search of gold, is frustrated by the challenges of city life, to which he is unaccustomed, having grown up in a village. Although he tries, he finds it difficult to adjust to an urban lifestyle fully; as a result, he decides to go back to his village but leaves behind a woman who loves him. She finally decides to follow her lover back home – to a village where she is a stranger. *Jim is Tired of Jo'burg* is a tragedy about village and small-town folk who flock to the cities to make a living, and are trapped by the shackles of a fast paced, alien world so different from their own.

Chapter 1

Leaving the Village

Today, Kgabalatsana was tall for his age. He had started going grey in early adolescence, the white hair protruding from his roots - something that would become his hallmark 'look' later in life and gave him the nickname *Toppie* - old *Manoja* (wise man), though he was still far from being a 'toppie'.

So, by the time he began his long journey in 1960, he already seemed older than his years. This long journey was to be the sequel of the story that had started when he had impregnated Nthabiseng Rethabile, a woman from his village Dinokana, near Zeerust in the former Western Transvaal in the Republic of South Africa. The year 1960 was to be one that would live in his memory for a long time.

On that fateful morning, while he was at school during his first year of secondary school, and unbeknown to him, a delegation of men from the village arrived at his homestead. His father had received a message late the previous night that *rre* Rethabile, Nthabiseng's father, was to dispatch men to report the impregnation of their daughter, and that they put the blame squarely on the young Monare son. After all, it isn't the king who kills you, but his court.

***

Dinokana, a village situated in the Lehurutshe district, was one of the largest villages in the area in the early 1960s, when the event that were to change Kgabalatsana's life forever took place. It was a place of vast historical and cultural significance. For example, there was the Ikalafeng Monument, built by the Bahurutse of Chief Ikalafeng, on the orders of General Pretorius, to symbolise peace between the

Tswana-speaking tribe and the Afrikaners. The monument had originally been a fortification used during the conflict between the two, and the people were, in later years, asked to demolish the fortification and pile the stones 5m high to form what became, and still is, a monument of peace.

Another place of importance worthy of mention was the Dinokana Mission at Lehurutshe, a Lutheran Mission built in 1889. Still standing today, above its altar is an original artwork, a painting of Christ dating back to the foundation year of the church.

Furthermore, there was the Church of St John the Baptist. Built in 1873, this was the third Anglican Church in the country to be built north of the Vaal River.

A national monument, the Hermannsburg Mission at Lehurutshe, is also worth noting. Established in 1859 to serve the Bahurutse of Chief Moiloa, it became both a church and school, at the chief's request. There was also the Kaditshwene Village Ruins, housing the remains of the Hurutshe headquarters and confirming the occupation of this land by the Tswana from the early 1800s.

Perhaps it was this rich genetic heritage that influenced and drove Kgabalatsana Monare, giving him the courage and initiative to venture into things of which a village boy would normally be wary.

***

Five men dressed in faded jackets, all wearing hats and carrying sticks, traipsed into the Monare homestead.

"*Re ka tsena* (may we come in)?" greeted the older man and head of the delegation as he opened the gate into the yard. They were met mid-way by Boysie, Kgabalatsana's elder brother.

"*Le ka tsena bo rra, kga agona dimpsha* (you may come in, gentlemen, there are no dogs)."

He guided them to a seating place under a tree at the side of the yard, where they were joined by Japheth Monare, father to Kgabalatsana and Boysie, and a relative and two neighbours, all of whom shook hands with the visitors, one by one.

"*Dumelang bo rra, le phela joang* (good morning, how are you)?"

"*Re sentse re tshela pele* (we are well)," responded the visitors.

Without much ado, Japheth welcomed the guests as they took sips of *bojwala ba Batswana* (sorghum beer) from a calabash, which was placed before the head of the delegation by women assisting MmaMonare, Japheth's wife.

"*Bo rra*, you are welcome at the Monare homestead and I can see that you look tired from the scorching heat of the Western Transvaal. First, let me thank you for informing us in time about your pending visit here; it has made life much easier for MmaMonare, and the women of the neighbourhood, who have been busy preparing for this visit. In the same vein, let me introduce members of my delegation."

Japheth glanced to his right and said, pointing:

"*Yo ke rre Twala, ke kgaitsedia mogatsake* (this is Mr Twala, a brother to my wife MmaMonare).

"*Gauffi le ene ke rre Mothusi, o nyetse nnakeago mogatse ke* (next to him is Mothusi, who is married to my wife's younger sister)."

The Monare delegation nodded in acknowledgment.

"*Re itumelela go le ntse lontlhe rre Monare* (we are pleased to know you all, rree Monare, and your delegation)," Sentoa, the head of the visiting delegation, responded.

"*Jaanong rre Sentoa, le bewa ke eng fano* (so, Mr Sentoa, what brings you here to the Monares)?"

Sentoa coughed lightly, clearing his throat, and responded:

"As you will know *rra*, as children grow, they mature in age - and maturing in age leads to all sorts of things that have been accepted by society as natural. That is how all or most of us came into being...."

"Mmm," agreed Monare, nodding at Sentoa, who continued.

"We are here as a result of a fall that happened at the Rethabiles. *Rre* Rethabile's daughter fell pregnant. *Mme* Rethabile noticed that the girl's face was starting to swell, and as you will know, women are always the first to notice any such signs from a girl, while we men usually notice certain traits in boys. Interrogating the girl, she then confessed to the family that the person responsible for this fall is your youngest son..."

At this point, there was a pause, with Sentoa whispering to a man next to him, who responded:

"Kgabalatsana."

"Yes, Kgabalatsana," said Sentoa.

"Ummm." A chorus of murmurings from Monare's delegation, while Sentoa pretended not to have noticed. It was then that it became the turn of the Monare delegation to respond to the news, with Japheth taking the floor on behalf of his delegation and as the head of the Monare family.

"Well! Well! Elders from the side of the Rethabile family, I am truly saddened by the affliction caused to the Rethabile family, whom I have known for some time now. As you all know, we attend the same church, the Anglican here in this very village, and we have attended a number of important other functions together here, too. As the old adage goes, 'boys will always be boys'."

There was a chorus of agreement with this statement.

"How true it is, *rre* Monare."

"And as such what has happened, has happened," said another, acknowledging and accepting Monare's viewpoint.

"You are talking like an elderly villager, Monare."

"Whilst this is not good news for the Monare family, I am sure that you, the Rethabile family, did not take this news lightly either," said Japheth.

"But again, what has happened has happened, and we, as the family responsible for the pain , will have to pay back in a manner that all African families do when such a thing has happened. And I would want to believe that at the right time we shall have to assemble to discuss the matter further."

"*O opile kgomo lenaka* (it is like that)," responded a member of the delegation.

"We are pleased with your response, *rre* Monare; we shall convey the good news to the Rethabiles and will revert to you in due course."

***

Meanwhile, three young men, Kgabalatsana Johannes Monare, son to Japheth and MmaMonare, Sechaba Modise and Dira Sekgametse, were walking the gravel roads of Dinokana village on their way back from school, when Sechaba said:

"*Bo rra*, as you might or might not know, we, the Modise family, are an old family rooted in the whole of the Western Transvaal up to Botswana, and as such, over the past few days, a distant relative of mine by the name of Tsepiso Sechedi had interesting things to say.

"Among these was regarding a friend of his, Ronald Diseko, who works for a mining recruitment company called the Native Recruitment Company (NRC)."

The loud talk and traipsing subsided as the boys came to a stop, converging closer to Sechaba, who knew that good actions are more nourishing to youth than words.

"He informed me that this company was founded by the Chamber of Mines in 1902 to acquire unskilled labour to work on the South African mines.

"He went on to say that the NRC has a representative office in Zeerust recruiting young men like us to work in the mines in Johannesburg."

"Work in the mines?" Kgabalatsana interrupted. "Why should young men like us go and work in the mines, when we are still young and have not even finished school? I am only 16 years old and my father will never allow me to do that; he wants me to attend secondary school in Mafikeng and after that to university in Fort Hare."

"But Sechaba, are you sure that this is for us?" asked Dira. "I also agree with Kgabalatsana; we are still young. My parents have greater ambitions for me, my father wants me to be educated, he wants me to be like a White man's child like those who heal cattle, sheep and other animals when they are sick. He wants me to know how to till the land like the fields of the rich farmers in the Western Transvaal."

Sechaba shrugged. "*Bo rra, bo rra*, (gentlemen) listen carefully to what I am saying, this was just information that I heard from Tsepiso. Perhaps I agree with you - he did not say to me that we should, or we should not take the opportunity.

"Who knows? Things might change; we might not be what our parents want us to be, and they might not have the means to take us further than secondary school. I propose that we keep this in our minds and remember the old African adage – 'one who enters the forest does not turn back when hearing twigs breaking in the brush.'"

"There might be truth in what he says; let us give this some thought," said Kgabalatsana.

An hour later, Kgabalatsana approached his home, where he found his father at the gate. As he entered the yard, Japheth yelled at him:

"Kgabalatsana, my boy! What you have done to this family and me is an aberration, a breach of good manners never heard of. At your age, impregnating a girl while you are still at school is a non-starter. How are you going to support her, let alone pay the damages that her family will expect from your mother and me? The Rethabile family are a decent lot, my boy, if you did not know, and for your information, only this morning a delegation was here in this very house of mine, bringing the bad news that their child is pregnant, impregnated by you, Kgabalatsana."

Kgabalatsana's forehead broke into sweat, which he wiped with the sleeve of his shirt. His eyes were fixed on the ground as Japheth threw another volley. "Tell me that it is not true that it is you who did this?"

"I do not know, *rra*."

"You say you do not know? They know you, and the Rethabile girl knows you, and she has confessed to her parents that it is you who impregnated her.

"Look at this kraal, my boy, it is getting empty, and the cattle are emaciated cadavers as a result of the drought that has been hitting us. The planting season is just around the corner, but the soil is scorched and I know not how one can plough in such conditions. The rivers are dry and there is no grazing land anymore worth mentioning here, Kgabalatsana.

"We are already struggling and you have done this terrible thing Let me remind you that what you have done to that family is something that you have to put right. There will be a child, who will need support and shall, and I say, *shall*, be your sole responsibility, for you have chosen to be a man. Where will you get the means to do so when you yourself are still under the support of your own family?

"Let me remind you that if we stand tall, it is because we stand on the backs of those who came before us."

Japheth continued showering Kgabalatsana with questions, not expecting him to answer, knowing that even if you know many things, you do not argue with the judge.

"Get out of my sight," said his father. Kgabalatsana, dragging his feet, eyes fixed on the ground, proceeded towards the house, where his mother was standing at the door. As she stepped aside for her son, she spoke softly.

"Your father is hurt, my son. I do not know what you will have to do to heal the wound in his heart - and it is not good for his health."

Leaving his parents' house, Kgabalatsana went to the hut he shared with his brother, Boysie. He threw his school bag onto the floor and collapsed on the bed, his mind meandering through the day's events.

The *first* flashback was the discussion brought about by Sechaba Modise.

The *second* was the recent confrontation with his father and the news about the impregnation of Nthabiseng.

***

Diseko began his introduction with a wry smile.

"Welcome to the Native Recruitment Corporation, Zeerust - the regional offices for the Western Transvaal. My name is Ronald Diseko, the Assistant Regional Manager."

"Welcome also to my close friend, Tsepiso Sechedi, who is your relative, Sechaba," he shifted his eyes to Sechaba. "We have been having discussions about creating a future for young people of the region – as carriers beyond their formative school years, so to speak. And we agreed with Tsepiso, who, as Sechaba would know, has been one of our most successful employees, working in one of our mines in the Orange Free State, in the Goldfield Mines. Now, *bo rra*, here is what you have been called to hear."

Mouths gaped in anticipation of good news.

"In a few weeks, there will be a new group of recruits, some of whom have already signed for employment."

He took a pile of files from his desk, brandishing them in front of his young audience.

"To be precise, the next group will be leaving for Johannesburg towards the end of the month of November.

"But before I come to that part, let me sketch for you what Teba is all about and what it has done for millions of people here in Southern Africa. It creates a lifeline that creates wealth for families...."

He pointed at a Mission and Vision Statement hanging on the wall on frosted glass, reading:

"Serving Mines, Enriching Communities."

"Our recruited employees have no sleepless nights – neither for themselves nor their families. Our mines in Johannesburg offer a lifestyle of which you have neither seen nor heard. The place is not called the City of Gold for nothing. You will live like princes and kings. So, gentlemen, the call is yours, our doors are opened. Think about the offer and we can have another day of discussion; that day, I believe, will be the day on which you sign your contracts."

With these dulcet tones, he captured the imagination of the young men before him.

"This sounds exciting," said one, while another chipped in: "Are men allowed to come with their wives or girlfriends to the mines?"

Diseko, looking a little uncomfortable, replied:

"Unfortunately not, *rra*. You see, the laws of the country forbid African men from migrating into the urban areas with families. The urban centres, such as Johannesburg, are places for white people to live in, whereas we Africans only are there because of our labour. Again, as I said, unfortunately the company is just following the laws set out in Pretoria and Cape Town. I hope I have answered your question, *rra*."

"You have answered my question, *rre* Diseko, and it will be our duty to mull over the information you have given us. We will come back to you through Sechaba, of course."

As they left the offices of the NRC, on their way back to the village, Kgabalatsana's mind was frantic with the events that had occurred in the last few hours.

He arrived home and went straight to the hut, rheumy-eyed, throwing his belongings on the bed. He stayed on the bed, staring at the roof, until he fell into a long, restless sleep, woken only the following morning by a knock at the door, even before his usual daily timekeeper, the crowing cock.

Kgabalatsana stumbled out of bed and shuffled towards the door, still half-asleep. He unlocked it to find his father standing there. A moment later, he felt a piercing slap between his eyes as he was pushed back into the hut. Falling on the floor, he doubled up in pain as kicks were aimed at his ribs and stomach.

"*Mmme! Mmme!* They are killing me," he cried out.

In the distance, he heard his mother shouting.

"Stop this nonsense, *rra*! Stop this nonsense, what are the people going to think of this house?"

She pulled her husband from Kgabalatsana, walking with Japheth out of the boys' hut towards their own.

"This boy needs to know who the head of this family is, MmaMonare."

"But not through assaulting the child, Japheth; he is still our child," responded MmaMonare. They went into the house, Japheth breathing heavily.

The words of his father – and the beating – would be with him for a long time. Indelible in his sub-conscious was the warning that surfaced again and again:

"There will be a child, my son, who will need to be support-ed; and this shall be your responsibility."

Clearly, he had crossed swords with his father. He was now going to be a father in his own right and thus needed to discuss his plans with Nthabiseng. It was at this juncture that he decided to meet with Nthabiseng to share with her his dilemma.

***

As the sun rose to the middle of the blue Western Transvaal sky, Kgabalatsana and Nthabiseng were seated on the banks of the river which cut through their village. This was a favourite rendezvous spot of theirs, which they had used for some time. Kgabalatsana looked at her stomach and caressed it with the softest of hands. Her whole body cringed.

"Please *rra*, do not do this to me." But she gave the slightest of satisfied smiles.

"*Moratiwa* (my dear), this is the most satisfactory moment in my whole life - to find myself seated next to you, as you are different today."

"What has happened and what have I done to deserve such compliments?"

"Many, many things; but primarily, you are now the mother-to-be of my child."

Nthabiseng looked away for some time, not speaking.

"I shall not go into the reasons why you did not tell me that your family would be coming to my home to report your pregnancy, for that has already happened; nonetheless, you are different to me at this very moment."

Nthabiseng turned to face him.

"Unfortunately, I did not know that the visit would take place either. My parents – my father, in particular – were very discreet about organising this. It wasn't done at our place, although I noticed that something was going on.

"All the preparations were conducted at *Ntate* Mashigo's house, a very close family friend. Even the delegation that went to your place went there from the Mashigo household. *Mme*, of all people, was also non-committal as if she knew nothing. She only raised the matter of my pregnancy in passing with me once."

"I never wanted to cast any aspersions on you, my dear, and if it is any consolation, I know that any seed planted into that womb would be mine. But there are other developments that have taken place in my life at home now.

"As a result of this, there are serious complications between my father and me."

Nthabiseng's mouth went slack, and she appeared alarmed, but recovered quickly.

"And what does that then mean?"

"I have decided that I will have to leave home."

"Leave home. No! Oh, no! Do not say that to me, *rra* - you are now hurting me."

"Listen carefully, *moratiwa* (dear), our situation has changed.

"There is a third person who will soon come into our lives; we have to think beyond the two of us now..."

Nthabiseng interrupted him impatiently.

"True, but what does that have to do with you leaving home? We could still think about him or her while together here in the village, and I have heard and believe that children are a reward for life?"

"That child has to be fended for, food has to be bought, nappies and clothing, and medicines too. The question is – what means do we have to deliver all these goods to the child? The answer is that, as the father of this child, I must leave school and go to work to support my new family. The upshot of this, *moratiwa*, is that I will have to go and seek work in the mines of Johannesburg."

"Johannesburg, you said, *rra*. Did I hear you properly? Over my dead body! No! Not that place!

She shrieked loudly, but quickly recovered her composure - Nthabiseng was a strong, practical girl. She breathed deeply and then looked squarely at Kgabalatsana.

"I have heard horrible stories about men from the villages of our region who went to look for work in that city and they either never come back to their villages, or they forget about their families, or they die paupers there. No, *rra*, tell me something else."

"It is true, what you have heard, and we have all heard such stories. But it is equally true that there are also those who come back home every Easter or December holidays; you see them in the streets of Zeerust, prosperous, walking tall, with pockets full of money. Nthabiseng, you have to trust me, for I have a reason for going to Johannesburg, and it is to work for my family, trust me on that, and this is the vow that I make to you."

After these words, she mellowed a little, with a hint of a smile.

"I understand you now, *rra*. And I put all our trust in you. You have never disappointed me and I, therefore, cannot expect that because you live far from me that I should doubt you, *rra*.

So, now, when are you planning to leave?"

"I, Sechaba Modise and Dira Sekgametse are in consultation with the office of the Native Recruitment Corporation, which is responsible for the recruitment of miners in Zeerust. We have been informed that we would be leaving for Johannesburg at midnight on 20 November."

"That is rather soon."

"Unfortunately. it is a fact."

"It is a sad day for me, it is sad news that you have just told me. Since the day I realised that I was pregnant, I started to dream of us. I dreamt of the family we would be building and more and more children and of a place of our own. Clearly these were but dreams."

She crossed both her hands on her chest.

"I was building castles in the air. I did not think of how all these dreams were going to be realised. Now I understand that families are not built on dreams only; they are built out of means and the means here is money. It's sad for me to think that you will be away from 'us', in a faraway place."

At that point, Kgabalatsana kissed Nthabiseng and brought her close to him. They fell on their backs, kissing and fondling for some time, before a shepherd driving his flock nearby whistled, not realising that he was intruding. The couple leapt to a seated position, waiting for the boy to pass by.

"With the clearest of consciences, *rra*, I now fully understand the decision that you have taken, and so let it be."

***

Kgabalatsana realised that he had been silent for a long time and was almost unaware of how engrossed he had been in playing back the events of the past few months. Now, he stood at the threshold of a future unknown to him.

The family of Kgabalatsana Monare believed that he had committed a grave social blunder. This, thanks to the unfortunate shadow it had cast on his reputation and character, was what caused him to be in this place now, at this ungodly hour.

The tower clock of the Nederduitse Gerevormeerde Kerk, nestled in the centre of the *dorpie* (small town) chimed midnight on that sweltering evening as the Teba mining recruitment agency's bakkie set out to carry the men on their long journey to the mines of the City of Gold, Johannesburg.

Kgabalatsana Monare, also known as Johannes, crammed together with two of his friends, Sechaba Modise and Dira Sekgametse and others from adjoining villages, whose names Kgabalatsana never cared to know, were all like sheep going as innocent and ignorant sheep at an abatoir. They were naïve village boys; their only preoccupation the fancy words used by the recruitment agent to woo them to Jo'burg, where roads were made of gold, and which never sleeps – that's what he had said, and that was the tempting mythology about this greatest of South African cities.

They travelled through the night while Kgabalatsana reminisced about his childhood and thought anxiously about what lay ahead of him. Most of the future lay blank, and tears fell down his cheeks. His dreams of school and university – gone, like dust.

Dira consoled him by patting his back.

He kept gazing towards the front of the bakkie, sometimes picking up the blurred outline of the driver's face from the dim light of the dashboard. From time to time, the driver would shout back to them, through the window: "We are still going fine, gentlemen!"

He never asked how they were, or if they needed anything.

Chapter 2

At the Mine

It was the crack of dawn when Kgabalatsana saw dim lights on the far-distant horizon and heard the driver shouting.

"Do you see those lights up there? That is Johannesburg! That is the City of Gold; brace yourselves for a new dawn - you are now entering the New Jerusalem."

As the sparkling lights lit the streets, mingling with the kaleidoscopes of scattered neon signs hanging on buildings, and tracing diamonds on the black surface covering the roads, Kgabalatsana noticed how suffocating the air was. He had been used to the clean, crisp air of the Western Transvaal, even where, in certain parts of their main town, Zeerust, there were lights such as these.

"Is this really the place called the City of Gold?"

After a long drive through a labyrinth of streets, they drove down a street which appeared to be taking them away from the city. The roads were becoming darker, and the flickering neon lights from the shop windows had disappeared as they drove into a dead-end street that led to a large gate, where the driver shouted at them:

"Mzilikazi Mine! Mzilikazi - we have arrived."

Outside the gate was a guard, carrying a baton and wearing a helmet. He waved the bakkie to a stop and shouted at them, too.

"*Yima wena lapha* - stop just there."

The driver slammed on the brakes in front of him. The guard was joined by a tall, hefty, scruffy white man in his thirties - somewhat reminiscent of cowboys from Texas. He went to the driver's side of the bakkie and greeted the driver.

"Welcome Stephan, we did not expect you so soon. Zeerust telephoned us when you left and here you are already." He looked at the passengers at the back, scratching his tangled red beard – the facial hair earning him his sobriquet, *Rooibaard* (red beard).

"It's a full load for this time of the year, Stephan; you are keeping us busy."

"It shows that business is booming and Zeerust is working hard, *baas* (boss) and people love our company."

"Tip your men out of the bakkie, Stephan. Banda," he said, addressing the guard, "count them and queue them inside the yard."

"*Wena phuma lapha* and *ngena pha* (out of the bakkie and wait inside the gate)," Banda directed the men as they jumped out of the bakkie with their knapsacks and suitcases and went through the gate to wait in line.

It was a strange place to Kgabalatsana, who was standing in the front row next to Sechaba.

The mine compound was surrounded by yellowish sand dunes, which later he came to understand was sand which had come out of the mine itself, accumulated over years.

"Is this the place called a mine?" he asked Sechaba.

"It is, Kgabalatsana, what else could it be?" responded his friend.

When they had all disembarked, *Rooibaard* and Banda led the men into the compound towards an office block. They were made to stand in a queue outside the office block when Kgabalatsana heard footsteps on the gravel road. Roughly 25 men shuffled past, dressed in blue overalls, helmets attached to their waists, hanging onto each other as if about to fall, eyes looking straight in front; so focused that they wouldn't have noticed a fly on either side of their faces.

Kgabalatsana was stunned by the fixated manner of their walk. They were quietly, sonorously, murmuring a song:

We are the workers of Mzilikazi.
The toilers of the deep mother earth.
It is we who are the creators of wealth.
And we love our work even if we know that we are
the least paid.
We know. We know.

They were led by two *indunas* (foremen or headmen) with clubs clutched in their hands.

Banda, seeing Kgabalatsana transfixed by the spectacle, yelled cheerfully, with a hint of mischief:

"Your turn will come when you will also be marching with that pride, when you will be among the greatest gold diggers like them. I only hope that this will come sooner than I die or you die under the belly of the earth. First things first. Pay attention to what you are here for."

And so, they waited.

***

The man was seated behind what used to be a grand mahogany table. It retained some dignity, owing to its wood; but it stood now on bricks. It must once have brought great pride to its owner.

But it was not clear to Kgabalatsana if Shearling, the young mine employee behind the desk, thought much of it, as it was old. It appeared that Shearling regarded the table as merely a work place – one at which he had been sitting for hours, and where, for the umpteenth time, he had been registering scruffy rural peasants who had come to this city in search of a means of survival. One by one, the men were called into the office.

"Name and surname *madala* (old man)?" he asked Johannes, who was standing in the front row, the first to be called in. He looked around as Shearling lifted his hand and repeated his question with emphasis and in *fanagalo* - the mine language which is a conglomeration of various languages:

"*Hey, wena miner, le betso who*? (You miner, what is your name?)"

Johannes, as he would now be known, fiddled with his hands, hesitating, not sure what to say as Shearling stood up from his seat. Remembering himself, Kgabalatsana regained his composure and answered.

"Johannes Monare, *baas*."

Shearling smiled, shaking his head and addressed him:

"You seem to be learning quite fast; that is the way to address me. The respect and dignity you bestow on your superiors is important here for your career. How I wish all of you were like him," he said, looking at the others.

The process of registering the men was painstaking, as some of them needed interpreters, and it was several hours before they were finished and had been handed work card permits – passes permitting them to leave and enter the mine, receive their pay and, most importantly, which would function as security/identity documents for the duration of their employment at the Mzilikazi Mine. The following words were inscribed on Kgabalatsana's card:

NAME: Johannes Monare
Employee Number: 50005
Employer: Mzilikazi Mine, Johannesburg
Date: 21 November 1960

To some, if not most of the men, it was intriguing that Shearling ascribed so much significance to the document.

"Keep this document safe and with you at all times, in the compound and most importantly, outside the mine. Without this piece of paper, you are nothing. And by the way, you might find yourself in jail, with a sentence of not less than three months' hard labour if you are found without it and deemed to be in an urban area without the necessary permits. Do you see the blue stamp across the card? It is worth a million pounds to you. You are warned. Do you have your *dompas* (pass) with you, Johannes?" asked Shearling.

"I do not have what you are asking me for, *baas*. In our village, we do not carry them."

Shearling shook his head.

"They will take you to the Bantu Affairs Commissioner office in Noord Street, where you have to apply for one. Anyone who does not have this book will have to do the same."

Kgabalatsana found it strange that he had to have a number, and a piece of paper, *nogal,* and he wondered why his name was not sufficient for identification. The dompas was a legal document required by all black South Africans – but in rural areas, people could get away without carrying them.

Directing Banda to get moving, Shearling turned to the recruits. "All of you will be housed in Section 2 of the compound. Your rations, blankets and one pillow per person have already been prepared; you will find them in your dormitory. Banda, show them the way."

Parrot-fashion, as if a trained robot, Banda barked out the orders: "*Hey wena, hamba lapha* (you, go that way). *Wena, ngena pha* (you, go to your section)."

Kgabalatsana was shocked by the language, which was foreign to him. It was only later that they learned about *fanagalo.*

As Banda opened the dormitory door, the men, having driven through the night in an open-air bakkie, filling their lungs with fresh air, gagged and cupped their hands around their noses at the stench and closeness of the rooms.

"Hey, *nina* (you lot), no time to play here, there is work to be done," Banda shouted.

Kgabalatsana began to realise that he was in another world. At home, he had slept in a decent bed most of his days. But here there were only double and triple bunks lined along the wall of compound Section 2. This was his new home. He glanced at Dira and shook his head. Dira shrugged.

Kgabalatsana whispered to Sechaba, who was already putting his suitcase on the bed next to his, "Do you know what is going to happen to us now? Will they allow us to rest? And what did Banda mean when he said that there is work to be done?"

"Like you, Kgabalatsana, I have no clue, and it seems that there is nobody who is going to tell us."

Just then, there was a crescendo of shouts from outside the nearby hall. Groups of men in single files were marching past the building, like a formation of soldiers going to war, their footsteps in unison, like a marching drill. This time, Sechaba noted, the group was quiet and not singing, and they looked tired.

"That is another morning shift reporting for duty, going to the cage that will take them underground," Banda said, noticing Sechaba's interest.

"Some of you will be getting used to that, just like them, while others might chicken out of this business. Mine working is not for women. And I hope all of you will learn that fast. Welcome to Mzilikazi Gold Mine."

He left the hall and the men began to settle, sitting among their unpacked bags and suitcases. A minute later, Banda's voice boomed outside the door again.

"Section 2 miners, get ready for the next order."

Banda reappeared.

"Stand to attention!" he shouted, coming into the room with two white men, *Rooibaard* and Shearling, who gave instructions. "One, two, three, four, five, six. Step outside."

Kgabalatsana was number four and they stepped outside of the hall, waiting for the next order.

Rooibaard came out of the hall where all the men were standing in three groups. He came to Kgabalatsana's group, looking intensely at each of them.

When he came to Kgabalatsana, he started scrutinising his feet, turning around him and then said: "Open your mouth, Johannes." The latter obeyed, opening his mouth so wide that *Rooibaard* could see the bottom of his jaw. He poked his teeth with the baton that he was holding.

"You have the teeth of an ox, Johannes." *Rooibaard* walked to each of the men, examining them carefully, and then shouted:

"All of you have been assigned to work under Shearling and your shift starts at 10 am." Shearling was by then standing next to the group, at attention.

Without waiting for *Rooibaard* to finish talking, he started marshalling the group to step aside.

"From here we all march to the other side of this building, where Shaft 2 is located, but before that, in the next ten minutes, Banda and others will be bringing you your working gear, which you will put on before being taken to the cage at 9.30 am to go underground." Shearling's voice was unusually soft.

Banda and his crew arrived with the packs, placing one in front of each man.

Shearling continued: "Now that you all have your packs, you have only ten minutes to go and change for the work ahead - the reason you came to Mzilikazi - and report back near Shaft 2. Banda will show you where it is and you will wait for us there."

Kgabalatsana was surprised by the precision with which these men had prepared for their arrival. He was not used to this type of routine, which seemed to be the order of the day.

"I have to pull through. I came here for one reason and that reason is for the future of Nthabiseng and the child," he thought morosely.

As they were standing in a queue next to the shaft, all dressed in their new garb, Kgabalatsana looked at his two friends and shook his head. He smiled at Sechaba.

"Remember, *rra*, it is because of you that we are here, you brought the idea of us coming to work in the mines. We have now arrived."

"Do you regret it, *rre* Kgabalatsana?"

"On the contrary, *rra* Sechaba. I have assigned myself a new mission in life and that is moving forward and not looking back. I left a family in Dinokana and as such, I will have to do the best that I can."

"Attention miners!" shouted Banda, as he walked to the front of the group.

"The hour of destiny has now arrived. Your new task will now begin. We are now going to march towards the shaft. When I count to three, you will all walk in two's please, and make space between each other. I do not want to hear a word from anyone; no sound but the shuffling of your new boots on the gravel road to the shaft. Miners, one, two, three, march forward!"

The group were a few metres from the shaft when the man, a Mosotho, marching next to Kgabalatsana suddenly fell to the ground. Shearling instructed one of his Mosotho foremen, Kgotso, to pour water on the man, as there was no time to waste.

"He will be OK in a second; we are used to the type, and it's just the shock of hearing that he is going underground."

As the group arrived at the entrance of the shaft, they waited for a second whilst Kgotso, who was guiding the Mosotho man, joined the group, together with Mzimela, a Swazi from Pilgrim's Rest in the Eastern Transvaal and Joseph, who was to be Kgabalatsana's foreman underground - and soon, a close friend.

After this they were assigned to their different groups and taken to a part of the compound where the teams were given orientation into their tasks. Kgabalatsane was assigned to Joseph where he was shown how the drilling machine worked and how the logs supporting the roof of the mine where they would be working in the underground were mounted.

It was this task that he was to perform permanently as a miner. When later he asked Joseph how they knew who was to do what, his answer was simple: "Everything here is done for a reason, and everyone assigned is based on that reason. Take note of that as it will take you far in your life as a miner. Look at how this machine works."

The shaft went down into the belly of the earth. The place was dark, only slightly illuminated by the torches attached to their helmets. The suffocating damp soil caught at Kgabalatsana's throat slightly as the cage came to a halt. Shearling unlocked it and they all disembarked to be readied for their very first task underground.

He switched on the heavy-looking drilling machine. Kgabalatsana closed his ears as the drilling machine kicked in, penetrating the hard rock. While he was watching Joseph with envy, Joseph switched it off and handed it over to Kgabalatsana. He showed him where the on/off switch was located and how he should switch it on.

Kgabalatsana did as he was told, but as soon as it kicked, he almost lost his hold. Joseph sprang forward, holding Kgabalatsana's hands together to stop the machine slipping from his grasp. Kgabalatsana pulled himself together and held the machine tightly to his body. Sweat dripping from his forehead, he doggedly gained control of the machine and felt the first flush of enjoyment as he drilled and pierced through rock.

"*Yibambe kahle* (hold it properly), Monare!" screamed Mzimela, encouraging Kgabalatsana to persevere.

Kgabalatsana continued drilling, now handling the machine with confidence until Joseph told him to stop. "From now on, I can see you will be a master driller, Monare. You handled the baby well and perhaps it was the right thing that the machine scared you."

Joseph became a friend to Kgabalatsana – it was as if he was sent from heaven. His demeanour, his modesty and the way they had struck a chord with each other from their first meeting underground pleased him; though he knew that, as far as long-term friendships went, only time would tell.

At the end of their shift, they were hoisted from the underground as the cage shaft shot up. As they reached the ground above, they emerged from the cage one by one, some dragging their feet while carrying their helmets. Kgabalatsana's head dipped forward, his neck and shoulders stiff and sore from the strength and power of the drilling machine. The new recruits loped back to their quarters, half-drunk with exhaustion.

Kgabalatsana was excited to share his experience with Dira and Sechaba, who were in separate underground groups.

"*Banna* (gentlemen), was I not scared when the damn cage was locked? Then the shaft going down into the underground. My head was spinning and I prayed till I heard it lock on the ground, then opened my eyes. Was I not relieved that I was still alive?

"Then came the drilling. It took our foreman, Joseph, an old hand at underground mining and an experienced driller, to orientate me about the job at hand. Kgabalatsana was also excited by the speed with which he learned. He was growing in confidence, feeling that he enjoyed the work – and had made the right decision to come to Johannesburg.

Dira, on the other hand, was not as positive.

"Banna, I do not want to lie, this is not the job for me. I am too small in limb, making it difficult for my body to cope with the strenuous nature of my task. The drilling, from the time the machine started, vibrated my body and limbs.

"I could feel my intestines shaking inside my stomach, my head was spinning and I do not know how I managed to stay conscious. By then, my eyes were half-closed, not knowing whether the drill was in the right position. My induna kept on asking me if I was alright. And when I told him that I was fine, he kept on saying, 'If you cannot cope on the first day, it means you are not fit for the job, Dira, but I will see how it goes.'"

"I know, my friend; after all, we forced you into this thing," said Kgabalatsana. "Me too, I was sceptical at first about coming here. But here I am today and I do not regret it. I am sure that you will be telling a different story soon."

He patted Dira on the shoulder.

"You would have changed your mind instantly if you had been with Joseph. In my short experience, Joseph showed himself to be the type of leader who finds solutions quickly, when he sees something go wrong. Do not worry, Morena, for I think you are just too hard on yourself."

Kgabalatsana grinned. "To me, the experience was as a dish fit for Gods – a game of two equal halves, in which my ancestors were looking after me."

They were dead tired by this time. At first, the chatter was animated, coming from all directions, with much joking and talking about their experiences. Kgabalatsana was sleeping on the bottom bunk, Dira in the middle and Sechaba on top. Kgabalatsana realised that Sechaba was becoming quieter and quieter, and so he continued talking to Dira. After a few minutes, Kgabalatsana realised that he was talking to himself. With Dira softly snoring, he realised that he was the only one awake. Kgabalatsana opened his small suitcase, which contained clothing and the little he was able to pack. He took out a pen and piece of paper, using the suitcase as a writing table. Sechaba stirred awake, watching.

"What is that supposed to mean now, Kgabalatsana, are you remembering your school days in the village high school - gone are those days, *rra*." Kgabalatsana ignored his friend and concentrated on what he was doing. He began to write.

Mzilikazi Mines
P.O. Box 1302
Booysens
Johannesburg
21 November 1960

My Dearest Nthabiseng
I hope with the sincerity of my heart that this letter will find you and the baby in good health. I cannot wait to see that tender little thing in my arms or watch her/him sucking the

mother's breasts. This is the end of my first working day at the Mzilikazi Mines, the day when we are both far apart, with no chance of us meeting before we sleep, as we used to. Distance is the thief in this instance. I write to you with a deep feeling that my mind will not rest until I have again repeated my deepest love for you; more so knowing that in that womb you carry our child.

I had my first experience working underground, and it was an experience words cannot fully tell, safe to say that I had a good day and this first day worked well for me. And I have to confess as I rest on my bed writing this letter that my body aches like it has been smashed with hammers. How pleasurable it would have been for you to have been here to soothe the stiffness out of it.

Enough about myself.

How are you and what have you been doing with yourself since I left? Please reply to this and tell me that you are doing well.

As I promised you when I left home, you will always be in my heart.

So long, my love

Kgabalatsana Monare

He finished writing the letter, folded it, kissed it and after that put it in an envelope. He licked the sticky side, sealed it and exclaimed:

"This goes for you *moratiwa*, fly postman to Zeerust." He placed the envelope carefully in his suitcase, locked the lid and shoved the case under the bed. The clock struck 10 pm as the lights were switched off and he fell into a deep slumber.

At 5 am the following morning, chimed by the booming mine clock, Kgabalatsana opened his eyes and looked around him as light flooded the big, dirty windows of their quarters. The light was blinding compared to the relative duskiness of his cosy hut at home, which had only one small window permitting the morning sun to enter. A man

Jim is Tired of Jo'burg

coughed and Kgabalatsana realised that it was the beginning of another day. His first morning waking up far from home. By this time, everyone was stretching and sighing their way out of sleep.

A bell rang and an induna was shunting back and forth outside the hall, shouting.

"*Ga gona kgomo ya boroko* (sleep is for the lazy), *wena vuka* - wake up.*" He rang the bell intermittently as his voice died away.

At 6 am, the men had finished washing up and were in the dining room - a long wide building lined with steel tables. From outside, the miners filed into the kitchen area two-by-two, where cooks, dressed in white uniforms, were ready to serve them soft mealie-meal porridge and slices of bread.

Breakfast was served on tin plates, with black coffee to go with the two thick slices of brown bread. After collecting their meals, the men sat at the tables.

That day's routine was identical to the procedure followed previously: Into the cage and down the shaft. But, to Kgabalatsana's surprise, Joseph handed the drill to him without uttering a word, watched with interest by Mzimela, who later related the event to his comrades:

"Kgabalatsana took the machine from Joseph with no hesitation, confident about what to do with it. He switched it on, it kicked and pierced through the black rock, which fell in big lumps in front of my feet. He fulfilled his task with the confidence that said, 'I am ready to be reckoned with.' As he took a break, *Rooibaard* came to him and patted him on his shoulder and said, '*Jy's 'n man, Johannes, ek kan sien* (you are a man, Johannes, I can see).'"

Mzimela patted him on the shoulder, too, smiling as he told the story.

Days and nights went by until one Thursday morning, as they were reporting for duty, Joseph came whispering in Kgabalatsana's ear:

"Prepare yourself. Tomorrow is Saturday- it has been a fortnight, and we will be getting paid. I need to go to the city to pay my accounts, and I would love you to accompany me."

Kgabalatsana did not hesitate.

"Yes, _rra_, I will. After all, there is a letter I need to post to Zeerust."

"You can do that at the Jeppe Post Office, it will be faster than posting it here in the compound post box," Joseph responded.

That Saturday, as soon as they had finished their breakfast, they left the compound, traipsing out of the gate with Joseph dressed in a style that Kgabalatsana never forgot. He was wearing a khaki shirt and matching khaki trousers, fastened with a brown and white stretch belt. His shoes were brown and white Crocket & Jones. Kgabalatsana envied this style of dress; he smiled and said:

"I hope that one day I will dress like you, Joseph."

"Your day will come soon, my friend."

As they walked through the streets of the city, Joseph, with a wide smile on his face, kept patting Kgabalatsana on his shoulder and hugging him. Kgabalatsana later noticed that at work, Joseph was Joseph the foreman and his senior, but as soon as they were off-duty, Joseph was just an ordinary man like him.

"Look, even now he has invited me to go with him to the city," Kgabalatsana later told his friends.

At the bus stop, which was just a short distance from the mine, Kgabalatsana realised the type of man Joseph was, for the moment Joseph stepped on the bus, the driver almost jumped out of his seat.

"_Sawubona_ - greetings Joseph!"

A commuter seated nearby also acknowledged the man, crying:

"_Dumela rra Joseph awu!_ (greetings Mr Joseph). Oh, yes, the man from the underground."

"*Dumelang bo rra.* (Good morning, sirs)."

It was "*Bra Joseph hier, Bra Joseph daar* (Brother Joseph here, Brother Jospeh there)." And he was all smiles as he shook hands with them.

"The first one who greeted me used to work in the mine before he left for a job in the factories," Joseph told Kgabalatsana.

"That one, I met him in the city; he was working, but do not ask me working doing what? You saw how he is dressed. He is always dressed like that, with his briefcase. But do not worry, Monare, you will get to know the sort here in Jozi."

Their first stop was in Bree Street, where Joseph went into a shoe repair shop to pick up his shoes, and from there they went straight to the Jeppe Post Office. On arrival, Joseph took coins from his pocket and gave them to Kgabalatsana. They went to the counter, where it was Joseph who talked to the post assistant, saying, "One postage stamp to Zeerust, *rra.*"

Watching Joseph negotiate his way around the place with ease, Kgabalatsana realised that he would have been lost without his friend's help. Joseph showed him how to post the letter, pointing to the big, round steel box outside the Post Office. Kgabalatsana slipped the precious letter into the box.

"It's gone to Zeerust now, my friend," Joseph smiled at the puzzled Kgabalatsana.

Further along, Joseph paused at a corner clothing shop.

"You see this shop, Kgabalatsana, it was the very first where I bought some of my earlier clothes. It was a craze amongst us neophytes in Johannesburg, and I still buy here at times."

"Why have you stopped frequenting it?"

"There are newer ones and they all compete in prices and the fashion seasons, so it depends on who gets his stock first."

Kgabalatsana wondered how long it had taken Joseph to get to know all of these shops and city street corners – and how much longer it would take him to do so. Clearly, Joseph was an old hand at city living and had worked at various mines before settling at Mzilikazi.

"You see, Kgabalatsana, walking in the streets of Johannesburg can be quite tricky. You must always be careful when you cross the streets because as you can see, these cars drive fast and the streets are wide. Look at this Eloff Street now," he said, as they were about to cross the street. "Wait here," he said and walked across the street. Sweat dripped down Kgabalatsana's face as he realised that Joseph had crossed already, leaving him to learn to cross the busy road by himself.

"Cross now, Kgabalatsana," he shouted from across the street. Kgabalatsana took one step forward just as an oncoming car screeched its tyres in front of him.

"*Voetsek*!" screamed a loud voice from the car window as the driver swerved past, impatient. Kgabalatsana took two tentative steps forward, with Joseph still shouting loudly at him.

"Run, Kgabalatsana, run!" He heard the voice drifting faintly until he found himself next to Joseph, who patted him on the shoulder in triumph.

"Man, *rra*!" panted Kgabalatsana. "This is never going to be an easy ride for me in the city of the white man. I am an ordinary Motswana village boy from Dinokana. This thing you call traffic just confuses me."

In a typically calm and collected voice, Joseph reassured his young friend.

"Well, traffic and wide streets confused us all in our early days here in the City of Gold, but here I am today, teaching you. It's just a matter of time – you will get used to it and I will not be surprised one day to hear that you are one of the clever men of Jozi."

"Speaking of which, I have noticed that your dress style is different from mine. I am still wearing the ragged old clothing that I brought with me from Dinokana. Do you think they fit the place?"

Joseph didn't. He took his friend through to Market Street, to another clothing shop called Kay's Outfitters.

"Do you see those shoes? Look at mine - the same, not so?"

"Yes, my friend, but they are quite expensive."

"It's easy. You put down a deposit and repay the balance every fortnight in instalments and when it is paid for, you get your parcel - that's how we dress in the city."

"OK, I see, you will have to bring me at month-end. I will also want to buy some for my father and my girlfriend Nthabiseng from other shops that sell women's clothes."

"All is yours. My role is to show you the ropes, but there are other places you have to know, real places in the city of Jozi - corners such as George Goch and Alexandra; the dark city as they at times call it."

After showing his friend around, they took a bus back to the mine.

"What is peculiar about George Goch and Alexandra?"

"You will see with your own eyes. Remember, I am not a teacher, but just a simple miner who has learnt life through experience."

"The last thing that I must remind you, Kgabalatsana. Do not forget your roots. Do not forget Nthabiseng and please keep in touch with her; remember she is carrying your baby. And finally, do not forget the cultural norms. At some stage, I will have to take you to a Sangoma, who will strengthen you and prescribe some medicines Sa Setswana. Do not be swallowed by the niceties of Gauteng."

Kgabalatsana remembered what Nthabiseng had told him in Dinokana – about men who leave their villages for the city and never return. As if picking up his thoughts, Joseph turned to Kgabalatsana, gazing at him seriously.

"Never forget these words, by the way, as this is only the beginning; you have not even seen half of Johannesburg, there are still other places of interest. The townships that I will have to show you, they are places of interest, with their own flavours of the city."

***

After work during the week, Kgabalatsana changed out of his overalls, took a shower and dressed himself in his new, nicely-pressed khaki trousers with matching shirt and takkies that he had bought at Kay's. He had copied this style from Joseph. He wore a saucer-plated black and white cap. Even when not leaving the compound, he'd wear these clothes proudly.

Sechaba once questioned him about this new Kgabalatsana.

"I do not understand you, Kgabalatsana, you seem to be changing by the day; only yesterday you were dressing like that village boy from Dinokana, and now all of a sudden you have changed. Look at how you are dressed, even though you are going nowhere."

Kgabalatsana smiled, doffing his hat at his friend.

"You snooze or you lose my brother - this is Jozi; if you cannot beat them, join them and Kgabalatsana has decided to join them."

"Even listen to your language, brother? What happened to *rra*? Jozi? When we still call it Johannesburg?"

One weekend, Kgabalatsana, now confident about going it alone into the city, decided to invite Sechaba and Dira to go with him, this time without his mentor Joseph. He was trying to prove to them that he understood city life and was in a position to show them around. They marvelled at the clothes displayed in shop windows, tempted by all that they saw – it was like a fairytale to a village child.

"*Rre* Kgabalatsana! I cannot believe my eyes that the place is so large, look at these thousands of people in the streets, is this not the gold that we were told about?"

As they were going from shop to shop, they met two guys who came to stand in front of them.

"Watches! The best in the market, guys, for sale! Cheap and genuine," said one of the hawkers. When there was no response from the three potential customers, the hawker exclaimed:

"*Die is net baries van die mines* (these are just rural guys from the mines)."

The hawkers moved on. When Dira and Sechaba looked around them, Kgabalatsana was nowhere to be seen.

"Where is Kgabalatsana?"

"What do you mean, 'where is Kgabalatsana', Sechaba?"

The next thing they heard was a voice calling.

"*Majita* (guys), *die ouens* (gentlemen)," called a voice from across the street. When Sechaba looked in the direction of the voice, he realised that it was Kgabalatsana.

"Do not cross now, look at the robots, they are red, do not cross yet!" he shouted.

"Hey, *julle moegoes* (hey you, village boys) stop shouting and making fools of yourselves, *die is Jozi* (this is Johannesburg)," muttered a man standing next to Kgabalatsana, who continued shouting as the traffic light turned green.

"Now cross fast but walk in-between the white lines," Kgabalatsana instructed them, as they crossed the street and joined him, panting and sweating.

"This is Jozi my friends, you have to learn fast."

"Was it necessary for you to have just disappeared, could you not have warned us?" asked Dira, but Kgabalatsana smiled.

"That would have defeated my intention."

They walked up the street, towards the south, leaving the city centre and travelling in the direction of the mine.

Sechaba was disappointed that this *tour de citi* seemed to be coming to an end when there were still so many fascinating sights to see.

"I was still enjoying myself, *rre* Kgabalatsana, and I still cannot believe my eyes."

"There will be another day, my friend. Unfortunately, we have to get back to the compound."

Later, when Joseph asked Kgabalatsana if he'd like to accompany him on another city jaunt, either to the city or, perhaps, Alexander township, the latter asked:

"Will it be possible, *rra,* that I can invite my two home-boys, Sechaba and Dira, to accompany us?"

Joseph replied, friendly but firm:

"Remember, *rra* Kgabalatsana, we have to draw the lines very clear here; the relationship we are starting to build is between you and me."

"I understand, *rra* Joseph, and I apologise."

Joseph nodded and suggested that they explore Alex this time.

"Alexandra? Us going to Alexandra! Only the other day I heard guys at the compound talking about this Alexandra, and I must confess I had mixed feelings, *rra* Joseph, part of me being excited whilst on the other hand being scared, but it is OK, when I am with you I have confidence that I will be in safe hands."

"I am happy to hear that, my friend, do not forget then it will be this coming Saturday."

Days later, as Kgabalatsana, Sechaba and Dira arrived at their sleeping quarters in the compound from the city, they found Joseph waiting at the entrance, paging through a copy of the Kay's Outfitters clothing catalogue.

"*Rra* Kgabalatsana, I thought that you had forgotten about our appointment for today as I have been waiting here for quite a while. Where have you been?"

Kgabalatsana shook Joseph's hand, apologetically.

"Just got delayed a bit - I took the guys to town."

"Oh, that's great, and how did you find the concrete jungle, *bo rra*?"

"Exciting and unbelievable – I still can hardly believe my eyes," Sechaba replied.

Kgabalatsana and Dira disappeared into the room and after a few minutes, Kgabalatsana joined Joseph who, surprised, noted his young friend's very snappy outfit. He was dressed in navy blue pants and shirt, a Dorian hat on his head and wearing black Crockett & Jones shoes. Joseph smiled, exclaiming:

"I like my boys to be smart and clean! Kgabalatsana, you are learning fast and I can already see you are well ahead of your two friends. Let us get going, my friend."

He flipped Kgabalatsana's hat slightly, tilting it sideways, as they left the compound.

They boarded a bus – Joseph paying the fare, as usual – and drove through the city into 2nd Avenue, Alexandra Township. Kgabalatsana was seated next to the window, staring outside, perplexed by the vision of houses whirring by.

"Wow! I did not expect to see such a big place, look at the crowded streets. The cars and the people. Where do so many people come from?"

"The place has a long history which you will live to learn. It was built over time. The people in the streets all live here in the shacks that you see. But there is life and vibrancy inside those shacks, as you will see for yourself. Let us prepare ourselves to disembark at the next bus stop at the corner of 1st and 2nd Avenue, near a shop."

The bus stopped and they got out and crossed over the street. They passed a general dealers' grocery store into 2nd Avenue. At the third house of corrugated iron, Joseph said to Kgabalatsana:

"Here we are, *rra*." As Joseph opened the gate into a small yard leading to a veranda, they were met by a thick-set, light-complexioned man in his thirties. Clean-shaven, bald head, black and white shirt and black trousers, shiny black shoes.

"*Heyta* (hi), *Bra* Sparks, how are you, my *bra*?"

"*Mojo, broer* (morning, brother) and how are you?"

"Great, cannot complain. Meet my *bra* (friend) Kgaba-latsana."

Sparks smirked and laughed.

"Hey man, *daai naam* (that name) is too long for Jozi. You have to reconsider it for it will not fit here. Look at yourself, you look smart, already greying at your age and the balding that is already appearing on your forehead. Maybe we will have to call you Toppie – which means old man - and later we might have to add something, I do not know."

Later indeed, Kgabalatsana was to be known as Toppie Manoja, which in township lingo means 'old wise man'.

"He has been working at Mzilikazi for a couple of weeks now."

"*Waarvanaf kom die ou* (where is the guy from)? *Ek weet hy is van jou span, Joseph* (I know he is on your team). *Ek meen sy kraal* - I was referring to his village."

"Oh, he comes from Western Transvaal, Dinokana village, near Zeerust."

"Oh well, welcome my bras, come in. In my house, there is plenty of space, otherwise I would not have welcomed you."

He hugged Kgabalatsana as they entered a spacious, corrugated iron dining room cum drinking room, where a handful of men were ranged around tables, chairs and sofas, glasses in hand, while others moved about, holding bottles of beer. Loud but melodious jazz music vibrated through the big speakers placed at opposite corners of the room. Joseph and Kgabalatsana took empty seats near a corner, and Sparks joined them.

"*Wat gaan die ouens drink, ek het alles soos jy nosh* (what are you guys going to drink, I have everything, as you know)."

"Castle Lager, *Bra* Sparks."

Kgabalatsana gaped. Joseph noticed this, saying:

"Well, there is also Coke, Fanta or Hubbly Bubbly."

"Castle will be fine."

Truth is, this would be the first time that Kgabalatsana had tasted alcohol. As he was thinking about this, a lady came out of a door that led to the kitchen. She seated herself between the two friends and introduced herself.

"*Dumelang, ou boetie* (elder brother Joseph) and *rra*?"

"Johannes," Joseph interrupted her.

"*Rra* Johannes, my name is Mampye." Bowing almost to her knees as she greeted them, with her eyes fixed on Johannes.

"Well, mine is Johannes, as my friend has said."

"Oh, don't even bother yourself about this one, everybody here knows him," said Mampye, hugging Joseph and asking:

"Long time no see, *ou boetie* Joseph. Are you well?"

"Everything is fine, Mampye, and you?"

"As you can see, I am still the same old Mampye, nice to meet you guys. Let me go and help in the kitchen." Mampye left Joseph and Johannes, patting his back as she went.

"Is she a friend of yours, or a wife to Sparks?"

"No, no, Johannes, just a friend of ours – part of a group of ladies who always hang around here. This is something else you'll notice in Johannesburg shebeens. You'll always find her type. Good, nice, decent ladies most of the time. Mampye was a friend of Sparks' late wife – and has remained so. I'm sure that you'll get to know her. She's a nice lady."

The night went on, Joseph becoming louder and louder as more beers came. Johannes had started taking it slowly, as he realised that his body temperature had changed, his vision was beginning to blur and he did not know what was wrong with him. Faintly he heard Joseph saying:

"Is everything fine with you, *rra*?"

He almost jerked out of the chair, responding:

"*Go seame rra* (I am fine, sir)."

"Let's go outside, it's starting to get hot here."

Joseph helped him out of the house and they went to stand near the fence. A cool breeze was what Kgabalatsana needed. He started to feel as if he had been sprayed in the face with cold water. He looked at Joseph and, seeing his blurred face, mumbled:

"Have I been sleeping all the time?"

"No, no my friend, you were enjoying yourself. That is what Castle Lager does."

Then Mampye came out of the house and saw them.

"I have been wondering where you two disappeared to." She turned back into the house, motioning for them to follow. Once inside, they took their seats and settled down, feeling refreshed.

The night went on and by this time the place was full of patrons shouting at one another as their voices were drowned by the music. Sparks came by.

"How are the gents from Mzilikazi doing?"

"Top notch, as you can see; we are cool, how else could the gents be in such a nice place?" Joseph yelled, standing up to give Sparks a hug.

"Ladies, bring us a tot of whiskey for the big man, on my account." And when one of Mampye's friends brought the shot of whiskey and two bottles of lager, placing them in front of the three, Joseph opened one bottle of lager, filled it up and said, as he lifted the glass:

"*Bo rra!*"

Johannes and Sparks followed suit.

"Drink and be merry, drink for human happiness gents, and as you can see, *keba Bo Mampye le Bo Julie* - here are the ladies, *ba tletse* - they are many. The choice is yours, Johannes, but just be careful and do not overdo it."

A round of applause followed Joseph's toast. Kgabalatsana shook Joseph's hand, thanking him.

"You have made my evening, Joseph, I did not know it was so nice in Alex. And so, this is how people spend their weekends here?"

"Right through my *bra*, it is like this. But please avoid the weekdays because that is your time to be at work; imagine going to work after such a hectic night, full of *babalaza* (hangover)."

It was almost 11 pm when Joseph bade farewell to *Bra* Sparks, who was standing with them.

"My *broer*, it's time for us to *phokala* , lets hit the road now, it is late."

"Check my *broer*, there is no public transport this time. But wait." Sparks stopped as if remembering something.

"There is *ou* (old) David here, he lives in Booysens, not far from Mzilikazi, let me go and talk to him."

Sparks disappeared into the crowd and came back with David.

"Gents *die is ou* David – this is old David." David nodded his head.

"Ou David, these guys live at Mzilikazi."

"Which is close by, my *kasi* (house)."

"Mojo David, please give them a lift and drop them right at the gate of the mine."

"Mojo *Bra* Sparks. Gents, you will signal me when you are ready - after all, I was also thinking of leaving." He disappeared into the crowd. Mampye was standing at the kitchen door, watching them talk. As Joseph put on his jacket, she turned and hugged him affectionately.

"Take care guys, I can see you are about to leave." She turned to Kgabalatsana and smiled, winningly.

"Till we meet next time. Joseph, do not forget to come with Johannes next time you visit Alex."

"He won't have the chance to leave me behind. I will be here, Mampye," said Johannes.

"Good, Johannes, and goodnight, gents."

Joseph found David, who was waiting with car keys dangling on his middle finger.

"Let's hit the road, gents."

Kgabalatsana sat at the back, with Joseph next to David, as the car drove through town towards Booysens, where David dropped the two at the main gate of the mine. Joseph was the first to get out of the car and opened the door for Kgabalatsana, who struggled to get up. Joseph helped him as the young man staggered, hit the ground, but quickly composed himself again. The men shuffled around to David's window.

"*Dankie my bra* (thank you, my brother), we shall ever remember you for this, hope to see you soon at Sparks." Joseph waved.

"It is my pleasure guys, take care and goodbye."

Joseph escorted Kgabalatsana to his compound, helped him to bed and closed the door softly behind him as he left.

The following morning was one Kgabalatsana would never forget. He woke to his head spinning like a wheel. Sechaba found him with his head hanging over the bunk, and asked in fright:

"*Rra* Monare, are you OK?"

Kgabalatsana only responded when Sechaba patted him firmly on the head. He opened his eyes, seeing Sechaba as a blur.

"Where am I?"

"You are in the compound."

By this time, some of his roommates were awake, including Dira.

One man brought a bottle of water and gave it to Kgabalatsana, who took it and gulped, but then vomited. Sechaba whispered in Dira's ear.

"Go and fetch Joseph, tell him that there is something wrong with Kgabalatsana, and he is not well."

One old man, who was sleeping in a far-end bunk, said:

"What is wrong with you, young men? There is nothing wrong with Kgabalatsana, just give him breathing space, open some windows or take him outside. He needs fresh air."

Dira came in with Joseph and went straight to where Kgabalatsana was seated next to Sechaba on his bunk. He looked at him and laughed.

"Easy, easy, take it easy, gents. There is nothing wrong with Kgabalatsana: it is normal after what happened last night…"

The old man in the corner chipped in.

"I told these young men that there was nothing wrong with the man. I knew that he was suffering from *babalaza*. But, realising that I was educating ignorant boys in terms of lifestyle, I decided that ignorance is bliss, and it is folly to be wise. Last night – no, this morning – I was awake when he came in with you, Joseph, and I guessed that you guys had gone on a spree."

Joseph chuckled and nodded.

"Old man Nzima has read the situation well. There is nothing wrong with Monare. You see gentlemen, this is what happens when you drink any alcoholic beverages. Always drink water after each and every glass of alcohol, be it beer, lager or the hot stuff."

But Sechaba chirped in.

"What is hot stuff Joseph, and why should one drink beer with water, since beer has already lots of water, I am told?"

Joseph responded slowly, and carefully, as though speaking to a child.

"Let me finish, *rra*. You see, alcohol consumes oxygen in your body when you drink it. Especially at the rate at which we did last night. It was heavy, I must say. And he is strong to have survived it. So, as more oxygen is consumed in our bodies, you then need to replace it by drinking water.

"Remember, water contains oxygen and carbon dioxide. From experience, and having listened to those who came before me in the field of alcohol consumption, this works, and when you apply it, you avoid the suffering that Monare went through, which is as old man Nzima there in the corner calls it - *babalaza* or hangover."

Dira seemed worried.

"Maybe the best thing is to avoid drinking these lagers, beers or hot stuff?" he asked.

Joseph look at Dira, shook his head and left.

Chapter 3

Knowing the City

Alex, or Alexandra, was the flavour of the time, but not the only spot where life was good for neophytes in the city of Jo'burg. There was also George Goch, Sophiatown and a few other places. George Goch was located on the Eastern border of the city.

According to the Flatinternational-South African audio archive on George Goch Mines Natives (an African song and dance troupe), the George Goch Amalgamated Mine was named after mining magnate George Goch and it had operated in Johannesburg from before the Boer War. Goch was the Mayor of Johannesburg from 1904-1905 and a township on the eastern side of the city was also named after him. Many mines had dance groups that often competed in formal competitions organised by the mine (See Hugh Tracey's book *African Dances of the Witwatersrand Gold Mines*).

Dillnutt recorded at least eight tracks with the group from George Goch Mine on April 27, 1912. The label states that the performers were using a "Native Piano", which sometimes refers to a thumb piano or mbira but in this case, it appears to be a xylophone-like instrument known as a timbila.

As Joseph had taken it upon himself to phase Kgabalatsana into city life, George Goch was his next target for orientation.

At month-end, he, Kgabalatsana and Mzimela left the compound early one Saturday morning to catch a bus. As they passed the guard on gate duty, he called after them.

"*Heita, majita* (hi guys), women are going to cry about where the gents are going, fare thee well *bafana bam* (my boys)."

They gathered at the bus stop next to the mine. Mzimela was dressed in baggy denims, takkies (running shoes) and a checked shirt, with an Ayers cap worn jauntily on his head. Joseph looked smart in his trademark khaki pants and shirt, with sandals. Kgabalatsana chose his Dorian hat, a faded white shirt, denims and takkies.

The boys were ready for a good day. The bus drove out of the city towards a place known as 'The Slums' – a sprawling row of shacks that mostly housed people who were working in the households of white employers and those working at the George Goch Mine. Kgabalatsana noted that and said to Mzimela:

"It is not as vibrant as Alexandra, it is more downtrodden and it looks shabby."

"It could not be the same, Monare, every place is different from the other."

The bus pulled up at a stop street at the entrance to the township.

Led by Mzimela, the group went to a white-washed, corrugated iron house at the corner of Mpanza Street. Mzimela opened the gate into a small yard. At the door, a plump lady in her forties greeted them.

"Welcome, gentlemen, to *Mme* Nori's, the best spot in George Goch; welcome my children."

Mme Nori followed them in and gave them chairs. When they had settled, a younger lady, Dikeledi, walked over and curtsied to Joseph.

"Can you bring us three Castle Lagers, Dikeledi?"

The woman disappeared into the kitchen and returned quickly with the orders, placing them on a crate in front of Mzimela. Four gentlemen and their female partners, seated nearby, noticed the group – and Joseph. One of the men hailed him.

"How could I forget *rre* Joseph, the big man from Mzilikazi? It is seldom I see you in George Goch. We from the George Goch Mine are blessed to see you."

"To you too, Tshawe, it has been years since I last saw you, and where are you working now?"

"I am in the trucking business now, delivering coal to various factories around Johannesburg."

Realising that he had not spoken to the other two gentlemen, he turned to Mzimela.

"*Awu! Nangu no Mzimela* (Oh, even Mzimela is here)!"

To Kgabalatsana, he nodded and said:

"*Sawubona Mnumzana* (greetings, my friend)."

"*Dumelang rra* (greetings sir)."

"*Hayi sizakunibona Madoda* (we will talk later, gentlemen)."

Joseph laughed and turned to Mzimela.

"That is Tshawe, Mzimela, the one and only Tshawe whom I found at Mzilikazi."

"We actually arrived on the same month," said Mzimela. "A difficult Xhosa man who always fought with the bosses."

Joseph smiled.

"How can one forget Tshawe?"

As they were finishing one bottle after the other, Joseph reminded Johannes:

"Do not forget what I told you about drinking water."

"How can I, Joseph, have you not been observing me?"

"Good."

It was around 10 pm before they left the *shebeen* (illegal tavern) to take the last bus to Mzilikazi. To Kgabalatsana's surprise, he was in control of his senses this time as they climbed in to take their seats.

"Do not worry about taking me to my sleeping quarters, I can handle myself this time," he told Joseph after they had arrived home.

"I am happy to hear that, Monare, and good night."

Kgabalatsana arrived at his quarters to find Sechaba and Dira playing drafts with two other colleagues.

"If it is not the trendsetter of Jozi, Johannes Monare, I do not know who it is," said Dira.

"*Dumelang die Kgosi* (good day gentlemen), I can see you are relaxed; me, I just want to go to bed now and I will see you tomorrow."

"I only hope that this time we will not have to call the mine ambulance."

"Sechaba my friend, Johannes is becoming a wiser man by the day, so relax - there will no need to call Joseph."

After a while, cosy in his bunk, he began snoring.

Alexandra became their visiting place of choice over weekends, surpassing even the temptations of George Goch. At times, they'd visit as individuals, since Joseph had set the agenda for them, and fostered introductions.

He had also done his work orientating Kgabalatsana into city life, having taken him there and back – to various locations – several times. Kgabalatsana, in turn, now felt confident leading Dira and Sechaba around the city, But Alex was Kgabalatsana's first love.

While Sechaba seemed to be catching on, Dira had not yet fully embraced the fascinations of city life. To his friends, Kgabalatsana seemed excited all the time – eager to leave for the city and explore.

"But *rre* Kgabalatsana, or as they now call you, Johannes, you are a changing man, you are behaving like a chameleon. I have been listening to your language," Dira grumbled one day.

"*Ouens, majita*, it's true, guys. You, Kgabalatsana, seldom use the village language of *rra*," said Sechaba, teasing.

Kgabalatsana laughed. "I told you long ago gents, you snooze, you lose. I have come here to learn and to work for my family; I am not going to allow myself to be a *moegoe* (a mere village boy) forever."

Interestingly enough, it was Dira who agreed with Kgabalatsana on that point. "Perhaps he is correct, Sechaba, what would be the point of coming to a new place and not learning the place's ways of life? We are no longer in our small village."

"Exactly!" shouted Kgabalatsana, pleased to have support. "And gents, henceforth, please, no embarrassment, forget about the name 'Kgabalatsana'. It is too long and too boring for city life."

"And what's the new one?" they asked.

"No, Sechaba, there is no new one. Johannes is the name and as you can see it is in my Employee card. *Ek is nou 'n clever van toeka* (I am now a 'clever' from long ago)."

Joseph nearly choked on laughter when Kgabalatsana repeated that to him one day.

* * *

One Monday after work, Kgabalatsana returned to his room in no mood to talk to his friends.

"Did you have another of your bad dreams last night *rra*?" asked Dira.

Kgabalatsana did not respond. He took off his work clothes and changed into casuals before taking out a pen and paper to draft a letter, which would accompany a money order telegram for Nthabiseng. After all, it was the beginning of the December holidays – and unfortunately, time was too short for him to visit home. He had not saved enough money and only managed to scrape together twenty pounds for her. He slipped off his bunk and whispered to Sechaba:

"Sechaba, Sechaba, do me a favour *rra*. As you had intimated that you were thinking of going home for your December holidays, if it is so, I am going to ask you to take a parcel for me to Nthabiseng."

"That should not create any problems my friend, it will give me a chance to see the mother-to-be."

He laughed, patting his friend on the cheek.

"Thanks, my *bra*."

Sechaba just looked at him with a wry smile.

***

The second week of December 1960, was the time when mines and factories closed for the festive season.

On Wednesday, 14 December, Sechaba caught the 6.30 pm train from Park Station to Zeerust – an emotional journey for him. Although he had only been in Johannesburg for a month, it felt that he'd been away from home for years.

Finding the better part of third class full, he managed to secure an empty compartment, where he dropped his suitcase and bags, making space for other passengers, should they wish to share the space. Sechaba sat next to the window, thinking of home.

At exactly 6.30 pm, the train whistle blew, there was a *chu-chu-chu* as the engine wheezed into life with a *chuck-chuck-chuuu*. Sechaba opened the window, leaning into the fresh air, marvelling at the industrial buildings passing the window with increasing speed as the train chugged past.

Once the train was out of the city, Sechaba closed the window and went back to his seat. The 300km-or-so journey unfolded without any hitches. He had privacy and plenty of rest time before two passengers from Rustenburg joined him. They were platinum miners.

"*Dumela*," they chorused, tripping each other up as they entered.

"*Re kopa tshwarêlô rra* (excuse us sir)," said one, who smelled strongly of liquor.

The strong smell of alcohol filled the coach, but Sechaba was used to that by now, as he was no longer a teetotaller. Imagine, he thought, if he still was?

The rowdy introductions eventually faded into a rhythmic silence, as the train wended its way towards Zeerust. The journey reminded Sechaba of the compositions set by Mrs Ntoeso at primary school, one of which had been about taking a train.

Was it not strange, he thought, that they had been asked to write about something which they had never experienced? He recalled another pupil asking this question, and what Mrs Ntoeso's response had been.

"Education trains your mind to think; to imagine the imaginable."

The pupils had been satisfied, if not a little mystified, by this answer. Sechaba, lulled by the train's gentle *shoosh-shooshing*, now understood what she meant.

He meandered through his childhood memories before falling asleep.

The following morning, at exactly 6 am, the train pulled in at the small Zeerust Station. He disembarked and found that he was not the only person going to Dinokana. Leaving the station gates, he saw dozens of taxis and bakkie drivers soliciting clients.

"Transport to Dinokana! Taxi to Lichtenburg! Taxi to Ramotswa!" they shouted *en masse,* a happy cacophony of eager service providers.

Sechaba and two miners went to a bakkie going to their village, put their luggage at the back and onto the bakkie they climbed. As they arrived at the village, Sechaba was the first one to be dropped off. He grabbed his luggage, paid the driver, bid farewell to his fellow passengers and eagerly turned for home. As he entered the gate into the yard, he saw his parents seated under the mimosa tree. His mother leapt up, shouting happily.

"My child! This is Sechaba, *Modimo* (my God)!" She ran to him, followed by his father. Sechaba dropped his luggage and hugged his mother, while his father waited patiently.

Reunited, relieved and happy, the family went inside and sat down at the dining room table. Sechaba's father looked at his son proudly.

"You look well, my boy, how is the city of the white men?"

"It is all well, *ntate*, different from our little Zeerust, and nothing to compare it to in our region."

Mme Diseko came back from the kitchen with a tray of biscuits and some Fanta soft drink. Sechaba opened the bottle and poured for his parents.

"It is for you, Sechaba, your mother never served me such drinks and biscuits, I do not know them, let alone when last I saw these glasses. I think they were waiting for you."

Sechaba looked lovingly at his parents.

"You look so well, dear parents, and I am so pleased to see that you are well. I have been thinking about you since I left home."

"It is the village that is keeping us well, Sechaba, and the drought has now subsided - we have had two rainfalls since you left."

"I can see that, *mme,* by the green grass on the side of the roads."

"How I wish it could rain more, Sechaba," added his father. "I cannot wait to start tilling the soil, as I noticed that there are already weeds sprouting out between the maize."

"I hope for the best, *ntate*, and I have brought you some seeds that I bought in the city - pumpkin, tomatoes, and I don't know what else. You will sort them out, you are better than me when it comes to agriculture."

"That will help your father, my child, for the upcoming planting season."

Sechaba turned to his mother, who was gazing at him, still smiling.

"*Mme*, I would like to go over to my hut to see if it is as I left it last, with my photographs and other precious things."

"I don't think that there is anything out of place, except that it is cleaner than when you left it. It is being cleaned as though someone was still living in it. You know your mother - she is a cleaning snob!"

Sechaba laughed as he stood up, taking his luggage and leaving the main house for his hut. As he walked through the familiar door, into the warm gloom, he paused and looked around.

"*Ntate* was right; it is as clean as a girl's house. Look at the mirror on this wall. There is not a fingerprint on it."

Throwing his luggage onto the bed, he walked about the room as though he was a guest who had just checked into a fancy hotel, surprised by the beauty of it, with its splendour and romantic setting.

"Typical of *mme*, I will always be the baby child, whom I was born to be, even though I am a grown-up now."

As he stood, appreciating the homeliness of his old quarters, he heard his parents calling to him.

"Sechaba, Sechaba, come over to us."

He found his parents seated under the mimosa tree again, in exactly the same position in which he had found them.

"I thought that you were asleep. Your father and I wanted to be sure that you are well."

"Everything is all well, *mme*, I was still marvelling at the state of my place."

"You are pleased, my boy, that it was intact and as you left it?" asked his father.

"That I can attest to, *ntate*. Thank-you very much, *mme*, for looking after it so well, the only form of material thing I possess."

His father was pleased that Sechaba had remembered his manners and still conducted himself with such sincere respect.

"I will be back. *Mme* disturbed me when I was unpacking my luggage, *mme* and *ntate*."

After sorting out clothes and some gifts for his parents, Sechaba returned to the main house. The sun had already set. He placed a large bundle of clothing on the table, including a navy-blue suit for his father.

"This is for you, *ntate*, and I hope that from now on, every Sunday, it will be your church suit I have heard you making excuses that you are tired of wearing your wedding suit on Sundays."

"*Kea leboga Sechaba ngwanaka* (thank you my child), it is true that the old suit will be buried and forgotten henceforth."

One by one he handed over the clothing items to his mother and father respectively. When he had finished, he took from his pocket an envelope and handed it over to his mother.

"This is the family parcel that I scraped from my meagre wages. I know it is not enough and that I could have done better, but I hope next time it will indeed be better."

"It is not the size that matters, my son, but what you can afford. We are simple village women and men here. Thank-you so much my child," she said.

When all was done and dusted, Sechaba stood by the door, looking at the far horizon of the village. He then turned to his parents.

"*Ntate le mme,* I have to go and pay a visit to the Monares and thereafter to the Sekgametse families, as I must report to them how their children, my friends, are doing in the city of the white men. It will look odd if I do not do that."

Sechaba noticed a subtle change in body language in both his parents. He couldn't quite fathom what it was, but something was different.

"That will be a good thing to visit the Monare family, my child," his mother said.

It was strange to Sechaba that she mentioned only the Monares – or perhaps he was reading into something that wasn't there? His first stop was the Sekgametse household, but a neighbour came out to say that nobody was home.

"There is nobody there, my son. *Ntate* and Mama Sekgametse left for Mafikeng for their holidays," the elderly woman said.

"*Dankie, mme* (thank you mother)."

He proceeded down the road to the Monare home. As he entered the yard, he saw *ntate* Monare and MmaMonare seated in the dining room. Kgabalatsana's parents stood up, excited to see him.

"I did not expect to see the city man so soon," exclaimed the old man. "You mean you could not wait to leave the city? It means that it is not true that village boys get swallowed by Johannesburg! Welcome, my son, have a seat."

"Look at him *rra*, he looks fresh, big and well looked after. They cook well for you at the mines my son," said MmaMonare.

"How is life in the white men's city, my son?"

"All is well, *ntate*, and greetings from Kgabalatsana. He has asked me to convey to all of you that you should not worry about him; he is well and is looking forward to seeing you soon."

"Thank you very much, Sechaba," said MmaMonare, as she stood up to fetch ginger beer and a plate of cakes from the kitchen.

"It is that time of the year when all the households have ginger beer and cookies. This I am sure is what the other guys are missing in Johannesburg," said Sechaba, wistfully.

"It is a reminder that you are at home, my son."

Sechaba started eating the cake and sipping the ginger beer, smiling at the Monares.

"What a time, what a reminder of how we were brought up. I thank you, my parents, for the nice Christmas cookies and *gemmer bier* (ginger beer). Without wasting your time, *mme le ntate*."

Sechaba dipped his hand into his jacket pocket.

"Kgabalatsana asked me to give *mme* this parcel."

He gave an envelope to MmaMonare, who took it and immediately gave it to her husband.

"It is very considerate of Kgabalatsana to think of home and parents, my son. This is how we all brought you up, and you should not forget your roots," *ntate* Monare said softly.

"How can we, *ntate le mme*? We have always been the children of Dinokana and city life should never change us."

"That is how I have known the teachings of your parents to have been, Sechaba, so keep it that way and never gets diverted from that upbringing, my child."

After a while with the Monare family, Sechaba asked to be released, saying that he should go home. He did not tell the old people that he planned on stopping at the Rethabile homestead first.

"Go well, my child, son of Diseko, and greetings to my son in Johannesburg - tell him that we are all well."

He left the Monare home and went to see Nthabiseng, who was alone when he arrived.

"*Rre* Sechaba, is this you, what a surprise! I did not expect you so soon. Tell me that he is as well as you look?"

"He is even better than me, I believe, and greetings from Kgabalatsana. He is always talking about Nthabiseng and the child-to-be and is excited to become a father."

As Sechaba was chatting, Nthabiseng was already in the kitchen, still talking to him.

"I recently received his letter, dated 21 November, and have been reading it every night before going to sleep. Sometime even when I wake up."

"That is good news and I am certain he will be happy to hear that, Nthabiseng. By the way, how are you doing, and how are your parents?"

"Ag, we are all fine, just excited that the child in this stomach is doing well. My parents are fine too - they have gone on holidays, *ntate* this time decided that he wanted to spend this Christmas with his in-laws in Phokeng, so I am left alone."

There was a pause as she entered the dining room with a cup of tea and biscuits. She put them in front of Sechaba and looked through the door. Sechaba noticed this sudden silence and asked:

"Is there something wrong, Nthabiseng?"

She recovered from her brief silence.

"No, no *rra*, I was just thinking. It is not important."

"What is not important, Nthabiseng?" Sechaba pressed her.

"*Rre* Sechaba, I do not want to bore you with family matters, but the truth is that there are problems in the Monare family and thus, in my own. To be honest with you – it is going to affect my relationship with Kgabalatsana. But, I beg you to do me a favour and swear by the Lord that you will never discuss this with him?"

Sechaba looked at her, wide-eyed, his hands trembling a little on the table. He put down his cup and nodded. Nthabiseng continued.

"You might not know, as I do not even think that he is aware of it, that in fact, Kgabalatsana and I are siblings."

Sechaba was shocked into silence. Nthabiseng stared at him, waiting for a reaction. The young man shook his head, trying to make sense of what he had just heard.

"What? What are you saying, Nthabiseng? You are what?"

Nthabiseng was anxious but explained more slowly.

"Siblings, *rre* Sechaba. *Ntate* Monare impregnated my mother before she got married to my father. The story is that they were supposed to have gotten married, but my mother's side of the family was vehemently opposed to their child marrying into the Monare family, and it was during this period of controversy that *mme* was already pregnant. A marriage was arranged wherein *mme* was betrothed to *ntate* Rethabile. And both families, that is, the Rethabiles and Monares, knew that by the time she got married she was already two months' pregnant."

"I cannot believe what you are telling me, Nthabiseng."

"You believe it or you do not. It is a fact and one which I heard directly from my mother. Unfortunately, this came out only after I was pregnant, when one evening I heard *ntate* and *mme* talking about the 'secret'. They were unaware that I was listening, of course. By the time that they became aware of my presence, *ntate* said that the secret was out and now had to be dealt with. As a result, *mme* shared this with me, under strict instructions not to tell anybody."

"So, this story gets to you when you were already pregnant?"

Nthabiseng nodded, downcast.

"Exactly, and I think that my parents had tried all these years to erase this issue from their minds, but unfortunately, my pregnancy resuscitated it. But when I look back at the time when *mme* realised that I was having a relationship with Kgabalatsana, I see now why she tried to discourage me. I remember her once saying, 'Do you think that you are in love with the right man?' and when I asked her, 'What do you mean, *mme*?' her response was that it was just a question from a concerned parent. Now I am just not sure if Kgabalatsana knows all this, for, as you know, the culture amongst our parents is to keep matters of this nature to themselves, without discussing them with the children – that is taboo."

"*Modimo* - oh my God!" exclaimed Sechaba, floored.

"Please keep this to yourself, Sechaba. I have the highest respect for you, *rra*, and know that you will not allow it to reach Kgabalatsana's ears via you."

"You have my promise, *mme*. By the way, what I came here for is not about what you have just revealed to me."

He took an envelope out of his pocket.

"This is for you, courtesy of *rre* Monare, jnr. He said I should tell you that you are always in his mind, that he loves you and hopes to see you soon."

Nthabiseng took the envelope from Sechaba and put it in her apron pocket, smiling in her pretty, womanly way.

"*Ke a leboa, rra* (thank you, sir)."

Sechaba thanked Nthabiseng with mixed feelings. On the one hand, he had good news to report to his friend – but on the other, there was a secret which his friend could never hear from him. This despite Kgabalatsana being his best friend. Sechaba felt torn and very sad.

The festive holidays flew past. Soon, Sechaba was on his way back to Johannesburg by overnight train, his mind ricocheting back to the conversation he had with Nthabiseng.

The new development folded and unfolded in his head repeatedly, but he knew that he had made a promise not to reveal it.

Sechaba arrived at Park Station very early, taking a bus from Noord Street back to Mzilikazi Mine. Luckily, he still had one more day off, so there was time to rest and relax with his friends before work began again.

On 25 January 1961, Kgabalatsana received a letter from Zeerust, which would have been posted at the end of the year. He grabbed the envelope and recognised Nthabiseng's handwriting. Lying on his belly in the compound, alone in his room on a hot summer's day, he ripped open the envelope, kissing the letter before reading it.

Dinokana Trading Store
Dinokana Village
Zeerust
30th December 1960

Dear Ou Boetie Kgabalatsana

I do hope that this letter finds you in good health in the land of the white man. I was elated when I received yours a month ago and only then did I realise how much you meant to me, because I noticed that you wrote that letter to me on your first day of arrival in Johannesburg.

The baby is growing well and my belly is growing bigger and bigger by the day, making it difficult for me at times to visit friends in the village, as if I am bragging of my pregnancy. You know how village people are. Just a few days ago I went to the village shop to fetch groceries for my parents and I met your mother, who greeted me so kindly, asking me how I was and then buying me a packet of XX Strong Mints, saying that I must eat one a day. But guess what? I finished them by the time I reached home.

As we begin the New Year, a great year in our calendar, as I will be giving birth to our child in April, I am hopeful that you will come and see her or him, for I think Easter weekend will fall during that month.

Rre Kgabalatsana, look after yourself and think about us, your family left behind.

You remain in our prayers.

Yours in-love

Nthabiseng Rethabile

As he finished reading the letter, tears rolled down his cheeks. He needed to give her a hug, but she wasn't there.

"Nthabi, I love you." He wiped the tears away as he heard footsteps coming down the hall and he folded the letter, putting it under his pillow.

Time has flown for Kgabalatsana. He was enjoying his work and he had good relations with his colleagues, especially Joseph and Mzimela, and with his bosses. The only sticky issue involved Shearling, and a question mark hung over that issue, which needed to be sorted out. One example was his insistence that he be called 'baas'. Not that Kgabalatsana opposed the address, but rather, he objected to the manner in which Shearling insisted on it. After all, any Western Transvaal person was used to calling white men 'baas', but why be so nasty about it? Kgabalatsana decided to stay away from Shearling as much as possible.

Composed now, he decided to waste no time in replying to Nthabiseng.

Mzilikazi Mines
P.O. Booysens
Johannesburg
25 January 1961

My Dearest Nthabiseng

What a day! What a lovely present you gave me this day when I received the warmth of your letter as it was safely delivered to me. I am in one hundred percent health, hoping that the same is with you and the baby. You are correct, moratiwa, the

*last letter I wrote to you was written on my very first night
of arrival in Johannesburg, I could not wait any longer to tell
you how much love I have for you and the child. And I am
pleased to hear that the child is growing well and I wonder
how big that stomach is now. I am sure you cannot hide it
anymore that you will soon be a mother of an amazon baby.*

*I will forever think of you and I know you will do the same
for me. Work is going well for me, I have made a number of
friends among my colleagues and my bosses, and am as hand
in glove with Sechaba and Dira as when we left home.*

*Moratiwa, I am looking forward to receiving another letter
soon from you so that I can hear how you are doing.*

Yours and Only

Kgabalatsana Monare

The Easter Weekend was nearing. Kgabalatsana, Sechaba
and Dira rested in the shade of their quarters, bare-chested
in the heat and playing draughts. Kgabalatsana interrupted the game for a moment.

"*Bo rra*, it will be my turn this time to take a long trip to
Dinokana to go and see my one and only, the mother of my
child, Nthabiseng. I cannot wait, *Bo rra* - the Easter Weekend
seemed to be years coming, when in fact it will be soon."

Sechaba nodded.

"It will be a good thing for you to do so, I am sure there
are a number of things you need to attend to, more so that
you will be a father soon. Remember when I was home this
Christmas season - it was like a gift from God for me to be
with my parents, so I know what it means."

A few days later, one Wednesday afternoon, when he was
on night shift, Kgabalatsana left the compound for Jeppe
Post Office, where he wrote a telegram to Nthabiseng.

Dear Nthabiseng

*I just wish to inform you that I will be arriving home on
Thursday, 30 March for the Good Friday long weekend.*

Kgabalatsana Monare

Chapter 4

Kgabalatsana Visits Home

At 6 pm on the dot, the train pulled out from the platform and he was already seated comfortably in a compartment with six other passengers

An old woman, who could easily have been Kgabalatsana's mother, made conversation to break the silence.

"It is just civil for us as Batswana to greet one another as we are meeting for the first time. *Nnna ke Mma Ntoaso* I am Mrs Ntoaso. *Ke tsoa Mahikeng* (I am from Mafikeng)."

"*Nnna Ke* (I am) Kgabalatsana Monare from Dinokana."

There was a pause and *mme* Ntoaso stared at a young man seated next to Kgabalatsana and said: "And *wena, mosimana* (and you, young man)?"

And as Kgabalatsana poked the young man in his rib, the young man just stared at him. The boy closed his eyes and looked at the roof. A lady who was seated next to *mme* Ntoaso whispered to her:

"He is disabled, deaf and dumb, *mme.*"

The old lady crossed her hand and exclaimed: "Pardon me, Lord, for I did not know."

As everybody in the compartment had settled, there was a knock on the door and a simultaneous voice.

"Tickets, tickets ready."

It was the conductor, a tall, stocky man. The young mute man presented a problem again when he was asked for his ticket, as there was no ticket. The conductor became agitated and started shouting, but was interrupted by *mme* Mtoaso, who explained the situation to him.

"*Baas, die kleintjie kan nie praat nie* (boss, this young man is dumb)."

"*Maar hy moes 'n kaartjie gehad het* (but he must be in possession of a ticket)."

The conductor was insistent, but nobody could answer on behalf of the boy. The conductor turned to Kgabalatsana.

"Boy, you have to talk to him."

"He is not travelling with me *meneer* (sir), there is nothing I can do."

Having run out of options, the conductor left the compartment, exasperated.

A woman travelling by herself, and who had slipped into an upper bunk, where she was listening to a Setswana radio station, called down in a superior voice.

"Can you listen to the Setswana that these people are speaking, Setswana, from back home? Not this *fanagalo* that is spoken in that Johannesburg, I can tell now that I am heading for my village, we Tswanas are cultured people, deeply rooted in our language."

A man seated near the door responded: "That is why we are the toilers of the gold mines of Johannesburg, forced to leave our villages while the other people, the Swazi, Tsonga and Ndebele, have filled their schools. We have turned our backs on our culture and left our women behind. Is this what makes you brag about the deeply rooted culture in our language - the only thing that should make us proud, lady?"

Mme Ntoaso nodded at the gentleman.

"I can hear that you are one of the educated ones, a teacher perhaps?"

Kgabalatsana joined the discussion.

"You see, my friends, there are reasons why I am travelling today and this discussion is far from that. I left my family just a few months ago, to work at the mines, as I had to do this for the survival of my new family. If all had gone according to plan, I would not have gone to Jo'burg, but this is where circumstances led me. I won't bore you with my predicament and challenges. However, to you, the lady up there, it is not only our language which sets us apart. It is also our skills and education – not just the beautiful Setswana we speak. So please, think differently, but continue listening to your Setswana radio and leave us alone."

Kgabalatsana turned his face away, hid his face behind his jersey and closed his eyes. When the train arrived in Zeerust, the passengers disembarked and left for their various destinations, while he and three men found a bakkie which was going to Dinokana. After he was dropped not far from his home, he passed the village shop close to his former school, where he paused and shook his head.

"It is like a hundred years since I walked through these gates, it was here where my future was being shaped, when the end came on that fateful day that I discovered, reminded by my father, that this was the end of the road for me as a school boy."

Kgabalatsana approached the family homestead, carrying the suitcase with which he had left the village; though now, it was accompanied by a large carry bag, striped in red, white and blue – a common bag used by migrant workers. He opened the gate and paused for a second, remembering the spot where he had been confronted by his father, and remembering what he had said.

"Kgabalatsana, my boy! What you have done to me and this family is an aberration, a solecism never heard of."

The words rang in his mind as he crossed the yard towards the house, where he was met by his mother.

"Kgabalatsana! *Ke* Kgabalatsana (it is my baby)."

"Dumelang, mme!"

"Dumela, ngwanaka (greetings to you also my child). I cannot believe my eyes. At least you could have sent us a telegram to tell us that you were coming. Look, now you arrive when your father has just left for Mafikeng on his church duties. But it does not matter, Boysie and I are here."

"How is *ntate, mme* (how is father doing, mother)?"

"He is fine, like everybody in the village, and as he would have told you if he were here, we had a few drops of rain, though we still need more. Your elder brother should be on his way home anytime now - he has gone to Zeerust to buy some things."

MmaMonare took her son's luggage and placed it inside, away from the front door, where Kgabalatsana had put it.

"Your hut is as you left it, perhaps you should take your things in there in the meantime while I prepare food; you must be hungry, and longing for home food."

Kgabalatsana took the luggage and went out of the main house into his hut. He looked at the wall above his bed, where his framed photo of Nthabiseng still hung. It – and everything else in the room – appeared to have been left exactly as it had been.

"I know my mother, she would have been the one who would have said, leave everything that belongs to Kgabalatsana. He will come back one day."

As he finished settling in, he heard his mother calling from outside: "Food is ready! Food is ready!"

Kgabalatsana left his room for the main house to find his mother with his elder brother, who was already seated at the table. They gave each other a familiar smirk.

"Kgabalatsana *Monna (man)*, I did not expect you so soon, welcome home, it is good to see you looking so well. You have grown in just a few months. This shows that city life likes you," Boysie said, as he stood up to embrace his brother.

The table was laid and their mother brought plates. She asked Kgabalatsana to pray for the meal and again, there was another silly smile on the brothers' faces. Boysie started asking for blessings for the food. They ate solemnly for a while until Kgabalatsana reached over and touched his brother.

"How is *ntate*, elder brother?"

"*Ntate* is well, brother, though you can see now that age is creeping up faster than we thought, as his movements are slow. Looking at his upper body, it is slightly bent, which is why he is now walking balancing with a stick and I can see he struggles to do the things that he used to do. Generally, though, he has no health problems. From time to time he asks about you. One day from out of the blue he said: 'Boysie, I think often about your brother, and I do hope that he is doing well.' Just the other day he called me aside to ask me whether or not I see the Rethabile girl and if she is well."

At this juncture, their mother rose to fetch more food from the kitchen.

After the meal, the boys thanked their mother and went to their hut, with Boysie reminding her to lock the front door. She nodded and said, "Goodnight, boys."

Kgabalatsana spent the night with his brother, asking him all sorts of questions.

"Elder brother, how is my Nthabiseng?"

"I often see her at the village general dealers and I must say everybody in the village, even children, now know that Sis Nthabiseng is going to have a child. I spoke to her only last week, she assured me that she was well and to my shock she told me that she received a letter from you and that you were doing well in the city; but never mentioned that you would be coming. Or was this supposed to be a secret?"

"Truth of the matter Boysie, I was and still am not sure whether *ntate* is still angry with me for what I have done. He was so cross with me at the time I left; hence, I wrote to none of you. But also, I have to say that I could not reconcile his temper and reaction with what I did."

Boysie did not respond to this last statement, keeping quiet.

Kgabalatsana looked at him and said:

"I understand, elder brother, I understand."

It must have been close to midnight when the brothers finally went to sleep, after having conversed about everything they needed to know from each other.

What struck Kgabalatsana was his brother's forthrightness about their father. He had even mentioned 'perceived adulterous behaviour' talk in the village.

However, when Kgabalatsana questioned him about this, asking if he was referring to his father's behaviour, Boysie had brushed the question aside, saying: "It is late, *rra*."

Kgabalatsana had not had such a peaceful sleep for months. No sounds of cars could be heard, only the occasional bellowing of the cows and crowing and singing of birds, until he was awoken by a cock that crowed below the window of his room. He opened his eyes, expecting to see the wide glass windows of their sleeping quarters, and when he wiped the sleep out of his eyes, remembered that he was sleeping at his parents' house in the village of Dinokana. Boysie, at this time, had long been awake but had stayed in bed until his brother woke.

"Is it not a good thing to wake up in the same bed that you have been sleeping in since you were a child?"

"Indeed, elder brother, home will always be home no matter what, and remember also that this is a holy day, Good Friday, and Happy Good Friday, elder brother."

"To you too, my brother."

Kgabalatsana went outside to look around, marvelling at the place of his birth, which was still as beautiful and rich in memory as it had been when he was a boy. He walked to the kraal, remembering what his father had told him about the gauntness of the herd, which in the last few months seemed to have improved. He then went to the main house to find his mother already busy at the hearth, preparing breakfast.

"*Dumela, mme*." He greeted his mother, who responded with a grin.

"*Dumela, ngwana wami*. Breakfast will be ready soon and I hope your brother is already awake."

"We are ready when *mme* is ready." He went back to the hut.

Minutes later, he returned for breakfast, carrying a parcel. MmaMonare looked at it quizzically. Boysie was already seated. Kgabalatsana addressed both of them.

"I had thought that this moment would happen when the whole family was around, but unfortunately, *mme, rra* is not around. And in his absence, I will then do what I planned to do."

He opened the parcel, that was wrapped in brown paper, and took out a pair of grey trousers, shoes and a jacket.

"This is for *ntate*." He handed them over to his mother.

"I am sure he will appreciate your generosity; I hope he comes when you are still around."

"I do not think he will find me here, *mme,* as I will be leaving on Monday and you had indicated that he was away for the weekend."

Kgabalatsana then took out another packet in the same wrapping, containing a black silk dress, black shoes and a headscarf, handing it over to her mother, who smiled broadly, her few remaining teeth prominent.

"This is for you, *mme*, how could I have forgotten you, the one and only who brought me into this world."

"What about your father, did he not?"

Kgabalatsana did not respond to the question, but rather looked at his brother, who refused eye contact with him. The last parcel was for his brother - a chalk-striped suit, a shirt and a hat. He took his seat at the table as the mother, on behalf of the family, thanked Kgabalatsana for the presents.

"I thank you, my child, for the generosity that you have shown to us. We all appreciate it, and I am sure had your father been here, he would have said the same. I hope that you did not forget your other family."

She looked at Boysie, eyes glittering with tears. Kgabalatsana was unsettled to hear these words from his mother.

"*Nya* - no, *mme* how could I? I actually plan to be with them today, this afternoon?"

"That will be important, and I will accompany you to her home," Boysie said.

Kgabalatsana adopted a formal, consenting tone of voice, acknowledging his elder brother's role as a senior family member.

"I think it will only be correct for an elder brother to accompany a younger when he is to visit the home of a woman to whom he has done damage. For what shall I do if I meet the woman's father at the gate, and he asks me who I am? I appreciate your support, my brother."

Their mother looked at her sons, wondering what this was all about. Boysie never spoke about Kgabalatsana impregnating the Rethabile girl. Did Boysie know about the 'other' relationship between the two families? As far as she knew, Boysie didn't know a thing. Hoping that this was still the case, she decided to avoid being dragged into the controversy, which would eventually have to be resolved one way or the other, as far as opening cans of worms go. But that day was not today – and MmaMonare would say nothing.

The day was warm on that Good Friday in 1961, when Kgabalatsana and his brother Boysie headed down the gravel road towards the lower end of the village, where Nthabiseng lived. They spoke very little. Kgabalatsana clutched a plastic packet, while Boysie carried his stick. As they turned into the yard, which was just beyond the church, Kgabalatsana was sure that he saw a shadow against the front window – it must be Nthabiseng! However, the shadow merged into nothingness; he was probably just desperate to see her, and so playing mind tricks on himself.

They paused at the gate, expecting a voice of welcome. None came. Boysie exclaimed suddenly:

"*Dumelang le lapa la* (good day to the house of Rethabile), *kenang* (may the visitors come in)?"

A voice from inside the house responded.

"You are already in, gentlemen. It is not necessary for us to welcome you in."

The two were met at the door by a woman of around MmaMonare's age.

"Please come in, welcome."

The woman led them into a sparsely-furnished dining room, fashionable in its day. On the walls were several family photographs, and a large one of an old man and his wife – the old woman who had welcomed them. Boysie gathered that it was the old man's wedding photograph.

Next to that picture was one of a young girl who looked much like Nthabiseng. This must have been her, as she was an only child. The brothers took their seats at a spacious wooden table, which filled most of the room.

"My name is MmaRethabile, mother to Nthabiseng, and my husband, *ntate* Rethabile, is unfortunately out on a church visit to another village. As you know, at this time of year, churchgoers are never at home. My daughter has gone to the shop. What can I help you with?"

Boysie cleared his throat, sitting up straight.

"My name is Boysie Monare, *mme*, and this is my younger brother, Kgabalatsana, who works in the mines. I do think that the name Kgabalatsana will be familiar in this home."

"How can it not be, my child, and as you entered the gate, I saw a replica of Japheth in your younger brother as I have known both your parents for a very long time."

"My brother arrived yesterday from the city of Johannesburg and he thought that it would be his pleasure to come and visit Nthabiseng," said Boysie.

"You are welcomed, my children, and as I said, she has gone to the shops, but should be here at any time from now. In the meantime, let me make you something to drink while you wait for her."

MmaRethabile vanished for a few moments and returned with a tea tray, soft drinks and biscuits. She served Kgabalatsana and Boysie, saying nothing more at first. After taking her seat, she looked directly at Kgabalatsana.

"*Rre* Kgabalatsana, you have been quiet since you came in. Feel free, my child, this is your home. How is the city of Johannesburg, my child?"

He took a sip of his drink and swallowed a biscuit before clearing his throat.

"I have not been quiet, *mme*. I was giving the elders a chance to talk as I, the youngest, must enter the conversation only when asked to. This is how *ntate* Monare and Mma-Monare taught us. And it was for this reason that I could not come here alone. The city of Johannesburg is an interesting place, with its up and downs. At times, it becomes too big for us not born there, though it is a place full of opportunities."

"Have you seen the gold lining the streets my child?" she asked, jokingly.

"That is another story, *mme*; what I have seen so far is the millions and millions of people roaming the streets, always rushing. I still have to see the gold, for even though we are the ones who dig it out of the soil, it is in a different form, just rough stones."

As he was still explaining to MmeRethabile about the city, he heard footsteps outside. His heart leapt, beating fast with excitement and fear. The person approaching might be Nthabiseng – or it might be *ntate* Rethabile.

Nthabiseng came in, seeing Boysie first. Then she spotted Kgabalatsana, and the parcels she carried slipped to the floor as she brought both hands to her chest, seemingly shocked and out of breath. Then her hands went to her head. Nthabiseng's mother led her to a chair and gave her a glass of warm water with sugar. After a few moments, the girl recovered. But it was her mother who spoke first.

"Nthabi, meet *rre* Boysie Monare and Kgabalatsana, his younger brother, whom I know needs no introduction to you. *Rre* Kgabalatsana arrived yesterday and they thought that they should visit you. So, feel free."

She left the room for the kitchen, leaving her daughter alone with the brothers. Boysie, by then, felt that he had done his job and should give Kgabalatsana some privacy. He asked Nthabiseng to call her mother to say goodbye. She accompanied him to the gate, turning back to address the couple.

"My children, it would be better if you go and use the room outside. I do not want to hear children's stories, I am old."

"There is nothing we are going to talk about, *mme*, that is secret."

"Go Nthabiseng and Monare, go, I want to clean this room."

"Understandable, if it is about *mme* cleaning the house," giggled Nthabiseng. They walked arm in arm to the hut outside.

"Were you not afraid to come to my place?"

"At first, I was, but when my brother told my mother that he would accompany me, I felt stronger and relieved."

"Now how do you feel?"

"I feel relieved that we were received with open arms by your mother, though I am not sure whether it would have been the same if your father was here."

"That is a million-dollar question, he is the unpredictable one here, it all depends on the mood in which you find him, and he is so not only to strangers like you."

"Can you stand up, *moratiwa*, so that I can see your stomach?"

Nthabiseng, with pride, stood up. Kgabalatsana was rather surprised that she did not have as much of a big, bulging body as he had expected.

"It is not all women who have those huge bellies, and I realised that I am one of them. At eight months, you would not believe that next month will be that great month of delivery."

"Do you think the baby will be a boy, and do you have a name for the child?"

"No, not really; I have not thought about it - and what about you?"

"Boy or girl, it will be a child to me. I just realised that I left a bag in the dining room, let me go and fetch it."

"Are you not afraid to go alone?"

"No, I am not, for the only reason that when we came in she welcomed us and said, 'Welcome to your home.' Therefore, I am not afraid."

Kgabalatsana walked out of the hut, across the yard and into the dining room, where he found Nthabiseng's mother seated.

"I left a parcel, *mme*, where I was seated; may I have it?"

"With pleasure, my child, there it is." Kgabalatsana took the plastic bag and went back to the hut.

"My mother is a very humble person, *rre* Kgabalatsana, I knew you would encounter no harm; if it was so, I would not have allowed you to go and fetch the parcel."

"I was not expecting any, to be honest, my *moratiwa*(darling)."

Kgabalatsana moved to take her hands in his face, giving her a deep kiss.

"You are killing me," she whispered.

"You have been killing me from the day I left the village. I could not wait for this moment."

She gently pushed him away and he complied. After a few minutes, Kgabalatsana and Nthabiseng were in intense discussion about how they had survived without each other over the past few months, with Kgabalatsana intermittently reminding her of how much he loved her and their unborn child. They fantasised about how they would sit together, the three of them, as they did now.

"It will be a great moment when that time comes, *rra*," she said.

"Well, now that I have heard that you are well, it is time to give you this."

He handed over the plastic bag.

"I am not going to open it, for I want you to do it in privacy. I do not want to see a woman crying."

She beamed and squeezed his hand.

"By the way, thank-you very much for the money you sent me just before Christmas; it came at the right time, not only for me, but for my family."

"It is my pleasure. Remember, we promised each other that we would support each other."

"I do remember that, but thank-you very much."

He took an envelope and handed it over, swelling with pride that he was able to continue providing for her financially.

Nthabiseng gave him a light kiss.

"By the way, when are you going back?"

"Early Easter Monday morning, my dear, I have to be back in Johannesburg, as on Tuesday I am reporting for the 6 am shift."

"But I am sure I will see you before that, for it is only Friday today, not so?"

"You are right, it is, and we will see each other tomorrow."

Nthabiseng and Kgabalatsana were the happiest couple in the world, thought MmeRethabile, as she watched her daughter accompany the young man out of the gate into the road.

"I do pray to God that they become successful in their affair; that there will be nothing devastating, for *ntate* Rethabile would say, 'I told you so'," she thought to herself.

Nthabiseng came back home to show her mother the things she had received, as well as the envelope containing a generous amount of cash. MmeRethabile was pleased – not only because of the money and clothes, but because her daughter seemed to be finding (and keeping) a husband.

Kgabalatsana arrived home, where his mother waited, busying herself in the kitchen. Handing him a glass of ginger beer and some cakes, she waited to hear about his visit.

"*Mme*," asked Kgabalatsana tentatively, "what is this

news – or rather, gossip – that I'm hearing around the village about *ntate's* infidelity?"

His mother was calm. "My child, it is not correct to delve into matters of the old people. Your father is a respected member of this family and the whole village. I do not want to discuss such things with children."

"But with him? Do you discuss these?"

"Kgabalatsana, my child, you know what, I said to you I do not discuss such things with children. It is taboo."

She turned back to the sink to continue washing her dishes.

Frustrated, Kgabalatsana realised that he would not be able to press his mother any further on the topic. However, she paused for a minute, hands poised above the water, and then turned to him.

"By the way, where did you get all this information? Who told you, if I may ask?"

"Let us leave it, *mme*."

MmaMonare looked at her boy and shook her head.

His love and respect for his mother worked on Kgabalatsana then. He was wrong to confront her with such delicate and unsubstantiated information. He did not think that it was his brother's intention to have him do so, either, when he had told Kgabalatsana about the rumours.

"The person with whom I should take up this matter is Boysie, not *mme*," he thought. "I think that I erred in this regard. But crying over spilt milk won't help."

Kgabalatsana returned to his hut for a nap. Feeling like a traitor, he buried his face in the pillow and slept for three hours.

***

Kgabalatsana was not looking forward to Sunday, as this was the day on which his father was now due to return from his church trip. He did not know how they would handle each other. Much depended on his father, and he was in no mood for confrontation, which would not come from his end. But, knowing his father's temperament, anything could happen. He tended to rely on his mother to diffuse tension.

It was late morning on Sunday before he finally woke and stretched.

"I have to wake up, in case the old man has already arrived. I will have to bow and scrape to avoid any misunderstanding with my father. If I don't, I will be giving him an excuse to get even with me for no apparent reason."

He washed and dressed, emerging into a yard scorched by the sun. Blinking, he saw Japheth arriving, carrying his suitcase in a jaunty, sauntering manner. Kgabalatsana rushed forward, taking the luggage from his father's hands.

"*Dumela, ntate.*"

"Kgabalatsana, when did you arrive?"

"I arrived on Thursday, father."

"I see. It is good to see you, my son."

No more was said, then. The father walked into his house, followed by the son.

Japheth greeted his wife while Kgabalatsana took the suitcase to his parents' bedroom. When he returned to the dining room, his father was seated at the table, waiting. A fly buzzed at his face, which Japheth flicked away with minor annoyance.

"This must be a sign of rain. So, Kgabalatsana how is the land of the white men? Did you experience the stories told of the city?"

"Some, yes, father, but it is not what people make it to be. Yes, it is big and there are many people when compared to our part of the country, father."

"It is interesting to hear that. And, when are you going back?"

"Tomorrow morning, father, I have to be on the road, as I am on duty early Tuesday."

"It is a pity that I missed your arrival, but church duties forced me. As you know, our diocese meets at this time of year."

MmaMonare placed food in front of her husband, and for a few minutes, he was silent, concentrating on his meal. Kgabalatsana's mother stared at her son intently, as though issuing a wordless warning. He interpreted this as a stern reminder not to talk about the infidelity rumours.

"*Mme le ntate*, I have to go and see family friends in the village - Sechaba and Dira's families - to tell them how they are doing in the city."

"That is fine, my child," said MmaMonare.

Kgabalatsana left the house, glad to be out in the fresh air.

The village was as quiet as a church mouse as Kgabalatsana walked along the rough road leading to Sechaba's home. With nothing in his hand, no present from him for his family, Kgabalatsana felt as empty as if he were casually visiting his own family, long after all gifts had been given.

"Still, this is not about presents or such niceties, but rather words to say that they are well, and told by a friend who knows them well and lives with them in the city," he mused. "That should be enough for Sechaba's parents."

As he entered the Sechaba homestead, he heard a scream.

"*Bathong! Bonang* (People! See) it is *rre* Kgabalatsana. I only hope that he is not bringing bad news?" An elderly lady of his mother's age climbed down the *stoep* (veranda) steps to greet him, wiping her hands on her dress.

"*Kena* (come in) *rre* Kgabalatsana, you are at home, tell me what happened to my child, Sechaba?"

He knew that now was not the time to waste on niceties, as the lady was already overwrought and imagining the worst.

"Good day, *mme*, I have not come for what you think of, but rather to tell you that Sechaba is well and working well at the mines in Johannesburg. I was with him the day I left Johannesburg and he asked me to convey to you good Easter wishes and tell you that he is well. And that he would be visiting home soon."

"But why did he not come with you?"

"We work shifts in the mines and both he and Dira are working this weekend."

Sechaba's mother nearly crumpled with relief. She broke into a smile.

"It a relief to hear that he is well. You know that we always hear stories about that city."

"I understand, *mme*, but it is not as bad as the news that you hear about in the village."

"That is comforting to hear."

"*Mme*, I will come back later, before I sleep, as this is my last day, and I would like to see Sechaba's sleeping place. He asked me to see what he could buy next time he comes; size of the bed, bedspreads and sheets."

"Go - there it is my child; it is as he left it."

He went into Sechaba's room to scout around.

After the visit, he went to Dira's place, where he found no one but a dog wagging its tail as he entered the yard. He knocked at the door and there was nobody at the house. He turned back towards his home, where he found his parents seated in the dining room.

He saw that his father was not relaxed and that his mother was still tense following the earlier discussion. She clearly was worried that he would bring it up. Kgabalatsana greeted them politely and then went back to his hut, where Boysie was relaxing on the bed.

"I am back, elder brother."

He threw himself down next to his sibling.

"I came back a few minutes ago expecting to find you home, but was told that you went out. I thought that you went to the Rethabiles?"

"Not at all, I will be going there later. I went to see Sechaba's family and found the mother, but unfortunately, I found nobody at Dira's place."

"As you know, this is holiday weekend and people tend to visit family and friends in other villages or churches. Remember, this is a big religious time for those who love the church, like our father."

"Talking about the old man, Boysie, he does not seem to be himself, is there any particular thing, except the one you raised the other day?"

"Not that I am aware of."

"Back to what you insinuated about his behaviour. What was it all about?"

Boysie looked the other way, not sure if he wanted to discuss the matter with his younger brother, but relented.

"You see, Kgabalatsana. You are no more a young boy, you are a grown-up, to be a father soon. You can decide between right and wrong. What I meant by our father's infidelity in the village…"

He hesitated, not quite sure how to continue.

"Let me help you out here. It has come out that what actually infuriated *ntate* about you impregnating the Rethabile girl had more to it. This was something that happened before MmeRethabile got married to *ntate* Rethabile and before *ntate* met *mme*. They, MmeRethabile and *ntate*, had an affair."

"Do not say that! When and who told you this?"

"It is irrelevant who told me or when I heard this story, but listen to it. The family of MmeRethabile, the Dithabanengs, were vehemently opposed to the affair and had always looked forward to their daughter getting married to the Rethabile boy. *Ntate* lost the bid, MmeRethabile ended the affair and she ultimately got married to *ntate* Rethabile.

"So, when you got involved with Nthabiseng, father always feared that that would bring forth old, healed wounds."

By this time, Kgabalatsana was on his feet, gyrating about in the room with his hands on his head.

"Where does that put me now with Nthabiseng?"

"It puts you nowhere, it's irrelevant. It was and still is a matter between father and his history – let bygones be bygones. After all, I am saying this because all damages for your impregnating the Rethabile girl have been paid, insisted on by our father."

"Do you not think that he had to do it so as not to open the old wounds that you talk about?"

"Whatever the reason, that should be irrelevant to you and me," said Boysie firmly.

Kgabalatsana looked at his watch, noticing that it was 6.30 pm. He looked at Boysie and said, "Brother, as you know, this is my last evening at home; as such I will be going to see Nthabiseng before it is too late, and if I do not come back, I will see you in the morning."

He took his jacket and left the homestead for Nthabiseng's home, finding her waiting at the gate, a small bag slung on her arm. They walked away from the house quickly, hoping to avoid a disapproving call from her mother, saying that she did not want Nthabiseng leaving home; but fortunately, this did not happen.

They went straight to Sechaba's place, where Kgabalatsana led Nthabiseng to the outside hut used by Sechaba. As they neared it, Sechaba's mother shouted from the kitchen window: "The door is not locked."

Nthabiseng looked at Kgabalatsana nervously, and he responded by placing their few belongings on the bed.

"Do not worry, Sechaba's mother has given me permission to use the place for rest whenever I need to."

That night was the most glorious one he had experienced since coming home. It wasn't that he had not enjoyed his first day back or the conversations with his brother; but this was different, as he was finally back with the one person who meant the world to him. And she was holding his baby in her womb. Kgabalatsana spent much time caressing her stomach, as though he was already able to touch the baby.

"Just hold your hand there for a while. What do you feel?"

"Nothing, just the warmth of your stomach," he replied.

"Oh! You are like any other man. I should have known."

"Ok, do it again."

The night went on and on, with the two playing as children, until at last, while they were sleeping, Kgabalatsana's hand on Nthabiseng's stomach, he suddenly felt a kick from deep within her belly and started, trying to rouse her awake.

"That was what I wanted you to feel earlier on," said Nthabiseng sleepily. "The child was kicking and he or she does it all the time, especially when I am asleep; as if it is waking me up."

When the first cock started to crow and the cows in the kraal began to bellow, Nthabiseng rose from the bed, softly waking Kgabalatsana.

"I have to go before my parents wake up."

They hurriedly dressed and went out of the house and yard, moving as quietly as possible to Nthabiseng's place, where she left him a distance from her house. He kissed her goodbye and said:

"I will write to you as soon as I arrive in Johannesburg."

Kgabalatsana went back home and slipped into the house.

The tranquility and the joy that he had had at Sechaba's place with Nthabiseng was short-lived. Just as it had that eventful day, when Kgabalatsana returned from school to be confronted by his father, another argument threatened. It was history repeating itself.

As he packed his belongings, Japheth stepped into the hut, eyes blazing – almost venomous, as it about to strike.

"You are the worst boy I ever brought into this world. Hardly had you greeted me and you disappeared, I came into your hut last night but you were nowhere to be found. Where were you, Kgabalatsana?"

"I was in the village, *rra*."

"Village, village, come to the main house."

They entered the main house to find MmaMonare standing next to the kitchen door.

"Here he is, not even able to tell me where he has been," said Japheth.

"*Ntate le mme*, I do not know what I have done? I came home, thinking that I was coming back to enjoy myself, and found *ntate* not at home, which was not a problem. But now, just as on the day when I made the decision to leave to work in the mines, *ntate* is again pushing me away from him for no apparent reason."

MmaMonare had kept quiet, not knowing what brought down such anger from her husband upon her son. But then, she sighed, and rounded on Japheth.

"Japheth, I do not understand where the problem is here? This boy told me and his brother yesterday, when he left, that he was going to his friends' places - Sechaba and Dira - to pass their messages to their parents; that further he would go and see the mother of his child. You never asked me where he was and seemingly you just presumed that he had left. Let us suppose that he did; is he no more than a schoolboy who has to report his every movement? I honestly do not understand what your problem is."

"My problem is that this boy, who does what he wants, he left us without seeking our permission."

"But you are the one who said that he has to work out how he is going to support his child, and this he is preparing himself to do."

Kgabalatsana looked at his father, feeling the puzzle pieces falling into place.

"Maybe, *ntate*, you have to tell me now where I have sinned or what your issue is? For I really do not understand. But I have my own suspicions and I think I am being used here as a scapegoat. Truth is, this is not about me; you are using me. Tell me, is it true that before you got married to *mme* you had an affair with MmeRethabile, before she got married?"

"Listen to the things said by this child. Where do you get all that nonsense? God help me!" MmaMonare held her hands over her head and sighed.

Kgabalatsana continued, agitated, and bristling.

"I know now that the woman I have impregnated is actually your daughter. Nthabiseng Rethabile is your daughter, that I know, and if you want me to tell you where I got this news, you will get it. *Ntate,* you have forced me, through your temperament, to say things that normally a child would not say to a parent. You have a big task on your shoulders now, for your grandchild is to be born soon, and born from both your children.

"And this matter is known in this village, by your friends and your equals. How that is solved or is going to be solved culturally, I do not know? You will have to figure that out. Unfortunately, that will be left with you. I am on my way back to work. One thing that I am not going to do is to leave my girlfriend because of a parent who has not been open with his children."

MmaMonare shrieked, stricken by her son's words, her hands still clutching her head. At that moment, Boysie came through the gate, saw his mother crying, and rushed into the house, where he found his brother and father facing each other like two Spanish bulls.

"The chickens have come home to roost, elder brother, the can of worms has been opened," Kgabalatsana said softly.

"What father thought would be a lifetime secret has now come out. I know now that the very woman I have impregnated is my father's daughter."

Boysie looked at his father, then went over to hug his mother. He turned to both and addressed them solemnly.

"I knew that one day this would come out and there it is, father, the truth of the matter. You have been too hard on your own, and not because he was at fault more than you. You were ashamed of your own faults. Let us allow Kgabalatsana to leave, as he has to report for duty tomorrow. Go, my brother, tough as it is going to be for you, we will see this resolved. There is no scandal that cannot be resolved in our custom. Father and the elders will have to guide us."

Kgabalatsana, by this time, had his suitcase next to him. He gazed at his mother for a long moment, tears brimming, and then took leave of his parents.

"I have to leave, my parents. *Ntate*, know that I leave home this time the most aggrieved person. I thought that when I first left home I was aggrieved, but this time my heart is torn apart."

Nthabiseng joined Kgabalatsana just as he was leaving his home street and slowly, hand in hand, they walked.

"I thought I should give you a surprise and walk you up to the store."

"It was very kind of you, *moratiwa*, and what a surprise; I needed your company."

"Truth is, yesterday I noticed that there were things bothering you, and look at your face now, it is as if you were crying. Or is it the feeling of the family last-born leaving his parents?"

"Maybe so."

As they reached the general dealer's store, there was a bakkie waiting to collect people going to Zeerust. They stopped at a distance from the bakkie, Kgabalatsana brushing Nthabiseng's stomach, and saying: "I can see growth in this baby."

"You talk of growth - it is kicking all the time and I think it cannot wait to come out."

The driver of the bakkie pressed the hooter and shouted.

"*Zeerust! Zeerust bo rra lebo mme* (transport for Zeerust ladies and gentlemen)."

Nthabiseng pulled her beloved by the hand and gently pushed him forward.

"Go now, *rre* Kgabalatsana, lest the transport leaves you behind, which you cannot afford, as you have a mission in Johannesburg."

They hugged, and Kgabalatsana gave her a light kiss on the cheek before stepping into the bakkie bound for Zeerust.

***

At Zeerust he found a half-full train station and after thirty minutes' wait, the train pulled out of the platform on its journey to Johannesburg, where it arrived just as the sun was dipping.

The journey seemed to have been short, because for most of the trip he fell into a deep sleep, despite the noise of the crowded carriage. It hadn't been a restful sleep, though. In his mind, his father's tormenting voice rang out at him, and he played over the second quarrel repeatedly, reliving his mother's shrieks of despair over this angry impasse between son and husband.

Kgabalatsana woke as they arrived at Park Station, from whence he took a bus to Booysens, where he and a group of mineworkers trudged back to Mzilikazi Mine. On arrival at their sleeping quarters, Kgabalatsana did not even have time to go and greet his friends, but instead, went straight to sleep.

In the morning, it was Dira who first saw Kgabalatsana in a queue, reporting for the first shift. He was excited to see his friend.

"Welcome back, home-boy! I hope you bring us good news from home. And I hope to catch up with you after work."

Kgabalatsana waved at him as he went into the shaft cage, the door slamming shut. Joseph was over the moon to see his friend.

"You seem rejuvenated. The weekend must have treated you well, and what luck that you can still go home when some of us have nothing left of what we used to call home. That is why we have adopted Johannesburg as our home."

Shouting beneath the background of the drilling machine, Kgabalatsana responded: "We will talk after work, let us now concentrate on the job at hand, lest we forget what we are here for."

Just several weeks later, in June, Kgabalatsana was made foreman of his group, as recommended by Joseph, who was in turn promoted to Shearling's position. The British expatriate had decided to retire and enjoy the benefits of having worked in South Africa's blossoming mining industry.

The promotion was a blessing for Kgabalatsana. It meant that his meagre wages were increased, and a move to a bigger, better compound, shared with only five men of his own rank.

The lights were even brighter here than in Section 2, where he had left his original home-boys. He also was free to leave the compound at any time, outside working hours, without seeking permission.

Only now did he fully understand and appreciate Joseph's lifestyle – and this bonded him more firmly to his mentor and friend.

The promotion news had to be communicated to Nthabiseng. After all, it meant that he was better able to provide her and the child with bigger luxuries now, and he was feeling quite fulfilled. Taking advantage of the quiet period in quarters after work, he took his writing paper and pen.

Mzilikazi Mines
Booysens
Johannesburg
June 1961

My Dear Loving Nthabiseng

This letter is further evidence of the love and dedication I feel towards you and our child. Travelling back to Johannesburg after my visit to you, and those last few moments spent with you before leaving, made me feel so much closer to you.

Great things are starting to happen here, for in the last days I have been promoted into a senior Induna position and what that means is that there will be a raise in my wages, better working conditions and privileges. We should all praise God for this achievement. I am also aware that the baby will have been born by now. I know that you asked me about a name for the child – that I will leave in your capable hands.

But despite these exciting developments, I have left behind huge problems at home. The relationship with my father has not helped much, thus putting a strain on my mother, who is a peace-loving person. I hope one day that I will have time to sit down with you to explain the complications of my situation.

Kgabalatsana never finished writing this letter. Truth be told, he did not want to air his family's dirty laundry and make it Nthabiseng's problem. He folded the half-written letter and said to himself: "I will come back to this at a later stage."

That later stage never came, for Kgabalatsana's lifestyle started to change dramatically, day by day.

His most-visited place of choice was Alexandra. He had fallen in love with it.

One afternoon, Sechaba noticed that Kgabalatsana and Joseph were having occasional conversations that included neither Dira nor him.

He was a little worried, but Dira reassured his friend.

"You are reading too much into something that is not worth reading into. After all, they will tell us if we need to know what they are up to, as they are our friends."

"I hope so," responded Sechaba.

It came out that there was nothing untoward about the whispered conversations. Joseph was trying to influence *Rooibaard* and his colleagues to allow Kgabalatsana to live outside the mining compound, thanks to a loophole in the mining regulations.

Mine Regulation 3000 stipulated that any mine worker ranked as junior induna was entitled to this privilege, regardless of the length of time in which they had been in the position.

When Joseph first made the recommendation to *Rooibaard*, the man brusquely replied: "But Joseph, Johannes is hardly long in this position."

Joseph hesitated, eyes to the ground, and then said:

"And there is no stipulation as to the time, sir."

The white man, realising that there was no more to argue about, agreed with Joseph.

Shortly afterwards, negotiations were successful and with permission from his bosses, Kgabalatsana was told that he would be allowed to stay outside the compound, should he wish to do so.

***

Kgabalatsana had had several promotions in the past two years. By this stage, he was a senior induna at Mzilikazi. Comparing his accommodation now to his hut in Dinokana – and the first shared compound at the mine – he felt that he had taken a big step up.

This was the springboard into his induction into an entirely new way of life, although he had not yet left the confines of the compound to live outside it. Alexandra became his playground and second home, thanks to him being coached and educated by the veteran miner, Joseph.

He also embarked on a stronger relationship with Mampye, which was becoming a serious matter. So serious, in fact, that Dira felt he had to step in.

"I have not heard you talking about Nthabiseng for a long time, my friend. The only words coming out of your mouth are Mampye here, Mampye there."

Kgabalatsana knew that Dira was right. Something inside him linked thinking about Nthabiseng with the horrible events at home – none of which, he believed, were of his making. He had been a scapegoat, owing to his father's indiscretions, and the issues surrounding Nthabiseng and the child had still not been resolved. If Nthabiseng hadn't fallen pregnant, then perhaps none of these secrets would have come out, he thought.

But he couldn't tell Dira this. Instead, he brushed off his friend's concerns with gruff, feigned annoyance.

"You are just jealous, man. Leave me alone. I have not forgotten Nthabiseng."

Sechaba was not as easily fooled.

"*Rre* Kgabalatsana, we have been noticing recent caucuses between you and Joseph. And you never share these with us, your own home-boys. What are these all about? We know, through *Bra* Sparks, that Mampye is scouting for a place for you in Alexandra. And that she says the place has an oversupply of accommodation, with every house-hold hiding a string of back rooms."

"Gents, you are casting too many aspersions on me. Give me my space and wait until I brief you on what my plans are. Please, not now. There is still a lot in my mind; too many things that need to be resolved in my life. As for what you are raising, Dira, it is nothing compared to what I am going through, so please bear with me, gents."

Much later, towards the end of December, 1963, not only was Kgabalatsana preparing to leave the compound, but also his job at Mzilikazi Mine. Leaving Mzilikazi would prove not to be an easy thing for Kgabalatsana, all his friends pounced on him for doing so, urging him to re-consider his intentions.

"You have a bright future here." Joseph urged him one day.

"This type of work is not a piece of cake, we all know Kgabalatsana, to sleep every night in a room full of men, without the opposite sex is even more strenuous. But think of home, family, children and girl-friend, my friend," Mzimela begged him. At last he did subdue himself to advice from friends, but was clear in his mind that ultimately, he would leave Mzilikazi for greener pastures.

Chapter 5

Life in Alexandra

Shortly before the mine closed for the festive season, Kgabalatsana handed his resignation letter to *Rooibaard*, citing 'going to greener pastures' as his reason for leaving. This rather shocked *Rooibaard*.

"Do you think it is a wise thing to do, Johannes? When the prospects for you in this mine are so great? And do you have a job that you will be going into after this one?"

Kgabalatsana was quick to defuse any concerns that he was not entirely sure about his future. Though the truth was, he had not found any job. He was just tired of working in the mine and wanted to try his luck with finding a job elsewhere. Of course, there was a danger that he might be kicked out of the city, as Joseph warned him.

"Remember, Kgabalatsana, you came into the city through the NCR contract and should you be found wanting, chances are that you will be deported back to Zeerust."

Kgabalatsana was unfazed. "I will take my chances, as many are doing, my friend."

"But also remember - the few pennies that you might get from Mzilikazi will not last you forever, Kgabalatsana."

"I will work hard, my brother, to get a job in one of the factories or shops."

By now, Joseph realised that his friend had chosen his own fate, and nothing that he did or said would change Kgabalatsana's mind. He reassured *Rooibaard* himself, saying: "Everything has been sorted out. Do not worry."

***

Alex is on the fringes of the affluent suburb of Sandton. Its history dates back to 1904, when a wealthy farmer,

Papenfus, bought several farms, including Zandfontein, which would later become Alexandra township, named for his wife, Alexandra. The farmer's first job was to build a mud hut, helped by his wife and their cook, Hey Nxele Mbanjwa. It would act as a donkey refreshment station for carts carrying his milk from the farm to Johannesburg.

The Mbanjwas brought their five-year-old daughter, Annie, with them when they moved. Annie married Phumeza Twala, and they had 10 children. Phumeza, a thatcher, plied his trade on many thatched roofs in the white suburbs of Johannesburg. Lured by job opportunities at the expanding mines, rural people settled near the Mbanjwas, and by 1912, Papenfus began dividing up Zandfontein into plots, selling them to black families with the intention of giving them the right to own land. But then, in 1913, the Land Act stripped them of this right.

Papenfus needed a name for the new township. Twala, the Mbanjwa's son, recalls Papenfus asking his grandparents which name might be suitable. They replied that he should choose his wife's name, Alexandra, as she loved people. And so, it became Alexandra.

Today, it is still Alexandra – but Papenfus would hardly recognise it. His wife would be aghast that a place named for her is a derelict hotbed of poverty, whose inhabitants are a forgotten lot.

Picture a warm, summery Saturday, just before midday, along a row of adjoining living quarters – most of which is going to hell in a handcart. Most big family houses hold dozens of illegal and legal residents, both within and without, in the back yards. These tenants, many down at heel, mingle about with each other, while others do their washing in tin or plastic buckets as they prepare themselves for Monday – those who are lucky enough to have jobs. Running water in households is a luxury which many residents cannot afford. Toilets are still the old 'bucket' system – the way it was when the place was founded so many years ago. Landlords and landladies supplement their meagre incomes by renting out rooms or tiny spaces, creating a little of something out of the nothing that others have.

WELCOME TO ALEXANDRA!

This is life in Alexandra, the Dark City, as it is often called. Although the conditions of these people leave much to be desired, to some, if not all, Alexandra is a way of life, a culture, a habitat that represents history. They were dyed-in-the-wool Alexandrans.

When Kgabalatsana left his job in the mines, he had organised a place there. Now, he was seated below a window in a house at the end of a row of identical houses. Clearly, he was transformed from village boy to city-clever man –even with a new name, TM ("Toppie Manoja"), which had replaced his old one here in Alex. With the money earned from the mine, he had bought himself a car – a red Dodge, with sparkly-white tyres. Together with his snappy city-dressing style, he had adopted a fancy new persona and could be heard bragging to his friends:

"I'm the clever one, I'm the only living example of one who comes from Dinokana and is still surviving in the Dark City, a mine driller of note at the Mzilikazi Mine until I was promoted to an induna. I have seen it all in this city of gold. Do you see that car parked outside there? It is the product of my sweat from working here in this city."

Kgabalatsana loved regaling his friends with his village boy-made-good tale.

"But listen further to the story, my *broer* and please, for the sake of brotherhood, listen to me carefully and attentively, David."

David Sithole, whom he had met at Sparks' place while working at the mine and frequenting Alex, had become one of TM's great friends and confidantes. Tall, slightly overweight and dressed in a green Viyella shirt, black Brentwood trousers, black and white Crockett & Jones shoes, and black and white Ayers cap on his head, nobody really knew where he came from originally, but he had been in Johannesburg long before TM. It was sometimes told that he hailed from the Northern Cape Province, from the town of Kimberley, but David neither confirmed nor denied this.

"Especially because I have noticed that of late you never take me seriously," continued TM. "Life is too short for one to be making jokes. I am far younger than you, David and there is still a long way for me to go to know the corners of Jozi as you do – and I have respect for you - but please take me seriously at times, because I am a serious guy.

"Look at you, you have a good life here in Alex. I am also comfortable with the new life that I am starting. Look at your Jewish clothing. All gotten at a discount and introduced, *no-gal*, by you and old Joseph. Just look at me now, *broer*."

TM admired himself. Bermuda shorts below-the-knee, a white vest and large, fawn Dorian hat covering his bald head – the hat being TM's trademark, and the outfit, his signature style. He was content with life and the independence of having his own place (though rented). He found solace in being one of the recognised inhabitants of Alex and that he had made a name for himself, despite an unknown future.

He clutched a cigarette between his teeth as he stroked at his shoes, flicking imaginary dust and checking the polish. He was slightly built, with a beer paunch. Clothing had always been a fascination, ever since that first meeting with Joseph at Mzilikazi Mine. The style of the time, and the fashion-consciousness of the age had 'got to him'.

A commotion erupted among the tenants, some dashing into their rooms as MamTshawe, the landlady, the *magriza*, the no-nonsense woman who took crap from nobody, bolted from her kitchen into the yard.

It was month end and renting out rooms was her only means of earning a living. Well-built, upright posture, big buttocks, tall and smartly dressed in a blue *Seshoeshoe* dress, she was wearing a *doek* (scarf) around her head and a "take-no-prisoners" expression on her face.

She passed the tenants slowly, fixing them with her unblinking eyes as if they were in a prison identification parade. She hand-picked and chose which ones would be greeted.

MamTshawe stood in front of TM and David, towering over them.

"*Molweni bafana bam* (good morning, my boys)!" she trilled. David took a step sideways, while TM stood up rapidly from the bench. They replied in unison, respectfully.

"*Sawubona, magogo* (greetings old lady)."

"Kgabalatsana, my boy. Do not play with me, I'm not a football game; and I'm not your age," retorted the old lady. TM looked at the lady as if he did not know what she was talking about.

"*Uzakundazi* (you will know me). Do not even try and pretend. Bring it, bring my rent money."

She stretched out her hand towards Kgabalatsana, who immediately turned his back on her and David, digging his right hand into his pocket. He did this to avoid them seeing how much money he had.

He took out R200 in notes and coins, handing them over to the lady. MamTshawe grabbed them, counting the notes, making sure that it was the right amount.

All the while, she kept a menacing eye on him.

"You've been warned several times, my boy," she said. "I've been telling you that I have long been in Johannesburg, and remember that I do not come from Dinokana, *andiphu-mi emaplazini mna kwedini* (I am not from the farms, my boy). Gone are the days of rent boycott, my boy, this is not the fifties – after all, you were not even there, you were just a nincompoop herding cattle in the *bundus* (rural areas).

"What do you think my children eat? Do you think I have buckets of money stored under my mattress? No man, Kgabalatsana, be serious."

"But, *magogo*, I have just paid you, why are you still complaining?" asked TM.

"Your problem is that you behave as if you're Croesus, drinking brandy and coke, gin and tonic, every day. Look at this David friend of yours. *Ugeziswa zezi beer zase* (you are spoilt by these beers) that Croesus David brings from the breweries and that shebeen that is almost your home on 14th Avenue. Everybody knows that when you, 'Toppie Manoja' enter the shebeens, tables will be full. Do that after you've paid the rent, boy, otherwise you will always be in trouble with MamTshawe."

She turned to the other tenants, pointing at them.

"And I must warn all of you that there is going to be a rent increase next month, so you'd better square me up."

Loud exclamations of shock could be heard from the tenants.

"No! *Magogo*. You can't do that to us, these are bad times."

"For all of us, times are bad," said MamTshawe. "I agree with you – these are bad times."

She turned away from them and walked across the yard to her house.

"Do not play with me, boys and girls," she called over her shoulder. "Check your calendars so that you know when your payments are due."

She closed her kitchen door with a bang, but then opened it again, shouting to TM.

"As for you, Kgabalatsana, you will never win this war. I've always been too smart for you, my son, and remember, and I repeat, I'm not from Dinokana." She then disappeared.

TM shook his head and was furious with himself and at the lady, and pointed a threatening finger at her, although she had long disappeared into the house, satisfied that she had achieved her objective. He looked to David for sympathy, but his friend just grinned, shaking his head.

"You are in for it, my friend. But TM, you're always creating problems for yourself, big problems for yourself, every month it's the same thing, you're just provoking the old lady. Give her money on time and she will get off your back.

I have noticed that you're always late and this puts you into a pot of trouble."

TM feigned shock.

"O-ho! Just listen who is talking? Big mouth David, *nye, nye* (yep, yep). You're just lucky because you have your palace in Booysens. You don't know the pain we rent-payers face. Jozi is tough my friend! Ask us, the rent-payers."

He walked into his room, followed by his friend.

His room was one large space serving as a bedroom, kitchen, lounge and everything else that a normal house should have – but minimised. This was life, squatter-style, in Alexandra.

TM's house was modestly furnished for the standards of Alexandra, thanks to the creativity of Mampye, who had spent hours scrubbing the floors, generally cleaning and taking some of her own bedding into their new shared accommodation. A double bed stood in the far-right corner, draped in a red silk-style bedspread, though it was really nothing to write home about. Above the bedposts, a large portrait of legendary South African jazz saxophonist Kippie 'Morolong' Moeketsi dominated. The icon of local jazz in the fifties, the country's answer to John Coltrane, he reminded TM of favoured hang-outs from yesteryear.

Next to the bed was a small, mahogany dressing table, which had seen better days. It was once a precious piece of furniture, clearly, in somebody else's high-end household. A wardrobe and two bedside tables completed the picture. The 'lounge' area housed a round coffee table, on top of which was piled a stack of long-play vinyl records. The 'kitchen' contained basic necessities, as well as a primus stove and green plastic water bucket, neatly covered with a white towel.

He has been living in these conditions for some time since he arrived in Alexandra, but his lot had not changed much, nor were there any expectations that it would. It was becoming clearer by the day that he had to persevere and look for a job, which was proving to be a struggle, as he was still unemployed after having left the mine. Living off hand-outs from people such as David and from time to time, his old friend Joseph. He threw his hat on the bed as he entered and wiped his bald head with a crisp white handkerchief.

"Shit! This landlady, my last two hundred rands." He looked at David, who was busy drinking.

"My *broer*, I am starting to get cheesed off with this place. No! No! For three full years now," lamented TM. "Working in the mines for nothing, look at me. The only meaningful thing I have worth mentioning is this old Dodge, which of course I love. *Ek raak moeg vir die plek broer* (I am getting tired of this place, brother). I have to change gear and I am sure vicissitude might come my way."

David, taken by surprise by the seriousness with which his friend spoke, realised that there may be other factors impacting on his old buddy's frustration.

"I did not realise that you were so educated, the English you've just used amazes me, and I have never seen you so serious. Your jokes and story-telling, which always make us laugh, are your trademark, but today you have shown me your other side, Kgabalatsana – a side I did not know."

"Hey, my *broer*, be careful. It's only my old man who addresses me by my full name, be careful, if you can't call me TM, then call me Toppie Manoja, but not my full name."

He sighed and smoothed down his shirt, absently brushing his shoes again, as he spoke.

"Exactly, exactly, my brother. You know what? It is all true what you just said. And the reality is that I was just putting up a facade, concealing a frustration that has been boiling and boiling inside me for some time. You know what, one Easter Weekend just before I left the mine, I visited my old folks and my wife-to-be."

"You mean you left Mampye in Jozi and visited another one in the villages, hey you migrants – always leaving ones in the village while there is a *vat-en-sit* (concubine) in the city."

"*Neh*, man, no man, *luister* (listen), David. Things just did not go well between me and my old man. In the first place, when I arrived, he was not at home, but that was not the problem: I never told them that I was coming. I had a nice time with the rest of the family, but boom, he arrived a day before I had to leave.

"Problems started, my *broer* (brother). You see, one of the reasons that drove me here was a clash I had with him when I impregnated a *cherry* (a girlfriend) of mine. My father was upset by that, and as he put it, 'I have disgraced the family'. He almost beat me for impregnating the woman.

"Now, the second incident. I discovered that the old man is or had been a Casanova in the village. He had a child before he got married to *mme*. When I confronted him about this, it became clear to me that things would never work between the two of us.

"I came back to work with a sore heart, not knowing whether I would dare go back home while he was still alive. This I cannot hide anymore; it is eating me inside. Look at me David, my brother, it is as if I have been in this damn Jo'burg for ages. But of course, there is the smog from all the cars that we are inhaling. This place called city, David. I am telling you."

David made clucking noises and held up his hand for TM to stop speaking.

"Just give me a break, my brother, you're again starting to stray into the narrative of a day dreamer."

TM recoiled slightly from his friend, frustrated and irritated. He turned to the dressing table and bent to look at himself in the mirror.

"I am growing older by the day, my brother," he sighed. "I have a five o'clock shadow on my face. Come and look at me, David, I'm balding too fast for my age, look at my hair. I know that it started greying when I was young, but at least it had life, shiny and beautiful. But now it is something else."

The seriousness in TM's voice worried David, for he seemed to have his head in the clouds.

"Where has that beauty disappeared to? Eaten by worries. All as a consequence of the carbon that we breathe from the millions of cars roaming around, some not even roadworthy. Half of Alex is full of *skorokoros* (old and rusty cars)!"

David burst into loud laughter, tinged with a little anxiety.

"No. Now you are really starting to scare the hell out of me. But tell me, what are you going to do with the situation at home? Jozi is not a place for the faint-hearted, TM. Jozi is not for sprinters but for marathon runners, men who are durable, guys who are made of steel.

"No. *Ag*, TM, let's go and drink our brandy outside."

TM nodded.

He opened the upper drawer of his dressing table and took out a white envelope, throwing it on top of the dressing table.

He then opened a second drawer, took out his red Viyella shirt and put it on, and then changed into navy blue trousers, and went outside.

"Bring me a glass from the stuff outside, brother, and neat, please!"

David came back carrying two glasses in his hand. When TM saw David, he covered his face with his hands. Alarmed, David stopped, not knowing what he had done wrong.

"*Maar* – but - David! I really do not know what language to use with you, the Xhosa in you at times comes out, irrespective of years in Jozi. I ask for bread, you give me cake. I asked for a shot of brandy, neat *nogal*. Look what you brought? Brandy mixed with coke."

To David's greater surprise, TM grabbed the glass and gulped its contents, despite his earlier complaint. He dropped the glass to the floor, watching impassively as David bent to pick it up, clearly not in the mood to argue with his friend, who appeared to have gone mad.

"And now? Is there a party? Why are you so smartly dressed?" asked David.

"Listen again. There goes my friend David! But *mara* (why), David, can't a man be smart, especially on a Saturday, in Alexandra *nogal*? You know the girls are roaming everywhere, chasing and fishing for guys like me. So, guys need to be presentable and how do they do that?"

He pointed at his trousers and shirt and pulled his trousers up, showing the pleats and the shiny shoes.

"Do you want to be seen in the same old, craggy gab you wore during the week? No, man just develop, get a grip on yourself. We are just going to the Post Office.

"There is an express mail I have to post, which has to reach its destination not later than next week."

He looked at his wristwatch and at the envelope lying on the dressing table.

David wondered at the letter's intended destination, but kept silent, fearing another lambasting. Better to let sleeping dogs lie.

"We've got to get moving, guy, time and tide wait for no man. Life is too short to be wasted."

TM took the envelope and his hat and once again lifted up his trousers, as though uncertain of whether or not it was the correct style for the day, brushing them with his hand.

As he motioned to go, he stopped suddenly, appearing to have forgotten something. He opened the drawer and took out a shoe brush to polish his shoes, which were already squeaky clean and shining. He looked at his friend with a smile and adjusted the collar of his shirt, much to the amusement of David, and said:

"I like my boys to be smart and clean, but not smarter than me."

My friend, my bosom friend, is a real character through and through, thought David, as they laughed and left home together.

TM locked the door and, in a leisurely fashion, they walked through the yard towards the gate, saluting and chatting to their neighbours along the way. A lady living at the first house next to MamTshawe's kitchen ululated and exclaimed: "Where are my days gone, how I wish I hadn't committed myself!"

David responded, "There is still time to disembark from that train!"

Laughter broke out among the other tenants. TM closed the gate and walked over to the next-door neighbour's yard, where he parked his car. The space was supposed to come with a fee, but the neighbour had given up the battle months ago, though not the war. TM just refused to pay, unless she put up a fight. This house belonged to MamTsamaye, a tall, heavily-built, light-complexioned lady who was about the same age as MamTshawe.

As she heard her gate opened, she peeped through the living room window, checking to see who it was. Just letting strangers into your premises could result in all sorts of misfortunes, she thought to herself. She recognised the two men and immediately recalled that TM had not paid his monthly rent for parking. More trouble was looming for the unsuspecting TM. Clearly, this was not a good day for the wise man of Alex. As TM was about to open the car door, with his friend already halfway inside, he heard a voice from the front door.

"Hey *wena* (you) TM - my parking money, don't you know that it is month end and you have not paid?"

TM paused and looked in the old lady's direction.

"*Nx!*" he said, irritably. "My ancestors are not on my side. Why is everybody pestering me like this? Can't these people realise that I'm not Harry Oppenheimer?"

He said it intentionally loudly. The lady took great umbrage, and strode out of the house, fists raised, walking straight to him and pummelling him with her hands, furious at this man's disrespect.

"Don't push me, Kgabalatsana Monare," she said. "Please don't even try it! There is no free parking here. Even when you park this big car, *o-batshi* (car guards) will expect from you not less than two rands just for parking for less than five minutes. A mere hundred rands a month, in a locked yard and you think it is too much. Go and park at the Jan Smuts Airport and you'll pay through your neck, I'm telling you, my boy! Give me my money. Kgabalatsana, I don't have time to play!"

She hit him repeatedly on the chest as she said it.

There was no place for TM to hide, so he took out a R100 note and gave it to the lady.

"You'll know me, my boy, I'm not your playing ground," she said smiling, satisfied that she had got what she wanted.

TM leapt into the car, glowering.

"Nx! One might think she has a friend in you."

He switched on the car engine and kicked the accelerator. The big Dodge, blood red in colour, pulled out of the yard and screeched into the road.

Windows open, the men could hear loud music pulsing from big Alpine speakers playing an O'Jay's tune as the car dashed through the streets of Alexandra.

Passers-by waved and ululated as TM blew the hooter.

"You see, David, I tell you my brother; Toppie Manoja is the most important person in this township. I tell you brother, if these councillors running Alexandra today were smart enough, they could take me in as their organiser and they would have the whole of the township in their bags."

David smiled at his friend the rodomontade, as he retrieved a small bottle of brandy and two glasses from the cubby hole, filling the glasses and handing one to TM.

They both took gulps simultaneously, as if they had practised this many a-time.

"What a taste this brandy has, the best men's transforming drink," David exclaimed.

"Nothing beats brandy, my brother!" TM agreed.

Encouraged by the about-turn in his friend's mood, David made the mistake of fiddling with the stereo player buttons. TM was not amused, and pushed David's hand away, shouting:

"There's only one pilot here, and that pilot is none other than me, TM, if you did not know the name. There can't be two drivers. Just sit, relax and enjoy the music, and pass me another shot please."

David quickly complied and filled another two glasses.

"This is life, TM, my *bra*," shouted David.

"I tell you, David my *broer*, life is here in Alex and nowhere else. That is why all the *moegoes* come and crowd this place. But the problem then is, once they are settled, problems start, blood flows, and you know what happens after that."

"*Maar*, TM, where were you during the days of Kippie Moeketsi?" asked David, as a song by the popular maestro began playing on the stereo. The car almost came to an abrupt stop; TM looked at his friend with a glowering, tough-as-nails expression.

"Hey, David! Why does it seem that you're here to upset me? *Wie's jy* (who are you) to ask me such an obvious question? You, you who found me here in this township! I taught you all the ropes of life, organised you a girlfriend and now you take the mickey out of me, no my friend, have respect man. Do you still remember that girl of yours from the Northern Transvaal, what was the place now, oh, Jane Firs, who used to live on 15th Avenue? What was her name? Say it man, how can you forget your very first girlfriend in Jozi."

"Leshabane, was the name," David said quietly. "Hey TM, please don't do that to me, that was my baby girl, what happened to her I do not want to know, she just disappeared into thin air."

"You're lying. You know what happened. Her boyfriend from the Transkei came to fetch her because she ran away from her village when her parents wanted to marry her to a guy she did not love, and *lobola* (bride money), *nogal*, had already been paid; and the guy traced her here."

"But why do you have to remind me of such a painful experience? I've deliberately erased that episode from my mind because it was not a nice experience."

TM suddenly made a sharp U-turn as he realised that he had passed the street where the Post Office was. He parked the car in front of the building and gave David the letter.

"Please see to it that it goes right into the box, my *broer*. That letter is extremely important and urgent."

As David was about to drop the letter into the post-box, he looked at it wonderingly, curious about its contents – and why it was so urgent and important. It was addressed to a Mr Japheth Monare in Zeerust. David had no intention of bringing up the subject with his friend, though. He returned to the car and hopped in as the Dodge skidded away.

Driving through the streets of Bramley on a Saturday had always been enjoyable for TM. The red, shiny Dodge always drew attention to Toppie Manoja, who craved it.

Oncoming cars were hooting and drivers waving at TM. He waved back with a satisfied, white-toothed grin.

"These oncoming cars are alerting you that the lights of the car are on, TM," David cautioned. "They are also warning you of the danger of being caught by traffic cops ahead."

Just at that moment, TM caught sight of a traffic cop, who was already indicating at him to move out of the road. A bit shocked, he swung the car to the kerb. The cop, short and plump, with red cheeks, sauntered over with a sly grin, ready for action.

"Kaffir, it is not necessary to have your lights on at this time of the day, save them for the evening and you'll be safe," he said, as he inspected the car slowly and then walked away to fetch his book. He turned back to TM, and asked: "And where is your licence?"

He took the licence out of the cubby-hole and gave it to the traffic cop.

"Damn stupid man, he is just jealous of my car," whispered TM. David said nothing.

"I know you, and I know you very well. You always disagree with my opinion even if it is the correct one, just for the sake of spiting me," TM snapped.

TM, who had already accepted the fact that he was going to be booked by the traffic cop for such a minor offence, was irked at the thought of being poorer now. As the traffic cop finished writing out the fine, and slipped it into his hand, TM melted into a pleading, anxious expression.

"*My baas, my kroon* (my boss, my crown). *Ek was nie bewis dat die ligte was aan nie* (I was truly not aware that the lights of the car were on). *Ek dink daar is 'n fout met die switch* (I think there is a problem with the switch)."

"*Van waaraf ken jy die taal, Kaffir* (where do you know Afrikaans from, Kaffir)?" asked the cop, smiling almost good-naturedly now.

"*Ek is oorspronklik van die Wes Transvaal, baas* (I am originally from the Western Transvaal, boss)." TM had responded in his most fluent, authentic Afrikaans. This flustered the traffic cop, and impressed him. He whipped back the fine slip and folded it into his pocket.

"*Dis die laaste keer, homeza* (this is your last warning, home-boy)."

TM looked at David with a smile as he pulled the car out into the road.

"You see, David, this is how you survive in this jungle; smear butter in their eyes."

He tapped the steering wheel, apparently deep in thought.

"*Jy weet wat* (you know what), David, I have a change of plan, I will have to drop you at your place after this and we will link up later."

David looked at his friend, confused, but not in the mood to argue.

"It's OK, my friend, if this is how friendship goes."

He climbed out of the car as TM pulled up outside a house in Booysen. David waved as the Dodge hot-footed away, tyres screeching.

TM drove straight to his old friend, Sparks, who was still running his business in 2nd Avenue. There he found Sparks, Joseph and Mampye seated in the lounge, chatting. They whooped when he walked in.

"This wise man of Alex, TM, our old friend, welcome my *broer*!" yelled Sparks.

"*Ja, neh* - it is so!" exclaimed Joseph.

TM pulled off his Dorian hat and seated himself. Sparks shouted to the kitchen for another glass and more beer.

"Remember the first day that I brought him here, Sparks," laughed Joseph, "fresh from the bundus, he was raw."

"Hey, do not talk about that evening; you were dropped by David at the gate at Mzilikazi, and he did not even know where he was, according to David. It is said that TM, in his drunken stupor, kept asking where Mampye was!"

Sparks and Joseph laughed at the memory.

"Do not worry, *moratiwa*, they are just trying to embarrass you these guys," said Mampye, coming to her lover's rescue.

"Enough gents, enough, I was just passing by to pick up my *moratiwa*."

He winked at Mampye, who was ready to go, holding jersey and handbag.

"I think you will be better off without these guys today, TM, for I can see it will be not your day here once they start this way," she giggled.

After another drink, TM winked at Mampye again and then stood, glass in hand. Joseph raised his glass.

"*En nou* (and now)? *Wat gaan aan* (what's going on)? Is this an engagement proposal?"

"Gents, let me propose a toast before we leave."

Jim is Tired of Jo'burg

TM puffed out his chest as Sparks shook his head, chuckling.

"In honour of our long friendship, thanks to Joseph for having brought us together," he started, but was interrupted by one of Sparks' lady employees, who was standing at the door of the kitchen.

"And for having made the introduction to Mampye, please do not forget that!"

"OK, Sarah, I will not forget that next time. Today, we are the greatest of buddies, but sorry, buddies, this is Mampye's night and we have to leave."

TM finished his toast as Mampye walked towards the door, waving.

The roads were full of people and cars, some drivers straddling the middle of the streets.

"It is Saturday and fortnight *nogal*, so all are millionaires and the taverns are full. This is life in Alex, not only on such days but right through the year," mused Mampye.

"The poor souls, what else can they do?" asked TM, as they stopped inside the yard of MamTsamaye and walked over to the house.

As they prepared to go to sleep, TM watched Mampye undressing, standing in front of the dressing table mirror. With her small body, one could mistake her for a much younger woman, although she was only five years younger than him. Stiff buttocks and long, straight legs made for supermodel material, he thought. Mampye became aware of his man-gaze, and turned around cheekily to ask what was wrong.

"You have been staring at me for some time, TM, where is the problem?"

"Marvelling at the shape of your body and nothing else," he said.

"Well, well, I would have thought that by now there was nothing to marvel at!"

"It is never so, if you care to hear, my dear."

As they lay side by side in the darkness, with only a slight light coming through the rather transparent curtains, closely enmeshed with each other, Mampye could smell her boyfriend's body odour as she caressed his chest and stomach, down to his crotch. TM lay still, as though asleep, but started to jerk as she moved further down his body.

"And then?" she asked in a low voice; and instead of getting an answer, TM suddenly moved his whole body and he was on top of her. For a long, long time they were moaning as TM straddled Mampye until he could do it no more, and they fell asleep, only to be woken hours later when Mampye leapt out of bed, rushed to the wash basin and filled it up with water.

"Damn it TM, why did you time the damn alarm for this time, I am supposed to have been at my place by now. I am accompanying my aunt to church."

She complained and muttered as she wiped herself down and dressed quickly.

"You will be there in no time, do not panic," mumbled TM lazily, quite content with the world.

***

To TM, the years were galloping by and he was unable to catch up with them. He was trying to adjust, having made enough friends for him to understand the intricacies of Jo'burg. There were Joseph, Sparks and now the likes of Mampye. He had left the mine and was right in the middle of life in Jo'burg, as Alexandra was. TM realised that he was hurtling towards the end of his seventh year in the City of Gold – but he had not yet found the gold he sought.

Chapter 6

A Letter from Johannesburg

People who come from small places, such as Kgabalatsana, tend to be attached to the 'smallness" and 'insignificance' of their towns. They tend to reminisce a lot about the beauty of their mountains, rivers and gorges, leading sometimes to an unexplained nostalgia.

Two village boys in their teens, dressed in shredded khaki shorts, upper bodies bare, walked leisurely through the gate of the general dealer shop owned by Mr Molewa and his wife. It was a small building, decorated with mediocre boards advertising Coca Cola, Lexington and Castle Lager beer, their colours long-faded from many years of scorching summers and piercingly-cold winter days. The placement of these boards was a win for the brands since shop owners such as Mr Molewa were unaware of the huge potential revenues available for renting out these spaces and so were probably exploited by corporates. Or perhaps the entrepreneurs did not really care, seeing their role only as sellers of basic products - mealie meal, bread, and samp.

One of the other non-revenue generating functions Mr Molewa's shop performed was to receive post from the Post Office on behalf of the whole community. One wonders if he ever received a day's remuneration for this vital service. The residents collected their post on special days when the postal packages were delivered from Zeerust. Behind the counter, seated and reading a Setswana newspaper, was old man Molewa. His wife was serving a customer.

He took his eyes from the headline news as he heard the boys coming in. He greeted them cheerily and went to fetch a small pack of letters, neatly arranged in a box. He knew the families in the villages very well and did not have to ask whose mail they had come to fetch. Old man Molewa handed over a letter to one of the boys. It was addressed to a Mr Boysie Monare.

Boysie, unlike his brother Kgabalatsana, was among the village boys who were never attracted by the myths and glamour of city life, but rather remained a rural person till this day. He still lived with his father Japheth and his mother Josephine MmaMonare, who were aged and very frail, almost ten years after Kgabalatsana left for the mines. He had stayed with his parents for their sake, although he was married and could have secured a home of his own.

The boys – curious to know from whom the letter had come – sauntered back home, their feet blistering in the midday sun.

"Where does it come from and to whom is it addressed?" asked the younger of the two boys.

"Give it to me so that I can read it for you. You are still uneducated, that is why you're in Miss Thuli's class and I am in Miss Serote's."

"You know yourself that all the students in my class are the most intelligent ones in our grade."

He grabbed the letter from his friend.

"I know it comes from Johannesburg, addressed to *rre* Monare. Do you still think I'm not educated?"

They arrived at the Monare household – a typical village homestead that was large by village standards and used to be the envy of the villagers, as Japheth Monare was a noble man, known in the whole of the Lehurutshe district for his cattle stock, goats, fertile fields and horse-drawn wagons. The only difference these days was that the wealth had long been eroded when his livestock diminished and had ceased to be a measure of wealth in Dinokana. The house had four rooms: a dining room, kitchen and two bedrooms. As one entered from the main front door, one came upon the sizeable dining room, old family photos hung on all four walls. Conspicuous amongst these was the largest of all, a wedding photograph of Japheth Monare and his wife Josephine There were also Standard Six school certificates for both Boysie and his brother, Kgabalatsana. The centre of the room had a large table that used to be brown, but had now faded into a non-descript colour.

The boys entered the house and greeted Uncle Boysie, as he was called by all children – even those as young as ten years, who normally would have named him 'grandfather'.

Boysie was a tall, dignified man, wearing a goatee beard, slightly lighter in complexion compared to his brother, and with hair as grey as ash.

He took the letter from the boys and thanked them and then stood up, stretching himself as he looked at it and noticed that it had a Bramley Post Office stamp.

The manner in which African families referred to their daughters-in-law was '*koti*', short for *makoti*, or referred to by the name of her first-born child with the prefix '*mme*'. Before they had children, women were referred to by the names of their husbands (or his surname), which most times, then, resulted in people not knowing women's real names. This was the case in the Monare family. Boysie's wife was named MmeBoysie, so named after her husband. She might have been named after her first child, but unfortunately, they had no children.

At the time of the boys' arrival, Boysie's parents were in the main house, where they spent most of their time, owing to their age. Boysie's mother had heard the noisy approach of the boys as they entered the yard and asked MmeBoysie who they were.

She replied that they were the neighbours' children. MmeBoysie came out of the kitchen into the dining room. She was dressed in a traditional brown SeShoeshoe dress, bare-footed. She wiped her hands on the sides of the dress and said, "*Rra,* I thought I heard you calling me. I'm here to hear what you've called me for?"

Boysie, without looking at his wife, handed her the letter.

"What is this now, *rra*, please don't make my heart stop." She looked at the stamp of origin and sighed.

"Didn't we many rains ago receive a letter with the same Bramley Post Office stamp in it?"

"Exactly, exactly, woman," retorted Boysie. "That is exactly what I told myself when I saw the name."

"But read it for yourself. Didn't your father take you to school; are you not proud that the education you got those years is far better than the one they give to the children today? Have you thought of it, woman, that the standards of these days are far below our standards? Did you ever think of it that way?"

MmeBoysie read the letter and when she finished, Boysie exclaimed:

"I can't believe my ears, I never thought that *rre* Kgabalatsana was still alive!"

"What if someone faked his name?"

"No, no, woman, I still remember his handwriting," said Boysie with confidence.

"I will not argue with you, *rra*."

"*Mosadi* (woman) my dear wife, will you please read the letter again? My knees feel weak and it would be better if I used my ears rather than my eyes to get the news."

She took a seat opposite her husband, cleared her throat and started reading the letter aloud.

***

Meanwhile, far away, in the busy downtown streets of Johannesburg, the ever-sparkling Dodge sedan belonging to TM made its way through the concrete jungle to stop in front of Patel Outfitters, where he bought and had his clothing mended. TM unfolded himself out of the car, swaggering and swinging a set of car keys held in a holder in his right hand. The wise man of the "Township" was wearing a green tweed jacket, navy blue trousers and his green-and-black Viyella shirt, feet shod with a black and white pair of Crockett & Jones shoes.

His rather large, shiny head was half concealed by a big-brimmed Dorian hat, which hid his baldness. He went around to the boot, taking out a paper bag, and then slammed the boot and locked the car before walking confidently up to the shopfront, aware of any eyes which may have watched him go.

Inside the dimly-lit shop, Faisal Patel, the owner, watched as the flamboyant swaggerer walked towards him.

"TM, my friend, it can only be you with that big-brimmed Stetson hat. Look at your suit, it is spectacular. Typical Jo'burg style. I always like my boys smart."

Faisal, tall and thin, stood up to receive his favourite customer.

"If this is not Toppie Manoja, my customer, then I must be day-dreaming. I would never have missed a gentle human being like you."

He came around the counter, opening his arms and hugged TM.

"Yes, you're right Mr Patel; it is none other than me. I am always like this, day in and day out."

"You see, that's exactly what I thought when you came in, that nobody in this Jo'burg forgets the Patel Tailor Shop in West Street. Do you know that even John Craig, the outfitters, know that we are the best - hence they are bringing all their tailoring to us?"

"Hey! Old man Patel knows the secrets of the job, the secret of this business.

"After all, why should I take my tailoring to the Desais, when I know that there will be no discount for me and here, discount is a given for good customers such as me. But this is not what I have come for; we need to talk business."

"Old Patel is listening, TM. Talk to me - that is my language."

TM looked around and, when he made sure that there was no one listening, leaned forward conspiratorially.

"I am to start a new job and you might like the place; it's Meyerton Garment Factory in Isando. The biggest fabric manufacturers in the country. An acquaintance of my friend is in charge of stores and I might -"

"Might, TM? Mmm, that does not sound promising."

"No, don't get scared, the job is already lined up for me in deliveries around Johannesburg city centre, which includes West Street. You see now where the interest might come your way?"

"Let's talk when you are in, TM."

"Sure, sure I just came here for an in-principle arrangement and thereafter will talk business. In the meantime, this suit needs diamond mending."

He took the clothing from the plastic bag that he was carrying and put it on the counter.

Old man Patel looked at the garment, picking through it sharply with the eye of a tailor.

"This khaki trouser is slightly loose, I have lost weight man, poverty is the reason, so it needs a slight adjustment in the waist line."

"That will be R80 for all to be collected and COD when the job is done."

"Can we agree on a future payment once I get the job?"

"You see now, my friend, that is not the way to do business. Money, TM, is the key, but OK, that is fine."

TM looked at his wristwatch, shaking his head.

"My friend, I have to hit the road for my next appointment."

"Till we meet again, good luck with your new job."

TM rushed out of the shop as if there was a place he was rushing to. He got into the car and drove off in the direction of Booysens, south of the city. As he reached the entrance to Mzilikazi Mine, a guard stood barring the gate, waving at him to stop.

"*Molweni rra* (good day sir), *wena where to* (where do you think you are going)?"

"*Mina bona* Joseph, Joseph Nduna."

"Oh! *Josefi, aa baasboy Josefi* (Joseph is a big boss). *Ngena lapha, jika light Josefi there* (come in, go right and you will find Josefi)."

"*Siyabonga Gadi* (thank-you guard)."

As he entered the compound, he went to Joseph's sleeping quarters to find his friend relaxing and reading a magazine.

"*Awu rre Monare*, I did not expect you here. Are you back looking for your job?"

TM laughed and shook Joseph's hand.

"On the contrary, *rra*, it is just a visit, seeing that I have not seen you and Sechaba for some time."

"It is good to keep in touch with old friends, this place can be lonely at times and one needs to see old faces from time to time."

Joseph stood up and took two bottles of beer from under his bed, opening both and handing one to his friend.

"*Banna* Kgabalatsana, I never thought of you arriving here."

"You are always on my mind Joseph, and it is for that reason that I came to see you and also, how is Sechaba?"

TM suddenly noticed a change in his friend's face when he mentioned the name Sechaba.

"Indeed, you have been away from here for some time now, Monare. It is today two months since a tragedy befell Sechaba. He was no more staying permanently in the compound but living with a girlfriend in George Goch, and to whom he had apparently promised marriage after their engagement. But, Sechaba got hooked up with another woman who was a friend of his fiancée. It was then when troubles started for him. One day he came back from work to find the fiancée had prepared his dinner, placing it neatly on the table, as usual. There was also a note telling him that she had gone home but would be back soon.

"Sechaba settled down to have supper, but it almost became the last supper, for as soon as he had finished eating, he started having stomach cramps. He drank water and went to sleep. The fiancée never came back. Sechaba was found, cramping badly, in his bed the next morning by a neighbour friend, who had noticed that the windows of the house were still closed, with nobody home. He became suspicious and went to the house, banging on the door until he decided to break the lock.

"Stone recalls that he found Sechaba seated on the bed, gazing into the distance, completely unfocused. He called his name and it was as if Sechaba was in Wonderland, just smiling and occasionally making a hissing sound. Stone then called a taxi and he took him to the General Hospital, where he was diagnosed with mental breakdown, which the doctors ascribed to a liquid substance that would have been administered in a drink.

"In short, *rre* Monare, Sechaba is in the Krugersdorp Mental Hospital as we speak. I and some colleagues visited him the day before yesterday and his condition was precarious. *Rooibaard* has done the decent thing by sending a telegram about his state of health to his family in Zeerust. So, *rra*, that is the situation with Sechaba."

"I will make time during the week to go and see him."

"That will be a great thing, for you never know, maybe it might change his condition. The more he sees familiar faces, the more we will know if he still recognises friends and family."

After receiving this sad news, TM felt that he could not bother Joseph with his own news – not yet.

"I will tell you some of my challenges when we meet next time, for they are not urgent."

Joseph took his friend out of the compound to where his car was parked. "Till next time, Monare," said Joseph, as TM climbed into his car and skidded away.

Joseph was worried about TM. He seemed to be falling into dementia – a state some of the man's friends, such as Sparks and Joseph, blamed on being a village boy transitioning into city life. It had happened many times in the early days.

"He needs a steady woman who will mould and tenderise him, that's all, and to visit a *sangoma* to give him some *muti* to strengthen his soul!" Sparks would say, laughing.

Joseph was not so sure. He wanted to chat to Sparks about it and went to visit him. Sitting in Sparks' lounge, nursing a beer each, Joseph said:

"By the way, Sparks, do not forget you have to talk to those friends of yours at Meyerton Garments – the ones who indicated to you that there might be a job coming. This I am sure could work well for TM."

Sparks looked into the distance, nodded his head.

"Ja - you are right Joseph, but I am sure some of them will pitch over the weekend at my place, as they always do."

And this was how TM secured a job as storeman at one of Jo'burg's finest and biggest garment factories. It was his first job since leaving Mzilikazi. The job was, naturally, an over-sized feather in TM's cap, as he loved the fashion industry. Always had. He immediately started firing on all cylinders by first visiting Faisal Patel to indicate to him that, as promised, he had got the job at the garment factory. The Indian man was keen to talk business.

"So now, TM, what is in it for me, and what does this job of yours entail?"

"Big! Big opportunity for both of us. You see, I am in charge of all dispatches going out of the factory, out of the stores. I control what goes out. I manage the drivers for the whole of Johannesburg, it's great."

"And explain."

"Just tell me how many metres of what fabric type you need, and it is loaded with one of the truck drivers, and from there it is delivered to West Street at the Patel Shop, and I get my share, simple and *klaar*, *meneer* (as simple as that, sir)."

"OK, I see TM, I will hear from you."

Things were starting to look bright for TM. A house, a girlfriend and now a job. Is this not what he came for in the City of Gold? Are these not the opportunities that Diseko talked about when he was recruiting them? These were the thoughts that went through TM's mind as he drove home from Patel's shop on his way to Sparks' place.

TM was caught up in the niceties of the City of Johannesburg, and he was starting to dream: dreaming of Kgabalatsana being the best amongst the best in the city. He was a big cheese amongst his peers.

Sparks was impressed. "TM, you have graduated beyond the bounds of many *moegoes* (village boys) I have known, who have come to this city and have failed to grasp the style of it."

"Well I just happened to have been born in a village; otherwise I was born a clever and not a *moegoe*, Sparks."

David, who had joined them, chuckled.

"He is beginning to be a fashionista amongst all in the city. Just look at the clothing he is wearing, this chalk-striped suit."

Sparks agreed, patting TM on the back.

"TM is amongst the elites who follow all the latest trends in the men's fashion, the mobility of a car offers him a bird's eye view of areas that normally he could not have reached had he not had the Dodge."

TM thanked his friends for their good wishes, swelled with pride.

"I had just come to say hello guys, and now I am saying goodbye."

***

By this time, TM was thinking less and less of home, let alone of Nthabiseng and the baby. His mother and brother were far from his thoughts – and his father even less on his mind. After all, he would tell himself, that man was the cause of his leaving home.

Meanwhile, Nthabiseng had found herself a job in Zeerust, working for Western Transvaal Furnishers. With the support of her parents, who looked after her daughter Rethabiseng while she was at work, Nthabiseng was doing well.

Boysie bumped into her while browsing her workplace for furniture. He hadn't realised that she was working there, and they were happy to see each other.

"*Mme* Nthabiseng, how pleased am I to meet you. How are you?" asked Boysie.

"We are well and good, *rra*, and, how are you?" responded Nthabiseng. "Except for not seeing each other, everybody is fine at home, mother, father..."

There was a pause, at which stage Nthabiseng realised that she was thinking of mentioning Kgabalatsana.

"And how is *rre* Kgabalatsana?" she asked Boysie, tentatively. He did not want to be lured into an uncomfortable discussion; instead, he turned the question around.

"I thought that you would have been the one who would be telling me. It is now a while that we have not heard from him. But you know village boys when they get to the cities, they forget home. I warned him about forgetting home, and the culture from which he comes. What can we do, maybe one day he will come back home and be with his people?"

Nthabiseng's eyes became teary. Boysie realised that he had said too much and decided to change topics and revert to his original intention – shopping for furniture.

"Please pass on my greetings to the little one and your parents, Nthabiseng," said Boysie.

The girl nodded, smiling wanly.

"I will do so, but please also pass on my greetings too, to your parents."

"I will, *mme*," he said.

Chapter 7

TM Meets Nancy Mabheka

As far as relationships went, TM had not had many affairs with girlfriends since his arrival in Jo'burg. One of his first was a short one with Susan Leshabane from Jane Firs in the Northern Transvaal. She was a domestic worker for a white family in Booysens. The affair was aborted when he quarrelled with Susan's employers, who had consistently denied him access to the premises, where she both lived and worked.

Mampye, his latest from Alexandra, had overlapped with Nancy Mabheka. TM would never forget the day that he met Nancy. It was rush hour, the intermingling of cars and pedestrians in downtown Johannesburg early Friday afternoon.

TM was slowly driving through the streets of the city on his way home. He reached the corner of Jeppe and Kerk Street, stopped, and saw a young school girl standing at the bus stop, waiting. He immediately made a U-turn and stopped the car close to the girl.

She was young at the time, dressed in a black and white school uniform. He approached her with a smile as if approaching someone that he knew.

"Hi, my doodle-do, I like your style, dressed in school uniform, standing alone, are you not scared of the vultures?"

Fiddling with her fingers, face to the ground, she replied:

"I am not, ou boetie - I use this place daily when going to school and coming back."

TM moved closer to the girl.

"By the way, what's your name, girlie? Mine is *Bra* TM."

He had moved even closer then, and the shy girl lifted her face slightly.

"Nancy Mabheka, ou boetie, and it's also nice to know you."

"Nancy is indeed a beautiful name."

He had held out his hand, and she shook it.

"What time is your bus arriving, girlie?"

"It was supposed to have arrived an hour ago, but it is late. However, it should be coming any time from now."

TM flashed the car keys, spinning them on his forefinger.

"You will be standing here until late, let me drop you at home. By the way, where do you say you stay?"

"I stay in Alexandra, ou boetie."

"Well, well. Easy-peasy. We are neighbours. Come, drop in the car, for there is enough space for the two of us."

Nancy took her school bag from the ground, and TM opened the front door for her. They climbed in and off they went.

There was silence for a few moments before TM spoke.

"What an innocent and pretty face. Has anyone ever told you how pretty this face is? Where did you come from before you arrived in Alexandra?"

"It is a long story, ou boetie."

"I love long stories - I suppose there is no hurry, as we are still far from Alex."

Nancy continued.

"I arrived in the City of Johannesburg after a horrible experience at home in King William's Town with my Uncle Thomas, my mother's brother, with whom I was staying after my parents passed away."

"My condolences, my dear."

"Well, Uncle Thomas was then in the process of arranging a marriage for me with a neighbour's son, a friend of his - they always drank beer together. I have heard of stories of arranged marriages and never thought that one day it would happen to me."

"Feel free, girlie, continue and tell *bra* TM."

"Until one day when I was coming from school, the front door was closed, which was unusual for the time of the day. I stopped outside and overheard my uncle talking. He was saying, 'You see, Zilindile, I told you long ago that it is high time that there is a bond between our two families'.

"I then became very curious and put my ear to the door. He then said, 'Nancy is ripe for marriage and there will be no complications in arranging the marriage. I am the head of this Mabheka family now since her parents passed away. Let us speed up the process. You just have to pay me R100 and a bottle of brandy', I overheard.

"I pulled back from the door and wanted to turn back but, on second thought, decided to brave it and go inside and see what my uncle's reaction would be. I opened the door and as I entered there was silence, and the uncle said, 'Come inside, my dear, you are early today'.

"I told him that it was Friday, so the usual time for that day. I had to greet Uncle Zilindile. They then went through to my uncle's room, where they continued speaking in low tones. I heard Uncle Zilindile say, 'Just look at her, look at her breasts, she is ready, though still in high school, but we can sort that out later'. Then my uncle said that it was fine and that they would proceed. Then Uncle Zilindile said, '*Hayi kulungile mmelwana ndiyakwenza njalo. Kodwa ke ndizakucel'indlela* (it is fine, neighbour, I shall do as we have discussed, but I must leave now)'."

Nancy had bowed her head, remembering the events as they unfolded, still fresh in her mind. She continued telling TM the story, word for word. He was a good listener.

Subsequently, the conversation between Nancy and her uncle had gone like this, she said: "I heard everything that you discussed with your friend, uncle, and I am just not amused. How dare you discuss my future without asking me what my plans are?"

Jim is Tired of Jo'burg

He had blushed, face turning purple-blue.

"*Uthetha ngantoni ntombazana* (what are you on about, girl)? *Yintoni lento undithyola ngayo* (what is this accusation)?"

"I have never met the man that you are planning for me to have as my husband and I do not care to know him. Truth be told, as a young girl, I have a playmate that would be called a boyfriend, and we are at school together."

"My goodness me!" the uncle had exclaimed.

"And for your information, uncle, we never do anything that I know some of my friends do, because, like my father, your brother, had always impressed upon me: 'Study and study and when you are through then decide what you want for your future.' Now even before the wishes of my father have been fulfilled, you jump the gun and decide behind my back what that future should be? You and your *nenz' amayelenqe* - you are conspiring my future. Uncle, it is not going to happen."

Nancy had really set the cat among the pigeons. Sitting down next to her uncle, she had awaited his response with interest.

"Nancy, that was my friend Zilindile, whom you might know lives in the neighbourhood. He has a son who has just come out of the circumcision school - two years ago to be precise - and he works in the factories in East London."

"What has that to do with me, uncle?"

"A very good question, my girl, that you asked, and this shows me that you have the interest to know."

"I was just asking, uncle."

"As you know, Nancy, you have no parents anymore and I have no full-time job, thus making it very difficult for me to look after you, let alone put you into high school next year. Therefore, I have come to the conclusion that the best thing for you to do is to get married, settle with a husband who will look after you, and who knows - he might even take you to high school."

"But uncle, I never said that I wanted to get married, and after all, if you cannot look after me, understandably so, but then why should the alternative be marriage? My priority in life now is to go to high school and after that do a teacher's training diploma, as my parents have always wished me to be a teacher."

"My dear, Nancy, I am sure you will appreciate that I am trying my best for you, but in the meantime, you can go. We will discuss this matter later."

Nancy had thought that this would be the end of the conversation, but her uncle continued to pressurise her and to invite Zilindile to the house to discuss the matter.

"I later discussed the matter with Nozi, a friend, and it was Nozi who advised me that I had to be careful, that Zilindile and his family could easily take me at night and make me their makoti – daughter-in-law - and more so that my uncle seemed to have already agreed with him. This was normal in the Xhosa tribe, Nozi warned me.

"I asked her how my uncle could possibly force me into something that I didn't want.

Nozi said that this was how customs went and that I had few options. She was going to work as a domestic in Johannesburg the following year and, since I had an aunt there too, I said that I would go with her. I tracked down my aunty and made contact with her.

"She was so pleased to hear from me, as she had no children and wanted me to come and stay with her and pursue my studies.

"I eventually told her my story, but I was very surprised that she was not bothered by what my uncle had tried to do. She said that he had always been conservative and had tried to do the same to her.

"And that, in short, ou boetie, is my tragic story," she said, as TM dropped her not far from her aunt's place.

***

The routine of the new job was interesting to TM, who enjoyed sorting out orders and dispatching them through to the various outlets. The process gave him many ideas on how to make extra money for himself. TM was starting to think like a shady entrepreneur.

He started inflating stock that was leaving the factory and diverting fabric to his friend in West Street, doing this in collaboration with truck drivers, with whom he shared the spoils. He would go to Faisal every Friday after work to collect what was owed to him.

"You see now my friend, you are really getting into the Jo'burg lifestyle," Faisal would tell him.

TM was, suddenly, a big shot among Alexandra's big shot suppliers. He enjoyed his new job, which had brought him some pride, especially since he no longer had to rely on friends for hand-outs – especially David, who had been keeping him afloat in a number of ways. He continued working for the garment factory for another four years. As the years passed by, he had all the connections at work in the various stores that were supplied with garments. The Patels, by this time, were among the key beneficiaries from the ill-gotten gains.

During a discussion with David at TM's quarters one night, the friends talked about a matter of common concern.

"You know, TM, there is something that I've long been wanting to tell you. You see, an African man needs to take stock of certain things – one of them being that, from time to time, one must go and see a Sangoma, a faith healer, so that they can check how things are with you."

TM looked at David thoughtfully, remembering that at the mine, Joseph had raised the same issue – and that he had never heeded his wise friend's advice.

"I have heard of those superstitions, my *broer*. I will see what I can do."

Chapter 8

Family Reunion

It was night-time, and Nancy had been asleep for several hours after returning from town. Before collapsing into bed, she had been so exhausted that she'd skipped supper – something she never usually did. Her Aunt Noluthando had called from her room: "The food is on the stove, girl, I only hope that it is warm!"

Nancy had thanked her aunt, whom she called 'Thando', and gone straight to her room.

Was it a dream or was she awake? She heard a voice.

"Nancy, my child, child of Mabheka, what is it that you are doing to us, why have you turned your back on us?"

She opened her eyes – at least, she thought that she had – and saw a tall, angel-like figure, dressed in a soft white silk dress, hovering near the ceiling. Its face was pale, as though dabbed with powder.

"Your father and I always reminisce and continuously talk of our little daughter, whom we left behind."

"But who are you?"

"Shame on you, my little angel, shame on you. Can you hear her, Nofuzile?" came the loud, melancholy voice of a man.

Nancy opened her eyes more fully, staring at the strange figure.

"Who are you talking about? Nofuzile? That was the name of my mother, who died a long time ago."

"Listen to our lost angel, ha ha ha!" said the man.

"Go, my child! Go look for your lost parents, for they do not know where to find you, they have been looking for you, go visit the place of your birth, where it will be easier for them to locate you. You are the only one who knows where this place is."

After this short encounter or dream, Nancy went into a deep sleep, and was awoken later by a knock on the door. Aunt Thando was up, and shouting orders.

"*Vuka, vuka* - wake up, wake up Nancy!"

She jumped out of bed, went to the mirror, and brushed the sleep from her face.

"I am awake, aunty."

***

"This on and off life in our relationship is not working, TM, we are no longer young, we have to mend our ways. And by the way, when last were you home?"

"Awu, Nancy! Of all people? I did not expect that question from you. And by the way, that question can be asked of you as well."

"Listen, my dear, we have had our share of differences; we almost share the same reasons for having come to Johannesburg, though they are slightly different. As you always said, you ran away from a situation. And, so did I."

"Get to the point, Nancy, let's get out of this cat and dog life. *Uthini sisi* (what are you saying sister)?"

"I am proposing that we take a long holiday, or, let us say, go on an outing to King William's Town. Blessings from the ancestors have always been part of ritual to us Xhosa-speaking people, but I would think it's the same for you, a Tswana. I believe that our ancestors are, by now, lost, not knowing where we are."

TM stared at Nancy thoughtfully.

"You might have a point there and I have to confess, it is only a fool who can argue against what you are saying."

"And by the way, TM, you will have to drop me at home. I promised Aunty Thando that I would accompany her to town."

"I am at your service, darling, when you are ready."

As Nancy and TM left the house through the yard, they strolled past the main house's kitchen, where MamTshawe appeared at the door.

"It is so nice seeing you two together. *Niy'aphi* (where are you off to)?"

"TM is dropping me at home, MamTshawe, see you later, bye-bye!"

On arrival at Nancy's, he parked the car and walked round to open the door for her. Nancy hopped out and accepted a kiss from TM before going inside.

She found her aunt seated in the dining room, sipping coffee. Thando shook her head as her niece walked in.

"What have I done now?"

"Nothing, Nancy *uyawandisukela mntwana ndini* - there is nothing, you are just provoking me, child. I was just thinking about you, saying that you must have forgotten our appointment."

"Nothing of the sort, aunty, how could I forget what I promised to do?"

After a while, they left the house for town, taking a bus. For a time, they were quiet, until Nancy broke the silence.

"Aunty, you know what? I was thinking of going home for a short holiday."

"Home?" Her aunt looked quite shocked.

"*Awu*, what's wrong with you, aunty, who said I cannot?"

"I am just shocked that you are raising that, for I thought that it was 'bygones are bygones' between you and King William's Town. You have never been home since you left all those years ago."

"Says who? Perhaps aunty does not even know where King William's Town is?"

"It won't be a bad idea, to be honest; one has to do it some stage, as there are many things to miss back home. When were you thinking of leaving, then?"

"I have not as yet decided, but it won't be long."

***

Except for short distances between townships, or from the township to Johannesburg, neither Nancy nor TM had ever been on a long-haul passenger train – apart from Nancy's one-way journey from King William's Town to the City of Gold all those years ago.

Now they were on a journey together to the Eastern Cape, driven by Nancy's dream about her parents. What that dream had meant, even Aunty Thando couldn't decipher. The only thing that she had said was: "The old aunts and uncles in *ema* Xhoseni in King William's Town might shed light on the meaning of it. Remember the Xhosa people love interpreting such dreams, always with the hope that there would be slaughter and *umqombothi*. So, don't be surprised if you're asked to *doumcimbi* (a customary event)."

The other important dimension to this journey was that it gave Nancy and TM an opportunity to mend their differences; to bond outside of the tensions of Johannesburg. This was evident in the relaxed banter within the privacy of their compartment.

"I hope you have all the necessities at hand, TM, and do not expect me to be your spokesperson."

"What does that mean?"

"*Yho! Akuwazi kanti amaXhosa* - you don't know the custom of the Xhosas, they might expect *lobola* (bride price), you cannot just live with their daughter *mahala* (for free)."

"Don't scare me, Nancy; they will have to understand that I am not a rich man."

Nancy gave him a wry smile as TM started fondling her breasts. Nancy's body jerked as TM put his hand between her thighs.

"Oh no! Not again!"

But she responded, opening her legs, as TM gently pushed her back against the bunk bed. At that moment, unfortunately, there was a knock at the door and a voice.

"*Kaartjies gereed* - tickets ready."

A sturdy conductor opened the door, searching for tickets. He clipped them and left the compartment. TM slid the door shut and went to stand in front of Nancy, who was seated. She clutched his stomach to her face as she felt his stiffness, and began unbuckling his belt, pulling his trousers down. TM followed her lead and they began making love. It was a long, serene love that seemed the very first of its kind.

"Oh! TM, hold it in that position."

"My God, Nancy, I never knew it was so different in a moving object."

After a while, TM slowly pulled himself off Nancy and put on his trousers, while she headed to the bathroom. She found him paging through a *Drum* magazine when she returned.

"Wow, TM, you are so serious - as if nothing happened just a few minutes ago. I have not even been out for ten minutes and look at you?"

"After action satisfaction, my dear."

She patted him on the shoulder, took her suitcase down and put on her nightie before settling down to sleep. TM did the same and then switched off the lights. They slept without interruption, lulled by the rattle of the train wheels clap-clapping through the night.

The train arrived at King William's Town station at 7 am on Saturday morning. A relaxed black couple disembarked, dressed to the nines, from the last coach. She in black jeans, a white silk top, large straw hat and high-heeled court shoes; he in a grey chalk-striped suit, blue shirt and red tie, with brown and white Crockett & Jones shoes. A young man offered to take their luggage and provide transport.

"There is a taxi parked just outside the gate, *mnumzana* (sir) that belongs to my uncle; it is the best and most reliable in town, let alone the most beautiful."

By the time Nancy and TM arrived at the black Chev Biscayne, a driver had already opened the front door and the back left one for his passengers.

"Welcome to King William's Town, *Mnumzana nawe Mama* (gentlemen and lady)."

"*Enkosi, mhlekazi* (thank you, sir)," responded Nancy, as she climbed in at the back, while TM settled himself into the front seat.

The driver took his seat and closed the door, looking at TM.

"*Ihambo iyakuphi, ke Mhlekazi* (where are you off to, gentleman)?"

"Zone 2 Kwa Zwelitsha, *bhuti* (elder brother), number 1023, next to the school," Nancy replied for TM.

The driver turned on the ignition and off the car drove towards the east of town to Zwelitsha. TM was all eyes, as though trying to find familiar landmarks.

"It is like any other township, though it is cleaner and quieter."

"Well, it is a rural township, as you can see, and there is no work for people - and you see this big factory on your left, that is the Da Gama Clothing Factory, the biggest in the Cape Province and employing most people of the township," said the driver.

"I can see by the smoke that it is a factory," TM commented.

The taxi parked in front of a house with a sign reading 1023. The driver swung out of his seat, rushing to open the door for Nancy.

"*Siyabulela mhlekazi* (thank you, sir)," Nancy said, grateful. The driver then did the same for TM. He was politeness personified. After Nancy paid the man his fare, he hauled their luggage out of the boot and took it to the door of the house. An old man, tall and slender, with silver hair, came to the door to meet the strangers. When Thomas, Nancy's uncle, realised that it was his niece, he exclaimed:

"*Hayi bo* (oh), it is Nancy, my sister's child!"

"*Molo tatomncinci* (morning, uncle). *Injani impilo* (how are you)?"

"*Hayi, Nancy kuyaphileka ngaphandle nje kwendlala apha kweli lase Mpuma Koloni* (we are well, except for the tough life here in the Eastern Cape), *sizakuthini ke* (what else can we do)?"

TM was observing the greetings exchange between Nancy and her uncle, wondering how they would be with each other after their last meeting – but that did not seem to be an issue now.

"*Hayi, tatomncinci mandikwazise ku mnumzana lo endihamba naye, igama lakhe ngu Kgabalatsana Monare abambiza u TM kwela lase Goli* (let me introduce you to the man I am with, his name is Kgabalatsana, though they call him TM in Johannesburg). *Lisoka lam* (he is my partner)."

TM, who had been seated on the step, stood up, bending down to Nancy's uncle, and shook his hand.

"I am pleased to see you, *rra.*" He sat down again, very deferentially. Thomas winked at Nancy and asked TM:

"*Khawusiphe ithuba khe siqgugule no mtshana mnumzana* (my apologies, sir, just give me some moments to talk to my niece)."

"This will give me time to go into the yard and see Zwelitsha, sir."

TM left them as they walked into the house and sat at the dining room table.

"*Khawutsho ke Nancy, unjani udade wethu u Noluthando kwela lakuni* (how is my sister Noluthando in Johannesburg)?"

"Aunty Thando is well in Johannesburg, uncle, and she said I should pass on her greetings and tell you that one day she will visit."

"*Kudala iminyaka ngeminyaka esitsho njalo, ndiyabona selimginyile I Rhauti* (she says she is coming every year, but I can see Johannesburg has swallowed her). "*Awu wasithatha ngesiquphe ke ntombazana, nencinci ke incwadi ethi usendleleni ezayo* (you took me by surprise. Not even a short letter saying that you are coming)."

"It was a sudden decision also on my side, this decision to come home, uncle. Actually, the thing that forced me to come was a funny dream that I had about my parents…"

Nancy related the whole episode to Thomas, who was listening attentively, intermittently interjecting.

"*Hayi bo*, (oh) do not say that! *Uthini na* (what are you telling me)?"

"I am telling you, uncle; I then discussed this with Aunty Thando, who advised that I come home and inform you, as you would be the one who could advise me. So here I am, uncle."

There was a pause, Thomas looking at the ceiling.

"Noluthando was correct, Nancy; even if she knew what the dream could have meant, she would have been handicapped and unable to give direction as to what needs to be done. It is true that there are many customary things that need to be done. The first one is that both your parents, especially Mpiyakhe, your father - *akazange akhatshwe* - no custom was done when he died. There would have been a cow slaughtered, and seeing that he and your mother Nofuzile are both no longer with us, we could, according to our custom, do a joint ceremony. This will be the main thing to do. Fail to do this, and they will continue troubling you - and they are doing so because you are past the age at which you should have attended to this custom already, my child."

"I understand, uncle, so when can this be done; is it something that I, or wc, can do whilc I am hcrc?"

"It all depends on you, Nancy; after all, the family is small, so there is no broad consultation -it is only you, myself and Noluthando. It would have been a good thing if she was here."

Thomas looked out the door, wondering where TM was.

"Oh, Ntombazana, I am sure your man must be wondering now why we are taking so long and might think that we are plotting against him! But, OK, we will discuss this later.

We still have tomorrow, depending on how long you are planning to stay."

"We will be around till next coming Friday, uncle."

"*Hay ke, kulungile* (it is fine then). As for sleeping arrangements, there is the room – the one that you left which you two can use; you will have to tidy it according to how you want it to look."

"There is no problem with that, uncle, as we have brought some bedding from Jo'burg and some groceries that should last us for the week. Aunty Thando bought us a few things."

"*Hayi, kulungile ke ntombazana* (it is fine, girl)."

Thomas and Nancy stood up, stretching their muscles, and went outside to find TM standing next to the front gate.

"You must be tired, TM, and bored?"

"Not at all, Nance, I was just viewing the place; I took a long walk down the road."

"Were you not afraid of getting lost?"

"I have been to enough places to not get lost here."

They went back into the house and Nancy went straight to the room to unpack their luggage and thereafter into the kitchen, leaving TM and Thomas in the dining room. As expected, Thomas was the first to engage.

"Yes, Mo…?"

"Monare."

"*Ewe*, Monaaare, you people in that Johannesburg all come from different places - and where do you come from?"

"I am from the Western Transvaal, *rra*, from a village called Dinokana."

"That must be far away."

"Just outside a town called Zeerust."

"And how and when did you go to Jwanesburg?"

"Wait, let me think, oh, it was in 1960."

"And do you still go home?"

At that juncture Nancy came out of the kitchen, carrying a tray of food. She placed it on the table and invited the two men to eat. Nancy went back to the kitchen while the two started eating. Silence, as if there was an angel passing and not a sound could be heard. When they were finished, Thomas thanked Nancy.

"The food was tasty. This shows how long I have been living alone in this house of the Mabhekas, cooking for myself or eating food from the tuck-shop next door."

"That is why I decided to come to King William's Town, uncle," Nancy called from the kitchen.

"Nancy, I will be taking *mnumzana* into the township to get a feeling for what Zwelitsha looks like."

"It is fine, uncle, but do not go too deep into the location (township) with him; his *isiXhosa* is zero. And by the way, I hope your usual old places - where the 'nice', temping things are - are out of bounds during this walk."

"*Yho*, and she is bombarding us with instructions. I would have thought that she had long outgrown that," Thomas said to TM. "She has been like that since she was a child – giving instructions even to my elder sister, who was her mother.

"But Nancy, your partner will have to learn as much as he has learnt of life in Johannesburg; why should Zwelitsha be an exception?"

Nancy did not reply. After they left, she enjoyed being alone in this house, which she had not seen for almost a decade now. Having Uncle Thomas and TM out gave her a chance to look around and reminisce about her childhood days spent here. This was originally her father's house; well, it would still have been, had he lived.

She went to her room, marvelling at the old pictures that were still hanging on the walls, like a marriage portrait of her parents just above the bedstead, in black and white. She took it off the wall to clean it, wiping it with a cloth.

"Good afternoon, mother and father, I know that you can see and hear me; what a pity that you are not physically with me, otherwise I could have been hugging and kissing you..."

She kissed the photograph as if she were kissing living beings.

"But as fate would have had it, you are no more. I am here, and I have responded in an appropriate manner, since you came to me in a dream, telling me to come home, where I could find you, my grandparents and the whole ancestry of the Mabheka, o Sidima, *o phuma-be-ngena*, o Satshaya - their clan names."

Tears slid down her face. She wiped them with the back of her hands and positioned the photograph in its place. Taking off the few sheets and pillows, she made up the bed with fresh linen.

"Oh, Uncle Thomas, what we have been through! My leaving this loving home was a result of you trying to force a stupid tradition on me.

"You are, after all, still a loving uncle – just look at these sheets and pillows. These are the same as those I left behind. Yes, they have been used, but you kept them for me; it means that you knew I would return one day, to my father and mother's house. And this is also Aunty Thando's house, and yours. After all, it is a Family Home."

She stripped the bed, put the changed bedding on the floor and took new ones from the bag that they had brought with them from Jozi.

***

Meanwhile, , near the community hall at Zone 1 was one of the most popular shebeens in the township, Kwa Mamjuqu, where the elite of Zwelitsha spent their time drinking and enjoying life in the township.

Thomas and TM stepped through the gate as Mamjuqu, the Shebeen Queen, was about to throw out water from a basin. She stopped in her tracks as she noticed the visitors coming her way.

"You almost got a shower, Matshaya."

"That would have been a beer *kaloku*, then Juqu."

"*Hayi ngenani manene* (come in gentlemen)."

Thomas and TM went into the dining room, took seats on empty benches that were lined against the walls and waited as the lady officially introduced herself to TM, with a curtsy.

"*Molo mhlekazi, mna ndingu Nomathemba Silinga, kodwa ke sendabizwa u MamJuqu* (afternoon sir, my name is Nomathemba Silinga but they call me MamJuqu, which is my clan name)."

TM stood up and shook hands.

"*Ke thabela kgo tseba mme* (I am glad to know you, madame). Mine is Kgabalatsana Monare from Johannesburg, and I am visiting *rra* Thomas."

"*Siyabulela* (thank you)," said MamJuqu jovially, and winked at Thomas.

"Thank you, Juqu, now we can quench the thirst, Monare has been travelling the whole night and has not even had time to rest; after all, there is ample time - the evening has not even started."

Thomas opened one bottle, poured beer into TM's glass and then his, put the bottle on the tray on a small table in front of them and then proposed a toast.

"Welcome, *Mnumzana* (sir), you have blessed us with your presence and have made my day by bringing my niece, my brother's child, whom I did not even know was still alive."

He lifted his glass and their glasses clinked together. They drank, and then put the glasses back on the tray. TM took a packet of Lexington cigarettes from his pocket and handed it over to Thomas, who took it, drew one out and handed the packet back to TM, who took his own cigarette. Thomas flicked out a lighter, and they began puffing their poison.

"Man, Monare, we seem to be cast in the same mould; you smoke, I smoke, you drink, I drink. Is this not a God-sent coincidence? Given time, I think we would make a good pair."

"I am pleased to hear that, *rre* Thomas, and I would love it to be that way."

As they finished the first bottle and started on the second one, which went down fast, Thomas said:

"By the way, Monare, I hope my niece did tell you a bit about the Xhosa culture."

TM took his cigarette out of his mouth, a little flustered, and thought to himself: "Here it comes. I was warned."

He responded cheerfully enough. "Not much really, Thomas, but having worked in the mines, where there were many amaXhosa speaking people, I got to know about their customs, such as circumcision, *umqombothi, umgqusho*."

"Yes, those are the obvious ones, Monare. Here specifically I was referring to the more substantial ones, for example *lobola*."

"Oh! That I understand quite well, we have it also among us Tswana, and I think all people have it in the country."

"Oh! No, that is fine, if you understand it. That is not what we came here for, that will be for another day, let us drink."

There was a pause after the mentioning of *lobola*. Thomas, who by now was becoming tipsy, began talking animatedly, straying onto another controversial topic.

"And did they tell old Monare that in our tradition, an unmarried man cannot sleep in the same room with a woman at her house?"

"No, *rre* Thomas, that did not arise and we in Johannesburg do not really adhere to the rigid customary details; after all, we are a melting pot of all traditions - Swazis, Rhodesians, Basotho and others. If you have to follow all these varied customs, life will stand still there."

"I hear you, Monare, but I was just mentioning this, so let us leave it for another day."

"I think I understand you well, *rre* Thomas. Is it not time for us to leave now, I think Nancy must be wondering where we are."

"Do not worry, Monare, she is a Xhosa girl and she knows quite well that when a man gets into the labyrinth of a village, he does not want to be disturbed. But I agree with you that there will be another day."

TM stood up, walked to the kitchen and went to bid farewell to MamJuqu.

"Thank you very much for your nice, ice-cold beer, *mme*. I have just started enjoying Xhosa hospitality. I also enjoyed the tranquility of your place and I hope to see you again soon, as I am still around for a while."

"Thank you, Mhlekazi, hope to see you soon. In my father's place, there are many rooms to stay and every day is tea time here; you know the place now and you do not need Thomas."

"Bye, Juqu," said Thomas, walking zigzaggedly out of the house and towards the gate for home.

As they arrived at home, Thomas paused in front of the door, seemingly in a drunken stupor. He took a deep breath and gestured.

"There is an alien smell coming from my house, what is happening here?"

Nancy was standing at the table in the dining room, and on hearing her uncle's comment, called out to them.

"*Ngenani, nifikile Kwa Mabheka ukuba beningazi* (come in, you have arrived at the Mabheka homestead, if you did not know)."

"We are already in, *mme*," responded TM, as they entered through the door.

"*Yho* Nancy, what a pleasant afternoon I had with *sbali* (brother-in-law); he showed me the whole of Zwelitsha."

"And all the famous shebeen houses of Zone 1," she interjected.

"Of course, my niece, what else is there to show him except Bartfare Grounds, the Community Hall and those places you just mentioned. The main thing is that we bonded, I got to know that there are common things between us."

The table had already been dressed in a white tablecloth. Plates and cutlery properly placed - and by then,

Nancy was busy dishing, while the two gentlemen faced each other.

"You see, *sbali*," said Thomas. "this is my elder brother's only child. Her father left her with me and before he closed his eyes, said to me, 'Thomas *mnakwethu* (my little brother), you must look after this girl, educate her until she is a grown-up woman and then she can decide what she wants to be'. And I can see now that she is indeed a grown-up woman, though I am not sure how far she went with her education - and one thing that we all know is that she has decided where she wants to be and that is in Johannesburg."

"That is true, *rre* Thomas."

They then settled in for a long quiet meal, with Uncle Thomas from time to time looking at TM with a big smile and patting him on his shoulder.

After the meal, Thomas was the first to go to his bedroom.

"*Banakwethu* (young people), I have to go and sleep now, it's late, *sbali*. I am not used to going to sleep so late. We will see about tomorrow morning. I am sure that there is a lot to talk about. You still have to tell me how Johannesburg is. Bye."

He was still talking as he walked into his room and closed the door.

Later TM followed Nancy into their room. She had placed a washing bowl of water on a chair in the corner. Nancy locked the door and started washing herself, while TM changed into his pyjamas.

When all was done, Nancy extinguished the paraffin lamp that was standing on the dressing table, and they lay down, tired.

"Good night, my dear."

"Without a kiss, TM? What happened to courtesy?"

He responded with a kiss.

"Goodnight, my sweet love."

***

In Alexandra Township, at Noluthando's house, it was early morning and the wash-line was full of clothes. A light breeze flung it to-and-fro. Aunty Thando stood at the door, watching the movement of the clothes, thinking aloud about her niece.

"How I hope that things went well between her and Thomas. I only pray that old wounds don't crop up – you never know with these children today. They are not like us, they are outspoken, but we will see how things pan out. I shall be the judge."

She then shouted:

"Lerato! Lerato! Come here my child!" as she saw the young teenage daughter of her neighbour, standing in the yard. Lerato came rushing over to Aunty Thando, as she was called by all in the area.

"Go to *ou boetie* Jwaneng and remind him that he should not forget to pick me up for the 6.30 pm train at Park Station."

"And where are you going Aunty, are you leaving us like Sis Nancy?"

Aunty Thando patted Lerato on her back smiling.

"I am just going for a week or so, Lerato. Go then, before Jwaneng disappears into the township."

"I will do so, aunty."

At 3.30 pm that same afternoon, Noluthando entered Park Station, Platform 2 in Braamfontein and walked to the ticket sales window.

"*Dumelang.*" She greeted a ticket sales person behind the burglar-barred, glass window. "Return ticket to King William's Town, please."

"Migrant workers are going back home," remarked the sales person behind the glass panel. Noluthando ignored him as she took her ticket, put it safely in her handbag and pulled her suitcase towards the waiting passenger train, where she stopped at the rear coach to find a spot in the third-class compartments. There were already two other passengers on board when she found her seat.

"*Sanibonani* (good evening)."

"*Sawubona*," they responded simultaneously, as she packed her luggage in the upper deck and settled down.

The train left Platform 2 at exactly 6.30 pm on its long trip to King William's Town in the Eastern Cape.

"This eleventh hour decision, I hope, will bear fruit," she thought. "I had to do it in support of my elder brother's child, as I am worried about Nancy's well-being and I think this is the time for me to intervene. I know that I should have done this a long time ago. She failed to fulfill the wishes of her father to get an education. On this score, my conscience is clear, though, and I know that my brother, in whatever world he finds himself, can bear witness; but Nancy went berserk-crazy with love for a man who I am really not sure is serious about her. I hope that her visit home will open up her mind for the sake of her future."

Noluthando thought about Nancy arriving in Jo'burg, her schooling, her relationship with TM and now, her visit to the place of her birth.

"Good night, people," one of the passengers said, as they settled down to sleep.

"Sleep well," responded Noluthando softly. She took some time to follow suit.

The train pulled in at King William's Town train station at 7 am. The conductor-cum-guard was the first to jump to the platform, whistle in mouth, signalling to the engine driver that he was in the right place to stop, which he did with precision. The train came to a shuddering halt.

Noluthando disembarked, and a young man came rushing to help her with her suitcase.

"There is a car outside the gate, mama, if you need transport."

"Yes, I will need one. I am going to Zwelitsha, number 1023, Zone 2, my child."

A taxi driver opened the boot of a Ford sedan, and Noluthando's suitcase was safely stowed, as she climbed into the taxi.

"*Molo sisi, igama lam ngu Mthuthuzeli Mabhongo* (morning sister, my name is Mthuthuzeli Mabhongo)."

"*Sawubona, mfondini* (morning, gentleman)."

As Nancy looked at the street from behind the lace curtain in the dining room, she saw a car stop at the gate. She could hardly believe who she saw climbing out.

"This cannot be!"

She unlocked the door and peered out. "Am I dreaming?"

"What is happening, *Ntombazana*, why are you talking to yourself?" asked her Uncle Thomas from his bedroom.

Nancy flew to the gate. "What are you doing to us? You just appear from nowhere, Aunty Thando?"

The taxi driver was already inside the house, following Noluthando, putting her luggage on the floor and receiving his fare.

"*Nisale kakuhle mama* (bye-bye, mother)."

He left the house as Nancy, Thomas and TM stood looking at Nancy's aunt for a moment before Nancy moved to hug her tightly.

"Welcome to King," TM said, with a friendly shrug.

"*Yin'ingathi ndiyaphupha* (am I dreaming)? Noluthando, *nguwe lo* (is this you)?" asked Thomas.

"It is me, *Bhuti*, my brother, your only living younger sister."

They hugged for a couple of minutes. Noluthando's eyes becoming watery, as she wept a little.

"The ancestors, our ancestors, only they could have made this to happen," exclaimed Thomas, looking at Nancy with a nod.

"Welcome, aunty, you've made our day."

"Thank you all, what a journey, I did not realise that King William's Town was so far!"

Nancy put away her aunt's luggage in the rear bedroom, while Noluthando took a seat. Nancy prepared coffee the way she knew her aunt liked it, and they sat together, as a family, at the table. Thomas was the first to break the silence.

"*Dade wethu* - my sister, welcome home.

I have no words to express how I feel, only yesterday was I surprised by the arrival of *mkhwenyana* (son-in-law), TM!"

The sister looked at Nancy and smiled, and Thomas continued.

"And Nancy, now it is you who did this, I'm sure. Did you all plan this and why did you not tell me, *Ntombazana*, that your aunt was coming?"

"She never told me, uncle. I am as surprised as you are."

"It cannot be such a coincidence, no, it cannot be."

TM, realising that there might be many family issues cropping up now, decided to make himself scarce. He left the dining room, saying: "It is that time of the day for my puff, good people."

He left them alone and went outside. Thomas waved and nodded, and then turned to his sister and niece.

"Well, well, well, the family, the only remaining grand and great-grandchildren of grandfather Mabheka. Now that we have all gathered in this unplanned manner, let me welcome you Noluthando, and I am sure that you are tired because of the overnight travelling. We are pleased that you arrived safely, and to let you know that we have had a wonderful time with Nancy and *Mkhwenyana* since they arrived."

"By the way, *Bhuti*, you have used the word '*mkhwenyana* (son-in-law) for the second time since I came. Are they married, is that what they told you?"

"No, no, nothing like that, *dade wethu* (my sister). It is just my way of showing respect because I cannot call my niece's man by his name, let alone his surname – it is too complicated for this Xhosa boy. By the way, now that you have raised the matter of their marriage. Is there anything you know, Noluthando?"

Nancy stood up, went to fetch a kettle from the stove and brought back boiling water, filling the cups of the two. Thomas and Noluthando looked at each other, blinking.

"Let me not tire you, we shall have enough time to discuss family matters. Nancy will prepare your room, and Nancy, you will see about arranging our sleeping quarters. There are still the outside rooms for whoever, but I leave that to you."

"No problems, uncle, I will see what I can do, and in the meantime, aunty, I will arrange the room for you, for I am sure you are tired."

She got up to make the necessary preparations.

Thomas and Noluthando finished their tea in silence. Shortly after that, Nancy called to her aunt from the bedroom.

"Aunty, I am done, my love."

Suddenly, it seemed to Nancy that her parents were right there, in that very room, owing to her aunt's unexpected arrival. She was still surprised, though pleasantly – her aunt had not hinted that she might follow her niece home. Thando had always been Nancy's mainstay and rock in Jo'burg – encouraging, steering and guiding her. Nancy, though, felt that she had failed her. Perhaps it was time to chat with Uncle Thomas and clear her conscience about the reasons why she had left home, after Uncle Thomas tried to organise a forced marriage with a man she did not know.

Then again, he had never been her favourite. He was nothing at all like her father; he lacked the finesse and openness which she had loved so much about him. All well and good, she thought, we'll see where this will end, I suppose.

Aunty Thando's appearance at the bedroom door distracted her from these thoughts.

"Wow, exactly as your mother used to keep this room. Did you know that your parents inherited the house when her parents died? Clearly, I will sleep like a real African Princess, rolling and tossing amid their blessings."

"Thank you very much, Aunt Thando, for that piece of history."

Nancy left the room and joined Uncle Thomas and TM in the dining room, where they were drinking coffee.

"I have sorted aunty out, uncle, and now it is time for TM."

"And what about you?"

"You are my host. TM, take the lead and let's go and check out the outside quarters, for I think that, as the youngest, we will have to move out of the main house. Though, seeing that you two seem so close, I may be the loser!"

They laughed uproariously and TM stood up, taking Nancy's hand, and went to inspect the outside rooms. These afforded the couple plenty of privacy – much like they had in Alex.

"It's like being in Alex", laughed TM, "except for the absence of Magogo and MamTsamaye."

"Oh shame, uMagogo and MamTsamaye - with their Kgabalatsana, they love you so much that they always treat you like a child-to-be-always-bullied. And talking about being bullied, be careful, I have a gut feeling aunty has a mission. I don't think that she came all the way from Johannesburg for nothing."

"What do you think that mission is?"

"No idea, my friend, just play it by ear; of one thing I am certain, you have captured uncle's attention, so it's up to you to do the same with my aunty now. She can be very unpredictable."

***

It was true that Aunty Thando didn't miss a beat. About a week into their stay in King William's Town, the Mabheka family, including their new 'son-in-law' were gelling like gelatin, TM and Thomas becoming the regulars at Mam-Juqu's. Thando, of course, had noticed this.

She queried her niece in a roundabout way.

"Hey, Nancy, it was a wise decision you took to come home."

Nancy looked at her aunt and shrugged nonchalantly. Aunty noticed this 'shrug' and wondered about it.

"I don't for a minute appreciate that casual approach, *Ntombazana*. Lines must be drawnn. I am your aunt."

"What have I done now, Aunty Thando?"

"Let's leave that for another day. It seems that your Uncle Thomas and TM are Siamese twins."

"Men, aunty! Many times – and I'm not sure if you've noticed – they become friends so quickly and easily through drinking at shebeens. TM is a social butterfly, aunty, and if that is stifled, he becomes like a tiger trapped in a cage."

"Well, while we are on this topic, what are your plans now that you seem so at ease with each other?"

This straight-as-an-arrow question rattled Nancy. Her aunt was known for being direct, but she knew that this was just the first of many salvos.

"You guys have to change your lifestyle. I am getting old, Nancy. And with what I have observed in the last few days here in King William's Town, and especially after the successful customary event done as a result of you and your dreams, I am satisfied and convinced that I should finally pack my things up in Johannesburg and return home, where I will wait for the day when I am to join others in that world which we do not know."

Nancy was quiet, watching her aunt with wide eyes.

"I will leave you and your TM with the house in Alexandra, as it is time that you build a future. But there is only one condition and it is that you have to get your ass out of your comfort zone, look for work – and by the way, you have to follow TM's example. I have already put out feelers with Gladys, our back opposite neighbour, and she promised me that she would try to organise you something at Edgars Stores."

"That will be great, aunty!" Nancy rose from her chair and rushed to her aunt's side to hug her tightly. Noluthando felt emotional as she held her niece close to her chest.

"When that is done and dusted, you will be settled. After that, I will move back to settle here. We have had time to discuss this with my brother and he is in full support and as he said, 'then the family would have reconciled.'"

That night, as they sat around the dining room table, Thomas' mind was swirling with confusion. He thought about how Noluthando and Nancy had treated him – how his niece had 'upped sticks' and disappeared to Johannesburg, with not a word of news for months. Now, here they were, sitting at home and having their last evening meal with him.

"It has been some fruitful and joyous time for me to have had you, Noluthando, Nancy and Monare, here at home. I have been living a lonely life and your presence has rejuvenated me, let alone the strong drinks that we consumed at Zone 1, TM, and your jokes which everybody so loved. All this has reminded me of the home when our parents were alive; they have resurrected. As for the customary event that you came here for, Nancy, you did the right thing to come home as it was obvious that your parents were lost, did not know where their child had disappeared to. Trust me, ancestors do wonders. The event was blessed and I know my brother and his wife and our parents, Noluthando, are happy where they are."

Noluthando smiled at her brother.

"All things happen for a reason, *Bhuti* Thomas. I left home for my own reasons, Nancy followed, and you decided to look after the family home, and we should all respect one another for the bond that we have formed. We brought you a *mkhwenyana* (son-in-law), *Bhuti*, and I am sure that you have formed your own opinion of him."

Thomas looked at TM and they winked at each other.

"Well, *Bhuti*, in the next few days we will be leaving, and I promise you this time you will be receiving letters and telegrams quite often, updating you how we are. We have spoken to the dead and I know that they have listened to us, happy that we brought their daughter and grand-daughter, as they commanded."

"Nancy and *sbali* (brother-in-law), from the bottom of my heart I wish you well and look forward to the day when I will be invited to the betrothal and the day that I receive that news will be the day when I know that it is time for me to join the rest in that other world," said Thomas.

Thomas looked at TM, puzzled by his uncharacteristic silence.

"It is your time now, *sbali*, to throw in a word. You have been too quiet."

TM stood up, buttoned his jacket and sat up straight.

"Well, well, well. What can I say when I am only a visitor in the Mabheka home? Firstly, thanks to my loving Nancy for having given me this opportunity to become part of your world – one which has been alien to me until now. Phasing me into the Xhosa culture has taught me much over this short period – I thank you, *rree* Mabheka."

He shifted his posture, turning to Aunty Thando.

"Aunty Thando, on behalf of Nancy and myself, I thank you for your presence here. It has strengthened the relationships in this family and has added something that was missing while you were not here. We will continue talking in Jo'burg. I thank you."

Two days later, Nancy, TM and Aunty Thando boarded a train back to Jo'burg – a journey that was full of love, joy and kinship.

Chapter 9

Nancy Gets a Job

It was one afternoon not long after the successful visit to King William's Town - an afternoon of love, calmness and togetherness, as the Mabheka family and TM gathered in Noluthando's dining room in 3rd Avenue, Alexandra Township.

Aunty Noluthando stood in front of a large wooden cupboard, facing her niece and TM, who were seated at the table. Aunty Thando continued her discussion.

"I think I had the most fulfilling two-week holiday in King William's Town. It was nostalgic, scary at first, as I did not know how my brother was going to receive me, after all my years of absence from home, or how he had taken Nancy's return either - and then there was the presence of TM, a thought of which caused me anxiety during my train trip there."

"So was it with me also, Aunty Thando, but one thing I told myself was that you cannot avoid home, no matter what the circumstances might be," Nancy said.

"True, that is true, *bo mme*," TM agreed. "You can imagine how it was with me, who did not have the full picture of what, first, Nancy's sudden desire was of going to the '*bundus*' and your sudden arrival, aunty, it really shocked me. I thought it was all about me, who had taken a woman without the permission of her parents."

Thando laughed. "But at the end of the day, all went well, I think. So, we have accomplished the first phase."

"First phase?" Nancy exclaimed.

"Oh yes, my dear, planning is the most important thing in the life of a human being. Thing is, as I mentioned to Nancy, TM, in King William's Town, you guys have to be serious now about life, about your future. You have to get out of your slumbers and Alexandra's artificial comfort zones – seriously, Nancy, you have to get a job soon and you too,TM, you have to get serious."

"But, aunty, do you think I am still employable?" asked Nancy.

"Only when you try will you have the answer; you are too impulsive and lack motivation and this is exactly the comfort zone I was referring to. Nancy, I have spoken again to Gladys and she assured me that she is working on something and that there is a colleague who is going on maternity leave, and so a replacement is going to be needed in her department. She promised me that I should give her until month end, which is just a matter of a week from now."

Nancy and TM looked at each other, hands clasped, thrilled with this news.

"Furthermore, lady and gentleman, I am still considering the options of living in Johannesburg."

"Meaning what, aunty?"

"Meaning, continuing to be a resident of Johannesburg. You see, Nancy, it had never been my intention to die here but to come and look for work, make money and go back home to support my parents; but fate did not work that way. And as I said, I am still considering my options, and you shall be informed when the right time comes."

True to her word, Gladys got back to Thando with good news. On Saturday, the two older women sat at Gladys's house, discussing the potential job.

"As I said, aunty, everything will now be in Nancy's hands," said Gladys. "She will have to come to work with me this Monday so that she can meet our human resources manager, who is the person with whom she must have an interview. I have to be upfront – all depends on what the manager thinks of Nancy; how she is assessed."

"But what are the chances, Gladys?"

"About 90/100, aunty. I have tried my best to canvas for Nancy, for I think she has the look for the type of ladies we need at a women's fashion store. I will pass your place on my way to work on Monday at 5.30 am."

"Thank-you very much, my dear. She will be ready."

She left Gladys, feeling happy.

Nancy was dropped at the front gate by TM as Thando came down the road. They went into the house together.

"Where are you from at this time of the day, aunty?"

"I have been seeing neighbours, Nancy. But I also passed by Gladys."

"And?"

"Curiosity killed the cat, Nancy."

"Oh, pardon me, aunty. I just can't wait to hear what you have to say!"

"Well, our dear Gladys has kept her promise and done her homework, it seems. You'll be going with her to work on Monday morning at 5.30 am to meet the human resources manager. You will be assessed. Once that's done, prepare yourself for another step towards your future."

"That sounds good, aunty! I will ask TM to drop us instead of taking a bus. He did mention that he had something to do in town on Monday, so I am sure that he won't mind."

"Well, sort that out in good time and once you know, go and tell Gladys."

"I will do that."

On Monday morning at exactly 6 am, TM and Nancy picked Gladys up at home.

"Gladys, this is TM, my boyfriend."

"Hi, Gladys, how do you do this morning, *mme*?"

"I am well and good, *ou boetie*."

They drove through to town in the already heavy Monday morning Johannesburg traffic.

"Hey, Johannesburg traffic, *bathong*!" Gladys exclaimed.

"Jozi, Jozi," laughed TM, used to the rush.

As they arrived in front of Edgars Stores, TM stopped the car and hopped out to open the doors for his passengers. He kissed Nancy lightly on the cheek.

"Good luck, my dear."

"Thanks, and goodbye." She kissed him back, glad to have his company for a few moments before going into the large building.

TM shook Gladys' hand and smiled.

"Thanks a million times for your assistance, Gladys. By the way, I will pick you guys up after work."

"It's my pleasure, *ou boetie* TM, and a pick-up will be nice."

Gladys and Nancy went up a flight of stairs into the store.

"Hi Thandi!" Gladys greeted a lady of around her age.

"Hi Gladsie, you're early today?"

"I got a lift from home to work, courtesy of this lady, Nancy Mabheka…"

Holding Nancy by the hand, she introduced her.

"She is my neighbour and will be having an interview with Florence today."

"Oh, that sounds good; welcome, Miss Mabheka! As Gladys has mentioned, I am Thandi, working in finance."

"Morning, Miss, and thank you."

Gladys took Nancy to a waiting room.

"Wait for me here, Nancy, we will see each other later."

Gladys disappeared behind an enclosure a short walk from Nancy's chair.

A tea lady came by with a cup of tea and coffee on a tray.

"*Sawubona, Sisi*, here is tea or coffee." She offered the tray to Nancy, who took a cup of tea with plenty of milk and sugar.

"*Siyabonga, Sisi*, this is nice of you."

Later, Nancy was called to a small office, where a middle-aged lady from Human Resources was seated behind a desk.

"Good morning, Miss Mabheka, my name is Florence Martins and I am the Head of Human Resources. Among other things, my responsibilities include hiring staff for our store."

She was by now standing on her feet, offering her hand to Nancy.

"Good morning, Ms Martins."

Nancy was polite but felt nervous, her voice shaking. Florence had a pad in front of her, to which she kept referring.

"I can see, Ms. Mabheka, that you have no work record, which of course is not a problem for us, for we like teaching and training new people such as you."

"True, ma'am, though I am willing to learn new things, which is the reason that I am here."

"I see. That is indeed intelligent and encouraging news for me."

She took Nancy through the job description.

"The job, Nancy, is that of trainee floor assistant. It entails receiving clients at the shop, co-ordinating with the senior staff whom they have come to see and ushering them to wherever they wish to go. For this, we need a person with good communication skills and a sweet voice, such as yours. If you are successful, you'll be on probation for two months while working under different managers. Any questions?"

Nancy shook her head, feeling marginally more confident.

"I do understand the job as explained and I have all the confidence that I can do it without any problems – the more so because I will be trained for it. I have no questions, except to thank you for having given me this opportunity to see you."

Florence stood up, shaking Nancy's hand.

"Welcome, Ms Mabheka, to the team. Somebody will take you through all the necessary documentation, which can be boring, but please take your time."

She walked Nancy out of her office and called:

"Gladys, please take Ms Mabheka to the registration office."

"Will do so, Florence."

They walked to the first floor where Gladys took her to an office with a number of ladies.

"Greta, here is your person. Florence said you know who she is and what she is here for?"

"What else could it be for Gladys? Everyone knows Greta's job here, make yourself comfortable, Ms Nancy!" said Greta, an exceptionally friendly and cheerful-looking lady.

"Thank you ma'am."

The day ended so fast that Nancy could not believe it.

TM picked them at the entrance of the store and saw a very excited Nancy standing next to a beaming Gladys.

"And?" he said, looking from one to the other.

"You can't even wait until we reach home, TM, you behave like a child."

"She got the job, *ou boetie* TM, she is now an employee of Edgars Stores."

TM broke into a wide grin and went to open the car door for Gladys.

"For Nancy first, *ou boetie*, this is her day." Gladys stepped back and allowed Nancy the honour.

"You are right, my dear."

He opened the door and Nancy took her seat. After settling Gladys, he drove the Dodge at a jaunty speed back home.

***

Working was a revelation to Nancy. Waking up in the morning to go to work became as natural to her as breathing.

"She is a fast learner, has all the qualities of an excellent employee. She has the politeness and the intelligence for the job," Florence told the two ladies seated in her office.

"I have been observing her from time to time when visiting the stores to do my rounds – she always dresses for the job, has a sweet voice and, given the right training and when the time comes, she might make an excellent sales person."

"Well if the two of you say so, I cannot object to the permanent employment of Ms Mabheka," said the third lady, a middle-aged, much-respected manager within the company.

When Florence conveyed the news to Nancy, the young girl became almost tearful.

"I can only thank you and Ms Martins. With no experience, you chose me out of many other women. I promise you that I will be the best employee at any Edgars Store across the country."

"Thank you for the confidence you show in our group, Nancy," Florence smiled, handing the girl a tissue.

But the new job, instead of being TM's salvation, became a source of friction between the lovers. Nancy tried and failed to understand what the problem was. She cast around to determine whether or not she was at fault; but clearly, she was not.

She tried discussing the issue with Gladys, who brushed her off, saying that it was the natural psychological development of a working, independent woman.

"I hope that you're not developing a guilty conscience, Nancy," her friend warned. "You have earned this independence, free of TM."

Nancy thought about what Gladys had said but still wasn't satisfied with the explanation.

"On the contrary, Gladys, it's just that TM is starting to behave differently."

Gladys shrugged, all-knowing. "Ok. Let's leave it at that, then."

Chapter 10

TM Goes to Jail

To the wise man of Alex, it was as though his world had been thrown into a centrifuge, his body a centrifugal object, tossed and damaged by continuous tribulations. The lively, jocular and fun-loving TM of yesteryear, who was always full of jokes, seemed to be fading. Standing in the bright, mid-morning sun, he looked at the dressing table, where two letters lay – and which he had been unable to open the previous night. He picked up the one from Nthabiseng and ripped it open.

Dinokana Trading Store
Dinokana Village
Zeerust
1 December 1976

My Dear Love, ou boetie Kgabalatsana

Minutes are going by the day, hours passed, days and years gone without a word from you. But your promises when you left home are still ringing in my ears. It is now 15years since I last saw your beautiful and lovely face and years since my letter to you was returned as 'No more in Mzilikazi'. I live in hope that you are well and alive.

Today I thought I should inform you that it is today the 15th anniversary of the birth of our lovely daughter, your lovely daughter whom my mother named Rethabiseng. She is growing to be a lovely and disciplined child, always asking who and where her father is and these, as you might know, are difficult questions to respond to, for an innocent child, though I hope that one day all will be clarified. It is unfortunate that I cannot convey my feelings and grief in written words, for it will only be through spoken words that I can convey my inner feelings.

Safe to say that I am still waiting for you.

Yours

Nthabiseng Rethabile

By the time he finished reading the last closing sentence, TM was as devastated as the day on which his father had confronted him about Nthabiseng's pregnancy. He put the letter on the bed, stood up and stretched his limbs.

"*Modimo* (oh my Lord), what have I done to deserve this?"

He took a glass from the table, scooped water from the plastic bucket and gulped it. He went back to the dressing table and picked up the next letter. His hands were shaking, fearful of what news it might contain. He lay down on the bed to read it.

Dinokana Trading Store

Dinokana Village

Zeerust

10 December 1976

My Dear Kgabalatsana

I am writing this letter to you after your long silence. It is true what your father used to say, that when village men go to the white men's cities they lose their roots. Ok, this is not why I wrote this letter to you but to inform you of the bad news that your father passed away a few weeks ago after a short illness. We buried him and he had a well-deserved farewell from family and friends around the whole region. Your girlfriend, Nthabiseng and daughter, Rethabiseng, came with her mother but without rre Rethabile.

My child, we all hope that the Lord is looking after you and you are still alive wherever you are. The second and last thing that I should inform you about is that just before your father passed on, he called the whole family and left us with a message that we should 'tell my boy Kgabalatsana that I ask for forgiveness for all that I did to him. It was not because of what he did to the Rethabile child, but my own conscience because of how I failed him by not telling him that Nthabiseng is my daughter, and therefore his sister'. He further went on to instruct Boysie to go and tell Ntoa in Ramotswa to do what the Monare custom dictates to be done, to cleanse his wrongs. We have done all that he asked us to do and rre Ntoa, who also attended the funeral, gave us feedback as to what steps he has already taken in this regard.

Do not forget to pass my regards to Sechaba and Dira.

My child, we are now working on attempts to resolve everything.

Hoping that this letter will reach you on time.

Your mother

MmaMonare

The world seemed to be collapsing around TM. He was devastated by the two letters. What was the panacea for all of this? Could his ancestors be turning their backs on him?

The more he tried to find answers to these questions, the more he found himself in a state of vertigo enveloping his body. He stood up and went to the window, his mind a blur. He held the wall below the window with one hand and regained his balance within a minute or so. He staggered to the table to fetch another cup of water from the plastic bucket. Then, he filled a dish with water, washed, had breakfast and dressed to go to town.

As he left the house, he came across MamTshawe, who was sweeping her *stoep*. She hailed him.

"*Kanti zitsha ngani wena* (what is going on with you), Kgabalatsana? You are hardly seen these days, *yini ngathi sowulal'emapayipini* (why does it seem that you have no place to sleep)?"

"I am around, old lady, I am around."

"*Yho, nayi mihlola, hamba* - I am seeing things, go Kgabalatsana."

TM crossed over into MamTsamaye's yard, to fetch his car. He skidded into the road and headed for Sparks' place, stopping the Dodge jerkily. Sparks was relaxing on his *stoep*, reading a magazine. He watched attentively as his friend slammed the car door and hastened through the yard.

"This is new Jewish you are wearing TM, why did you not tell me that there was new stock at Patel's, look at the Alpaca jersey, striped nogal, *yho*, you are hot, man."

"This is old stuff, Sparks, otherwise?."

"No *mkathakatha broer*, everything is *mojo* - all is well, my brother."

Sparks stood up and left TM, disappearing into the house and returning minutes later with cold beer and glasses. They drank in silence for a minute before TM broke it.

"Hey Sparks, I am in *shundies* (in problems), my *broer*, everything is just not going in the right direction for me, letters from home, lot of problems, I have not heard from Mampye nor Nancy who since she started with her new job seems to be busier than the busiest of business people. I am just a lonely wolf with no direction and I don't know what to do."

Sparks filled the glasses and shook his head.

"*Broer*, life is a bitch. Today things go well, but tomorrow it turns against you. We all have our challenges; the key thing is how we solve them. You keep things inside yourself for too long and they eat you inside. They eat your soul, *broer*, and I think that is where your problem is. Think about it and don't rush and you will find solutions to what you think are problems. Some of us have been in worse situations."

"*Ya neh*? You've said a mouthful, my *broer*, I will try."

"Not try, TM, you just have to do it, otherwise *jy is in shit* (you are in the shit) my *broer*, real *shundies*," said Sparks.

They chatted some more, and then TM bid his friend

farewell.

From Sparks' place, TM was just roaming around the township in circles, not knowing what to do until late afternoon, when he went to a tavern in 2nd Avenue, a place he hardly frequented, and had some drinks until late at night. At about 8 pm that night, half-drunk, he saw Mampye entering with a man. TM ducked to avoid her seeing him, but she had already seen his car outside. After some time, she came over to greet him, leaving the gentleman with whom she had come in. They seemed to be good friends.

Mampye and TM stood looking at each other for a while. Then Mampwe cocked her eyebrow.

"I trusted you with all my heart, I set you up here in this Alex and you spat me out like saliva. You, TM, of all people."

"It was just a misunderstanding, Mampye, and you never gave me a chance to explain myself."

"Explain yourself when you are with a woman in 'our' house, the very house that I organised for you? What was there to explain? That is TM again, with all his tricks."

"And who is that *moegoe* you are with?" he asked.

"My boyfriend," she chipped in without looking at him, turned on her heels and walked away.

TM looked at Mampye as she shook her back, walking towards her 'boyfriend'. TM didn't believe this story and knew that she was just trying to make him jealous. When TM next looked in their direction, he noticed that the gentleman was gone and that Mampye was now seated with two other women. TM soon joined them.

Hours later, as he was getting ready to leave, Mampye's 'boyfriend' returned. Suddenly, without warning, TM felt a blunt object slamming the back of his neck. Women started screaming.

TM whipped around, grabbing an empty beer bottle, and swung it at his attacker. The bottle broke, leaving the jagged neck in his hand. A second assailant charged at TM, meeting the broken bottle instead. Blood gushed from between his eyes.

TM heard gunshots – a first and then a second, which hit the roof of the lounge.

Mampye shouted above the chaos: "What are you doing, Justice, I told you there is nothing between the two of us, why are you stupidly jealous of nothing?"

TM rushed at one of the men, who was carrying a revolver, and hit him on the back of the head with another bottle. The gun flew into the air and both the attackers ran from the house as police sirens wailed in their direction. TM absently picked up the revolver and then promptly dropped it as the policemen rushed in – but not before they had seen him holding it.

"No point, my friend, that is evidence," the police officer told him.

"It is not mine!" shouted TM.

"You will tell that to the magistrate, not me."

TM was taken to the police station for questioning. He did not know where Mampye was, or the other men.

"I do not even know *die moegoes* (those nincompoops), to be honest." TM talked politely to the officer taking his statement, assuring him that he was an innocent party.

"Sergeant, I think it will be important for me to start the story from the beginning. We were socialising at Stan's place with friends when a guy came in with Mampye…"

"And who is this Mampye?" asked the policeman.

"She is my former girlfriend."

"OK, proceed."

"Socialising or drinking, Mr Monare?" asked a second policeman.

"Socialising, sir," responded TM.

"Much later in the evening, the guy who was with Mampye left to come back later with another man, who from the look of things, was his friend. I was by then talking to Mampye and two ladies whom she was with, facing the door, and so I saw them approaching. Mampye's 'friend' was brandishing a knife while his friend had what looked like a revolver, which was in his hand, covered by the sleeve of his jacket. I lifted my head to stand upright, concentrating on them.

"The one with a knife charged at me and I side-stepped and he hit the corner of the table. I hit him with a full beer bottle behind his back as hard as I could and he fell on the ground. And as he was on the ground, I heard a gunshot, which I presumed was from his fried. By this time, there was pandemonium inside the lounge, ladies screaming and men taking cover. In that confusion, I heard Mampye's voice."

"So, you hit someone with a bottle?"

"Self-defence sergeant, what else could I do? I heard it breaking and when I turned I saw blood spurting in my face and heard Mampye's voice shouting: 'What are you doing Justice? I told you there is nothing between him and me, why are you stupidly jealous of nothing'."

"So, this is the same Mampye, your girlfriend?"

"Former girlfriend," TM corrected, and the policeman continued:

"She knew the man?"

"I presume so, but I cannot speak for her."

"Proceed, Monare."

"I heard a second gunshot, and I presume that it was from the same person, I do not know and I heard Mampye's scream, 'He has shot me, he has shot me' and when I looked in the direction where Mampye's voice came from I saw and realised that it was this Justice who might have shot Mampye. I charged at him, hiding behind two guys and hit him with another beer bottle, directly this time, between his eyes and he fell, with his gun flying in the air. I picked it up as it fell on the ground.

"That was when I heard a police siren and you guys found me with the gun in my hand."

"Did you by then realise that the first gunshot hit a person or the bullet ricocheted and hit him?"

"No, I was not aware, but I heard Mampye scream, 'He has shot me, he has shot me' but I was hearing it for the first time."

"And do you know that the man is as we speak in a critical state in hospital?"

"No, I am not aware, sergeant."

"Are you aware that Mampye got a direct shot in her chest and she is dead?"

"May her soul rest in peace, she was a good girl who got shot in the crossfire."

"And that it was the same gun that was found in your possession that led to this man's hospitalisation and Mampye's death?"

"I am not aware, sergeant."

The second policeman, who was standing next to the door as the statement was being taken, commented: "Are you aware of the seriousness of your predicament? Possession of an illegal firearm, which might be stolen or has been involved in other misdemeanours, forensic will verify all this, injury with aggravating circumstances, death with a firearm.

"Monare, I am afraid we will have to lock you up and you will appear before a magistrate tomorrow on charges of possession of a firearm, attempted murder, public violence and drinking in an illegal place. These are serious charges, but the magistrate is more competent in expanding on them."

TM was asked to leave all his valuable possessions - watch, wallet and belt - at the desk, where they were registered and put in a bag, after which he was taken to the police station cells.

The following morning Kgabalatsana Johannes Monare appeared before magistrate Ken Vosloo, where he pleaded not guilty to all charges and his case was remanded for Thursday, 20 March. When his trial reached the bench on that warm summer's day, Johannes Kgabalatsana was sentenced to an effective three-year jail term and, as the magistrate put it when he handed down sentence:

"There is overwhelming evidence that you were found with the gun that caused the mayhem that fateful evening and this is beyond doubt; and, as in your own admission in your statement, you still had the weapon in your hands; therefore, all blame for whatever happened is on your shoulders. This very weapon has been used in horrific crimes as far as Lourenco Marques, as evidenced by forensic experts. Mr Monare, the odds are against you in this case. According to evidence in front of me here from the police forensic department, your fingerprints are all over the weapon and in that case, I have no option but to find you guilty."

Years later, TM's mind meandered through the memory of that day in the dock.

He had had his fair share of the City of Gold. The three-year jail term was spent at Fort Prison for an offence he continually maintained he did not commit. If he had not done what he had done, he argued to all who would hear, he would have been six feet underground.

In prison, TM became a darling of his prison inmates because of the stories he related and the jokes he shared with the prison warders. His knowledge of Afrikaans made him a likeable and popular inmate.

"*Maar Johannes, jy is mos van die Wes Transvaal, wat soek jy in 'n plek soos Johannesburg, jy is ook nie 'n jong man nie* - but Johannes, you are from the Western Transvaal, you are not young, not so? What are you doing in Johannesburg, and *jy's ook slim* - and you are wise," said Botha, the prison warder responsible for the section in which TM stayed.

From that day onwards, the prison warders and some of his peers referred to him as 'Toppie', (or 'old man') Manoja (wise).

"Prison is not and will never be a nice place to be, though," TM mused.

He realised this on the first day of his arrival at the Fort Prison. He was devastated by the sentence and as they were driven in a big *Khwelakhwela* prison van which was carrying approximately 50 people, but was actually only big enough for 20, he was anxious about his fate.

"Old man this is not a taxi, sit properly," a light-complexioned, middle-aged man said to TM, shoving him.

"Like you and your Ma and *vok off* (fuck off)," TM retorted.

"We will see when we arrive in prison who is the boss." the man sneered.

"And you will see who will be dancing," answered TM, irritated.

The man was, by this time, starting to search through TM's pockets, looking for money, taking a packet of Boxer tobacco and his wrist watch.

"Where is the money, old man? You see, it just does not help to slaughter the white man's sheep, look now where you are. But do not worry, I look after you when we are locked in those cells."

"Kleintjie, *los die ou, man* (leave the man alone, man)." A heavily-tattooed inmate, with the number '26' etched on his forehead, jostled Kleintjie.

"*Ek speel net met die mpathas, my broer* (I am just joking with this rural man)," Kleintjie said.

Shock gripped TM as they arrived at the prison gate, sweaty and claustrophobic from the cramped, bumpy ride. A heavy steel gate was opened and they were shouted into rows by the prison warders. It was like herding animals at an auction.

"*Voer hulle* (feed them)!" Adrian Fourie, the prison warder, screamed at his men as the inmates jumped from the truck into a queue. Two lines, seated, heads facing the ground.

"*Hoeveel is die lot* (how many is this lot)?" asked another warder, De La Rey, who was standing some distance from the prisoners.

"*Vyftig, meneer* (50, sir)," replied Fourie, a junior warden.

They were taken one by one into the registration office, where their particulars, name, surname, date of birth, tribe, and so on were recorded in a black Croxley book, after which they were told: "*Klere uit, ons soek nie luise hier nie* (take off your clothes, we do not want lice here)!"

It was Fourie again – a small, shrill-voiced man.

"*Hande op die kop* (hands on your heads)!" Fourie screamed, angling for some violence. He hit the top of TM's penis with his baton and did the same to several others.

"*Groot piele! Party van julle maak net gemors met die groot piele. Wie is vir rape hier* (some of you have big penises and these penises are used to commit crimes – which of you is here for rape)?" yelled De La Ray.

"It's me, sir," answered a young man of about thirty.

"*Ek ook, Makhosi* (and me, sir)," said another.

Fourie went to the first respondent, looked him in the eye for a minute or so, and then yelled: "*Sir is jou ma, bandiet* (you call your mother 'sir', prisoner), *verstaan jy my* (do you understand me)?"

He hit the young man on the penis with such force that the inmate screamed.

"*Eina! Eina!*"

The boy fell to the ground as Fourie followed up with a stomach-crunching punch. He turned to the second rape confessor and pushed at his chin with his baton.

"You are going to know what rape is when they do it to you in this prison. Wait and see how it feels."

When they were finished with registration, they were all taken to a shower room and lined up under the shower taps, which blasted ice cold water onto their hot bodies. There were screams as the icy water touched bodies, followed quickly by hot water and then cold again. This happened at least three times, TM counted.

"It was the most terrible experience I had had in my whole life," TM recalled, years later.

Not waiting for their bodies to dry, Fourie, helped by long-serving prisoners, allocated uniforms: short khaki pants and shirts, socks and shoes. They were the most uncomfortable and ridiculous clothes worn by TM for as long as he could remember. For example, he wore a size 38 pants but was assigned a 48, and, because no belts were allowed in prison, lest prisoners hung themselves, TM had to tear off part of his shirt to fasten the trousers more tightly.

The shirt was easily a size 40, as well, while he wore a 36. He didn't want to talk about the shoes. When he complained, the warder snapped they did not have the correct sizes in the shoe stores, and that, after all, he would only be wearing them for three years.

They were then divided into two groups, one that was housed in Section 1 of the prison facility next to the hospital, and the second in Section 14, near the kitchen. TM was put in Section 1. He found prisoners already staying in his section and when the ten of them came in carrying their bedding, one thin soft cloth for the mattress, and two faded grey blankets, the stench of the previous owners was overpowering.

TM was leading his group as they entered the cell. He did not know which way to go. He peered into the far right-hand corner, searching for space and a bed. A prisoner was seated on a bed, with a stack of close to 20 mattresses forming his mattress, together with a pile of grey blankets and two pillows.

He was reading a magazine and he kept looking in TM's direction. When TM found a spot on the left-hand side, the prisoner called to him.

"*Sbotshwa* (prisoner) come and stay next to me. Can't you see there is an open space here?"

TM ignored him and proceeded in his chosen direction. As he settled in, the door was flung open with a bang.

"Eating time! Eating time! *Bandiete*! (prisoners)" called out a prison warder, who was their section head. They formed a queue of two outside of the cells in an open space, where there was a row of steel tables set for the evening meal: white mealies, a cup of black coffee each and a slice of brown bread for the Africans, while the Coloureds were given mealie-rice, coffee with milk and a slice of white bread.

After being given their meal, they sat in rows of two on the floor of the yard. Prison warder Fourie came into the yard, observing them from a distance, and then called over one of the prisoners working in the kitchen.

"*Het jy genoeg kos om almal te voer* (do you have enough food to feed them all)?" TM was conscious that he used the word '*voer*', which relates to feeding animals, not humans.

"*Genoeg, makhosi* (enough, sir)," the prisoner replied.

Fourie walked between the rows, staring intently at each prisoner, before coming to an abrupt stop behind the two men who had confessed to rape earlier.

"Japie!" Fourie called to a prison warder standing guard.

"After supper, take these two to Section 5."

"What does that mean?" TM asked an inmate sitting beside him.

"Section 5 is where the prison gang inmates with serious, long-term offences are kept, mostly the 28s, a gang known for committing murders in prison among their counterparts, the 26s. The 26 Gang are known thieves who sell drugs, dagga, anything that has value, including the life of an inmate."

"How do you know all these things, man?" TM asked, incredulous.

"You have to have spent time here to know all these things, *broer*."

"Are you one of them?" TM asked.

"Me, no, not a member of either of the two. I belong to the 25s. We are the least troublesome in prisons, our sin, perhaps, is only in our attempts to escape from prisons. Finish and *klaar*. We do not harm anybody."

"What about the guy in our cell, who was seated on a pile of mattresses?"

"Oh, though I am not from your section, that must be Drake, the General of the 28s, die *makhuluman* - the big guy of prisons. He is serving a 50-year sentence and is known to be the Big General for all prisons in the country. So dangerous is he that he does not work outside like other long-term prisoners. Word is that he controls some of the prison warders here, he instructs them whenever there is something that he needs. Watch him, he always smokes cigarettes, never a *zol* (a cigarette rolled out of newspaper or brown paper) like most prisoners do. Under those mats he has his own special supplies. When there are raids, he is always alerted by some warders, who create a mock raid before the main one, thus taking Drake's property but what you will notice after the raid is that you will see him with his things back. This is not unusual for the likes of Drake, they run prisons."

TM was grateful for the information. He introduced himself.: "By the way, my name is TM, Toppie Manoja from Alexandra."

"I am Zonke. And what are you in for, *bra* TM?"

"Murder."

"Mmm, heavy stuff. They will like that."

"Who will like that?"

"Time up! Back to your cells prisoners," Fourie shouted so loudly that spit flayed the floor.

They all filed to their cells, which were locked at exactly 6 pm. And as the clicking-locking of the cell doors was going on and on and TM took to his bed, on his first day ever in prison, he thought of how many more days and months and years this was going to happen to him.

The prison routine was a continuous pattern that never changed, day in and day out, and was thus – waking up was at 5.30 am sharp without fail, making up the beds, standing against the wall, waiting for prison inspection, and being counted like animals. Fourie or any of the prison warders of his rank - Hannes, Hennie, Schalk and many others who

Jim is Tired of Jo'burg

worked in shifts - would conduct such inspections to check if all prisoners were in, lest one of the 25s had escaped overnight or if there had been a killing of someone overnight.

As days, weeks and months went by, TM made friends with a young man who was sleeping four places down from him. He soon noticed that he was not like most of the inmates, as he was always alone or talking to one person at a time and had books that he read constantly after working duties – a supply that he was officially given from time to time by the warders from the prison library. TM further discovered that the young man worked in the prison library. One day he approached him as they came back from work in the prison fields.

"*Sawubona, mfana*, (good day, young man), my name is *bra* TM, I am from Alexandra."

"I am Lebohang Mangoana, from Thokoza in the East Rand."

"What are you in for?"

"Tax avoidance and white-collar crimes."

"Man, this is heavy stuff - and what do you do for a living?"

"A practicing lawyer, but with this criminal record now I have to look into other avenues."

"Oh, I see."

He left the young man and went to his bed; and just as he was beginning to relax, he heard a voice calling.

"*Hey wena*, TM *sbotshwa, zwakala hier* (hey you, TM prisoner, come here)."

It was none other than Drake, his nemesis. He got out of bed and slowly walked to where Drake was seated.

"Sit down." Drake meant business.

"By the way, what is your call here? And *ungubani ngempela* - who are you really? I checked your credentials and they are nowhere to be found."

TM didn't flinch from the seasoned criminal's gaze.

"Let me start from the beginning. My name is Johannes Kgabalatsana Monare, but I am known as TM, which stands for Toppie Manoja, as that is my name in Alexandra and in Jozi generally. Secondly, I am here for murder. And *jy* (you)?"

"*Hulle noem my Drake* (they call me Drake)."

"Drake *wie* (Drake who)?"

Drake extinguished the fag on the mat and stretched his arms. There was deathly silence in the cell, all eyes on TM and Drake. He looked as if he was not going to answer TM, at first.

"Drake Meintjies, from Senoane in Soweto, but I live in prisons such as these all over the country."

"I am pleased to hear that, Drake."

"Well, there is still a lot between the two of us that we should talk about, we do not like newcomers to just arrive and run the show, people that we do not know, for this is our territory. As you are still going to be with us for the next three years, I am going to serve this sentence with you and you will leave me here. So, let's take one thing at a time, my *broer*."

TM stood up and walked away. The inmates were watching this interaction, surprised.

TM became very friendly with Lebohang the lawyer, and moved his bedding next to him. He began to learn much about the law from the earnest young man, as well as an inside knowledge of prison life and procedures. It was Lebohang who had advised TM to appeal his case after hearing about the trial. He would help TM to make the application, he said.

"It is common practice, in my profession, to be involved in such cases, *bra* TM," he said. "Helping people like you is what I do. Had you had a lawyer in the first place, I doubt that you'd be here today."

Indeed, as he had promised, TM and Lebohang worked on the case. After that, TM filed the applications at the Johannesburg High Court. Some weeks later, TM was called to the offices of the prison head, Captain Vosloo, where he showed him, in the presence of his lawyer, Lebohang, a letter from high court, acknowledging receipt of the application and an assurance that a response would be received in due course.

TM's first visitor was Sparks, one Thursday afternoon.

He was taken by surprise when his name was called by a warder through the prison intercom system, instructing him to go to the visitors' room. And as he arrived in the small hall, through the glass wall he saw his friend waving at him as he took a seat on a hard chair. TM sat down opposite him.

"Big man, you look well under these conditions; we have heard about your tragedy and what befell Mampye, may her soul rest in peace.

"I heard from a friend what happened. He kept us spellbound about your battle with those thugs. Thank God you were not hurt. And the unfortunate squabble with the *moegoes*, you did them good, die *moerskonts* (the devils). They deserved it."

Sparks had worked himself up and was shouting. He calmed down quickly after glancing at the grim-looking prison guards.

"Look, we left you R500 at the reception for you to buy all the nice things, it was a collection from all of us. Nancy, Gladys, MamTshawe and MamTsamaye all say to keep well. We are looking forward to your coming back home one day, my *broer*."

Sparks had given TM no chance to talk, which he did not mind, as his friend was the visitor, after all.

"And look, the two girls, Nancy and Gladys, will be the next to pay you a visit, so behave like a gentleman please towards Nancy, things are still sour, and be warned, the women are taking a hard line, believing that you are at fault, but don't blame her, birds of a feather flock together *broer*, just be calm and don't argue when they visit, just listen. Will see you next time, *broer*."

***

The Fort Prison was different from all other prisons in the Transvaal or the country as a whole, as it had housed some of the most notorious of guys in Jozi, including the infamous Msomi Gang. Now it was home to TM, who had never so much as sniffed at a prison door.

One evening as he was preparing to sleep, an inmate crept up to him, almost sneaking so as not to draw attention to himself.

He knelt down and whispered: "My *broer*, welcome to The Fort, our home, we were expecting you, for we received a message from *die Groot Ou* (from the Big Guy), through *ou* Drake, when you were first arrested and your two appearances in court. Our guys spoke well of you, *moord* (murder) and possession of a firearm, they thought that you are well-connected and they sent a message immediately to Drake that should you come to the Fort, as we expected that you would, we must look well after you. That you are a great wise man."

The man gave TM a thumbs-up and slipped away into the gathering gloom.

TM was not happy with the news. Firstly, he hadn't committed the murder; secondly, he had no connections whatsoever, regardless of what they believed; thirdly, he did not want to find himself back in the salt mine, owing to these tenuous links to Drake and his gang. TM had heard much about the danger of prison gang relationships, be it the 28s or any other. He didn't want to jeopardise his chance of parole or remission of sentence. However, he did not say this to the inmate who had brought the news. After all, what was the point of shooting the messenger?

Unfortunately for TM, he was a sitting duck. One night, as they were preparing to sleep, and just as the lights were switched off, Drake's friend lit a match, and when TM looked at him, he noticed that there was no cigarette. He heard a rattling sound, and spotted two men apparently sleeping near the toilet section. The men charged in his direction. He jumped out of bed as a steel mug hit him on the forehead, followed by someone covering him with a blanket. A commotion ensued, everybody brawling, the prisoners hitting one another with any missiles to hand.

TM noticed that his head was bleeding. The prison siren sounded and a group of prison warders descended, bringing with them barking, snarling dogs, which they let loose in the cells. Batons were wielded and chaos erupted for nearly an hour. A whistle blew, and the warders stopped beating, calling their dogs off.

"26s one side!" bellowed Sergeant Pierce. "And 28s against the wall. All others in the middle."

TM stood in the middle of the hall, but Pierce shouted at him.

"Prisoner Monare, join the other side, there with the 28s."

TM took offence to being associated with the gangsters, but he did as he was told.

"All 26s out of their cells!"

Pierce marched the men to a different section of the prison. He turned back to yell at the 28s: *"Ek soek nie kak nie van enige man nie, hoor julle my* (I want no nonsense from any of you, do you hear me)?"

"Ja, makhosi (yes, sir)." The response was muted.

Pierce turned to TM. "Johannes Monare, report to my office."

TM was taken out by a black warder to Pierce's office, where he found three senior warders waiting, including a Van Dyck and a Du Toit, according to their name badges. They greeted him amiably enough.

"Well, well, if it is not the murderer of Alexandra, I do not know who it is," chuckled Van Dyck, as he stood up to shake TM's hand.

"Johannes. *My naam is* (my name is) Bertrand Van Dyck, Provincial Commissioner of Prisons in the Transvaal, and what this means is that I am in control of all prisons in this province."

He picked up a large brown envelope, opened it and handed over the contents to Du Toit, his deputy, who reviewed the file quickly.

"*Jy is mos 'n complicated man* (you are a complicated man), Monare. Our records show that you had no criminal record before the murder conviction that led you here. But man, you associate with wrong people. First, the person whose gun killed the lady in a *shebeen* and critically injured another who is still in a coma in hospital. Did you know that he, Justice, was a member of the 28s prison gang, and that he was having an affair with your former girlfriend – the one who was killed by the gun found in your possession that night?"

"*Nee, makhosi* - I did not know that, sir." TM had no clue why he was being told this, or what line Du Toit was going to take next.

"Ja, Monare. It is possible that you did not know, but this is not a question but a fact. Do you know a man called Drake?"

"If you are referring to the Drake who is serving a 50-year sentence here in this prison, *makhosi*, I can safely say that I do not know him because I met him for the first time on my arrival here."

"OK, OK, Monare, I can see you are playing it safe. Let me tell you, Drake made a recommendation to his gangsters here at the Fort long before you came here, actually still when your trial was on, that you must be well looked after in any prison in which you might be serving your sentence. That we know and I am not going to ask you if it is true or not and again, this is a fact that we know."

TM shook his head, which was starting to spin, for he wondered where this was leading. He thought about the appeal application and what this would mean for him.

"Can you tell us about the fight between the 28s and the 26s? How did it start? For our information is that you were the first to be attacked and you were thereafter covered with a blanket? Why?" Van Dyck chipped in.

"Sir, no sorry, *makhosi*, it happened so fast that the only thing I remember was seeing a flicker of light in the cell, I do not know from whom. Then I was hit with a mug on my head, I started bleeding immediately and a blanket, as you just mentioned, was thrown over my head. What, why this happened to me I do not know."

Whether or not they believed him, he was beginning to reach a stage at which he did not care. The prison officials looked at one another and then Van Dyck said something that TM found interesting.

"Monare, *jy moet versigtig wees* (you must be careful). We will be in touch with you and we expect your full cooperation. Pierce, take him to his cell."

TM took refuge in his bed, exhausted by an hour of prison interrogation. He was angry about this supposed conspiracy and the way that he was being treated by both officials and prisoners. There was nothing more to do but sleep. Seemingly moments later, he was woken for daily inspection. Prison was starting to take its toll on TM; too many things were happening that he did not understand, let alone how he had landed there in the first place.

The prison uniform was getting bigger and bigger and he had continually to find ways of holding his pants up, as they fell easily past his waist. He started thinking of the days in his house in Alexandra, and Nancy and Mampye were starting to haunt him all the time. He found himself mumbling repetitively: "It will be alright soon."

Nostalgia, ironically, made him stronger. He developed an inclination to hold his head above water. He realised that surviving in prison had to be his focus. One sunny Monday, as they finished up breakfast and were preparing to go to work, Pierce jogged into the yard, calling:

"Johannes Monare! Johannes Monare."

"Take your belongings, you are needed at the offices."

He did as he was told, and after gathering his insignificant bits and pieces, went to the office, where he found Van Dyck seated with another man.

"Monare, this is lawyer Van Schalkwyk from Van Schalk-wyk & Schoeman Attorneys in Pretoria and instructed by a prison friend of yours – an advocate Lebohang Mangoana, who had filed an application for the review of your sentence. I will leave the rest to the gentleman to explain."

"It is true what the Commissioner just said, Mr Monare, I have been instructed by advocate Mangoana and have been working on your appeal. The High Court in Johannesburg sat in the last few days and heard your case. The presiding judges accepted our arguments for your release. You are therefore now a free man, as soon as the prison officials have finalised your release. You shall be out of the doors of Fort Prison. Lastly, Mr Monare, we have made contact with your friends in Alexandra. They are, I think, already on their way to take you home."

That was a good day. After more than two years in prison, TM was a free man.

***

Stepping out of the Fort prison gates was like stepping out of a grave. The clock struck freedom at 10 am for TM, who carried with him a plastic bag holding a few meagre belongings.

As he set foot on free soil, allowed to go in any direction he chose, vertigo hit him as the prospect of being a free man came to him. He could decide when he wanted to sleep, or not; he was out of the clutches of prison gangs and warders; he was a bird.

He became elated, seeing his buddies, Sparks and David – and an unexpected guest. Nancy Mabheka, his long-time lover, had also come to take him home. His heart thumped, not knowing what to think. Fortunately, there was little time to think, as she ran towards him, enveloping him in a fierce embrace. TM's friends hung back, giving the couple space.

Holding hands, TM and Nancy followed David and Sparks to David's car. They all talked at once, overjoyed to

Jim is Tired of Jo'burg

be reunited.

"Welcome, my brother," said Sparks. "You've left Fort. I hope that you had a good time with those *ouens* (guys)," he chuckled.

"You talk as if you were once in there, Sparks, my brother!" said TM. "Prison can never be good, my friend. It is tough, stinking and bad – you are always on the look-out for warders who might plant something on you, or the gangs who are always ready to do something to you.

"Otherwise, though, it was not too bad, except for thoughts of this baby next to me," he added, hugging Nancy close, and kissing her.

Sparks whooped: "Not in public, my brother – watch out! You might end up going back!"

The group drove to Noluthando's house, where they found several of Nancy's new friends, including Gladys and Angela, as well as neighbours. All were cooking in the kitchen, happily preparing a meal for the released man.

Noluthando shrieked with excitement as TM walked through the front door.

"Welcome, TM! You look good, my man. Take a seat and relax."

Nancy interrupted her aunt: "Aunty, remember what we said? There is new clothing on the bed and TM will want to refresh himself first. Come *ou boetie*, TM." She ushered him through to the bedroom, where he found his chalk-striped suit, white shirt and black trousers.

"Everything is in the shower room outside, ou boetie, so take your time."

Nancy patted TM on the cheek and then left him.

Feeling clean and energised, TM later joined the rest of the group in the dining room. They were listening to Noluthando singing a hymn – *Nkosi Sihlangeni, Lord We Are Gathered Here* – with an angelic voice that reminded Nancy of her childhood, when Aunty Thando was a choir girl at the Methodist Church in Zwelitsha.

After the performance, Sipho, a neighbour and uncle to Gladys, prayed, thanking the Lord for having looked after TM in jail, and welcoming him back amongst his own. TM gave a vote of thanks to Noluthando, Nancy and his friends.

"I never thought that I would see some of you again. I have learned my lessons. I would not have landed in that jail had I not been in the wrong place, at the wrong time. I thank you, aunty, for having allowed me to join all my friends at your place."

TM held his hat in his hands, humbly.

The day was festive and soon became a party, with food and drinks in abundance. David brought stock from work, and the men drank freely.

Hour later, Nancy and TM retreated to her bedroom, leaving Noluthando and Gladys to clean up. TM gave a deep sigh as he joined Nancy in bed.

"It is like a dream," he whispered.

Chapter 11

A Visit to a Sangoma

L ife in the city was bedevilling TM.

"This is the last straw for me; I'm in real Sh...."

He looked at himself in the mirror and pinched his cheeks. Two days after the terrible incident of TM's receipt of the letter from the attorneys he found himself driving through a dirt road in Krugersdorp, west of Johannesburg slowly negotiating the car down the curvy roads. The car windows were wide open allowing a fresh breeze was passing in.

He came to a stop at a *cul de sac* leading to a gate in front of a hut. An old emaciated dog ,wagging its tail lazily, began smelling at his feet as he got out of the car. He kicked the dog, looking around to see if anybody was watching him – 'dogs of today have dog rights,' he thought to himself.

The front door of the hut opened, and a thickset lady dressed in *Sangoma* (traditional doctor) attire came out, carrying a horsetail whip, wagging it up and down and spitting on the ground as she ushered TM into a darkly lit hut next to her main house.

In the middle of the room, covering the floor, was a white sheepskin with bones laid in a lump. The lady of the house motioned TM to sit down directly opposite her, and she continuously spat from left to right and at times on the bones.

"Vumani!" (Agree with me)

"Savuma!" (I agree), responds TM,

"Vumani!" said the Sangoma louder

"Savuma!" responded TM.

She patted him with the whip on his shoulders and started shuffling the bones.

"My bones tell me that you are in a severe dilemma, *Vumani!*"

"*Savuma!*" retorted TM.

"*Mhh! Ahh!*" growled the Sangoma, "my bones show me that you're the most worried man, confused, not knowing what to do with the predicament you find yourself. I see a beautiful lady who is in the same difficulty, disappointed, hurt and bitter. *Vumani?*"

TM kept quiet. The woman lifted her eyes from the bones, shook the beads concealing her face and continued, staring at the man opposite her,

"*Vumani!*" She dipped her whip in a bucket and beat TM on his shoulders, and a watery substance splashed onto his face.

"*Vumani!*"

"*Savuma!*" replied TM this time, intimidated by the stare of the lady.

"*Makhosi!* (A call to the ancestors) Your way is now opened," groaned the Sangoma, "for you have recognised your troubles."

She stood up, leaving the room and came back with a bottle of medicine and handed it over to TM.

"Take a spoon of this, mix it with water in your washing bucket in the mornings and evenings before you sleep. Take a teaspoon and gargle once a day. After having finished this bottle, make contact with your lady and your problems would be solved.

"I now send you home, my child, and may your ancestors be with you."

She bade farewell to her client as he got into his car and drove through the gate with the dog barking lazily, as if a long-time friend was deserting the household. The lady went back to her hut and came back with a bucket with a wet substance and sprinkled the tracks of the car up till the gate. Having finished this ritual, she disappeared into the house.

***

To TM, the time spent behind bars was an experience that dealt with his being. He knew that he had to go back to the drawing board, as it is usually said in other circumstances, but in his situation, he had to take stock of his life and livelihood.

His macabre experiences and the dire straits in which he found himself in the City of Gold forced him to think of that fateful evening, in 1960, when with two of his friends, Sechaba and Dira, he left their village to look for 'gold' – a better future that would help them become decent beings He realised that he had forgotten about his old friends.

"Where is Dira?" he asked himself and he could not find an answer. "What happened to Sechaba?"

He had promised Joseph that he would visit Sechaba at the Krugersdorp Mental Hospital where he had last heard that he was languishing.

He experienced a sense of betrayal to his two friends and as a result of this realisation, he took a decision that he would find out where they were and whatever he did moving forward, he could give an account one day to their families, for he thought that this would also be what they would want to do in future.

The thought left him with a sense of fulfillment even though he knew that it was still a long way to Jericho, that there might be hurdles ahead. And a few days later he took a drive south west of Johannesburg towards Krugersdorp, looking for the mental hospital and as he drove into the facility, he experienced a sense of depression.

He gasped: "I cannot imagine a human being entering this place and coming back sane."

He stopped in front of the reception. Slowly he walked towards a counter manned by depressed-looking men and women draped in white doctors' and nurses' uniforms. At one stage, he thought of going back but proceeded to fulfill his mission. He went to a nurse who was scribbling something in a book.

"May I help you, Sir?" she asked.

"I have come to look for Sechaba Sekgametsi who, at the time he was hospitalised here, was working at the Mzilikazi Mine in Booysens."

The nurse lifted her gaze and responded: "When was this when he was admitted here?".

TM stammered, and sweat dropped down his forehead, and when he had regained his strength, he responded,

"It is a long, long time ago, which I cannot remember."

Another nursing sister who was listening said to her colleague: "Let the gentleman wait for a while and I will check with the registry at archives, the more so when the gentleman uses words such as 'a long time ago'."

"We will help you, Sir, just take a seat and we will be with you soon."

He took a seat, not knowing whether he was at the right place and right time, for he started to fear for the worst news of his life.

Soon thereafter, the nurse who went to registry came back carrying a brown file and whispered at her colleague and handed over the file. He was called to come forward and the nurse who started helping him said;

"Sir, *rre*, Sechaba Sekgametsi indeed was admitted at this very hospital, but regret to tell you that he passed away. Unfortunately, the hospital could not trace his relatives and he was buried at the Krugersdorp cemetery for Bantus. But this cemetery has long been demolished and is now housing the Whites Only Krugerdorp Villa."

He stared at the lady, who was talking to him as if she was reciting a poem, but in truth she was telling him what had happened to his friend, Sechaba. He thanked the nurse and left the hospital, traumatised.

At that point he decided that he would not venture to look for Dira, for he was scared that he might hear the same about him too, He decided to let sleeping dogs lie.

Chapter 12

Jim is Tired of Jo'burg

After 20 years of living in the City of Gold, the tragedies that had befallen TM were taking their toll on him. His two-year prison term, trouble with Nancy, loss of his father and his close friends and the loneliness of life without a girlfriend or his buddies caused him untold heartache.

Time flies when things go well, but drags when they are bad. He was trapped in the nuances and chaos of city life, and some his troubles he had brought with him from the village – his quarrels with his father and separation from the mother of his child. These constant nightmares had been dealt with privately, except on one occasion, when he wrote to tell his mother about his woes.

TM was realising that staying in the city was not good for him. He needed to see Joseph – the one person whose advice he had always cherished.

"Look at me," he would think aloud to himself, in the seclusion of his room.

"Where is Dira today? Sechaba is dead. I am without Nancy today. I feel naked in the midst of the Alexandra crowds."

TM had to leave Jo'burg, before it killed him. "My time is up in this City of Gold," he whispered, staring at the bare walls of his room.

The decision made the present a little easier to bear. Wearing Nancy's apron while listening to light radio music, his mind wandered away from the jazzy Miles Davis tune. He noticed a half-full glass of brandy on the dressing table and got up to drink it.

Alas! It tasted very different – either because his taste buds were no longer accustomed to brandy, or because it had been standing too long. He drank some water to cleanse his palate and tried again.

"Wake up, man."

He slapped his cheeks, grinning.

His eyes swept over the stove, where he noticed smoke seeping from one of the pots. He rushed to take off the lid, but the pot fell from his hand, knocking over a second pot, which overturned onto the floor. The plastic tiles were pooling with hot soup and boiling water.

He held his head, shouting: "Oh God. Help me. Damn, Nancy, what are you doing to me? Cooking, washing, going to the shops for bread and milk; even the shopkeeper's children in the cafe keep asking me where my girlfriend is. It hasn't been easy. I never knew the absence created when a woman has left – such a vacuum! It has not been easy, I tell you."

He took off the apron and threw it on the floor.

"Just like that? Yesterday it was Nancy, today it is none other than my old friends Joseph - my bosom friend *nogal* - and Sparks, who tutored me about life in Jo'burg.

"The man I spent the most of my life with here in Jozi, *nogal*. But where did I go wrong? What sins have I committed to be treated like this? Though, I cry not for you, Argentina, but myself."

He slammed and locked the front door and window, closed the curtains and collapsed in bed, mind racing, memories crowding. He recalled a near-confrontation with Sparks and Joseph once, at Sparks' house, a while after he had been released from prison.

"But TM, my *broer*, it was not by accident that I coined this name for you, you looked smart, you were one of the chaps in whom I noticed potential. Look at you now, *jy lyk klaar*, my *bra* -you are ragweed, mentally."

The ever-observant Joseph, added: "I took him by his hand the very first day of his arrival at Mzilikazi. He was then fresh from the bundus of the Western Transvaal, but I also saw a witty, though shy, man. I remember taking him through all the corners of the city of Jozi.

"Hey man, cheer us up and be the man we built for the rough Jozi life, this is just not you."

Joseph was almost tearful. Sparks, too; wiped his eyes with a crisp-white handkerchief while shaking his head slowly, forlornly.

"I once did this to many of my girlfriends, but not to my men friends. You force me to do this to you for the sake of your being and more so, I like my boys to be smart and clean, TM."

Sparks brought the trio Lion Lager and glasses, poured, and then proposed a toast.

"In the spirit of the revival of our friend, TM."

TM was pulled from his reverie by a sharp knock at the door. "TM! TM! *Vula* - open."

It was MamTshawe, who had been deeply involved in the Nancy-TM saga, and found herself unwittingly tangled up in the life of her tenant. TM ignored her knock.

"TM! TM!" She banged the door until it shook. "Come, come here, there's a letter for you. Foolish man!"

TM opened the door a crack, looking tipsy and sorry for himself.

"You're still asleep at this time of the day? Wake up! It is already daytime. Look at the sun. You have to pull up your socks, boy. Since you came to this Alexandra and left your job in the mines and became this Topie Manoja, you have turned into something else. We must run after you for our rent and parking money all the time!"

"You disturbed me, old lady, I was fast asleep, having a beautiful dream. Have you ever dreamed of being on the moon?"

"Dream, dream, my foot!"

The old lady pointed her finger at TM, frowning.

"I really do not know what to do with you, Kgabalatsana. At times, I really begin to think that you are cursed. I have never seen a man as cursed as you are. Perhaps you have to go to that Dinokana of yours so that they can slaughter the fattest of the white goats. Definitely, you are not well and it is only a non-African human being who would disagree with me that all these problems of yours could only be re-solved by the slaughter of a goat and not just a goat, but it must be a white one. Just listen to yourself, dreaming of the most ridiculous of all dreams – being on the moon? This is news to me."

She paused for breath.

"May the Lord help me. There's something wrong with you, Kgabalatsana Monare. Don't say I did not warn you, my boy, there are lots of young men out there; they are go-ing to take her from you."

TM looked the other way. He took the letter from the old lady and closed the door behind him, eager to read it.

Dear Mr Monare

We hereby write to you under instruction from our client, Tony Factor Furnishers, to inform you that your furniture account of R400 is now in arrears following non-payment for three months.

Failure to settle this amount within 21 days will lead to legal action being taken against you.

M & M Attorneys

He threw the letter on the floor.

"Fucking bastards."

He took another sip of brandy, rancid as it was.

"Too many things piling up on me now. Nancy ditched me." He wiped a single tear from his left eye. "All the people I thought were my friends, I thought that they had respect for me, for who I was. They are all running away from me, real fair-weather friends. All these things make me feel like a fish out of water. This is the last straw for me, I'm in real sh...".

He paused, looking at himself in the mirror, and pinch-ing his cheeks.

"But here am I alone, and alone in this City of Gold."

After 21 days, with TM having failed to settle his furniture account, a delivery van sporting bold letters – 'Tony Factor Furnishers' – stopped in front of MamTshawe's place one morning. Two men, one carrying a stack of papers, walked up to the old lady, who was seated on her *stoep* under the corrugated roof that did very little to shield her from the shimmering summer heat.

She stood up as she saw the two men, knowing exactly what the problem was – TM.

"*Sawubona, magogo.* Am I right that this is house number 1502?"

The man with the bundle of papers in his hand greeted the old lady politely.

"That's right, my boy," responded MamTshawe. "I can see that you are an educated young man."

He smiled without responding. He had been in the job for some time and could smell a fight brewing. He didn't want to pick one this early in the day. He was quite pleasant and conversational with 'clients', especially when there was no delivery to be made and only repossessions to be carried out.

"We're looking for Mr Johannes Kgabalatsana Monare, ma'm."

"He lives in the backyard. Go around - he is in his room."

The men immediately moved towards the backyard, no longer needing the lady's permission to go to the house, since the number and location had been confirmed.

The old lady, however, shuffled after them and placed herself between the men and TM's door.

"Mr Kgabalatsana Monare!"

One of the men called loudly – loud enough for MamTshawe's neighbours to wonder what was going on. She quietly stepped aside, realising that it was foolish to become involved.

TM jumped out of bed.

"Yes? Who are you?"

He flung open the door, seeing strangers carrying documents.

"*Dumela, mnumzana*. We are from Tony Factor Furnishers."

"I can see your signage and what about that and what does that have to do with TM?"

"*Rra*, we have come to repossess what you owe the store for furniture bought some time back and you never settled the account, though letters have been written to you."

"Never! Never! You are not going to enter my house and you are not taking any furniture, that would be illegal."

He blocked the door with his body, but the two men forced their way into the house under the watchful eyes of neighbours.

The men began moving the dressing table, bed and wardrobe. TM jumped towards the wardrobe, protecting it with his body. While he was doing this, the second man took bedding off the bed and tossed it to the floor. TM realised that he wasn't winning.

"Gents, could we discuss this?"

"*Rre* Monare, that is not what we are sent here for, you can go to town and discuss your problems with our offices."

By this time, one by one, the furniture was being taken out of the house and placed outside near the van.

By now, MamTshawe had been joined by MamTsamaye, the women watching from MamTshawe's kitchen door.

"I am not surprised this is all happening, TM has not been working but still driving this big red car."

MamTsamaye clicked her tongue, holding her hands to her head.

"Do not forget that he has been depending on Nancy since she started working, car petrol money, Nancy, rent money, Nancy and even money to buy cigarettes comes from Nancy. Where have you heard of that? Other men support their *vat-en-sit* (women they cohabitate with)."

A melee broke out as the men began loading the furniture.

"This is illegal!" TM yelled, becoming overwrought. "You cannot do this, I'm going to report you to my lawyers!"

They ignored him, and when they had taken all the things that they wanted, they got into the van and drove off.

Neighbours watching the spectacle gossiped among themselves.

"He has always been a creepy one amongst us in this yard, playing big in a small town."

"But also, Joe, the old ladies here have been hero-worshipping him, look now. Where is he going to sleep?"

"On the floor of course, unless perhaps he is going to sleep at his Nancy's place."

"But Joe, are they still together, I have not seen her for some time now?"

Things settled down, and everybody continued about their business. TM closed his door and sat on the table – one of the few remaining items in the room.

"When the music changes, so does the dance."

As he sat, he thought about Nthabiseng, feeling like a man lost in a void.

"You know, Joseph once warned and advised me that I should go to a Sangoma - traditional healer, as all Africans do at some point, and that he or she would strengthen me. I hesitated and took a long time to follow his advice and when I finally did it, it seems that it was almost when I am on a precipice. Perhaps I was supposed to have done what he told me to do at the time when he advised me to do so and I would a different person to what I am now, but I now know the old African adage to be true: 'A man who takes advice, is still a man who acts in his own free will'."

He scooped up some water from the bucket and gulped it down.

"I remember someone saying to me once; 'he who was not taught by his mother will be taught by the world.' I now realise that I was young when I left my village, and at times I wonder if I am not reaping the fruits of my own making?

I left a woman who was in her early pregnancy stage. I lost my roots and gave my back to those whom I would now have been relying on."

The few letters that he had received from Nthabiseng in the past came to mind. He thought of the ones that he wrote and never posted. He remembered the old Zulu saying: "A person who won't take advice, gets knowledge when trouble overtakes him."

"This is true. I now realise that troubles have overtaken me."

He was disturbed by a knock at the door. When he opened it, Nancy stood there, holding a bag and a large brown paper packet.

"I did not realise that it was this late. I know that I have taken you by surprise when maybe you have taken me off your love-list. We have not been together for some time, but I have come to mend our differences now."

She smiled at him and stepped across the threshold. As she noticed the empty room, she gasped, stumbling backwards.

"Come in Nance, it is as you see it, almost everything has been wiped out by the furniture sharks."

"TM! TM! What are you saying?"

"The furniture has been repossessed by Tony Factor."

Nancy then came in, kissed TM on his cheek and stood next to him in front of the table.

"But TM, I really do not understand that after all this time, you could not finish the balance on that account. I recently gave you pocket money, I give you petrol money on top of that. And what do you do with the pocket money I give you? Come on, tell me something!"

"Nancy, this is not the time for confrontation, my mind is still roaming around about many things."

"What are these things that I do not know, TM? Please do not play with my mind. Only recently did we have a good, healthy discussion about our future. I thought we had solved our problems. I really do not understand."

"Let us shelve it, Nancy, for a later date."

"When what would happen TM? Look, I do not have time to play. I have a future to plan, I work my butt off while you are playing. I am doing all in my power to nurse this affair but it seems I am the only one playing the game."

She stared at him, waiting for a reply, but he said nothing. Eyes filling with tears, she picked up her bags and left. Later, seated at the back of a taxi, she thought about the jolly old days spent with TM and the future which they had planned together. As the taxi criss-crossed through the narrow streets of Alex, she thought to herself: "Looking back, I do not know how it came about that I fell in love with him, though I vividly remember where and when we met. But, *ag*! Love is love and it has no age limit. Here I am now, having grown to love the man for so long.

"I remember the first time. So, after all these years staying almost as husband and wife, two abortions because we would not have afforded to bring up the children. This is how it happened. We were in the second month of our affair, I was an ignorant young schoolgirl, knowing nothing about protection from pregnancy. TM had all the experience, so in my stupidity, I relied on him. From time to time he would pick me up at either the bus stop or at the gate at school and we would go to where he stayed at MamTshawe's place. We would have unprotected sex. One month I missed my period, followed by the second month. One evening I started vomiting, I was at my Aunty Thando's house and she heard me vomiting into the toilet. When I came out, she was standing in front of the door, waiting for me, the next thing I heard was her shouting at me: 'What is this vomiting nonsense, *ntombazana* (girl)?' I was shocked, as I knew that if she used my full name, all hell would break loose.

"I felt paralysed, not knowing what to say. Her next question was to ask when my last period was. I choked, as I had not prepared myself for such a question. She repeated it and I had to tell her that it had been two months.

"She yelled at me, saying, 'My god! What the hell?' What did I tell you about coming back late from school and that red car that drops you at the corner of our street?'

"I didn't answer. I was scared that aunty knew about my affair with the man far older than me. The following morning was a Saturday. I was woken up early in the morning and taken to a house at 10th Avenue belonging to an old lady. I did not know where I was being taken to, but only realised when we entered the house and aunty and the lady of the house went into a room where they were for a few minutes and I was then called in.

"An abortion was done. I have never seen such an amount of blood in my life, it was painful and thereafter we left the place in a taxi back home, where I was nursed by aunty for two weeks.

"When I was fully recovered, I had a long meeting with aunty, who by then had got to know TM. She said, 'I do not want to see that man near you, *uyandiva* (do you get me)?' I agreed and accepted.

"From that day on, I realised that aunty was totally against my affair with TM, though, truth be told, any affair would have been a no-brainer to her; after all, I was just a school girl."

Nancy closed her eyes, lulled to sleep by memory and the swish-swaying of the taxi

Chapter 13

Don't Cry for Me Argentina

It never rains, but it pours. Seated at home alone, TM was stunned and silent. Hours later, he made himself a makeshift bed on the floor. "It's like what we did in the Fort," he said. He fell asleep on the floor. The year 1981 would be starting with things looking worse for TM, he thought.

A postman dropped a letter in front of MamTshawe's place. She had a round tin for a post-box, with a little hole for incoming mail. The old lady heard the thwack of the mail and went to fetch it, sorting through the letters one by one. She usually looked for personal letters first, hidden among the usual account statements – especially the furniture shops, which sent out letters diligently each month.

She stopped suddenly, holding one of the letters in her right hand, and walked through the back door into the yard, shouting: "Nancy! Nancy! Where is this child? She is again glued to that mirror, a thing I never understand, does she not know her features by now at her age?"

MamTshawe walked through the yard, talking to herself. Neighbours peered through lace curtains, hearing Nancy's name, curious. TM, too. He opened the door and MamTshawe shoved the letter at his chest. After she had left, TM read the letter and then threw it onto the table.

He then took a wash basin and filled it with water, started washing and then dressed in his fancy drapery, before locking the door and walking through the yard, greeting neighbours cheerfully as he went.

"Gents, I see you."

"*Heyta, bra* TM, *mojo,* my *broer* (hi we are fine)," they responded, as he disappeared out of the yard into MamTsamaye's yard, where he unlocked his car and drove off to Sparks' place.

As usual, Sparks was reading. This time, a *World* newspaper. He leapt up as he saw the snappily-dressed TM step out of the car.

"My *broer*, my *bra*, how nice to see you, take a seat. *Wat drink jy vandag* (what do you want to drink today?"

"*Neh, moenie worry vir drink my broer, gee my net pure water, met ys* (no, do not worry yourself with drinks today, just give me pure water, with ice)."

"*Wat gaan aan TM, wat is die shundies* (what's going on, and where is the problem)?"

"It's a long story, my *broer, nie vandag nie, my kop draai net nou op* (not today my brother, my head is mixed up)."

"*Ja neh, ek sien* (OK, I understand), and *hoe is ou Nancy* (how is old Nancy)?"

"Part of the *shundies*, Sparks."

"I was just passing by, *broer*, just to greet and I have to leave and not bother you with my problems."

"It was a real flying visit, *maar ouens wat nie drink nie, jy's so boring nou* (guys who do not drink are boring)."

"So long, my brother, we will see some other day."

When TM arrived home, he found the lights on.

"What the hell, what's going on?"

He turned the door handle as quietly as he could, pushed open the door and was hit by the aroma of Glenryck tinned fish and fresh bread. Nancy was in the kitchen.

"Hi," she said, with her back to him.

"Hi, Nancy."

He took off his hat and threw it on the blankets on the floor. Nancy's eyes shifted to the bedding, where TM had thrown the letter.

Jim is Tired of Jo'burg

"Shit! Shit!" TM muttered to himself.

"Well, well, unfortunately as we say in Xhosa, '*imfene yam iphale kahle*' (I arrived just in time), I found it lying ready to be read by anyone."

TM stumbled, picked up the letter from the floor, sweat dripping down his face.

"What can I say? It is all there, Nancy and there is no way I can deny it, I have been having a rough time."

"Who has not, TM? What worries me in all this is that you refuse to take me into your confidence, and I think there is nothing that I can do to make you change."

"It is not like that, Nancy."

But she ignored him and continued.

"I committed myself to you and your whole life, support-ing you at all times – you promised me the world and now you're telling me of 'your' intentions, no mention of 'our' intentions because you've been hiding this from me, and in your small mind failed to remind yourself that people in this whole township know about your plans, making me the laughing stock of town, the only fool who did not know that you are planning to leave town for a lousy village you do not even know, nor do you know if whatever you left behind still exists? Is this how I get paid in the end – is this the climax and closure of decades of togetherness?

"By the way, for your information, my aunt warned me about this relationship a long time ago, but being the lady that I am, I resisted because I gave all my life to you. How I wish I could have taken heed of her caution. But again, 'love is blind', as the old adage goes."

TM opened his arms to Nancy and said: "Do not use such harsh words to drive your point for you know deep in your heart that I still love you and we will continue loving each other, we are peas in a pod, though I must admit that we are going through a rough time."

"Why don't you say something rather than just looking at me, just opening your arms at me means nothing."

She hit him with a wet dishcloth picked up from the table.

"Do I have any role in your life? Or should I just forget about you?"

"Just relax and listen to me, Nancy, you are missing the point here. You've always been part of my life and you will continue to be."

"Always, always?" she interjected, throwing her hands in the air. "Oh, my Lord! It's finished. They were right – it's finished."

"Let me finish," said TM in a low, subdued voice and Nancy looked at him with blazing eyes. "Let me finish, please, Nancy."

"Listen here, TM, watch your step." She threw herself on the bed and hid her face in the large pillow.

TM fidgeted like a restless animal waiting to be slaughtered. It had been a long time since he had seen Nancy in such a state.

"You are a fool, TM, that is the only thing I can tell you, you still cannot see how much love I have for you after all these years. Do you think that you're the only one who is frustrated by life in the City of Gold? We all are, to an extent, but we're now here and we have to fend for ourselves. Go back to your dusty rural Dinokana. But 'don't cry for me, Argentina'. This is the very last time that you will see me. Let bygones be bygones."

"Shall I drop you?"

"Do not waste my time." Nancy left TM abruptly, banging the door behind her.

When Nancy arrived home, she heard her aunt washing dishes. Passing through the dining room, she heard Noluthando shouting from the kitchen.

"So early! I did not expect you would be back, thinking that that boyfriend of yours was going to detain you."

"No, aunty, it was not my intention to sleep there. I have work tomorrow."

She escaped to her bedroom, stared at herself in the mirror for a few moments and then prepared for sleep. Exhausted by her exchange with TM, she was convinced that it was over between them.

Lying in bed, she reminisced about her arrival in Jo'burg and the moments they'd shared together – at shebeens, drinking, laughing, TM's womanising, his love of fashion. But what else, Kgabalatsana, she thought – what else have you achieved? She remembered how he would take off his hat after arriving home, wipe his clean-shaven head with a white handkerchief. His mannerisms were ritualistic.

She thought about the hardships that he had endured, and his two-year jail term at Fort Prison. Of how she had waited for him all that time. This afternoon, she had gone to his house in an attempt to heal the relationship. And then? Then she had found the letter.

"They still know his address, after all these years, when last did he write to them? You're a damn bastard of a man, Kgabalatsana."

She had been angry with him when he confessed.

"Yes, Nance. The letter is indeed from my elder brother. You see, sometime ago I jokingly wrote to him, telling him that one day I will be coming back home to re-establish myself and settle."

Nancy berated herself. Why had she not taken heed of Thando's suspicions? But it didn't matter now. Nancy would erase TM from her mind. She resolved to do it.

***

The letter that TM had written to his mother took time to reach the village; after all, it is common knowledge that post to the villages takes ages.

22nd Avenue,
Block 1,
Alexandra Township
Johannesburg
10 January 1981

My Dear Loving Mother,

I write this letter to you with the utmost admiration for what you have done for me, bringing me up to be what I am today, and I say this with the deepest honesty and conviction to you, as my mother. This, to an extent will also go for Ntate, even though you know the tragedy that led me to be where I am today and the last quarrel that we had that fateful Easter Weekend when I last visited home, which has made an indelible misery in my mind and soul. Be it as it may, he still remains my father even in his grave.

This put me in a difficult position, a position which put me in a situation of doubt as to whether or not I wanted to engage with him. The news of Ntate's infidelity in our village came as a shock to me. It was worse than knowing that the woman whom I impregnated was, in fact, my own sibling.

I have no experience in knowing how the Tswana culture and custom resolve a matter of this nature. Do I forget about her being my sibling? What about the child that we have? How do we explain to the child? I am at a loss, mme, and I need your indulgence on this matter.

Though I would have loved to not make this your problem, unfortunately, you are the only living person who can help to resolve this for me. And as to your inquiry about Sechaba and Dira, I have to inform you that Sechaba is no more and I do not know what happened to Dira. The City of Gold is a gigantic place with people always moving in different directions, so have we.

I will wait for your reply. Pass my greetings to all at home.
Your   *Son*
Kgabalatsana Monare

Boysie put down the letter after reading it a second time.

"What a controversial piece of news from Kgabalatsana. How will we deal with this matter? *Mme* is now old. I do not think that she should be exposed to such issues."

"And how do you plan to proceed with it then?" his wife asked.

"I will have to think of a way, there are always ways that our customs deal with such matters."

"And what is that way?"

"At this point in time, I do not have a solution to this dilemma, to this mystery, one that will not engulf the family in a calamitous situation that might pit us against one another. You read my brother's tone and thus, his feelings on the subject. Let me handle this. At the right time, you will know what I am going to do."

He put the letter in his pocket.

It was the worst of times for Boysie, as he was caught up in a complex family conundrum that couldn't, unfortunately, be resolved by his mother alone. African culture and customs, at times, prevent a woman from taking part in matters that are seen as taboo for them. Boysie realised that his mother, MmaMonare, knew that she was in this dilemma. How would she resolve the matter of her husband's infidelity, for example? Boysie was left with no option but to lead. He decided that the first step was to consult with his mother.

"*Mme*, there is an outstanding matter that must be resolved before it gets out of hand. How are we going to resolve this matter of Kgabalatsana and Nthabiseng?"

The old woman looked intently at her son, and then looked away. She knew what Boysie was saying, but she was unsure how to proceed.

"What do you have in mind, Boysie?"

"This is not a matter for me as a child, *mme*, and that is why I am soliciting your advice."

"How I wish that nobody had told Kgabalatsana. You see, Boysie, it just does not solve the problem - it is a conundrum for all of us as a family."

"*Mme*, Kgabalatsana already knows it, *ntate* knew it. And I am not sure how the Rethabile family are handling it. That is the dilemma that we are in and it is for that reason that I seek your advice."

"Look, my child. I appreciate your concern and I fully agree with you that it has to be resolved.

I think you should take a journey and visit your distant uncle, *rre* Ntoa, in a village called Ramotswa, in Botswana. This village has an interesting history in that before the present borders were created it was the same, hence till this day when we older generation talk of it, we understand it to be borderless. Your father's father and Ntoa's fathers were brothers. He would be the one who could advise how this matter could be resolved.

"There is no disgrace in African custom that cannot be resolved, for I know for a fact that in other customs this could be as simple as slaughtering a white goat and offering it to the elders on behalf of the disgrace that your father has caused in the name of the family, and to talk to the ancestors and apologise on his behalf. I would not be surprised that in this case, it could be the same."

"I hear you, *Mme*. I will do as you advise in due course."

Two days before Boysie's journey to Ramotswa, he talked to his mother in the dining room. He had hoped that she would understand his plan and that, should there be a problem with it, she would rescue him.

The mother had changed with age. She tended to be unpredictable, and that was why Boysie was approaching her with all the necessary caution.

"*Mme*, I can see that you are sipping your coffee, but your mind is far away. What is on your mind? Tell your son."

The mother gazed at Boysie, her eyes glazed.

"Oh, Boysie, my mind is far away in a distant land where my father and mother and their parents are. In a world where, when you go, you never come back to report on it. We can only imagine, though I know that, wherever they are, they are resting in peace. It is only us who are still alive who do not know where we will end up.

"There are too many temptations that lead us to do things that we should normally not do, my child. You will grow to learn what I mean. Is there any special thing that you want to raise with me, my child?"

"Yes, indeed *mme*, just the other day I was thinking about the broader Monare family in the Western Transvaal and I remembered you and father once talking about an uncle, who lives in Ramotswa. What is his name?"

"Ntoa, Ntoa, my child. How you still remember all the Monare tribe more than I. We used to visit them with your father when we were still young." The old lady took a sip from her thoughtfully.

"You were correct the other day when you suggested that I pay them a visit, *mme*, more so we have not seen them for some time. It will be correct therefore of me to travel to Ramotswa and make a link with the broader Monare clan. You are getting old and we will continue not knowing family and that is not correct in our culture. You did not bring us up that way."

Boysie concluded his carefully-prepared speech, scrutinising his mother's body language closely.

"You will be doing the right thing, Boysie, and remember that you are the eldest son in this family and you will have to do what you think is right for the family. When are you planning to leave?"

"Within two days, *mme*, I should be on my way and spending at least two days there."

"Prepare yourself properly and do not be absorbed by the trivial ties of the Tswana people."

"*Dankie*, *mme*, for your support."

Boysie stood up and left his parents' side of the house, satisfied to have received his mother's blessing.

***

Early the next morning, Boysie left his father's homestead, criss-crossing the village towards the local taxi rank, where he would catch transport to his great-uncle in Ramotswa.

***

Ramotswa *is a village in the South-East District of Bo-*
tswana, southwest of the capital of Gaborone. The popula-
tion was 27,760 in the 2011 census. It is the tribal capital
of the BaLete, an ethnic minority springing from the Nguni
tribe. Kgosi Mosadi Seboko of Ramotswa was the first woman
to serve as a paramount chief in Botswana. Seboko took on
her role as a village leader and representative of the House
of Chiefs after her brother Kgosi Seboko II died in 2000. Her
presence in the House of Chiefs was hailed as a victory for
women's rights in southern Africa.

The nearby hamlet of Otse is the site for Moeding College,
originally a colonial secondary school and a school for the
disabled run by the Campbill Rankoromane Community ed-
ucational centre. Police XI, Botswana Premier League cham-
pions for 2006, are also based in Otse.

The climate is semi-arid, vegetation is a tree and shrub
savanna. Only a fifth of the area is farmed but the density of
cattle and goats and sheep is high.

Otse is overlooked by cliffs from which a colony of vul-
tures is easily visible on most days.
Source: Wikipedia.

***

Branches of the Monare family had moved from Dinokana
to settle in Botswana when Ntoa's father became a teacher
in the village, together with his wife, also a teacher. After
retiring, and owing to the Apartheid Laws enacted in South
Africa, they decided to settle in racially-unsegregated Botswana.

They had never relinquished their Dinokana roots, as a
number of people in Ramotswa knew that they were from
the Republic, as the Batswana people referred to South Africa. As to the rest, Boysie had only his imagination and
family tales to guide his impressions of his distant uncle.

The taxi dropped him at the village entrance at midday, from whence he was directed to the homestead of *rre*
Ntoa Monare, which was within close walking distance.

Not knowing the area, it took Boysie about 30 minutes to find the house, and when he did, he was welcomed by a big, black dog, which ushered him towards the front door. Boysie, being used to dogs, knew that he was harmless. An old man appeared at the door to meet him, and gently shushed the dog.

"*Dumela, ngoana waka* (good day, my child)."

"*Dumela, rra.*"

The man took him inside and gave him a chair. The elderly host had still not identified himself or asked for introductions, and Boysie knew that he would have to initiate the discussion.

"My name is Boysie Monare, son of Japheth and Josephine Monare from Dinokana in Zeerust, in the Republic."

The old man lifted his hand.

"Not necessary, my child, I can see a Monare from afar, identifying yourself is not necessary, as you are not a stranger in your own home. How is Josephine?"

"Age is taking its toll on her now, uncle, but she is well, as the Lord is still looking after her, *rra.*"

A lady of approximately the same age as his mother came through an interleading door.

"*Dumela, ngoanaka* (good day, my child)."

"*Dumela, mme.*"

She took a chair next to the man.

"This is my wife, your aunt Sebine, known as MmaMonare in the village. I am sure you will not find it surprising that she shares the Monare family name with your mother – this is the traditional way of the Tswana people," said Ntoa, with the confidence typical of a Monare.

Boysie had noted his uncle's self-assurance – the way he conducted himself, the words he spoke and how he sat – and felt confident that he had come to the right place, and would receive frank and open counsel from *rre* Ntoa. MmaMonare rose from her chair and smiled at her nephew, before leaving the men to their talk.

"So, Boysie my son, tell me more about Dinokana. You know what, it is decades now since I have been home, if I can still call it that, except for the short time when we went to bury your father. I only have vivid memories of the childhood leading to boyhood to manhood stage growing there. And does the mind forget such reminiscences? No, they remain with you until doomsday."

"Dinokana, *rra*, is not what you might know it to have been. The landscape and landmarks that you know are still there, mostly appreciated by tourists from all over the country and the world, relics in which some of us see no value. Lands are still nurtured, but unfortunately not to the extent that uncle might think of as during your times. Most, if not all the old families of your time still exist, though in most instances, it is the children and grandchildren looking after the homesteads. What else can I say, uncle?"

"I hear you, my boy, and again, welcome home, hoping that you will spend some days with us, we need family company from time to time and unfortunately with the distance of our abode, which again was not any making of our own, we seldom meet…"

MmaMonare returned to the room, carrying a tray of food.

"Boysie, my child, meet your mother properly, my wife, from as long as I can remember. This is the woman who keeps my mind and body working, otherwise I could have long been domesticated in this house."

"*Dumelang mme, ke thabela go bona* - good day mother, I am pleased to meet you," Boysie greeted his aunt again, feeling quite at home.

"Same to you my child. *Hawu*, you can see a real Monare in him."

"I always tell you, *Mosadi,* that even if you can put a thousand people in this room I can easily tell you a Monare. Oh, what big plates, *Mosadi*?"

"Are you complaining, *rra*? Let us ask for grace."

The gracious old woman led them in prayer.

"Thank you, oh Lord, for the food that you give us, the strength that we get from your food, Amen."

"Amen," her husband and Boysie responded in unison. They ate in companionable silence, Boysie clearing his plate. MmaMonare stood up after the meal, putting her hand on Boysie's shoulder.

"*Rra*, I suggest we allow Boysie to have a rest, Dinokana is far, let alone the uncomfortable taxis that he used. You will use the spare room..." she said, pointing to the door leading to his quarters. "In the meantime, I will put a basin of water in the room."

"Thank you, *mme*," said Boysie.

"Go now, my child, as your aunt has instructed, your father will keep on talking until you collapse; your mother knows him well. We shall meet later."

Boysie took his small bag into the bedroom, where he changed out of his travelling clothes into shorts and the vest which he wore under his shirt. He lay down on clean, neat, cool sheets and fell into a deep, restful sleep.

After long hours of sleep, Boysie woke up and went into the dining room to find his uncle seated near the door, looking far away into the distant horizon.

He was inexorably clear about his reason for coming to see his uncle, despite the matter being delicate. His uncle's advanced age and wisdom meant that he was the right person to help with this dilemma. He pondered this, until his uncle spoke.

"You look fresh and relaxed now, son. The travel fatigue that you had subjected your body to seems to have vanished."

"It was a rest worth taking, *Ntate*. Thanks to *mme* for the advice."

"Let us go and sit under the tree; it is much cooler there, my son." His uncle directed them to a shady tree in the yard.

The detailed manner in which Boysie elucidated his uncle about the family's problems took him more than two hours – from the infidelity and village gossip, to the revelations about Nthabiseng Rethabile's true parentage and various bits of hearsay along the community grapevine.

"What? Don't say that to me!"

Ntoa was understandably shocked.

The impregnation of Nthabiseng by Kgabalatsana, Japheth's youngest son, was the biggest and most controversial shock in the whole saga – and which had resulted in the stand-off and tension between Japheth and his son, Boysie explained.

"This just does not sound good for my brother, dead or alive," Ntoa sighed, ringing his hands, occasionally taking a sip of water.

After the long briefing, which Boysie carried out with utmost precision, and without prevarication, his uncle showed himself to be a most scholarly, respectful man, with the innate ability to listen well, and without interruption. It was only when Ntoa saw that Boysie had nothing more to say, having exhausted himself emotionally, that he spoke. He stood up, stretching.

"You are a real Monare, my child, you remind me of your grandfather and father. Your father was a forthright man who curried no favours, a gentleman who called a stone a stone. Your mother was correct to have directed you to me, this matter is far beyond your control, it needs the elders in the Monare clan, and fortunately I am amongst those, but what I will need to do would be to assemble the Monares from all over the Republic and here in Botswana for us to find a once and for all, lasting solution to this tribulation that has befallen my brother, for it was also beyond him, as he was directly affected. Worry not, there is nothing that cannot be resolved in African situations such as these, even where there has been murder, say, within the family. It is always resolvable."

Boysie was relieved that his mother's advice had been right and that she had encouraged him to travel to Ramotswa, where he had now spoken candidly to an elder in the Monare clan.

"I appreciate your comforting words of encouragement, *Ntate*. I was confused, not knowing whether this could ever be resolved, and here am I, being shown the light."

"That is what is called family, Boysie; as the old adage goes: '*mothu ke mothu ka batho* (we help each other as family in time of need)'. Let us go to the house, as I kept on seeing your mother looking in our direction, which is an indication that it is time for taking something."

They proceeded towards the house, where they were already awaited by MmaMonare, who led them to the table, which was set with a meal ready to be served.

There was happiness in the eyes of both Ntoa and Boysie.

"This was the most fruitful discussion I have had in a long time, *ntate*, and I have to thank *mme* for having sent me here to Ramotswa."

While Boysie was relieved, his uncle was aware of the challenge and great task lying ahead. He knew that he had to think, and then consult with the broader Monare family, most of whom would be distant relatives – but who would be the best guides on a subject of this nature. He had no doubt that he would achieve his objective in the shortest possible time.

Later that evening, before they slept, the men had another brief discussion, in which *ntate* gave Boysie more sage counsel.

"Boysie, my child, when you see your mother, please do not mollycoddle her. Give her all the details of our discussions; assure her that everyone has our unequivocal support and that this matter will be resolved sooner, rather than later. Do not let this news go to the ears of anyone, we know what it is that needs to be done. As already indicated, your aunt and I feel that you must take the earliest transport home, as we do not have much time."

"I will do so, uncle."

***

At around 8 am the following day, Boysie took a taxi back to Dinokana. The return journey seemed shorter, as he felt lighter and more content. He arrived home at 2 pm, the sun blistering the Western Transvaal sky, to find his mother sitting under the great tree in the yard; it was a landmark of home – a place of rest under which elders had waited for news and received visitors for so many years.

MmaMonare was delighted to receive news from Ntoa. Boysie only told his mother the rest of his news once he had relaxed and they were alone.

Chapter 14

"You Asked for it, My Brother"

TM drove through the afternoon traffic of downtown Johannesburg, arriving at the offices of a second-hand car dealership. The dealer took his car for a spin and a test. TM waited.

The salesman was seated behind the desk, flanked by several merit certificates showing off his career achievements. A portable fan swung to and fro, blowing hot air into the man's shiny, red face. For a moment, the salesman turned the fan towards him, full blast, convinced that it would cool him down.

"Well, sir, we have tested your car and found it to be in mint condition," smiled the salesman. "We are definitely interested, and if all motorists could keep theirs in a similar state, it would do our roads the world of good, let alone the environment."

"As I said to you over the phone earlier, you'll fall in love with it. It's true that the taste of the pudding is in the eating," laughed TM.

The man did not respond, though he remained polite. He had heard this type of cheap talk from car sellers who wanted nothing short of a good price.

He flipped through a small booklet, hesitated, and then looked at TM.

"You said that you're the second owner of this car, and that, therefore, there have only been two drivers behind its steering wheel? Do you then want to tell me that you've never even given it to your wife?"

"My wife, no ways. This baby is only driven by me."

TM began feeling uncomfortable with this line of questioning. He felt annoyed with the man but kept his cool.

"Ask anybody in the township, they only knew me behind the steering wheel."

"Well, my friend, I do not have the slightest of doubts about the truth of your statement and your car's credentials. But as you will know, there are standards that we follow when buying and selling cars.

"There is what is called the depreciation value of a car which is, amongst other things, dependent on the year in which the car was manufactured; yours has already seen its years."

TM looked at the man with menacing eyes. "And then what does that mean?"

"And as you might have realised, we do not deal in vintage cars; nonetheless, yours is still not one, luckily. Having said that my friend, we will be considerate with the price."

TM smiled, convinced that his run of bad luck was about to change.

"We will give you the generous amount of R900, but because you've kept it in such a clean state, we could settle on R950."

"Never, over my dead body, my Dodge, stereo tape, leather seats, Alpine speakers. No ways, brother, never."

He was on his feet.

"Sit down, Mr Monare, and relax. We're not yet through. And tell me, how much were you expecting to get for the car?"

TM scratched his head, and reality dawned that he had no clue.

"R9000 is the price."

"You're in a wrong place, then, sir. Best bet for you, sell the car out of hand, not through people like us and if you are lucky you might hit a jackpot."

He stood up, lit a cigarette and gave TM his business card.

"Goodbye my friend, that's my card if you change your mind, I have to get moving for my next meeting. I have a car to deliver in Sandton."

"I'm sure you'll do the same and you have my details if you need me," said TM, in a boastful manner.

***

Life in the city of Jo'burg was taking its toll on TM, leading him to shy away from public life. Though truth be told, as everyone now knows, it had not been a good year for the whole of the country, which was on fire – the politics of the country were fractious.

For the wise man of Alexandra, hope was fading. He had lost Mampye, his very first Jo'burg girlfriend, and now Nancy had left him – and he did not know if they would ever be able to reconnect again after such a long, painful separation.

He had also spent time in prison and, as a result, felt justified in calling himself a victim.

"I have become a *rara avis*," he mumbled to himself. Despite his, at times, paralysing self-pity, he was beginning to feel forced to think about leaving Jo'burg and returning to Dinokana. Nostalgia, among other things, propelled him, and he forged ahead with his objective, finally frustrated by his failure to find the fabled gold of 'Jozi, the City of Gold'.

Busying himself with pots of food, wearing Nancy's navy-blue apron and listening to light music on the radio, TM felt almost – but not quite – content. Soon he felt like a drink and drained some brandy from a glass. Searching around for more, he found a half-full bottle in the cupboard – Nancy had left it there on the night that she'd visited and found the letter.

TM drank some more. Once again, as he had done before, he became distracted and forgot about the pots on the stove. They bubbled over, spilling potato stew onto the floor.

TM dropped his glass, shattering it. He yelled angrily, thinking that if Nancy had stayed to take care of him, he wouldn't be such a domestic disaster.

"Nancy, why? Why did you leave? Damn, Nancy. Damn you!"

A voice answered him from behind the front door.

"Don't dare blame her, blame yourself."

Sparks let himself in. He almost slipped on the puddle of stew, but quickly composed himself.

"What's going on? Why are you talking to yourself?"

TM growled at him, bending to pick up bits of broken glass.

"You must watch your step, buddy. You can't just show up at someone's door, just as if you're walking into a kraal. Look what you did just now – you almost lost your legs."

TM burst out laughing, suddenly conscious of the hilarity of the situation and with his apron splashed with steaming potato bits.

"Welcome to the real world," he said, motioning to the stove and floor.

"You asked for it, my brother," said Sparks, shrugging. "How did you think that it would end? Life is never easy without a woman. Both of you should wake up and stop playing games."

Sparks picked up the brandy bottle and poured himself a shot.

"Otherwise, how is life, *broer*?"

TM pointed at the floor and at his soiled apron and shirt. "Well, see for yourself!"

"All this cooking, washing and going to the shops. It's like I'm being looked at with binoculars. Everybody is still asking where Nancy is. Even the children. I'm afraid to leave the house these days. I have to confess to you – it's not easy stuff for a guy like me, my brother. It's tough. But, it's not the end of the world."

"*Ja neh* – it is true." Sparks nodded philosophically, pulling at the dregs of brandy in his glass.

TM changed the topic, suddenly animated.

"You know what, yesterday I went to Elridge's Garage in town; trying to sell the Dodge. Guess what? The *moegoe* offers me R900, can you imagine, for that machine?"

"And what then, my *broer*? Is there anything wrong with the offer from Elridge?"

"No, my *bra*, I told him to forget about it and bugger off, and I left his place."

Sparks smiled. TM would never change, he thought.

"So, TM, tell me, what is the next move between you and Nancy?" TM looked at Sparks, rather surprised by his question – or pretending to be.

"OK. Detective Sparks, let me be open with you. I've not yet made up my mind about the next move. Is that fine? Is your question answered?"

Sparks ignored him. "Second question – did you call her, check on her, to see how she is doing?"

TM made a face.

"Did she check on *me*? Shouldn't that be your next question?"

"*Ag*, you're behaving like a primary school child, TM!"

TM poured more brandy for them both, and slumped to the floor, balancing the glass on his knee.

"We are best friends when we're drinking, and boring when we poke our noses into each other's business," he said curtly.

"But, is that not what friends are supposed to be like?" asked Sparks.

"Let's change the 'Nancy, Nancy' subject. You're boring, my *bra*."

"If you say so, that's fine with me. But don't cry over her, my *bra*. One thing you must know is that she is a beautiful lady, smart, has a decent job, and looks very young for her age. You know, there are lots of vultures out there. So, if you waste your time, *walala wasala* (you snooze you lose)."

"Just like that? Yesterday it was Nancy, today it is none other than my old *Bra* Sparks, my bosom friend, *nogal* (by the way), you taught me the corners of Jozi and I respect you for that. The man I almost spent the rest of my life with here in Jozi, *nogal*, threatening me with boys who will snatch my beautiful Nancy from me. What have I done? What sins have I committed to be treated like this? It is true that one came alone into this world, and so shall he leave it."

Sparks shook his head, chuckling silently. TM was TM and that was that.

"Hey, *broer*, I am not here to stay. I was just passing by, but I have to be back home, the gents will start flocking in and I have to manage them. Bye then. Till next time."

TM staggered as he followed Sparks out of the house. He almost fell but grabbed at the corner of the door. He could not stand by himself. He struggled back inside, balancing against the table and finally managing to hold himself upright, flung himself onto the makeshift bed on the floor.

His sleep was peppered with strange and fitful dreams.

He was seeing Nancy in town, dressed in school uniform, standing in a queue at the bus stop, carrying her bag. It was exactly as it had been on the first day that they'd met. TM was standing there, watching the beautiful young girl. When he approached her, she almost slipped, but he stopped her from falling. The dream came and went in fits and starts, picking bits from real life. He asked her name, and she told him: "Nancy Mabheka." She was shy.

"Mine is Johannes Monare, but Nancy is a beautiful name."

At that moment, he jumped out of bed, realising that he was dreaming. Clearly, this woman was haunting him. He had been thinking about his Nancy non-stop but had no idea why, or what the outcome would be. His main preoccupation was to return to Dinokana. He would think about Nancy later.

Indeed, TM was haunted by his own thoughts. His mind had been going around and around in circles for the past few years, observing the situations in which he found himself, and realising, finally, that he had nothing – absolutely nothing – except the car and half of his furniture. The rest of the little bit of nothing had been repossessed.

"I have earned nothing here in this Jozi. *Ek is moeg vir die plek* (I am tired of this place called Jozi). And my only solution now is to go back to Dinokana."

Clearly, he was in a Catch-22 situation. He had not erased Nancy from his thoughts. He still harboured the illusion that nothing could come between them, that time would tell, and he'd still take his chances with her. The question was, though, if she would wait for him. If she did not, he would be responsible.

***

A double-decker bus drove through the city streets in the early evening. Nancy Mabheka was seated on the upper deck in the back row, wiping her face with a tissue. As usual, she was casually dressed in a white dress, black hat and white shoes. Gladys was seated next to her, wearing a blue denim skirt, white, short-sleeved blouse and a red beret, as well as designer sunglasses.

"My girlfriend," said Gladys, looking at Nancy, "I still reckon that both of you are still in love, whatever the present differences are from what I hear, day in and day out, about TM. Though I must confess that I do not know much except from the snippets that you often tell me during lunch or on the bus, when we come from work. No love built over such a long period of time could or should suddenly disappear overnight.

"You complicated the situation by not communicating your intentions to each other – let's face it and get me straight, I'm not taking your side here. TM messed up by not talking to you about his problems while you also did the same by not asking for an explanation from him when people sensitised you to what he was planning to do. Men need to be pushed at times to come out with the gospel truth that is close to their chests."

Nancy looked at her friend in bewilderment.

"Both of us messing up?" she asked. "Did I hear you well, girlfriend? Whose side are you on? Do I have a friend in you?"

Gladys ignored the remark, for she understood her friend's state of mind; that Nancy was not thinking straight. Why, otherwise, should she pick an argument unnecessarily when it would yield no positive results?

"Look at me. Straight in my eyes, girlfriend. Have you really thought through TM's plans of action? Do you in the name of twenty devils think that TM can survive in a village, how he will afford to live there? No job, no friends, and no nothing. There is something else up TM's sleeves and I am convinced it is definitely not settling at Dinokana, whatever that place is called.

"Give him his space and time. Watch him closely and at the right time you might have the right strategies to deal with his situation. But before we agree on this, Nancy, I'm going to ask you to stop behaving like a child."

Gladys looked at Nancy sternly.

"No! No! My friend, you are not going to succeed with that arrogance. And don't ever look at me like that," Nancy retorted, slapping her friend lightly on the lap.

"Why are you pushing TM to the vultures? There are many women in Jo'burg. He will get one and forget about you."

"Why do you have to threaten me with Johannesburg bitches?"

"I'm not, but am reminding you of them, because if you don't resolve your differences, he will have no choice but to do exactly that."

Nancy blinked, considering her friend's words.

"You know, I never thought of it that way, Gladys; now I realise, should that happen, it would be too ghastly a thing to contemplate."

She hugged her friend and remarked with a deep feeling of honesty: "What would I do without you, Gladys? You're a real friend. You saved me from unemployment and made me what I am today. Please advise me, what should I do under these circumstances?"

"Just be calm and listen to advice in times like these; one's mind needs support and I am here to give you exactly that."

At that moment, there was a sudden noise on the lower deck and the bus came to a complete stop in the middle of the road. Nancy and Gladys rushed down the steps to investigate.

"Is the bus on fire?" Nancy asked anxiously.

"I really don't know," Gladys replied.

They saw a middle-aged man being held by the scruff of his neck by two fashionably-dressed youths in dark suits and hats. They were kicking, punching and slapping him.

"Where is it, where is my wallet, you think we are *moe-goes*?"

They continued with the assault, as he yelled and screamed: "No! No! It was not me, it was my friends," he cried, pointing at two ladies seated at the back. He was summarily dragged towards the ladies, who were on their feet in seconds, trying to escape.

"Where is it?" said one of the men, pointing at the frightened women. "Give us the wallet, or else you'll be killed! Where is the wallet?"

The ladies didn't answer, frightened into silence. One of them was grabbed and her blouse ripped open. A thick, brown wallet tumbled to the floor. The men exclaimed, and then reached towards the ladies, cornered their accomplice and dragged all three off the bus.

Nancy and Gladys jumped off the bus onto the pavement. They quickly crossed the street, keen to avoid being fingered as witnesses by the police. As they reached the other side, two young men, aged around 20, approached them.

"Hi, my sisters," said one of the two young men. "May we join you?"

Within a second or two, one was close to Nancy, the other holding Gladys by the hand. The women were taken aback, and irritated by their presumptuousness.

"You have no manners, boys. Don't you have elder sisters, can't you see that we are your mothers? One can see that you were badly brought up," Nancy remonstrated.

"Go and look for girls at the high school, damn nincompoops."

They walked off briskly away from the intruders.

"You know, this is one of the modern-day situations which I at times cannot understand; how young boys like these give chase or think that they can have affairs with their own mothers."

Nancy nodded in agreement.

"Is it not what we read in newspapers, that there are cougars and their cubs – elderly women dating young men. Maybe, as they say, these are the times, but sorry, I do not subscribe to that nonsense. And on the other hand, the choice is with the women and what we have just demonstrated is an utter rejection of the acceptance, by us women, of this practice; and the best way of doing it is to reject it from the onset."

Gladys smiled. Nancy had, indeed, grown up.

***

MamTshawe wiped her hands on the sides of her dress, stepped into the yard, and looked around to make sure that no neighbours were eavesdropping. She called TM's name, loudly and boldly.

"TM! Kgabalatsana, where is this man? *Uyawalele lo* TM (you are again sleeping)."

"*Yebo, magogo.*"

He came rushing out of his house, fastening his belt, and when he reached MamTshawe, she took him by the hand, getting closer to him, and stood face to face, whispering: "I do not want *bo-ndaba* - gossipers - to hear what I'm going to tell you, my child. Everybody in this township knows that you are frustrated by life in this Johannesburg. People are saying you are even afraid of being seen in the streets, even children at the shops are asking where Nancy, beautiful Nancy, is. But the worst is that you are tired of Jo'burg and you are planning to leave town for your home village. Even small children know about this, but I'm surprised that you seem to be the only one who does not know this and this is what is worrying me, for it makes you look like a fool. Is it just gossiping or real *mntwanam* - my child?"

"No! No! No! Not at all, *magogo.*"

TM began giggling – he couldn't stop himself. MamTshawe was so intense and serious. The old lady was unimpressed by his reaction, especially since she was only trying to help. TM noticed her annoyance.

"No, no, old lady, I do not believe this. Tell me that it is not true?"

"I'm only telling you what people told me. Well, ask yourself why it is that you are the only one who does not know about this?"

She looked him squarely in the eyes, unblinking.

"Well! Well! Gossip or not, MamTshawe has conveyed to you what she heard, as simple and straightforward as that. But Kgabalatsana, my child, I'm just doing what any woman, of my age and dignity, *nogal*, would do - inform an innocent man like you of what your detractors might be spreading. I cannot verify the truthfulness of this, only time will tell. But be open-minded, watch and listen for any sign coming your way."

MamTshawe went back up the bench. And TM went back to the house, dizzy, and unaware of his neighbours in the shadows, listening and watching.

***

As soon as he had arrived home, and hardly settled, TM thought of his old friend, Faisal Patel. and no sooner than he arrived home he was back outside getting into his car and driving straight to West Street.

He parked and took a paper bag out of the boot before walking to the shop. Inside the gloomy interior of the tailor shop, Faisal Patel, owner and entrepreneur, stood waiting for customers. Tall and rangy, in his late sixties, he looked up eagerly as he heard the door open. Eyesight not as sharp as it once was, Patel failed to recognise the elegantly-dressed figure at first.

He took off his thick-rimmed glasses and placed them on the counter, wiped his eyes, and gazed at the man, who politely removed his hat. Patel replaced his glasses, and recognition dawned.

"I thought that I knew this face! It seemed familiar! Old man Patel is now growing old to forget his old customers so fast."

He came around the counter, opening his arms to TM for a hug.

"Yes, you're right, Mr Patel, it is none other than me, Kgabalatsana from Mzilikazi Mine."

"Now I can remember you well, my friend. A friend of Joseph's, who one Saturday came to introduce you as a new customer. What can I do for you, my friend? Where do you mend your trousers these days?

"You've not been here for a long time; you know that Patel is still the best in town. Remember – once a good tailor, ever a good tailor. That's our motto."

"How can I forget that, Mr Patel," chuckled TM, bashfully.

"You see, that's what I meant, nobody in this Jo'burg forgets the Patel Tailor Shop in West Street. Do you know that even John Craig knows that – they bring all their tailoring to us!"

TM nodded enthusiastically. "Hey! Old man Patel knows the secrets of the job, the secrets of this business."

"So, tell me? What brings you here today? I hope you're bringing Patel good news, and the good news is money to an old Indian man."

TM emptied the contents of the paper bag onto the counter.

"You see, Mr Patel, I stick to tradition. I value old relationships."

"Be careful, TM, remember, old Patel is originally from Andhra Pradesh, and the Naidoos are my home-boys here in Jo'burg," joked Patel.

"By the way, when last were you in Zeerust to see your brother – what is his name again?" asked TM.

"Yusuf – Yusuf is the name. Where else can he go to, as business is going well for him there, more so we are told that there is lots of platinum there. It is because of this that you are asking all these interesting questions?" said the old man, patting TM on the shoulder.

"You know us *Charras* (Indians). We don't just move around, only one thing attracts us, and that is business."

TM smiled at his long-time pal.

"You are like any *Charra*, Mr Patel."

Patel nodded.

"Do you think that he is different from me? No, he is not, my friend."

TM smoothed out the suits which he had brought with him. "Mr Patel, I need these suits mended. Look at these stitches."

Patel clucked approvingly. "Oh yes, they are none other than Faisal Patel's."

"Diamond mending, please, Mr Patel."

"It can only be diamond, TM. That is Patel's signature."

"How much will it be, Mr Patel?"

"Fifty rands," replied Patel, without hesitation, looking TM squarely in the eyes. "Take it or leave it, my friend."

"Fifty rands, my friend? You know my situation – unemployed and still living in a back yard."

Patel laughed. "Oho! You think old man Patel is blind? TM, I saw the big red car parked outside. Old Patel is driving a battered Volkswagen Beetle, second-hand. You remember the one I bought in Fordsburg. It is still going strong!

"On top of that, you still owe me money from long ago."

Damn Indian, thought TM. By that time, Patel was behind the counter, shuffling old papers and coming back to TM with a receipt.

"You still owe me ninety rands – lots of money, my friend."

"No, no, Mr Patel, let bygones be bygones, man, we are friends."

He suddenly thought of a plan to distract his friend from the old debt.

"Let's not dig into history. Let's be forward-looking. There are bigger things that we have to do together. Remember I asked you about your brother in Zeerust?"

Patel stopped in his tracks and took off his glasses. TM continued, realising that he had captured the wily businessman's attention.

"Remember a long time ago when we talked about a business opportunity there, in Dinokana in particular?

"I've been working on that proposal because the time is ripe for us to re-look at it. That is the history that we could dig up, rather than this debt. The land my father left me when he passed away is being kept by my brother on my behalf."

Patel stood close to TM, intrigued. He recalled the time, years ago, when he had told his brother in Zeerust about the potential investment in Dinokana. Nothing had come of it then.

Jim is Tired of Jo'burg

"You know what, TM, in recent times, Yusuf asked me about this and because I had lost contact with you, I told him that I had not seen you for some time, but that when I did, I would ask you about it."

"Take it from me, my friend, as you've always known me – TM is always there when there is gold to be had. Why did you think that I came to Jo'burg in the first place?"

Patel giggled.

"You now think like a real Indian, TM. Business and business."

TM shook his head.

"No, Mr Patel, like an African! Many years ago, when I came to Jo'burg, the sole reason was to get a brick of gold. And I was told that the streets were tarred with that precious metal – but where am I now?"

He dipped his hands into his pockets, turning them inside out.

"Not a cent, my friend."

Patel ruminated, nodding thoughtfully.

"Ok, my friend, let's forget the money for the mending. I will do it for free and clear the debt, for old time's sake. Come next time so that we can have tea and samoosas.

TM chuckled and gave his friend a naughty smile.

"We will do that, we most certainly will."

***

Hardly a week had passed since TM's visit to West Street when he was back again to have a 'serious' business discussion with Faisal Patel. This time he was anxious to gain something concrete from the wily entrepreneur.

They sat in the dining room above the tailor shop, deep in discussion over a large plate of samoosas and a pot of tea.

"So, TM, do you think that this land of yours in Dinokana is worth it – are you sure that it is in the mineral-rich part of the village? We have to make sure so that the Patels don't miss the opportunity of being one of the wealthiest mining magnate families in the country," he said, standing up and looking through the window at the fast-moving cars purring along West Street.

"Mr Patel, Dinokana is the place where I grew up. I know every inch of that land. I walked through that soil and through all the rivers that pass through it. I've proposed to girls on the banks of those rivers and helped them to carry heavy buckets of water.

"Page through the *Hansard* and you will not get a shred of this information – but ask anybody in that village, and they will tell you the same story. Trust me and trust my instincts, judgement and, most of all, honesty. Together, we are beginning to climb the ladder. You have the bucks, and I have the land."

TM was at his best, convincing the man of an opportunity that he had not even proved yet. Although the tales of a mineral-rich tract in the village abounded amongst its inhabitants, no exploration had actually been done. Some people had also spread unproven stories about diamonds being picked up along riverbeds.

But Patel was hooked.

"This is what I have been waiting for all of my life. I knew that one day it would come. What a surprise that this opportunity comes through none other than my old friend, Kgabalatsana Monare, once my client, and now my business partner. The thing that I did not ask, TM, is – what is in it for me in this whole deal? Remember, you've been raising this land business with me for some time now, but what's in it for me? I'm still not clear – will you clarify, please, my friend?"

He stood up again and went to the window. TM followed suit, realising that Patel was firmly on his side – but needed one more push to seal the deal.

"Oh yes, this is Jozi, Mr Patel, the City of Gold," he exclaimed, dramatically.

Memories of his arrival in the city flashed through his mind – shebeens, drinking, women, fashion, et al. But what else, Kgabalatsana? What else have you achieved? TM took off his hat and wiped his head with the ever-present clean white handkerchief.

He went back to the table and took another sip of tea. He thought about the hardships he had endured: the two-year jail term at the Fort, incarcerated for an offence that he did not commit, having been caught in the wrong place, at the wrong time, one fateful Saturday night.

He had come full circle now, with this opportunity. He could not allow it to slip through his fingers.

"Mr Patel, in answering your question, let me first say that we need to agree on broad principles here. The most urgent thing that I need from you is a verbal assurance that you'll support me in all my efforts to relocate to Dinokana.

"For this, I am going to need money, as you might know. Remember, I have to impress upon my brother that I have been working and have earned a living while in Jo'burg. Driving a flashy car is not enough, although it will certainly give some of the villagers a good impression.

"I'm sure through your brother there in Zeerust, I can get basic groceries and general support to survive. People there live on simple things – mealie meal, samp, beans, sugar, and so on."

The old man turned away from the window and went back to his seat.

"Well, if that is all you need, that is easy for old Patel. I can get you groceries from my sister's shop in Fordsburg."

TM looked at his wristwatch and stood up, satisfied that he had achieved the first part of his plan.

"Thank-you, Mr Patel. I have to rush back to Alex, as I have an appointment there. We will keep on talking."

***

Mr Patel was having an earnest telephone conversation with his brother, Yusuf.

"I'm telling you, this is a genuine man. I've known him for years and he even used to work for me. Let's keep in touch, for he was here at the shop. He is a sincere man. He also comes from Zeerust; I think that he said the place is called Zeenocana."

"No, no, Faisal, if it is Zeerust, then it can only be Dinokana."

"Okay, yes, that's right. OK, brother, you've heard what I had to say. Can you write down his number, please?"

Patel heard Yusuf calling to his assistant, Tommy, for a pen and paper to job down TM's name and number.

"We call him TM here, but you can call him Kgabalatsana Monare – yes, that is his real name."

Patel waited as his brother chatted to Tommy again for a few moments, before returning to the line.

"Ok, Faisal, suck as much information as you can out of this man. I am also doing my homework on this side and things are going well. I have my Tommy here who knows everybody in the village. I will meet the chief again to discuss the matter further. Hopefully, this will be the last meeting before the deal is signed."

Yusuf hung up abruptly. Patel put down the phone and went to switch on the kettle.

"You know," he said to himself, "my father used to talk of perseverance. He used to talk about the patience of an Indian trader who would sell bananas for years, add apples and then pears – and the next thing, you would see that he'd opened a small corner shop.

"He used to say that Indian business people are like tortoises; they take their time in business. But, once they have taken off, there is no stopping them. I think the Patels are reaching that take-off stage now. Nothing is going to stop them."

Patel realised that his wife had been standing behind him, listening. He blushed.

"At least you could have coughed to indicate that I was not alone," he muttered.

His tiny wife, dressed smartly in a blue and silver sari, smiled affectionately at her husband.

"I did not want to disturb your dreams."

Patel looked astonished. "You call this a dream?"

She shrugged knowingly. "What else can I call it?"

***

Zeerust

Through the dusty roads of the village, a white Toyota van drove slowly. Seated behind the steering wheel was an Indian man; next to him, an African boy in approximately his mid-twenties.

"Tommy! Are you sure that we're on the right track?" asked the driver, exasperated. "We've been travelling for quite some time now. Why should it take us so long to travel from Zeerust to Dinokana?"

"We're not far now, sir," replied Tommy, pointing down the road. "Remember, sir, that you're a slow driver. If I were driving, we would have arrived a long time ago."

His comment was aimed at prompting the Indian to finally consider teaching Tommy how to drive – a chance that the young man had been dreaming of for some time. However, his boss had always had an excuse to avoid it.

Yusuf Patel, the wealthy man of Zeerust, looked at his employee with pride but shook his head.

"Your time will come, Tommy. One day it will come; you're in too much of a hurry. You are right in one respect, though, Tommy, and that is that Mr Patel is a cautious driver, not slow, but careful, Tommy. You see, I am saving petrol – you know how costly it is these days."

They came upon a neat-looking street.

"Here is the house, sir, slow down."

Patel applied brakes and brought the van to a standstill before pulling it off the road and parking next to a fence.

They climbed out of the car and headed towards the yard of the royal residence, where the chief's aide ushered them to the large bluegum tree at the far end. There were four chairs under the sprawling branches – Tommy and Yusuf sat next to each other, while the chief sat a little further away, his aide seated slightly behind him.

The chief introduced the visitors to his aide.

"Mr Yusuf Patel is an old family friend, a wealthy and important person in Zeerust. For some time now, we have been discussing with Mr Patel various business interests, such as developing the land here in Dinokana.

"You see, there is a lot that we Africans can learn from people such as Patel."

He looked at the Indian man intently, winking at him and then turning to his aide with a smile.

"Yes, four pieces of land which Patel intends buying and then building businesses that would create jobs for our people, bring wealth to the tribe so that it can be recognised as a wealthy group amongst others," the aide added.

"Mr Patel," continued the chief, "is a vital person amongst the Tswana people, right up to the borders in Botswana, and his efforts in the development of the Tswanas is well-known, yes, well-known."

The aide looked at the chief and then at Patel, nodding his head in agreement.

"Yes, we must support the efforts of good people like Mr Patel. *Kgosi*, it is true that our people need the support of wealthy persons who have the means to kick-start development. Our livestock alone cannot lead to sustainable development because this type of venture needs people with money, which in this case, cannot be measured by cows and fields."

The chief nodded enthusiastically, encouraging his aide to continue.

"Do you want to give us any more information, Mr Patel? How soon do you want to start the project? I cannot wait to see tractors and bulldozers working in the village, because this will without doubt bring pride and confidence to our people."

Patel whispered in Tommy's ear. The latter stood up and walked out of the yard, returning with two envelopes – one large and one small. He handed then to Patel, who bowed to the chief and handed over the large envelope to him. He turned to the aide and gave him the small one, smiling politely.

Both chief and aide put the envelopes into their pockets as if used to this type of exchange – and knowing that nobody should see it. Patel bowed and then took his seat when the chief indicated, with a wave of his hand, that he may do so.

"Thank-you very much, *Kgosi!*" Patel said, beaming. "As you've already said, and correctly so, the Patel family is part of the Bahurutse tribe, as my father used to say, and has been doing business here for more than sixty years since our arrival from Andhra Pradesh in India.

"While most Indian families chose to settle in the big cities of Durban and Johannesburg, and some in the smaller towns of Krugersdorp and Potchefstroom, my father decided to come and live in Zeerust. The family has done a lot for the people here.

"Look at little Tommy. He is now educated and trained in running a shop – he is an experienced shopkeeper and I rely on him a lot.

"We are still committed to building modern businesses right here in rural Dinokana. We are ready to start as soon as you indicate readiness on your side, *Kgosi*. Our commitment is beyond any shred of doubt."

"*Rre* Patel, I'm proud that I have the support of people such as you, who are always prepared to support the royal families and their aides, of course," said the chief, looking at his aide, who smiled like a Cheshire cat.

"Men such as you, who not only help their chiefs but are always on their side."

His eyes wandered to the old Ford sedan parked in the opposite corner of the yard.

"I usually drive it only when I take my family to church and Zeerust. A sign of the benevolence of people such as you, Mr Patel. I will be convening a *lekgotla* soon, and we will be discussing the allocation of land to interested parties such as you.

"Do not worry, as my aide will be dealing with all applications. It is for that reason that I invited him to take part in this meeting. He is my most trusted man in the village."

The aide shook his head, sporting a wide, toothy smile, nodding in agreement with his chief, whom he was more than ready to assist now, following the receipt of the envelope.

The chief stood up, shaking hands with Patel. He asked his aide to escort the men out of the yard as he returned to his house, satisfied with the outcome of the discussion.

Chapter 15

"I am Now Tired of Jo'burg"

It was the beginning of the year, and the final lap of TM's stay in the City of Gold. He had, by this time, given up all hopes of getting the gold for which he had come.

It was as though he was stuck between the rock and a hard place; but he was not without an option. He knew that he had a home that he could go back to – his village of Dinokana in Zeerust.

It was an auspicious, tranquil morning, as the rays of the sun were about to appear beyond the horizon of the mountain ranges; dawn was settling in, bringing with it another day. The sun's rays created a flare of beautiful blue skyline as Kgabalatsana meandered the Dodge through the curves and precipices of the narrow roads and ridges of the Western Transvaal. Luckily for him, the traffic had not yet started to fill the usually busy, narrow roads. He was in an ecstatic mood, content with himself about the decision that he had made – he was leaving Johannesburg.

"I am tired of Jo'burg," he said to himself, again and again. "I am tired of Jo'burg. This is enough now, Kgabalatsana. I will tell Boysie that I am on my way home for good."

He realised that he was using the name that had remained hidden, forgotten, for so long. The man was as restless as the sea, desperate to claw back some sense of security and familiarity. He had lost the ability to concentrate on anything much for long, and nothing could calm his anxiety.

Friends and neighbours believed that TM had lost his marbles. The jovial Toppie Manoja was no more; he had faded into depression, with no apparent cause. He was in and out of the house most days. That last day, though, was different; he had headed to Jeppe Post Office to send a telegram to his older brother, informing him of his homecoming.

Chapter 16

Opening Up a Can of Worms

Long after Boysie received his brother's letter, and as promised to his mother, he went to see the chief of his village, Chief Moiloa.

Arriving at the kraal, he was met by a tall man in his fifties, who was wearing a leopard skin draped around his middle. They exchanged greetings, and Boysie was ushered towards a large, umbrella-shaped eucalyptus tree – the ideal meeting place for an important discussion. Boysie sat in one of the two chairs arranged beneath the welcoming canopy.

"This summer has not been kind to our livestock and fields, *rra*," he said to the chief's assistant.

"True. It has not been kind, *rre* Monare," answered the man, gravely. "How long is it since we have had good rains to soak our fields? It seems that those days are a thing of the past. Usually, at this time of the year, the land would have been as green as a gourd. Cattle would be grazing in the meadows and goats mingling with the sheep along the rivers."

Boysie nodded.

"What happened? What have we done to deserve such harsh treatment, I wonder?"

They continued discussing the weather for a few minutes until the chief appeared. Boysie stood up respectfully.

"Good morning, *rre* Monare." The chief spoke in a deep, solemn voice. "Please, take your seat. I hope that the hospitality of Moiloa has been accorded to you?"

Boysie watched as the assistant disappeared into the house and returned with a calabash of *bojwala BaseTswana* (traditional beer), took a sip and then left it in front of their Monare guest.

"It would have been rather a sacrilege if a guest of the Moiloa had left this homestead without a drop in his mouth," the chief commented, sitting down. "Welcome, Monare, my child, to your home – this very chair on which you sit was once sat on by your father, Japheth, many times, when I summoned him for advice.

"Your father was a man amongst men and one of the few in this village who came not about problems with his family, but in order to solve the problems of other families. And, what can I do for you on this day?"

Boysie cleared his throat and spoke aloud what he had rehearsed several times in silence.

"Praise to the chief and may the ancestors of the Bahurutse be with you, great chief," he started.

The chief interrupted him, gently.

"Always remember, Monare, that chiefs are here to serve their people, especially in times of need and despair. Both when there is peace within families and when there are misunderstandings. This role has been played by my father and his father before him.

"So, shall it be for those who will come after me also. Ask any royalty the world over – it is so. My ears are here, *rre* Monare."

"*Kgosi*, it is exactly for that reason that I felt I should come for an audience with the Lion of Bahurutse, in order to shed light on the problems of my family. You, being the only person who can help us in this time of need. My family has always relied on your wisdom; my father used to tell us that this was so from time immemorial."

"Japheth, your father, was a great man. An honourable and wise man in this village and in the wider Lehurutshe district," mused the chief, gazing into the distance, as though caught in a happy memory.

"*Kgosi*, my problem might sound simple, but nevertheless, it is a problem. Yes, it could become a big problem if not attended to in time.

"Sometime back, we received a letter from my brother Kgabalatsana, who lives in Hauteng, in the city of Johannesburg. As you might recall, *Kgosi*, he left the village a long time ago, after the last rains, and before the drought that almost brought total collapse to our land. And to be precise, it now close to twenty two years since he left his father's place, though occasionally he would drop a note such as the one in point.

"We all thought that he had long passed from this world into the land of the dead, as he had not written to us for some decades. Now, he is telling us that he is coming home."

"Home?" exclaimed the chief, surprised. "Is he serious? After all these years have passed? I have heard stories, but this one sounds more like a fairy tale. It reminds me of the Shakespearean tales that I read at school. No! *Rre* Monare, tell me that it is not true, and I shall believe you."

"It is as I tell you, *Kgosi*. He tells us that he is tired of life in the cities and is considering returning here in the very near future. He is in conversation with people in business in Hauteng and these people intend investing in our village. He wants to use *ntate*'s land for that purpose.

"To be fair to him, he asked me to come and discuss the matter with you, chief, as custodian of the land on behalf of all of us."

He looked earnestly at the chief, who sat with downcast, ponderous eyes. Boysie continued.

"He would want to develop land in partnership with these investors."

The chief raised his hand to speak.

"Did he mention the names of these investors, these 'people', of his?"

Boysie shook his head. "He did not, Great Lion. He further reminds us that all land is kept in trust by the chief on behalf of the people. He recalled our father telling him stories about such practices and therefore believes that it is still so today."

"As a son of this tribe, you are aware that issues of this nature are discussed with the elders of the village, who then advise me on how to proceed. I will therefore convene a *lekgotla* of the elders here in the royal kraal, and you can expect to present your case to them."

The chief stood, ending the meeting. Boysie saluted him and left the yard, feeling a little concerned that the chief had not engaged as positively with the issue as he had expected.

However, as the chief had promised, Boysie received a message from the royal aide a few days later. He was instructed to attend a meeting of the elders the following Monday at 10 am and should be ready to make his case if needed. Any changes would be communicated timeously, it read.

Boysie was pleased that the chief appeared to view the subject as a priority, but he still felt worried. He decided to prepare properly by inviting a few elders to his home beforehand in order to discuss the matter in detail.

The Monare homestead was a busy one on the morning of the meeting. Villagers' horses were being tied to wooden hitching rails and neighbours' fences; children peeped into the yard, curious; women rushed about, attending to bubbling pots and brewing beer.

Under the gigantic eucalyptus tree, three elderly men were seated on benches, drinking African beer, sharing the calabash between them. They were enjoying the refreshment, which had been brewing for several days.

Kgabo, a village elder of great renown, and one of the true wise men of Dinokana, was an oral historian who prided himself on having acquired the knowledge of eons from his father, who had, in turn, received it from his father before him.

African history is known for this oral method of passing along information, rather than using the written form. Of course, men of Kgabo's age had never seen a classroom; but nobody could match him, despite his lack of formal education, when it came to customary and traditional matters.

Dressed in a rugged grey jacket long past its prime and neatly-pressed khaki trousers, he smiled contentedly at his peers, eyes twinkling above a thick, grey beard.

"*Yoh, yoh, yoh*! It is still amazing that women in this village brew such tasty brew," he commented, wiping bits of the fragrant froth from his beard.

"Nobody will disagree when told that MmaMonare comes from the belly of a good Tswana woman."

They all laughed in agreement.

One of the elders, Lehotoana, took pleasure in reminding his peers that he was the eldest among them and thus the most experienced; he enjoyed teasing Kgabo about memories of him as a young boy herding cattle in the meadows and hunting rabbits in the forests.

He reminisced about how nervous old Kgabo had been at his very first *lekgotla* in the chief's royal residence. Yes, Lehotoana had an abundance of memories to share, and despite his advancing years, was a strong, fit man with a short, stout physique and well-trimmed white beard.

"I always tell people that the Tswana are the most cultured, the most modest and the most intelligent of the tribes of this country," he quipped. There was a chorus of agreement.

Dikeledi, Boysie's wife stood watching the men from her door, waiting until she saw her husband, Boysie, stand up to address the gathering, before turning back to her kitchen. She heard his voice filtering from the yard – strong, diffident and sure.

Boysie bent to put down the calabash, put on his hat – African men never drink sorghum beer, or even water, while wearing hats – and began his speech.

"Elders! Friends to the man who built this homestead, and my villagers. As I have said already to some of you, this letter recently received from my brother Kgabalatsana, is at the heart of the matter. We have not seen him for a long, long time.

"If my memory serves me well, he left after the last long rains and before the terrible drought which destroyed the livestock of our entire people – a catastrophe from which we have never recovered."

The men murmured in unison, recalling the suffering of their people.

"It was this drought, as you will recall, that led to a number of our brothers leaving for the cities, because there were no fields left to be worked on and no cattle to be reared. My brother was among those who left Dinokana as well.

"In this letter, my brother writes that he is preparing to come home for good. He says that he is tired of the city and longs to be amongst his own – something he cannot find in the big city."

Kgabo rose from his chair, exclaiming: "Coming back home! Does he know where that home is? Will he find his way to his father's homestead? What home is he talking about? What does he know of home – a home that he deserted and turned his back on for decades. Oh, no, this is unacceptable!"

After a pause, he took his seat, but not before Lehotoana had risen and, in a soft, low voice, took the floor.

"I have seen many days in my life. I have heard and presided over many disputes in my father's land; but never have I heard men prattle the way the two last speakers have. Never have I heard old men of the age of Kgabo talk in a tone such as I have just heard.

"Gentlemen, children of my father, grandchildren of Chief Moiloa, the father of our tribe, son of Monare and Kgabo: I wonder what your fathers will think of you as they listen to such childish tittle-tattle?

"Boysie, let me address myself to you directly. You brought this matter to us. It is about a brother of yours who disappeared and who was swallowed by the city of Hauteng; a brother who was dead. I say so because you did not know if he was alive or not, though he has suddenly surfaced from the grave, which Hauteng has become for him.

"Thanks to his frustrations with city life, he remembered that there was a place called home. He remembered that there was a village called Dinokana, where he was born, and where his father left him an inheritance.

"He remembered his village and that there was a man called a chief. He asked you, his only brother, to convey his intentions to the chief – a noble gesture, civil and respectful. He has shown you and us dignity, pride and remembrance. Now, when Japheth's son, your sibling, your blood brother, decides that he has had enough of the City of Gold, he has to come home.

"You bring the matter to us, asking for our advice. I would have been happy if you were telling us that you were making preparations to receive the lost sheep and inviting us to a feast for the lost brother, who has been lost for all of these decades."

Looking at Kgabo, he continued.

"To you, Kgabo, with your wisdom and age: I thought that you would have been a guiding light to young Boysie Monare, a child of both of us, but nay, you confused him, leading him towards the wrong conclusion, which is bound to lead to the wrong decision, which would be refusing to open the doors of his father to his brother.

"No! No, children of my tribe. Boysie, it would be folly of you and Dikeledi to turn your backs on Kgabalatsana. Give him what belongs to him and to nobody else. You have many times fantasised about the day you long to see the land of your father resurrected, but because of lack of money, you also longed for the day when your brother would come back to help you fulfill this dream."

Lehotoana paused for breath and prepared to take his seat. MmaMonare appeared just then, carrying two calabashes.

They immediately changed the subject – though she was no stranger to old men's intrigues, she knew that they did not want her to overhear their discussions. She placed the calabashes in front of the men and left.

"Gentleman," Lehotoana continued, "let us give to Caesar what belongs to Caesar."

He settled into his chair. Boysie was as quiet as a church mouse, eyes fixed to the ground.

He glanced up furtively now and again, watching the elders pass around the calabash. After some time, having finished the business of the day, they rose to bid farewell to Boysie, who thanked them for their audience.

As Kgabo and Lehotoana left together, they paused at the gate.

"Kgabo, tell me, what was it that Boysie called us for? Was he soliciting our support or opinion?"

Kgabo, realising that he had not conducted himself appropriately when responding during the meeting, knew that the older man's questions were leading somewhere, and so took a moment to frame his answer.

"To be honest with you, Lehotoana, now that you're raising the matter, I'm also confused. But I think he was soliciting support, rather than our opinion or advice, because I feel that his main aim is to block his brother from coming back home."

Lehotoana chipped in: "That is precisely my problem. Why should he have a problem with his brother coming home? Is there something that we do not know? You see, Kgabo, my wife and I are the ones who closed Japheth's eyes. I was there when that grand old man passed away. He called all of us, in the presence of his wife, and told us not to forget that he had two boys, Boysie and the younger Kgabalatsana.

"Before he closed his eyes, he said that the land where his fields were should be looked after for his younger son and given over to him once he had reached manhood. I'm not sure if Boysie knows that I have this information, but that is the story, Kgabo. I'm suspicious of Boysie's intentions."

The two old men shuffled off down the road to their respective households.

***

Dawn was breaking. The morning sun appeared behind far-distant hills as shepherds walked their livestock to the rather patchy meadows, while men and boys began toiling the fields, already busy with their daily schedules.

As the sunlight brightened the village, elders streamed in groups of two, three and four towards the royal house. Some were dismounting from horses and tethering the sleepy animals to fences and posts, or handing them over to young boys assigned to care for them.

This was to be the most exciting day for the young people of the village – it was a *lekgotla*. The sense of proud duty at being given responsibility for the horses was part of an age-old tradition, once which had been part of the village for as long as anyone could remember. The boys would tease each other about the speed or health of each horse.

Inside the yard, seated on higher ground, under a tree, sat the chief, whose subjects walked in deferentially, saluting and singing his praises. Women, wearing colourful traditional dresses, mingled among the men, serving traditional brew. This was a high moment of the festivities, with the women, as dictated by tradition, taking the first sip of the beer, in order to ensure that it had not been poisoned. A strange part of African culture, this, putting women on the front line in this manner.

The festive mood was disrupted by the arrival of the praise-singer, who was already singing loudly to his chief and elders. He danced and shouted, drumming up dry, red soil, which seemed to flame as fiery air beneath his feet. He continued to perform, even when told by the chief to desist.

It is a normal African tradition that a praise-singer's status allows him to go against the chief's wishes. After a while, at his own pace and in his own time, the performer moved slowly towards his own seat but still insisted that nobody had the right to stop him.

"Not even you, lion of the Bahurutse, dare touch me; this honour and respect has been bestowed on me by your father, the father of the tribe – Moiloa. Who are you then to touch me?" asked the praise-singer, causing men to burst into laughter and applause. The chief, too, enjoyed the defiant speech.

"Yes, indeed, my children, who am I to tell our praise singer what to do? I'm just your ordinary shepherd fulfilling his duties," said the chief.

After that brief comment, he called on the gathering to be silent, as he began his address.

"My father, my grandchildren of the Great Chief Moiloa, my father, our father, the father of this tribe, I greet you all."

"*Kgosi*!" A choir of chorused voices resonated, creating an atmosphere of community togetherness.

"The chronology of events and makgotla which we held over the years is beyond my recollection. The number of times we have gathered here to discuss matters of bread and butter – that which affects our people – cannot be repeated, since you are all conversant with what I am talking about."

"*Kgosi*!" the gathering answered.

"The chrysalis of our resolve to shape our destiny is beyond doubt, otherwise you would have been tilling your fields, you would have been guiding the young shepherds caring for your livestock, and you would have been helping the boys in the meadows. But, instead, you prefer to come and listen to what you were called for?"

The language, the rousing speech, the praise and the vigour of the moment filled the gathering with a flowering energy. This was going to be the *lekgotla* of the year. The men did wonder, though, why they had been called, since they knew that only the chief's inner circle would be privy to this information.

"Elders and wise men of the village of Dinokana, this is a place known for its wisdom, for its wealth of experience amongst our Tswana nation in the face of difficult challenges, has found itself with problems, at times, that seem to threaten the heavens falling upon us.

"But, we have always come out the victors. Today, I called you to discuss some issues referred to earlier. What you will hear will make or break the destiny of our people."

A wave of grumbling washed over the gathering, who were agitating for the chief to make his point and stop beating about the bush.

"Today, we are going to deliberate on matters of economic and business substance. It is for this reason that I urge you – I repeat, urge you, my children – to be attentive, so that at the end of the day, you can make sober, well-informed decisions. I will pause here."

The chief took his seat and looked at his aide, a close associate, and one of the more educated men among the villagers. The aide stood up, as though he and the chief had rehearsed this procedure several times.

"*Kgosi*! *Kgosi*, son of Moiloa, father of our tribe, the mighty lion who raised and nourished us with the wisdom sucked from your great-great-grandfathers. You have touched on the cornerstone of why we are here. You are raising long-overdue matters.

"We do not doubt your leadership, your congenital instinct, your vision as to where you want to take this tribe, putting it among the best in the country. Who would we have been without your skills, knowledge and leadership, *Kgosi*?"

The men shouted in agreement, roused to interest again.

"Other villages in this region are way ahead of us in terms of development. They have mines, they have shopping centres, they have stadiums and playgrounds, but, where are we? Are we counted among those? The answer is a big, big, NO! Let me, therefore, as you have instructed me to, *Kgosi*, report to this *lekgotla* that we have been inundated with applications and requests coming from afar – important businesspeople are eager to buy land here, people want to build businesses, they want to prospect for minerals – all sorts of minerals, some of which may be unfamiliar to you.

"Notables in the field of business want to build bridges, roads and infrastructure here in our region, which has a dearth of these."

He brandished papers in his hand.

"We've done well over the years in terms of allocating land to ourselves and to our children; now we are faced with the possibility of making Dinokana accessible to all, even to people who do not have their roots here."

A voice from the crowd interjected vehemently.

"Did I hear you well, Moabi? Or are my ears betraying me? Pardon me if they are, as I have seen days, I've witnessed conflagrations in this very same place of my great and respected chief, *Kgosi*."

The speaker, an old man, saluted the chief and begged his pardon again for any rudeness. The chief nodded his head approvingly.

"Please tell me that my ears are not betraying me, Moabi?"

Moabi continued smoothly, as though there had been no interjection. The elderly man took his seat, content to have made his point.

"This was because of the gold that was supposed to be so copious in our land. Some mineral prospectors have been writing in journals and now it is attracting these people. It is imperative to ask ourselves a number of questions, chief among these being – will Dinokana still be considered the land of the Bahurutse when we have among ourselves other nationalities and tribes? Will these people pay the same respect to our customs?"

Another voice rose from the crowd now.

"Obviously not, Moabi. Let's stop the rigmarole, let's stop pointing out the obvious. How can one pay respect and practice customs and traditions of a tribe to which one does not belong? They will only pay lip service to the chief, Moabi. Their aim is to rape our land of its bountiful resources."

There was laughter and agreement, with a smattering of disagreement, among the men.

"Moabi, what is it that you have called us here for? Is it to listen to your seemingly priggish prattle? I have been to *makgotla* all my days. I've heard men prank us as you are doing today, wasting our precious time when we could have been tilling our fields or grazing our stock in the meadows.

"Moabi, I believe that it was the intention of our honourable chief for people such as you to get directly to the point and to address the matters of economic importance – you are wasting our time."

The speaker, a seasoned elder with a gristly, crisply-cut beard, grunted and sat down. The gathering murmured, seemingly restless.

The chief's face was a mask. He looked down, possibly pondering the elders' responses, or perhaps devising his own response. What was in his mind? Did Moabi indeed represent his intentions, or were they playing hide and seek? Only these two, who hatched the plot, could know what the strategy was. The chief's eyes shifted to Moabi, who prepared to take the floor again.

Hopefully, thought the chief, he'll deliver some sense this time, and garner support.

"Will our customs and beliefs be adhered to? Someone asked this earlier. I can only say that there are some things we need to consider as we come to our conclusion. Gentlemen, I have here applications from the people to whom I referred earlier."

He pointed a finger at a young man, Sentle, who was clearly attending a *lekgotla* for the first time, so green about the ears was he. Being under the gaze of Moabi was a baptism of fire and he fervently wished that he had not chosen this day to attend.

Sentle came to the middle of the gathering, nervous and shaking. He wore a dark suit and hat – a smart contrast to the creased, old jackets and hats worn by his fathers and grandfathers.

"Should he not be at school? Look at how he is dressed!" mocked one of the elders, but not unpleasantly.

"He reminds me of the interpreter at the magistrate's court in Zeerust," said another.

"Times have changed, *rre* Matholoana. Men like him are now ripe for the experience of life. And *makgotla* are the best schools for this kind," a sallow-faced, kindly elder said, understanding how Sentle felt just then.

"Ag, perhaps you are right. Let us give him our ears, *rre*," quipped Matholoana, with a hint of sarcasm.

Sentle bowed to the chief as a sign of respect.

"*Kgosi*," he said, in a small voice. Then he saluted and greeted the chief again.

"Father of us all," he continued, taking a pile of papers from under his arm. "I will start by reading the letter from Mr Giron Levison from Mafikeng."

A hush swept through the gathering, as Sentle began reading the letter, clearly and loudly.

Dear Chief Lentsoe

I have the pleasure in writing to you, honourable chief, although we never met, but I deemed it necessary to introduce myself and my vision of the development of your area. It has come to our attention that your part of the country offers a great possibility for business development.

And let me not hesitate to indicate that my business partners, that is, the Levison family, have taken a deliberate decision to invest in the development of infrastructure, be it roads, bridges or whatever else, in your village. Please therefore, Kgosi, receive this application for the allocation of land ERF no 1007, which as we know according to customary laws falls under your jurisdiction.

There was laughter and surprise at the tone of the letter.

"Where did he get all this information? Which land is this? Who owns it? Young man, land here is named after families, what is this 'ERF' number that the mister – what did you say his name was – talks of?" an elder asked.

"Levison," someone responded.

"Yes, that name, where did he get all this information? How could a stranger have known about all of this?"

The questioner sat down without waiting for an answer. Boysie Monare, who had been very quiet, seated at the far end of the crowd, looked at the chief, also wondering if the land to which the letter referred was his father's; plot numbers were not something with which he was acquainted, as plots were known only by association with neighbouring ones, such as, for example: 'the plot next to the church'.

Sentle continued without responding or arguing – he could not question or criticise his elders or their questions. All he had been asked to do was read the applications. Moabi and the chief would respond at the appropriate time, he thought. He continued reading the letter.

Our intention is to start a mine and build a factory that will employ 200 people. We will at the same time build houses of the modern type and a school for the workers of the factory and the mine.

This, I believe, Kgosi, will be a contribution to the development of your village that you accept.

Thanking you

Giron Levison & Family

The chief, realising that there was going to be a confrontation between the elders should the meeting continue, realised that he had to take action. There was increased murmuring and grumbling following the reading of the letter, and the young man tasked with reading them was starting to sweat and stammer. This wasn't his usual demeanour, having been chosen as an intelligent, educated young recruit for the royal house.

The chief had a liking for the educated lot, being one himself. Unfortunately, though, after completing high school, he had been persuaded by village elders to take the royal post. Reluctantly, after much consultation, he accepted the duty, when really, he had wanted to study law at the University of Fort Hare. It was this educational background that informed his running of the royal house – and not everybody approved of his methods. He called on Sentle to take his seat.

"My children, I guess that you must be very hungry and tired. I see that from how you respond to these issues. Some of you are not concentrating, so we will not be able to conclude this business today.

"Perhaps we have been here for too long and may still be here for some time. I, therefore, beg you to take a break and we will resume after lunch."

He stood up, followed by his aide, and went to his house, leaving the men breaking into little groups of urgent discussion and support-canvassing.

The women of the royal residence emerged almost immediately to serve the elders food and African beer, almost intuitively knowing that the recess would be called when it was. A joyous atmosphere ensued as the drink and food flowed. The gathering was soon at peace with itself again.

A grey-bearded man – tall, dark of complexion and probably in his eighties – balanced his walking stick as he wiped his mouth and handed the calabash to a friend.

"You know, Sentsoe, I have problems with the application just read by the educated young man, Sentle. This young boy is smart; his mannerism reminds me of his father, with whom I grew up. I appreciate the foresight of our chief in bringing the young under his tutelage. It is a good thing the chief is doing, yes, a good practice.

"Perhaps let me start with the application, then, from the white man named Levison. Where and how did he get these facts? Does any one of you know which plots he talks about? It will be interesting to see and hear if any applications come from our own people – and I am not just talking about our own people here in the village, because I do not think that they are so developed, or have the necessary means.

"If Levison does what he says he will do, oh, if that materialises, imagine mines and factories and businesses here? And employment for so many people? So many households – that's when we will talk of real progress in Dinokana. And it would be turned into a city the size of Zeerust, if not bigger, and more than anything, it will stop our people from going to the cities to work there."

The man paused, waiting for his turn to drink from the calabash again.

"When I talked earlier about our people, I was referring to African business people countrywide – those who know about these things. People who have big monies in the banks."

Matholoana overheard the conversation and joined in.

"I wonder if they know about all these opportunities we are told about?" he said.

"My problem," said another man, "is our culture, religion, customs and general way of life. Imagine Dinokana being swamped by all these foreigners? I do not understand the language of these foreigners? It scares me. I pray to God that decisions on such matters have not already been taken behind our backs and that we are being used merely as sounding boards."

A stocky elder, hunched over a plate of stew, shook his head impatiently.

"I do not think that we need to be scared of that at all. Any decision will be deliberated here and we will give our opinions, guiding our chief towards what he needs to do.

"Remember and appreciate, though, that we are nothing but his advisors. The thought of such developments coming our way might be an answer from our ancestors, bringing progress rather than a depressed and poor village. Our children are hewers of wood and drawers of water in foreign lands because there is no means of survival here.

"A development such as this one promised by Levison is something we should look at carefully and objectively, lest we regret not taking the opportunity and perpetuate the poverty of the next generations. We shouldn't be myopic and lose out, or blind, lest we regret it in the long run," he concluded.

Within the chief's royal residence, tempers flared and men were pointing fingers. Despite the rumpus, the chief said little, keenly aware of not being seen to be taking sides. He ignored the abusive language being thrown about by the royal court and kept his cool, as all good leaders do.

He had a strategy, but would it work? The elders were clearly very concerned. This was a culture shock for them and the implications of bringing strangers into their world was a decision not easily accepted. Their families had lived here, in seclusion, for centuries.

The royal household trooped back to the *lekgotla* area. The mood was expectant.

Old man Lehotoana stood up, shouting loudly for calm and waving his stick as if going to beat someone. He walked to the centre of the gathering. An immediate silence descended and the chief dropped his eyes to the ground as Lehotoana looked at him intently.

"King and his subjects," the old man boomed. "I plead for calm, sons of Moiloa, I beg for restraint, children of Lentsoe. *Kgosi*," he saluted the chief in an age-old sign of respect, and the chief nodded and smiled.

"How can I be dreaming when my eyes are open? How does a man of my age dream when he is awake, ploughing and tilling his land? I am ashamed of myself and of our behaviour in front of our father. Pardon us, *Kgosi*, for we do not know what we are doing.

"Perhaps we are shocked by the news read to us here. Maybe we are scared of what will become of our tribe when, in our midst, we will find ourselves living side by side with foreigners. I do not know what the right answer is, nor what the implications of any decision would be, sons of Moiloa, indeed, I do not know."

He paused, wiping his eyes with a khaki handkerchief, as the gathering watched him in silence. He looked at Kgabo, who was seated next to the chief and beat the ground with his stick.

"Let us not forget that we are custodians of our culture, thoughts, beliefs and practices. We are the forebears of our children's future. We are the creators of a belief system loved by our friends and enemies alike, and we should be remembered and appreciated by the coming generations.

"*Kgosi*, *Tau Tona*, respected guide of our times, father of our nation, this land, and the land bequeathed to us by our ancestors, your father's fathers, as well as its culture, customs and beliefs,must be maintained. Why should we then be subjected to this barrage of applications from people who have no link with this great land?

"Why do we not invite our children, some of whom are still roaming around the big cities in the mines and factories, to come and invest their meagre earnings here and get things right in this village of theirs, rather than considering applications such as the ones we have heard today?

"Should we not have turned this opportunity into a benefit for our own children? Gentlemen, I am just an old man who knows nothing about matters of economic importance. I am just an uneducated man."

He walked sedately back to his seat, respectful silence following in his wake.

Nobody said a word for a few moments after the veteran had spoken. Some men nodded in agreement, while others shook their heads, stubborn in their resistance. The chief recognised that his plans could be quickly scuttled, especially after a man of Lehotoana's stature had spoken. He knew that there were no brave men willing to oppose the respected wise man, a known strategist who had been close to the royal house for many, many moons.

The chief stood up. Normally, he would have spoken to his subjects seated, but this time decided to do it differently – perhaps working on the sentiments of those who might have the courage to disagree with Lehotoana.

"My children, men of great respect and honour, we've been deliberating on this subject for the whole day, clearly without any possibilities of reaching a consensus. You've all heard Lehotoana's input on this matter and as usual, he was the Lehotoana everybody knows.

"You have tired me, and I would want to believe that we are all tired. I, therefore, think that it will do us all good if we take a break until tomorrow morning, for I know that when the mind is fresh, it comes with fresh ideas, tolerance and good reasoning."

He stopped abruptly, greeted the elders and walked away from the gathering, back to his house, followed by his aides.

***

Later that day in the vicinity of Dinokana, on a dusty road which meandered through mealie fields, a van sped along the gravel towards the village, heading for the chief's royal residence. It slowed down as it approached the gate, which swung open from the inside; clearly, the visitors were either expected or had been spotted early.

A young man climbed out of the van and saw the chief standing in his doorway, closely attended by his wife. The man walked up to the chief and greeted him cheerfully.

"*Kgosi*! *Tau Tona*! Mr Levison sent me over here, *Kgosi*, and asked me to hand this over to you personally – to you alone."

He took a large, brown envelope from a bag and gave it to the chief, who immediately passed it over to his wife.

"You still remember Mr Levison?" the chief said to his wife, smiling. She shook her head, perplexed. "Oh *mosadi* (woman), that is the man who donated the fifty heads of livestock to us last summer."

His wife looked at the envelope with suspicion, saying to herself: "Why does this man prod me into doing this?"

The chief thanked the man and asked him to pass on a message of appreciation to Mr Levison and to convey his family's greetings.

Life works in mysterious ways, thought the wife. It appeared that those who were most entangled in such devious behaviour were often men of status, such as chiefs and kings. They took bribes from the rich and powerful – the likes of the Levisons of this world. The question was though, she wondered, where it would end? She looked at the envelope with thinly-veiled disgust, but said nothing.

Chapter 17

The Prodigal Son Returns

In Dinokana

Although the journey was a two to three-hour drive, TM did not feel it, as he was in no hurry. He drove at a leisurely pace, as if he was not sure of the direction he was taking, and as he entered the dusty rural town of Zeerust, the music pouring from his Alpine speakers was so loud, that onlookers couldn't help but hear it, and marvel at it – and the shiny Dodge, with its smart-looking driver.

Shopkeepers came out of their shops, waving at the Jo'burg man-about-town - a strangely normal routine in South Africa's rural areas, where people would throng the streets at the sight of something new – especially if it came from the city. Of course, TM was thoroughly enjoying the attention.

After all. as a boy in the same town some decades back, he used to be the same onlooker, marvelling at the motorists of the big city, the men travelling in their flashy cars along the very same dusty roads. He swung the car into a garage to get petrol. He left the ignition on as the music continued playing. He casually asked a petrol attendant for assistance.

"Full tank and write me a slip, *rra*." TM smiled at the awed attendant and went into the shop.

His pit stop was not without incident, though, for TM, having spent so much time in more liberal Jo'burg, had forgotten about the tight screws of apartheid law in the rural towns. There were still strictly-enforced separate entrances for blacks and whites here in the conservative enclave of Zeerust. The signage was everywhere, reminding: "Slegs Blankes" (Whites Only); and "Slegs Nie-Blankes" (Non-Whites Only). Unfortunately, he went through the wrong entrance, and was only reminded of his error when a group of old white folk pointed it out to him.

"Your entrance is the other side. I know that you city dwellers do not respect the laws of this country, *die is die ou Wes Transvaal* (this is the Western Transvaal)."

"Jesus," responded the city dweller, "*hoe kan ek vergeet* (how can I forget)? My boss, next time I will go to the right place. You see, these signs mean nothing to us in Jozi – it's money that talks."

By this time, he was approaching the counter.

"A packet of 20's Gold Dollar, baas, a packet of fish and chips and please add a Russian sausage."

He took out two R20 notes and shoved them to the man behind the counter.

"Money talks," said the Greek shop owner, as he took the notes from TM, put the money into his till and shouted to his assistant: "One chips, one fish, salt and vinegar please."

TM looked over at the white man, who was still standing watching the scene.

The lady assistant handed the food over the counter to TM. He took the parcel and left, not glancing back. The petrol attendant gave him the receipt, he paid, and then moved to park under a mimosa tree, where he ate his lunch in the shade. After handing over part of his meal to two scruffy boys who had been hovering near the car, TM got out, stretched, and then hopped back in, readying himself for the last lap of his journey home.

As he manoeuvred back onto the main road, a traffic cop waved at him to stop. He swung the car off the road, and the cop loped over to him, taking out a pen and notebook.

Realising that he was about to get a fine, TM fixed a broad smile to his face, waiting for the familiar exchange.

"Why do you Bantus from the cities like bringing attention to yourselves all the time? You are bent on disturbing the peace and tranquility of our small town – so arrogant."

He spoke with a strong Afrikaans accent, intent on ridiculing TM.

"Have you not realised how we white people in small towns hate noise and I have to emphasise to you, my boy, that I'm one of those who hates noise.

"What is this show-off? I heard the loudness of the music that came from this car the moment you entered town. Just look at you, you are so full of yourself, enjoying the attention of the small-town envy."

He was scribbling in his book, walking about as he talked.

"I have to say I'm not amongst those that you impress, but rather, you are depressing me."

When he had finished writing out the fine. he threw the receipt on TM's lap without giving him the chance to reply.

"*My baas* (my boss). Why don't we discuss this matter?" pleaded TM. "It is a small matter and I think that we can easily solve it."

"Solve it, can't you see that it is already solved? Better pay the fine, Kaffir boy, soon, or else you will end up in jail."

He left TM and walked in the opposite direction.

"Welcome to rural Zeerust," TM thought to himself. "'Don't cry for me, Argentina', I was told in Jo'burg."

TM's curious admirers, who only a few minutes earlier had been marvelling at him, started making remarks about city dwellers who did not understand the arrogance and importance of white traffic officers. They mumbled that Zeerust was a small place where big city behaviour had no place.

Some, of course, were intuitively sympathetic to this stranger; he was, though they didn't realise it yet, one of them. TM headed his car out of town in a northerly direction, clear about where he was going. He was, indeed, a child of this soil.

After such a long absence from the place, he still knew each and every corner, and the reality of the matter was that the place had not changed much since he had left, except for the gravel road that had been well levelled. When he saw the general dealer's shop from which he used to buy groceries, accompanied by his mother – a journey planned well in advance, back in the day – he felt nostalgic memories flooding back. He remembered Kgabalatsana, the child so excited to be going into town.

For a village boy to go to town was a great privilege, he thought to himself. Are these the experiences that led him to decide to come back to the village? Maybe or maybe not? The car went along the dusty gravel road leading to Dinokana until it came to a stop in front of his father's place.

The car drove slowly into the yard, through a gate already open, as though they had been expecting him. A man stepped out of the house, while a woman peeped through the window. No car had entered their yard for a very long time.

"*Mosadi* (woman), come and see, your husband is day-dreaming. It can only be my brother, Kgabalatsana!"

MmaMonare, hearing herself being called, was already making her way outside.

"*Rre* Kgabalatsana!" she shouted. "Is this really you? The family never thought that they were ever going to see you alive again."

Boysie, overwhelmed, said softly: "I now remember you did say in a letter sometime back. I never took it seriously."

He wiped his eyes and hugged his brother, who by then was standing between himself and the woman.

"Greet your sister-in-law, my wife MmaMonare."

Hand-in-hand, the two brothers, with Kgabalatsana's sister-in-law at their side, walked towards the house. Kgabalatsana was puzzled as his eyes took in the familiar scenery. The place had, indeed, changed, though.

"I can see that you are lost, little brother. Come into the house."

They went into a large, spacious sitting room, full of modern furniture and flooded with light from two large glass windows – a design feature unheard of in villages.

"Dreams do come true," said Boysie, as they took their seats at the table. "I never thought that this day would ever come, when my own blood would be standing next to me alive. You look well, my father's child."

"Well, I've tried to keep myself upright, Hauteng was not an easy place, but you learn over time to adjust and adapt, it is the survival of the fittest - but also the death of the weakest - and this is what I've tried to do all these years. But tell me, elder brother and sister, this beautiful house, look at both of you, you have done well for yourselves. What is the secret of this opulence?"

"I don't know about opulence. You have not even heard anything about your family and you already jump on opulence. There is enough time, you are now back, though I do not even know whether it is just a holiday?"

Kgabalatsana looked the other way, shaking his head.

"We will talk later, elder brother. But let me thank both of you for having received me so warmly."

"What else did you expect, you are at home now."

Boysie stood up and looked through the window, shaking his head. He then turned back to look at his brother.

"*Mme*. I have to take Kgabalatsana to the Big House, as I can see he is out of place here."

"I will be preparing a meal in the meantime, and by the time you are back, it will be ready," she replied.

The two brothers went out of Boysie's side of the household, with Boysie carrying one of Kgabalatsana's suitcases, while he was carrying another suitcase and a huge red and white plastic bag. Boysie paused, turning back to point in the direction from whence they had come.

"You see, Kgabalatsana, that part of the house is where the main kraal used to be. It goes down towards the small field where *ntate* and *mme* used to plant vegetables."

"Now I can see, this is the old part of the homestead."

"I knew that this part you would never forget."

Boysie unlocked the door, turned the handle and flung the door open for Kgabalatsana to go in. Following behind him, Kgabalatsana stood next to a big table, which in its days was indeed one of a kind.

He looked at the walls, which were adorned with an assortment of family pictures, including the much-loved portrait of his parents' wedding day. Positioned next to a family photograph was another of two young boys. The 'visitor' immediately recognised himself and his brother. Kgabalatsana must have been eight years old then. Boysie came to stand next to him, taking a handkerchief from his pocket to wipe his parents' photograph.

"It can only be them," exclaimed Kgabalatsana. At that sombre moment, the brothers were disturbed by Mma-Monare coming in through the front door, carrying tea and biscuits on a cloth-covered tray.

"I have always wondered when these cups and cloths would be used – only to find that they were waiting for you, brother."

She left the room to fetch more snacks and, when she returned, Boysie grabbed her by the hand.

"Kgabalatsana, my little brother, as you will recall, at the time you left home I was still a bachelor, although not as young as you. Meet my wife, your sister-in-law... Ms Matlhare from across the river."

Kgabalatsana smiled warmly.

"How could I forget her, the lady from across the river Mntumbe, whose arrow pierced my brother's heart?"

"Your memory is good; I never thought that you'd remember her."

"How could I forget?" asked Kgabalatsana.

"I remember one Saturday morning when you overslept. The previous night the two of you had gone to a church concert at the church hall and arrived late at home. Mama, the early bird, was up at the crack of dawn, she saw you taking her out, and it caused a stir for you for some time with the old man."

They all laughed.

"We ultimately got married and have been together since."

"You must be tired, *rre* Monare," said Dikeledi to her brother-in-law, embarrassed about childhood matters that she no longer wanted to recall. "Gauteng is far."

"Not really," said Kgabalatsana, "although I was driving slowly, afraid of traffic cops on the rural roads."

***

Kgabalatsana had had his first night's sleep in his father's homestead, in the tranquility and serenity of rural Dinokana, where evenings occasionally resonate with the howls of a jackal, the whistle of birds or the bellowing of a bull in a nearby kraal. For the first time, after a long spell, he had slumbered like a child, waking only once.

He stretched himself under the clean sheets, which seemed brand new. It was as though they had always been expecting him to come home. Kgabalatsana opened his eyes, wiped away sleep and then remembered his beautiful dream about the heydays in Jo'burg, Mampye and Nancy.

"What were those about?" he wondered. For one reason or another, the dream images quickly evaporated, as hard as he tried to clutch onto them.

"Ah! Forget it, TM. What's the point?"

A soft knock came from the bedroom door and his elder brother stood on the threshold.

"What a wonderful sleep!" Kgabalatsana said. "Not a sound from cars, no screeching of tyres on noisy Johannesburg roads. I slept like a child. This has not happened to me for a very long time."

"Home can be heaven," laughed Boysie.

The two brothers walked out of the house, holding enamel cups filled with coffee and brought by Boysie from the house. Kgabalatsana looked at his cup, and said:

"Do not tell me that these are the same mugs that I know?"

"The one and only ones, little brother, bought by your mother in one of the Indian shops in Zeerust. You'll be surprised at how many of the old people's things we still have. The day you get married, you'll not need to buy many things, because the old man left them intact and most are still packed in mother's kist."

He looked at his brother out of the corner of his eye, but Kgabalatsana looked the other way, and Boysie decided not to pursue the subject.

"It is a pity that when they passed on you were not here, it was difficult for both of them to close their eyes and your mother kept on asking my wife, 'MmaMonare, when will Kgabalatsana come and close my eyes, they are becoming heavy.'

"The old man, in his last minutes, said to me, thinking that he was talking to you, 'Kgabalatsana, bring me my blanket and cover my feet.' Your mother responded, '*Nyaa rra* – no sir, this is not Kgabalatsana but Boysie.'

"Those were the last words that your father uttered and he was gone. May their souls rest in peace."

Boysie sipped at his coffee. Kgabalatsana was silent.

"Well, young brother, ours was a lucky one, I'm telling you brother, when this village is divided, it is like heaven is falling on it. The question of land ownership is a hot potato and the division is between what I would call the traditionalists and the enlightened, depending on what side of the river you live. When the first Christian churches and priests came to settle in our part of the land, there were those who welcomed them with open arms, and others who did not. It is the same with the land issue."

Boysie pointed to the far end of the village, on the other side of the river, near the church and village shop.

"The rich and educated on that side, while on ours, the traditionalists, and mostly those who never went to school. They wore traditional dress and shied from suits. Although, I must say that nowadays, that physical distinction seems blurred. We are caught up in a historical creation by the missionaries.

"I discussed with the chief the issue of father's inheritance, and he said that the matter would be for a discussion between me and my brother the day he came back to the village and as a result of that, my little brother, I then divided the land into two sections.

"The one where the new homestead has been built is for myself and my wife, and the rest of the land is meant for you, and I want to believe that this is how the old people would have wanted it to be. And by the way, I did inform *Rangwana* (uncle) Ntoa in Ramotswa and he thought that it was civil for me to have thought that way."

"Tell me, my brother," said Kgabalatsana, "do you know that you are still the old brother that I have known from the time I was a child – always concerned with the welfare of the family, bridging gaps where they seem to be falling? Your consultation with *Rangwana* Ntoa on this matter I would easily have overlooked."

"Remember Kgabalatsana, I watched the ways in which the old people were doing things here at home, and most of that was through eavesdropping. As you will appreciate, children would at times never be involved when many family issues were planned; you would only know about it when implementation time came."

"I do appreciate what you have done and believe that goodness is never wholly absent from the woods and goodness is never wholly absent from people."

"Who am I to negate good, encouraging words from a little brother?" Boysie looked in the direction of his house and saw Dikeledi waving a hand at him.

"The *Mosadi Wa lelapa* (lady of the home) is ready to fatten us again, *rra*."

Leisurely, they walked towards the house.

Kgabalatsana looked at his elder brother with appreciation and patted him on his shoulder.

"Now tell me about yourself, your family, because I think you have taken me through the broad Monare issues. What has kept you looking so well? Look at your kraal, it is full, and the fields there are well maintained."

"It's a long story, little brother, which should not be told while one is walking, we have to sit down and have a calabash of *bojwala ba Batswana* (sorghum beer) in a calm and quiet place, under a tree, for example."

"I am looking forward to that, elder brother."

The dining room table was neatly laid with plates, forks, knives and side plates. Boysie ushered Kgabalatsana to a chair between himself and Dikeledi. As Kgabalatsana settled in at the table, MmaMonare brought in two rather large dishes, one full of rice and the other stewed meat.

"That smells really good, *mosadi*, you are going all out to treat us to a feast," Boysie said delightedly.

"It is a big day for us, *rra,* having been joined by *rre* Kgabalatsana, of whom we had given up hope of ever seeing again. God does wonders."

"It is true, *mosadi*."

"That is what the city of the white man does to us people. When first you hear stories, you never think that it will happen to you. I am just pleased that I am back home intact," said Kgabalatsana.

Dikeledi scooped a spoonful of rice and put it on her husband's plate, and thereafter did the same with her brother-in-law's one. She did this standing and then dished stewed meat for all. When she had finished, she sat down and turned to Boysie.

"Will you please say a grace, *rra*?"

Boysie said the grace as they bowed their heads.

MmaMonare then invited them all to eat. It was silent, as though an angel was passing through the room. They concentrated on their plates, Dikeledi keeping watch, ready to dish second helpings. She then stood up to fetch a large jug of Kool-Aid, stirred it with a wooden spoon and then poured the drink into the men's glasses.

"*Dankie, mme*," said Kgabalatsana, as he took a sip.

Boysie cleared his throat and turned to his little brother.

"You earlier asked me how I have kept myself going to become what I am today – the answer to that question is not to be found very far away, little brother, just look at the food in front of us. Was it not for her, we would not be eating all these fresh vegetables that we have. Our garden produces more than what we can chew, and with the surplus, we barter at the local trading store for things that we cannot grow ourselves, such as rice, soaps, and so on.

"Dikeledi tills the soil, while having a job at the local clinic, working three days a week."

"It is really to keep me busy, *rra*, rather than just staying at home doing nothing," chipped in Dikeledi.

Boysie continued: "As for myself, my reconnection with Ramotswa was an eye-opener. Ever since, *Rangwana* Ntoa has persuaded and encouraged me to study via correspondence, which I did, finally passing my Standard Ten, after which I was appointed deputy principal at your old primary school, which, by the way, is now also a high school. The meagre salary that we both get has made us what we are today. We are not rich, but we are living comfortably.

"And, Kgabalatsana, the beautiful one that you left in her mother's womb is a pupil at my school. You will not believe it when you see her, as she is a replica of *Mme*."

"Indeed, you have done well for yourselves and I am proud of you. Maybe, had I been patient too, I would have been what you are, instead of having wasted my time in the City of Gold."

"I would want to think there are things you have learned about being away from home and from the city, *rra*," said, Dikeledi consoling Kgabalatsana.

"Talking about the little one, how is she and her mother and grandparents?"

"The old people have passed on. Nthabiseng is living at her parents' place with her daughter, and actually she is working as a nurse at the same clinic where Dikeledi works."

There was another brief silence after the mention of Nthabiseng's name. Kgabalatsana's mind went back to the time when he last communicated with her, to what he remembered – and what he could not.

"I can now feel satisfied that I am back in the family fold and have a lot to do to catch up with the years I wasted in Johannesburg."

"If you can walk, you can dance; if you can talk, you can sing, my little brother, and let me, in the same vein, remind you that a man who takes advice is still a man who acts of his own free will," said Boysie.

"We are all here, *rra*, to put our hands together."

She smiled at her brother-in-law, trying to cheer him up.

"Well, well!" said Boysie, getting up. "That's enough for the day, I believe. There will be a lot of catching up to do, little brother. I am sure that by now, news has spread about the big red car seen at the Monare homestead."

"You are right, elder brother, there are a lot of places where I will have to touch base."

"Actually, Nthabiseng is off-duty today, *rre* Kgabalatsana," said Dikeledi, warmly.

"Thank you, *mme*, for that extra information."

The brothers left the table as she began clearing.

***

Like a well-working, cordial, and good marriage before a divorce, the relationship between the two brothers was not to last for long. Kgabalatsana was to contend with the greater skeletons up the sleeve of the brother, while on the other hand, Boysie himself might even have got to know that his own brother was conniving with the Patels to sell a portion of the land – none of them knew each other's connivances as was to be seen in a conversation held between the two one day.

"I'm telling you, brother, when this village is divided, it is like heaven is falling on it," said Boysie, worriedly. "The question of land ownership is a hot potato and the division is between what I would call the traditionalists and the enlightened, depending on what side of the river you live.

"So, we are caught up in this historical creation. I discussed with the chief the issue of the inheritance left by our father. The chief said that the matter would be discussed at a *lekgotla* to be held in due course. But, let me warn you, this is not going to be an easy matter, for the reasons mentioned earlier."

Kgabalatsana was not happy.

"Tell me, my brother, why should this be a complicated matter? Does tradition here not dictate that the land belongs to the tribe, which is us, the Bahurutse, and that the chief is keeping it in trust on our behalf?

"Therefore, if that be the case, as you seem to agree, I, the son of Japheth, have all the rights to get it back?"

"That is why I just said I do not see why it should be complicated," said Boysie, looking at his brother with disappointment. "I thought you people in the cities understood these things."

He held his brother by the shoulder. "You see, little brother, it is clear that you've been away from home for too long and you do not understand the modern Dinokana. You imagine a traditional village of the fifties – the one that you left.

"The Dinokana of our fathers is what you think still exists. Old habits and practices have changed; practices are interpreted according to group interests now, and at times these interests are not based on tribal interests, but on friendship, business or otherwise.

"You'll be surprised by the way the tribe has become morally degenerated. Raping of women is commonplace now, and gone are the days when a woman could walk alone at night. Pregnancy among children is rife. You'll see these things yourself as you stay longer. Strange people and cars are reported to be seen at odd hours at the chief's royal residence, for what business, none of us know."

"Doing what" asked Kgabalatsana. "What do his aides say?"

"The grapevine has it that they might be part of the big game or shall I say, some of them," said Boysie, "Dinokana of the old has changed, brother, and is yielding place to the new Dinokana, but welcome to the new village, little brother.

"Only a few days ago your sister-in-law was telling me that she saw a van belonging to one of the rich Indian shop owners from Zeerust at the chief's royal residence."

Kgabalatsana suddenly changed his focus, keeping quiet, thinking to himself that this might have been one of his connections. It could have been Faisal's brother.

"Are you okay, little brother, or are you still tired after your long journey from Hauteng?"

"Oh, no," said Kgabalatsana, "my mind was on something else."

Boysie looked at his watch. "By the way, we have to prepare for the meeting at the royal residence. I have to formally introduce you to the chief as a matter of protocol."

After a while, Kgabalatsana went to his bedroom and started preparing himself for the *lekgotla*. He took the bottle of medicine given to him by the Sangoma in Krugersdorp and gurgled it from a cup.

In his own room, Boysie was assisted by Dikeledi in putting on his jacket. She brushed the dust from the shoulders, pulling the jacket downwards, as though it had shrunk.

"You have not worn this for a very long time!" she exclaimed.

"Where would I have worn it, *mosadi*?"

"You will have to play your part very well in that meeting, for it will not be as easy as your brother thinks. He will need all your support, for he does not know how these rural matters are conducted; try and avoid him talking, because I'm not even sure of his Setswana," Dikeledi giggled.

"Trust me, woman, I have traversed places. The thing that worries me is why the chief decided to leave me out of a meeting he called recently?"

"Oh, you know how he operates. This is an enlightened chief who at times does things according to what he learned from the college, and when he does that, he consults with his peers. That should not preoccupy your mind, because I do not for a moment believe that there was malice on his part.

"He has the utmost respect for the Monare family and we never disappointed him following the death of your father. People like you have very little role to play when strategies are being devised. English is the order of the day and the educated play the leading role."

"I hope that you are right, *Mosadi*, and I will rely on your wisdom and remember your words."

Boysie left the house to join his brother, who was already in the car. Kgabalatsana opened the door from his driver's seat.

"*Banna* (man!) you've helped me! I was not sure that I was going to know how to open it." Boysie slipped into the passenger seat. "The real sons of Japheth. Imagine how he would have felt seated with us now? Imagine what the villagers are saying and thinking now about us?"

The car cruised along the gravel road. They hadn't needed to use the car but wanted to show off to the villagers.

"This must have cost you many cows," said Boysie, brushing the dashboard.

"Two thousand rands," Kgabalatsana retorted, exaggerating wildly.

"What? You could have filled a whole kraal and still remained with money under your mattress, brother."

They arrived at the chief's residence and parked.

The chief emerged to welcome them, and Boysie held back for a moment, eager for his superior to see the car.

The chief held Boysie by the hand and together they walked to a secluded corner of the yard, a distance from the gate.

"Boysie, I see that you have become a VIP overnight, chauffeur-driven and in a beautiful vehicle," he said, looking at Kgabalatsana, who had not yet been introduced. The latter had been warned to take his cue from his brother.

"The success of black people in the cities, at times, makes me envy them. Look at the car, it is still sparkling, even though it has been driving through our dusty roads."

"*Kgosi*, allow me to introduce my younger brother," said Boysie. "Kgabalatsana is the one whom we talked about a few days ago, when we received a letter from him saying that he would be coming home. You see the fatigue in his eyes – he arrived only yesterday."

The chief smiled courteously. "Every Muhurutse belongs here. Welcome home, *rra*, and welcome to my humble house – a place left to me by my father."

The two men bowed to their chief.

The chief turned to Kgabalatsana. "*Rre* Kgabalatsana, one sees opulence and success in you, attesting to your long years of hard work in the city of Hauteng.

"You gentlemen must know that as children of your village, your father, Japheth Monare, was a most respected man here and known for his wisdom and honesty. My father relied on him and you will perhaps recall stories about how he was my father's chief advisor on traditional matters.

"It is, therefore, for this reason, that I felt I should call you two so that I could personally receive your brother, Boysie."

"We are grateful, *Kgosi*," said Boysie.

"I hope, Boysie, that you informed your brother of the problem we have with the land left for him by your father? It is not only your land, *rre* Kgabalatsana that we are busy with – there are others, too.

"This matter is causing divisions within the village and we are here trying to resolve it but rest assured that there is nothing that is beyond our reach."

The two brothers nodded.

"It is not going to be an easy matter, but we shall try," the chief declared.

Kgabalatsana looked at his brother questioningly, but Boysie motioned to him to say nothing, fearful of any damage that his words might do – just as his wife had cautioned.

"Thank-you very much, *Kgosi*, for the audience that you have given us. This is a manifestation of the honour placed on our family, *Kgosi*. We respect and honour you for that. Again, I thank you for having received my brother personally and the great, encouraging words you expressed to us about our late father.

"As to the matter of land, I do believe that my brother has heard it for himself."

He looked at Kgabalatsana, who nodded vigorously.

"Yes, *Kgosi*," he said, almost obsequiously, "we had time to deliberate over the matter as a family."

The chief bowed his head and turned towards his house, bidding them farewell. He knew that Boysie would handle the rest.

The siblings drove off. Once home, Boysie was out of the car first. Boysie's wife watched them from the kitchen window – she saw that the tension between the boys had lifted.

Kgabalatsana pulled at Boysie by his shirt.

"Brother, tell me, do you honestly think that this will be an easy matter to resolve?"

He spotted Dikeledi at the window, realising that she was listening. She ducked back into the kitchen.

"I trust so, brother, as the chief said, even though it is a difficult question. We only depend on the wisdom of the chief and the elders of the village. But at this juncture, no one can tell what the outcome will be. As I told you earlier, there are too many interests and influential groups here."

***

Boysie and his wife were seated in their dining room, drinking tea in silence, Boysie engrossed in puffing his pipe. After a spell, his wife spoke.

"I really do not like the way that things are going, *rra*," she said in a small but resolute voice. "Sooner, rather than later, *rre* Kgabalatsana is bound to know the truth about this. Don't you think that it would have been honourable of you to short-circuit all of this? How would you have felt if this had happened to you?"

Boysie glared at his wife, but she ignored him.

"I maintain that you're being dishonourable to your own," she said, standing up and brushing her hands on her dress. "Truth is truth and nothing else but the truth."

"Since when have you become a lawyer, *mosadi*?" said Boysie, glowering with the utter arrogance of male chauvinism.

Dikeledi lifted her eyebrows contemptuously.

"I find it surprising that you and nobody else – you, the one who used to brag about the good and well-mannered way in which you were both brought up as brothers – could display such behaviour towards one of your own.

"What happened to the sentiment of brotherhood? You are blood brothers – and brothers don't cheat each other. They support and defend each other in times of need. Get it straight – you will find no sympathy from me when this reaches *rre* Kgabalatsana's ears. Expect that I will not be on your side, for I cannot be on the side of wrongdoers."

With that, she stormed from the room and into the kitchen.

At that moment, Kgabalatsana arrived home, greeted his brother and hung his hat on the back of the door. Excitedly, he opened a letter which he had just collected from the village shop. He had seen that it was from Hauteng. Boysie saw his brother's face change rapidly from joy to despair, as the latter allowed the paper to drop to the ground.

"What is the matter with you, little brother? What bad news has this piece of paper brought?" asked Boysie. Dikeledi appeared at the kitchen door, watching and listening.

"You know, I don't need this." Kgabalatsana almost spat out the words. She decided to leave the room, fearing that the land secret had been exposed.

"What is it, Kgabalatsana? Don't keep us in suspense. Tell me?"

"The letter is from Hauteng, brother. Everything in my house has been repossessed by the furniture shop owners."

Dikeledi was relieved to hear that, as she stood quietly behind the door. Boysie stocked his pipe, which had long since extinguished. The tension evaporated as he began puffing.

"They say that I owe them money," Kgabalatsana said flatly.

"They say? You say 'they say'? What do you say? Do you owe them or not? Stop using city language here," Boysie said angrily. "You either owe the white man money or you don't. There can be no middle road here, otherwise they would not repossess the furniture?"

Kgabalatsana shrugged sheepishly.

"Mistakes do occur, brother, especially these days. I will have to phone a friend in Johannesburg to help me out and resolve this matter soon."

Boysie looked away, staring out of the window, feeling irritated.

"By the way, brother, on another note, where are the papers for the land? I mean, the ownership papers that stipulate the land belongs to us? I remember that at the time father had passed away, the chief – or was it the magistrate in Zeerust? – was busy preparing them for us, so I am reliably informed."

Boysie flared with annoyance, but it quickly subsided.

"Indeed, brother, you have been in exile for too long," he clucked, feeling sorry for his sibling. Dikeledi came into the room as he continued. "Little brother, all such papers are kept at the royal residence, remember, according to customary practices here. All land belongs to the people of Dinokana, and it is the prerogative of the chief as to how it is allocated."

"I know that, elder brother. And that process was completed when the land was allocated to *ntate* – father – who in turn gave it over to me."

"Listen, Kgabalatsana, let me finish," Boysie interrupted, glancing sideways at his wife. "This, by the way, is for everyone who has land here and not just the Monare family."

He stocked his pipe again for the umpteenth time, using a matchstick, and then stood suddenly, brushing his hair flat.

"What you imply, then, is that I should ask *Kgosi* for the papers? Is that what you are saying, big brother?"

"I did not say that. I was just relating to you about the custodianship of papers. How you access them is another matter."

"And can you then tell me how I can access them from *Kgosi*?"

Clearly, Boysie was now beside himself with emotion and restrained anger. He was answering silly questions in front of his wife, who had just a short while ago raised the issue with him. Couldn't Kgabalatsana have raised these matters in the absence of his wife? Is this how men in the cities dealt with domestic issues? Did they not know that there were limitations as what a man discusses in the presence of a woman?

Boysie realised that he had to learn to understand his brother better. For now, though, the damage had already been done, as his wife had been party to the discussion – and there was no way that she would now disengage herself from a topic on which she had a strong opinion.

"Remember, my brother, what the chief said? Let us, therefore, wait for him to resolve this, as he promised he would do."

"And what did the chief say, *rre* Kgabalatsana, if I may ask, and now that my ears have allowed me to be a part of this?" the lady of the house asked, curtly.

"Well, he said that this matter would be dealt with at the *lekgotla*," said Kgabalatsana.

"By the way, what is this matter you two keep referring to, *bo-rra*? This matter, this matter – what is it?"

It was only then that Kgabalatsana realised that there was something more to the situation than his brother had let on. But still, Boysie said nothing. Kgabalatsana felt annoyed and worried. He stood up and left the room, fuming with anger.

***

As dawn broke, the sun's rays streaming through thick tree branches and the teeth-like crevices of the mountain tips, the silhouette of figures of men and cattle-drawn sleighs emerged in the fields of the toiling men of Dinokana.

This was the bread basket of agriculture in the district of Lehurutshe, whose people have, for centuries, been tillers of that land. Today, men and boys woke early, why have a break as soon as possible. Their chief had called a *lekgotla* – a call to which no man could fail to respond. The chief was an active man who always brought forth new things, especially at times when the villagers were in conflict.

At about 10 am, groups of elderly villagers were already shuffling towards the royal residence, with many more galloping towards the house on horses and in donkey carts, as they all made their way along the dusty roads to the venerable household.

Under the big bluegum tree was an elevated platform, where the chief usually sat in a high chair, surrounded by a circle of men. Women ululated as they mingled, placing calabashes of *bojwala baBatswana* (sorghum beer) in front of the gathered parties.

The chief emerged from the house wearing a leopard skin around his loins. Strapped across his shoulders was a belt of animal skin. Legend had it that the skin was that of a lion killed with his bare hands when he was young boy.

"*Kgosi*! Tau Tona!" saluted the men, standing and bowing their heads. He motioned that they should remain seated. A praise singer appeared from the crowd, singing praises to the chief.

> *Lion of the Bahurutse*
> *child of Moiloa*
> *our great father*
> *who defied the forces of evil*
> *when they tried to dethrone*
> *You as chief of our tribe*
> *You who dared tell the evil forces*
> *that the land belonged to your people*
> *And nobody else.*
> *Kgosi, Tau Tuna.*

He proceeded to his seat as he finished his praises. The chief stood up, addressing his subjects.

"My children, elders of the Bahurutse tribe; I greet you this morning with love."

"Long live the chief! Long live our chief, son of Moiloa," responded the elders.

"Today, we are going to start our *lekgotla* with a prayer. I have asked our priest, the Reverend Kgabarane, to be with us and to bless our *lekgotla* – you may witness his presence here today."

He pointed in the direction of the priest.

"I shall therefore ask you, *muruti* (priest) Kgabarane, to lead us in a prayer."

The priest stood up, walked to the platform and stood behind the rostrum, just in front of the priest.

"Thank-you, *Kgosi*, thank-you, great chief of this noble tribe. As a servant of the people, as a messenger of the Lord

Almighty, it is my duty to respond to instructions made to me, especially where and when the message of the Lord has to be delivered.

"An invitation to such an august gathering is a manifestation of the seriousness you pay to the word of the Almighty, in allowing and facilitating a link between us as priests, the royal family and the people of this village at large. Let us, therefore, close our eyes and pray. Oh, Heavenly Father…"

Following the soulful prayer, the priest stepped back and sat down.

Dinokana, at times, depending on one's appreciation – or lack thereof – was of a rural setting, and was a kaleidoscope and microcosm of any town in South Africa. Many went about their daily business, earning their bread and butter, ignorant of the pressing issues being hotly debated by town and city fathers at the centre of their communities.

"We shall now start our meeting," the chief declared. He looked in the direction of the young man Sentle, who was conspicuously dressed in an outfit that set him apart from the rest of the gathering, making clear his age and academic status: grey trousers, black jacket, smart white shirt and tie. He held a pile of papers under his arm.

Sentle stepped forward jerkily, beads of sweat already forming on his smooth, youthful forehead. He seemed to have rehearsed this moment many times – but now that it had come, he still looked ill-prepared.

"Will you, young man Sentle," the chief intoned, "take us through and remind us of where we stopped last time with our programme? I do hope that those who attended the last meeting will remember the issues that we discussed. Please, let us not waste any more time by repeating what we already know. For those who were not present, I do hope that you consulted those who were present last time. Over to you, young man, Sentle."

"Thank you, great chief, and thank you my elders of this noble village. As you will recall, most of the applications of the allocation of land have been presented and dealt with,

with the exception of the application for the land along the river that belongs to…"

Sentle paused briefly, as he paged through his papers, seemingly confused. Old man Moabi immediately stood up, ready to heckle. He pointed a finger at the boy.

"Young man, we have no time to play here. Our heads are scorched in this burning sun and we are sweating. Look how it is already killing the very little vegetation that remains from the last rains. Our land needs ploughing, our livestock are wandering the meadows and will destroy our fields.

"*Kgosi* asked you to remind us where we stopped, simple and *klaar* – finished! Why is it that when such a simple explanation had to be made, you then must look through those papers – are those details not supposed to be in your head already? What are they teaching you at these colleges?"

Other voices rose in agreement.

"No! No! We are just wasting our money sending you people to school! This is the result of involving children in the affairs of the elderly – *makgotla* were never meant for children!"

The elders chuckled at this; but Sentle had learnt a few tricks from them after his last appearance here – he kept his cool and refused to be provoked by their insults.

"The land next to the river belongs to *rre* Montsho and the family still has issues to discuss among themselves. The other application is…" he shuffled through his papers again, drawing clicks and sighs from the crowd, "It is – oh."

Sentle composed himself and continued.

"The other application is for the land belonging to the Monare family. But I have to stress again that, as with the previous one, there are issues that need to be settled and clarified by the two children of *Ntate* Japheth Monare. But, as they are among us today, I think that they will be in a position to enlighten us as to where the matter stands."

He stood back, allowing the gathering's full gaze to rest on the Monare brothers.

Kgabalatsana, who had seated himself next to his brother, whispered to him: "What is the boy talking about? What is it that we are supposed to settle, brother? Are there things that I'm supposed to know?"

Boysie, irritated, shushed him.

"How am I supposed to know what he is talking about when we have only just arrived? Shut up, keep quiet and listen to the proceedings. Learn something from this and then ask questions later."

"I will pause there, *Kgosi*," said Sentle, as he took his seat, his forehead sweating from the heat of both the sun and his critical elders.

Kgabo stood up as Sentle sat down, wiped his face with a handkerchief that was so worn and used, one could not tell if it was white or khaki, and straightened his jacket swiftly.

"Young people of today. Oh! Chief, I'm scared as to what will happen to the traditions of our people when we are no more. I wonder at times what our fathers will say to us, men of my generation; whether we groomed these young men properly for the tasks ahead. Is it my failure? Perhaps, yes, *Kgosi*.

"Keorapetse Sentle, father to this young man, a man of honour and integrity whom we all know, one of the hitherto most enlightened men in our village, is unfortunately no more amongst us. He spent his last penny and took young Sentle to university, educating this boy to be an asset to his community. Young man, stand up and tell your fathers the last decisions we took in relation to the two matters in our last meeting."

A voice interjected from the crowd.

"Decisions? What decisions? Did I hear you well, *rre* Kgabo? My understanding was that we were asked by the chief to discuss matters that Sentle had just presented and then we would have the time to discuss them and take decisions. *Kgosi* pointed out clearly that the young man should not dwell on matters already presented in our last meeting - that I understood to mean that we should first take off from where we left off in our last meeting and thereafter then discuss the two subjects just presented by the young man."

"That is precisely the point, you are right," another elder shouted, as he stood up.

"Kgabo has always been a dreamer from the time he was a boy. *Rre* Kgabo, please do not waste our time. If there are things that you know outside these meetings, keep those to yourself and do not cause confusion here. The young man has made his presentation professionally and to the point. There were no decisions made, Kgabo, otherwise we would not be here."

Commotion and pandemonium erupted, with men shouting at Kgabo to sit down. The old man sat down.

The chief realised that, once again, there would be little progress today. He called to Kgabo, Sentle and a few elders to join him on the platform. He noticed, too, that Boysie and Kgabalatsana were arguing. The situation was fraught with tension.

At this point, an old man, aged mid-eighties and leaning heavily on a gnarled walking stick, slowly stood up. He cut a fine appearance – tall and dignified, his worn grey tweed jacket, brown shirt, hat and trousers were elegant throwbacks to a bygone era. As he began walking towards the platform, silence descended.

Ntate Mogolo (old father) Seemela was the oldest man of the village, a veteran of Dinokana *makgotlas* since the time of chief Moiloa, father of the current chief. In a soft, commanding voice, he was able to sway the crowd to hushed reverence; some even appeared to have their tails between their legs, chastened by his respectable demeanour.

"*Kgosi*. Great Father of the Tribe and descendant of our forefathers. This, indeed, is a time of hope, this is a time of joy – yet this seems to be a moment of despair and confusion also. Elders howling at the young, grey men shouting at one another. I used the last words deliberately, great chief, for it seems as if the heavens are about to fall on us, yet it is not so.

"How interesting it is for me to meander through my last days of these *makgotla*, pierced by the sun. This *lekgotla* reminds me of the one that we had many, many moons ago. The last moon when we had the longest rains that fell and nourished our land. When our livestock became so fat that we did not know what to do with them, for they could not pull our ploughs and wagons. When the cocks used to be the timekeepers of our time and the hyenas the ones telling us that it was sleeping time.

"Those were the good times. As elders of this great and noble place, as your advisors, *Kgosi*, a few moments ago as I was watching you, you seemed in a state of quandary, yet I know that deep in your heart, you were not.

"When things are as they seem to be, wisdom, experience, always tell me that we need to take a pause. Look back. Retreat to our homes and ponder a way forward in the peace of our huts. I'm sure by now our wives are wondering as to why at this hour of the day we are not yet finished with our business. I do not think we give a good impression of ourselves and to them. Let us not undermine the institution of our families, for we might think that we are alone when in fact, they are with us.

"By now, our sour milk and porridge have started to get dry. In short, *Kgosi*, I beg you allow us to take a break, how long that will be, I'll leave to your discretion, *Kgosi*. This shouting and grumbling coming from the elders of this village tires me. I've no more strength remaining in my bones, the marrow has depleted over the years. I beg you chief to allow us to go home."

At that juncture, the praise singer jumped to the stage, as if he knew that the old man had finished the business of the day.

Bayethe!

Tau Tona, Bayethe
Lion of the Bahurutse
Who are we to stand here
In the way of the wise
the old Seemela
who are we to ignore his wise words
when it is clear that all of us are tired
Everybody agrees with old man Seemela
that we need to soothe our tired minds,
Kgosi.

He saluted the chief as he threw himself onto the ground. The chief stood up and addressed the gathering. "We shall break and you'll be notified when we will continue with the meeting."

Followed by his aides, the chief returned to his house. In small groups, the men left the royal residence, tired but encouraged by the wise words of the veteran Seemela.

After the *lekgotla*, Kgabalatsana and Boysie walked home together in silence. And when they arrived home, Kgabalatsana hung his hat on the back of the front door, while the latter took off to his bedroom.

Kgabalatsana's eye caught sight of a note on the table, which he quickly picked up, opened and quickly read before Boysie came back. After he finished reading it, he folded it and put it back onto the table; after all, Boysie had not seen it yet. As his brother came back from the bedroom, his eye caught sight of the note, too. He looked at his brother with suspicion, seemingly cheesed off by this "intruder" from the cities.

Kgabalatsana looked away, pretending not to have seen his brother opening the envelope and then putting it in his pocket. This double game of hide and seek was reminiscent of their childhood days. Indeed, at times, men do behave like children; but, after all, perhaps we are children still?

Boysie walked back to the bedroom and returned minutes later, expression unchanged.

"Is there anything that I should know, brother. You look tense; your face seems to have contorted? And as a matter of fact, you've been quiet since we came back from the *lekgotla*," asked Kgabalatsana.

"You know what I said, little brother," said Boysie, "this is not what *mme* would have expected from us, her only children who were brought up and grew up like twins. Everybody in this village knew us as such."

"I'm aware that it has been a very long time since we've lived together and I respect the privacy that you've been used to and if my arrival might have affected it, I do not know."

Kgabalatsana left the dining room, not expecting any response from his brother. He came back from the bedroom. and asked his brother;

"Tell me, brother, there were some things that I could not follow at the *lekgotla* and I recall that you told me that the subject of our land was to be discussed?"

"Well, as I previously told you, little brother," said Boysie, in an arrogant voice, "the village elders are still divided on the issue. I really do not know when this will be resolved. And as you have been there, the meeting ended without any conclusion, but the matter was indeed supposed to have been placed on the agenda, as promised by the Chief to me."

He paused as if he still wanted to say something, but took his pipe out of his pocket instead.

"And when the chief realised that divisions were about to start again and would have disrupted the meeting, which could have led to a rumpus, wise man Seemela saved the day by advising the chief to adjourn the *lekgotla*. So it was, little brother, and the meeting was adjourned, thanks to the skills and experience of the old man."

Kgabalatsana was surprised at the artfulness with which his elder brother was able to spin stories to his advantage

– and with such apparent interest. He was convincing, but what he said always left Kgabalatsana with more questions than answers. There must have been something that he was hiding – but what?

"Am I just being naive, trusting my own blood?" thought Kgabalatsana, trying, but battling, to divert his mind from such thoughts.

"Divisions amongst the elders which are caused by such seemingly simple matters tend to cause chaos. Remember what the chief said to us, and I repeat, he said that the matter would not be easy to resolve," said Boysie.

Kgabalatsana said nothing, concentrating on his dinner plate. Then he looked up.

"By the way, where is the mother of the house? Is there something I need to be told about?"

"No," Boysie chipped in with a stern and resolute reply. "There is nothing for you to know."

He got up from the table and went to stand at the door, looking outside. He turned and stared at his brother, a vicious expression on his face.

"Let's get things straight, little brother, my affairs and the relationship between me and my wife is my business, and nobody else's. I repeat, little brother, it is nobody else's, not even you. Where she was should be none of your business? How dare you prod into my life? Where did you get the courage to do so? Did I ask you where you were last night? Even when I know that you came back in the early hours of the morning. Oh! No, I didn't, for that was not my business."

Kgabalatsana, who by this time had a better understanding of the tricks and craftiness of his brother, refused to be deterred by his pretence and continued baiting him.

"Oh! By the way, elder brother, will I be correct in assuming that it all has to do with the land, my inheritance left for me by our parents?"

Boysie gave his brother a stern look as if he was going to devour him.

"You'd better count your words, young man, otherwise you're going to get hurt," said Boysie in a threatening voice.

"By the way, your temper reminds me," said Kgabalatsana calmly, "of an incident when we were still young when you behaved exactly in the same manner when you tried to hit me after a quarrel. It was about a mistake I had made - and after having apologised, you still fumed like a wounded buffalo; and were it not for the intervention of mama and *ntate*, you would have devoured me, but you were sternly warned that the day one lifted a finger to the other would be the day when we would have to leave their place. Brother, elder brother, remember that this is still Japheth's and mama's house; this is a family home."

Boysie shifted his eyes to his parents' photograph hanging on the wall and when he looked more closely at it, it was as if they were looking at him and saying, "You dare do it, Boysie."

"I asked you about the papers of registration and what did you say? Now I know that everything you told me about the land was not true. It was only last night that I saw papers from someone who lives in the very same village. I can attest that there are no papers kept by the chief, you were just making up an excuse for something that you know."

At that moment, the kitchen door cracked open and Dikeledi entered the house and walked through the dining room towards the bedroom, carrying a suitcase.

"Greetings sister-in-law," said Kgabalatsana. "why did you not tell me that you were on your way, because I would have picked you up at least at the bus stop. It is not good for your health to be walking in this scorching sun when I could have fetched you even from Zeerust."

"Don't worry, *rre* Kgabalatsana, I'm a village woman and I'm used to walking."

Boysie shook his head and Kgabalatsana walked into the kitchen to prepare food for his sister-in-law. Minutes later, he placed it on the table.

"Food is ready, *mme,* and it is as if I knew that you were coming back."

"I'm coming, *rre* Kgabalatsana, thank you very much - the food will do me good."

She came to the table and started eating. Boysie looked at his brother with threatening eyes as if saying, "You dare continue with the discussion in front of my wife and you will get me."

"You came just in time," said Kgabalatsana.

She looked up questioningly.

"Just in time for what, *Rre* Kgabalatsana?"

At this point, Boysie could not hold himself together and lost his temper.

"I'm warning you!"

The lady then realised that there was something untoward between the two brothers.

"I thought that by coming back home I was coming to the old Monare homestead that I knew. Hardly did I know that the situation was not as I left it – old order changed, yielding place to new. It could have been worse, sister-in-law, had it not been for your arrival."

Kgabalatsana narrated to his sister-in-law the history of the land left by his father, how he had left Johannesburg with high hopes of one day settling back home when he had saved enough to return and develop his father's place for the benefit of the whole family.

Dikeledi shifted her gaze to her husband, furious.

"Shame on you, Boysie Monare, shame on you! All these years I've known you to be an honourable man. The problem with you is that you've been living in a fool's paradise for too long, convinced that your brother had long since died. I've suspected that there was something up your sleeve. Many years ago, I asked you about the plot along the river and what was your answer? I knew then that you were lying to me."

Kgabalatsana was on his feet, looking down at his brother.

"You were so greedy and desperate for money – and to do what with it? I do not know. How could you do that, elder brother?"

Kgabalatsana let out a cry, years of hurt and misery erupting. If the neighbours had been listening, they would have heard the wails of an old man.

"The last and only inheritance that *ntate* left for me, the only reason for me having left the city of Hauteng to be told that there was no land? Tell me brother that it is not true what my sister-in-law has just said, tell me!"

He held his brother by the jacket, crying.

"Tell your little brother the truth, Boysie," said Dikeledi. "The time for lies has now passed. The truth is needed, for you're the only one who knows what you did with the money that you might have received out the sale of the land. How I hoped that you kept that money safe so that you could now be giving it to your brother."

But again, truth be told, though Boysie, with the connivance of the chief, had indeed intended to sell the land and because Boysie had not been truthful, taking his wife into his confidence on the matter, he got stuck with this guilt.

Kgabalatsana went to the window and looked into the horizon, his eyes blurring as if about to faint.

Boysie stood like a zombie, mute. Dikeledi was the only person who seemed alive in the room, watching the two brothers seemingly paralysed by what she had just revealed.

Kgabalatsana's mind raced with thoughts of the village of Dinokana, seeing the mountain range at a distance, the valley in the south and the cattle grazing in the meadows. This was the place of his birth – the land to which he had been known from childhood. Now it seemed as barren as the city he'd left. Could a man ever win in this world?

The words of his Alexandra friends echoed: "Don't cry for me Argentina."

Kgabalatsana turned to his sister-in-law and hugged her tightly for some time.

"Thank you, *mme*, you're a true sister - a sister in need is a sister indeed. You are a *rara avis* and your forthright, mature handling of this matter has opened my eyes. I have suddenly woken up and realised that whilst there are many rapscallions in this world, equally so there are also rare people such as you, who will always stand by the truth and defend that truth with honour and dignity."

Kgabalatsana's words pierced Boysie's heart. He looked at his brother and then at his wife.

These were the only two people I've lived for in my whole life, he thought to himself, and yet, what had happened?

"We're all in this boat," she said, realising what was on her husband's mind. She had been with him long enough to know him well. "We have to resolve this matter in the interests of these two."

She pointed at the portrait of the parents.

"Look how they are looking at us, why then are we disappointing them?" asked Dikeledi, encouraged by the words of her brother-in-law. Kgabalatsana wiped the dripping tears from his eyes.

***

The village of Dinokana, like many in the district of Lehurutshe, is a beautifully multi-coloured, scattered assortment of rondavels, roughly hand-painted with a variety of amber colours smeared in circular patterns.

Four elderly men, among the oldest in the village, were seated around a large table in a rondavel hut artfully decorated with white and brown amber, the roof neatly covered with dark brown straw forming a hat-like shape at the edges and cone-shaped top. The large dining room table filled most of the room, allowing space only at the edges for family members and friends who might move around serving guests.

Along the walls of the room hung an assortment of animal skins. A spear and shield hung on the wall, facing the front door, as though placed deliberately to welcome guests entering the hut.

Kgabo, Sentle, Seemela and Moabi were scattered about the table, drinking African beer from a calabash. A tall, beautiful, light-coloured lady, slightly younger than the men, was serving food. She dressed prettily in a blue *SeShoeShoe* outfit, a black scarf covering her head. Her movements were leisurely and diligent. One could see that she had been performing these ritualistic acts since marrying into the family. After all, human beings are born with different attributes, and hers was the preparation of food for family and guests. She strongly believed that this was an Act of God. Serving guests in her house that day came easily and naturally to her.

She could often be heard telling friends and lecturing girls – especially those at college – of the merits of being the mother of a household in an African society.

"What a delicious smell, woman," said old man Seemela. "You people are masters when it comes to these things." He looked in the direction of Moabi. "Moabi, tell me, where would you have started if you were asked to prepare all these delicacies?"

Moabi smiled and responded to the provocative question from the veteran.

"The Almighty knew what he was doing when he created Adam and Eve. It was not an accident. Seemela."

There was laughter around the table at the succinct manner in which Moabi answered the always provocative Seemela. At that moment, the chief entered the room from the far end door, dressed in his leopard skin outfit and already waving his hand.

"Remain seated, please."

He took the chair beneath the wall-mounted shield and spear.

Most men gathered there had no clue why they had been summoned to the royal palace; let alone why they were being entertained in the chief's private dining room, which was normally reserved for the entertainment of guests who came from afar, mostly from among royalty. The chief whispered something in Sentle's ear, covering his mouth so that the others could not hear. Then, he addressed his audience.

"Gentlemen, my children, trusted warriors of this tribe! You must be wondering why I called you to the royal house on such short notice, why this gathering is taking place in a room that is usually utilised for members of the royal families. There were times when my father used to do the same."

He looked in the direction of Seemela, who amongst most of those present could attest to the chief's testimony; and Seemela rose slightly, nodding his head in agreement.

"It is indeed so, great chief," Seemela said. "I can still recall a number of such gatherings called during odd hours of the night by your illustrious father, *Kgosi*."

"This is your place, this is your entitlement and I have decided that from time to time I shall do so," responded the chief, much to his guests' amusement. "The reason I decided to call this meeting is because of the issues that we've been deliberating in the broader *makgotla* without any progress. You've been deliberately selected to participate in this discussion so as to guide me, so that by the time I address a full gathering, I will know exactly where each and every one of you stands."

He looked at the young man Sentle, seated a distance from the main table, slightly removed from his elders.

"You will notice that of late, this young man has been my spokesperson and presenter on matters that are new to me and to most of you, if not all. Dinokana, as a traditional village, has been known for its adherence to culture, traditions and norms, but now we have to gear our knowledge towards new things.

"I refer here to what some of you see as intrusions into your domain. Into matters that used to be for the sole discretion of you, the elders only. Gone are those days, gentlemen. Very soon every South African will have the right to live where he or she wants to live. To give a précis, I'm opening a discussion on the issue of the allocation of land to those who do not belong to this tribe – people you may refer to as outsiders. We will have to finalise the outstanding dispute of the Monare sons and other applications."

The chief looked at Seemela, trying to indicate to him that he was expected to respond and Seemela, realising what the chief was expecting of him, cleared his throat as he prepared himself to take the floor.

"I will not be offended if you remain seated as you address the meeting, Seemela."

"*Kgosi*." responded the old man. "Thank-you very much. On behalf of all of us, we are humbled by the confidence you've shown to us, respect that some of us have enjoyed even during the reign of your father, the great chief Moiloa. Thank you very much, *Kgosi*.

"It was not an accident that you chose these elders for this important gathering here today. For without them, the whole village would go astray. They have the wisdom and the experience to guide the tribe as they command the respect of all its people. It is these men who are supposed to chart the direction of our people's affairs.

"At times, we have to swallow our pride and do what other tribes decided long ago to do. I refer here to the path of development. The question might, therefore, be asked: what type of development and in whose interest and at whose expense? We are now starting to be the laughing stock of the women in this village because they see us every day coming to and fro to the royal residence. They ask themselves - what is it that these men cannot resolve all these days? Our children are starting to wonder why we are no longer seen in the fields, thus wondering whether we no longer care about producing food for our families."

The gathered men nodded in agreement.

"But, great *Kgosi*. For me to advise this meeting properly, there are a number of questions that I have, questions that I could not find answers to.

"Your father ruled this tribe with honour and openness. So have you, honourable chief, since you assumed your role as the father of this great tribe."

There was a pause and Moabi chipped in.

"*Kgosi*. Tau Tona, it is unfortunate that people like Seemela have chosen to be diplomats. Men such as him have now taken the role such as those who are at the Organisation of African Unity - people who like to beat about the bush. We are divided as a nation on the issue of land allocation, *Kgosi*. Perhaps we are dealing with this matter at a time when there are changes in society as a whole.

"Correctly, as you said earlier on - every South African will soon have the right to live where he or she wants to live. Our forefathers have long agreed on this fundamental principle and it is for that reason that people from far away, people with no connection to this tribe, find it easy to want to come and stay with us. What, then, should our response be to this new change? The issue in my mind is not whether they should or should not, but rather how we should manage the process.

"Great *Kgosi*, I said earlier on that people such as Seemela have become diplomats. The reality of the matter is that there are rumours doing the rounds here that there are deals and promises that have already been made to certain business people from as near as Zeerust and Kimberley, as we have noted in the last gathering."

The chief did not flinch at the mention of land deals.

"Rumours abound that vans and beautiful cars are seen here at the royal residence at odd hours. Doing what? I do not know. But perhaps there are people here who could enlighten me as to whether we are dealing with rumours, or with realities. Some of us here in this village are seen wearing new clothes on Sundays. Where does this money come from to buy such beautiful and expensive outfits? I do not know.

"Maybe, honestly, these things come from decently-living, loving people. The compounding of these rumours, therefore, *Kgosi*, has resulted in jealousy and ill-feeling among villagers."

He took his seat.

It became obvious to the chief that there was something that the gentlemen knew, and therefore he had to be direct and to the point in his responses; he should not allow further input on this matter, lest there be more direct accusations. He decided that he was going to keep a stiff upper lip.

The chief rose to his feet, in direct contradiction to his earlier inference that they all remain seated, as friends. He was smart enough to play with the traditional sentiments of his tribesmen and knew that he had made his point.

"Gentlemen, my children, sons of Moiloa. I've presided over many meetings in my lifetime. I've attended many *makgotla* over the years in my father's place. Never, oh! No, never have I seen such division amongst my people. As a result of this, I have decided to call my most trusted, my most experienced tribesmen, men that I trust are not intimidated and will give me an honest opinion."

He looked at Seemela and then Moabi.

"These rumours did come to my ears, as you know that the chief has his ears on the ground all the time. Your own mother, my wife, raised this rumour-mongering with me when she heard about them. Let me then set the record straight."

He paused and took a glass of water that sat in front of him.

"It is indeed true that from time to time, as it is normal with any chief's residence, that different strangers, at different times, visit for various matters, some of which I resolve and some I refer to my consuls. It is equally true that at times gifts were presented."

He looked behind him and paused.

"You see all these fancy things hanging on the walls of this room, this shield and spear, for example? All were given to me by a gentleman from the Transkei whose father's father was once a priest here in this very village of Dinokana. Nobody ever asked me where I got some of them from. So it is with many artefacts of value that we have in your royal palace.

"Ask any chief and he will tell you that it is normal practice. Is there anything wrong in receiving gifts? This question might also be posed to the aides who work with me who might receive such gifts, but they will at the right time answer for themselves."

There was nodding from around the table, with the exception of Moabi and Seemela, whose body language seemed to suggest that they were not satisfied with the chief's explanation. He was quick to spot this.

"I will urge that we start the business of the day, with the applications that have been tabled. You have the power in your hands to advise me and thereafter formulate conclusions.

"What happens if the decisions that we come to are in contradiction to the rumours you hear? The deals that have been concluded with business people from Zeerust? What will you say? For these decisions will have been taken by you. My children, let us exercise restraint, lest we fall prey to baseless rumour-mongering."

He sat down.

"*Kgosi*. Son of Moiloa, I propose that we delay taking decisions on the Monare matter until such time that we have clarification as to whether Boysie and Kgabalatsana have resolved their differences on the matter," said Kgabo. "As for the other case of the Montsho, I have been informed that neither of the family members could be traced.

"Rumour is that both sons who inherited the land passed away while working in the mines in Hauteng and as we know and see for ourselves, the huts are run down and have not been used for more than twenty years."

"The information given to us by *rre* Kgabo does take us forward. Yes, it does take us forward, and I'm pleased *Kgosi* that we are starting to make progress," said Seemela. "The Monare issue seems to be the one we are not clear about, but I have seen a stranger with a beautiful car these days in Japheth's house."

"It is his younger son, Kgabalatsana, who has recently come back from the big city after a long absence." said the chief.

"Perhaps then, *Kgosi*, it would be easy for the two boys to clarify the issue in the next meeting that might be called," Kgabo suggested.

There was agreement from the table on the last proposal. The chief again realised that there was still an uncomfortable silence among some of the elders, and he suspected that this was not accidental, but deliberate. He moved forward with the discussion.

"What do you then say about the actual applications? How are we supposed to respond to other applications that have been submitted? We have an obligation to respond to them. We are a civilised people who're supposed to respond in a decent manner to other people.

"As to the Monare family misunderstanding, both boys recently paid me a visit. Boysie came to introduce his brother and at the same time to indicate to me that he intended staying at Dinokana now, as he does not have any further intention of returning to the big city of Hauteng, where he spent many years. "

"*Awu!*" exclaimed Moabi from the other side of the table.

"Yes, *rre* Moabi, he does not have any intention of returning to Hauteng. He related to me the pain of having lived in a foreign land without a house of his own, knowing that Japheth left him land on which he could build himself a big house for his family. I, as his father, sympathised with him and have to report here that I promised both brothers that we'll do everything to resolve the matter at the right time.

"I therefore do believe that he should be given back what belonged to the Monares, as there was - or was supposed to have been - no dispute on the matter; thus, we should take it to the *lekgotla,* which I will convene soon. I thank you, my children."

The chief shook hands with all the elders and left the room. They were shocked by the easy manner in which he had resolved the matter. The elders finished eating and discussed how stupid and foolish some of them had been in listening to rumours, instead of raising the matter with the chief directly, long before it surfaced at this meeting. Seemela and Moabi were dumb-founded, not knowing where to hide their faces.

"I'm pleased with myself that I had the courage to raise the matter, late as it might seem. My conscience is clear, and I do believe that the chief will bear me no grudge. Had I not raised the matter, it would have been a different case today," said Seemela.

"Truth is, I'm not sure where I stand, because I believe that I did not put my case as I should have done. I went through a rigmarole which might have left more questions than answers for the chief," said Kgabo.

Young Sentle was enjoying himself listening to the veterans analysing their faults.

"Yes, Moabi missed it completely," he thought. "And he became too emotional."

***

Boysie might have considered his brother's insistence on unearthing a long-buried matter much ado about nothing.

But to Kgabalatsana, the matter of his right to an inheritance left by his father was a matter of life and death – and one over which he had drawn battle lines. The matter preyed on his mind. It was unfortunate for Boysie that his own wife had not taken his side; it was now a battle of wills. Kgabalatsana and Boysie's wife Dikeledi were ranged on one side, and Boysie on the other.

The bone of contention was a piece of land comprising wide-open grassland next to the river – it was known to be one of the most fertile areas in Dinokana. The envy of village inhabitants, it had brought to Japheth Monare, a noble gentleman of the village, much wealth, thanks to his hard work in tilling the patch, which rewarded him with the title of the most successful tribesman of his time.

It was early morning, with shepherds herding their flocks to dewy grasses, and girls carrying buckets of water on their heads, walking carefully up the steep slopes of the riverbank. Dikeledi and Kgabalatsana were out strolling; they came to a stop at a glorious stretch overlooking the river. Flocks of goats and sheeps were dotted about, and cattle scattered as far as the eye could see, grazing.

Emotional and bereft, Kgabalatsana exclaimed: "Is this flock not supposed to have been the livestock of the Monares? Was this grass not grazed by our own? Look now what is happening – it makes my heart bleed. I'm not blaming the poor animals, for they do not know any better. I am lamenting the tragedy that my own blood brother, your husband, has created."

Dikeledi , dressed elegantly in her usual *SeShoeshoe* dress and headscarf, held her brother-in-law by the hand.

"Indeed, this is the land in dispute. This is the very land that your father bequeathed unto you, *rre* Kgabalatsana. I remember so well, when I fell in love with your brother, how proud he used to be of this place. He used to boast to everybody, dreaming about how one day you would come back from the city with money and re-build what your father left for you. How do we resurrect the Monare name in this village? I long for the day when we will bury the hatchet and live together as a happy family."

Kgabalatsana listened carefully, comforted by Dikeledi's support.

"I still cannot believe that this is the work of my own, but he is still my own blood. He is my mother's child, and that I cannot undo. One cannot choose relatives. Even when the devil encroaches into ourselves. Even when men's souls are driven by evil spirits, and integrity ceases."

Dikeledi bowed her head, smiling sadly.

"But remember that he is also my husband and the only one whom I vowed would be so until death and all other things do us part."

Kgabalatsana took his sister-in-law by the hand and walked her away in the direction of the car.

***

Zeerust

In a modestly-furnished house, decorated with typically Indian flare and colour, sat two gentlemen of longstanding association. They laughed and joked affectionately, as though they had not seen each other for some time.

Faisal Patel, Kgabalatsana's friend from West Street, Johannesburg, lounged in a comfortable chair at the far corner of the sumptuous room, while his brother Yusuf sat opposite him, stirring tea thoughtfully.

His wife, Samira, a beautiful woman who enjoyed relating the story of how Yusuf had been blinded by her looks many years ago, in the dusty streets of Fordsburg, laid on a feast of Indian cuisine for the brothers.

"I've not cooked this dish since last you were here, Faisal," she teased. "You know how your mother used to insist that I prepare it when you guys were all together at home? This takes me back there, all the way down memory lane.

"The only problem here in Zeerust, nowadays, is with preparing real Indian food – it is not easy finding the good spices. How I wished that I had known you were coming! Are there still any good spices and curry powders in Fordsburg?"

Faisal grinned at his sister-in-law, of whom he had always been fond.

"As long as there are Indians, there will always be good curry and spices in South Africa. It cannot change, because remember that the country has the biggest Indian community outside India. We are good at bringing in the best cooking goods from any corner of India! But, we in Jo'burg are not so particular, my sister; the Robertson's products are quite good and our taste buds have become used to them!"

"*Ag!* Don't tell me that, Faisal," interrupted Samira. "What is good food without good Indian curry and spices? No, man, you don't know what you're talking about! Eat and enjoy."

She left the two brothers, as she was not in the mood for debate, knowing that she could never win.

Yusuf took a samoosa, eager to continue their prior discussion.

"Tell me Faisal, do you think that this friend of yours is still here in Zeerust? What about this other friend of his, what did you say his name was?"

"David Mokoena."

"That surname sounds familiar."

"Oh! No, brother, grow up - that is almost like the Naidoos amongst the Indians. It is a common surname amongst the southern Sotho group."

"I see you've become such an expert in African languages that you are bound to correct the slightest mistake I make," said Yusuf, mildly jealous of his brother's mastery of African family names.

"You see, brother, David has now become an important link in this business we are working on, as TM has known him for decades and has been his closest friend and confidante. He will come in handy for us. You see, there is a letter TM wrote to me a week ago telling me that his application for the return of the land will be approved at any time now. He and his brother met the chief and they presented the matter and the chief promised that it would be resolved in due course. TM further informed me in the letter that he has told his brother about my - "

"Our," chipped in Yusuf. "Remember that, Faisal, don't cut me out of the business so early in the process, please. Understand that, brother; 'our' involvement."

Yusuf stood up and took off his spectacles, realising that his brother had not even started eating.

"Please eat, brother - Indian food is as good as it is hot!"

Samira walked in and the family sat down together to enjoy what she had prepared, chatting idly about family matters and business in Johannesburg. After the meal, the brothers walked outside to the front of the house.

"Now, brother, tell me then – does this mean that I'll have to withdraw my application because it seems to me, from what you've said, that we don't need to complicate matters for the chief?" asked Yusuf. "We don't need to double-pay when the deal is already on a silver platter for the Patel family – am I correct?"

Yusuf was a wily and detail-oriented businessman. He demanded clear facts and due process before throwing himself into an investment. Faisal knew this and appreciated it.

"You see," he explained, "initially, what was going to happen was that we're buying the land from the chief and thereafter, we'll develop it – but for now, there is no need to do that, because TM wants us to become partners in the development. So, of course we'll build him a house on the same land. Building costs are not huge in rural areas."

Yusuf liked what he was hearing.

"Now I see your plan. It works well for me, if this is what your TM also wants. Yes, let's save the chief's reputation in the eyes of his people; he tried to do what he could. We'll need him in the future, for bigger things. I'll send a message to Tommy, who is well-known to the chief and his aide. I envy you city folks for your fast thinking."

Faisal chuckled. "You see, brother, remember what father used to say about me? That I have eyes like a hawk, business in my veins and how I've survived in that Jo'burg all these years."

Yusuf dismissed his brother's bragging, focusing instead on the golden opportunity within their grasp. They had been working hard without any meaningful business breakthroughs for the past few decades. The tailor shop run by Faisal was a good one, and respectable, but it would not bring the family name into the right circles. The Dinokana deal, however, could.

"Tommy will have to move fast and alert the chief about the application withdrawal," said Faisal. "He might be calling another meeting at any time."

"Fine, brother," Yusuf agreed. "We've got the plan cut out for ourselves now. There's no turning back."

***

The Monare homestead was tensely quiet. How strange that, within such a short space of time, relations between Boysie and his younger brother had changed so dramatically? Only yesterday, they were the apple of each other's eye – living in peace and fraternal happiness.

Dikeledi was no push-over; this had contributed to the general sense of doom and gloom. She was not the type of woman to give up her rights for the sake of her husband – or to keep silent when she knew that something was wrong. Lying in bed as her husband lay sleeping, she turned over the issue in her mind.

Boysie stirred next to her, and she looked at him. He felt a lump rising in his throat, sure that she was about to berate him again. She had become so erratic and unpredictable these days, he thought, as though she had a chip on her shoulder, and blamed him for it all.

"I went to see the land with *rre* Kgabalatsana the other day," she said flatly. "Boysie, he broke my heart; his eyes were brimming with tears from the moment we touched foot on your father's land. He couldn't hide his feelings. Your name is mud, my husband, and you must do something about this. This is not the Boysie I know."

Boysie sighed and returned his wife's resolute gaze.

"You know what he said?" continued Dikeledi. "That you are still and will always remain his elder brother, no matter what. But I've never seen him so hurt. Explain to your sibling, whatever mistake you've committed, that you will make things right. I guarantee you that he'll be the most pleased man on earth for that – he needs you! Remember that you two come from the same womb."

She moved closer to her husband, touching his face with the palm of her hand. Boysie felt a tremor; it had been some time since he had felt the warmth of a woman's hands in bed.

"For the sake of peace in the family, you must tell him the truth," she whispered. "Why you sold the land and what you did with the money. You cannot keep quiet as though nothing has happened."

Boysie's arms enveloped his wife's shoulders, holding her close. She felt a thrill shudder through her – a sense of positive joy not experienced for so long. This was the Boysie she knew; this was like the old days.

"I do not know where to start with the mess that I got myself into," said Boysie after a long while. "The most painful thing is that people think I sold my father's land, squandered the money; when in fact, not a cent changed hands between me and the person who wanted to buy the land.

"People think that the land does not belong to us anymore. No, this is not so! The land still belongs to the Monare family. Let me give you a rundown of what happened. I also owe you an explanation, albeit that this is difficult, because, my wife, I was supposed to have told you all of this long ago."

Boysie felt a wave of relief as he finally unburdened himself to his wife.

"Long time ago, there were people who were interested in acquiring the land, but nothing came of it. To this day, I cannot tell you why, or what happened. We were informed that there were problems with the partners who intended buying it. But, alas! Thanks to our ancestors, this did not materialise.

"At that time, as you will recall, I used to talk about the day when Kgabalatsana would come back and develop the land. I was already dreaming of the money that we would have received from selling part of it, the truth is that he was not telling the truth, for he had no intention to do so. I never thought that my brother would ever come back home again. And, I must be honest, the deal being discussed was for only thirty percent of the land – we would have retained ownership of the rest.

"So, technically, the land still belonged to the Monares – to Kgabalatsana Monare. I must apologise for having been tempted to sell, though. What would I have done with the money? My conscience is quite clear. I swear on Japheth's grave that I would have kept it for my brother and you, my wife, would have been told about it."

Dikeledi – relieved, overjoyed and choked with emotion – kissed her husband and stroked his back tenderly; it was as though she had found a new love. His body relaxed against hers, gratefully. He was home again.

"That will relieve *rre* Kgabalatsana; he will be so pleased to hear about this news you've shared with me tonight, *rra*."

Boysie nodded. "Yes. Let's wait to see what the outcome of the *lekgotla* will be – but I'm confident that the chief will resolve the matter."

***

In Alexandra

"How could I at this hour of the day?" MamTshawe shouted so loudly that it was possible for the neighbours in the backyard house to hear her. She had seen a lady dressed in smart-casual attire disembarking from a taxi in front of her house. MamTshawe was seated on the verandah as Nancy came through the gate.

She called to her next-door neighbour, MamTsamaye, who came rushing from her house, overjoyed to see Nancy. They walked together into MamTshawe's sitting room, the two older ladies sandwiching Nancy between them on the sofa.

"Just look at our child, MamTsamaye; we were talking about her just yesterday, saying that she will turn up one of these days."

"Exactly, *mosadi*, it was only yesterday, but look at her, there must be someone already looking well after her, otherwise how could she keep her beauty during what is supposed to be hard times for her?"

They all laughed, with Nancy rather looking shy.

"Children do not discuss matters of love with their mothers. You make me feel shy, you two," she said, blushing.

"These are women from the township, my child, we're not rural women and we understand these things, remember we have been down the same road. Tell us then, what made you think of us after such a long absence?"

"I was coming from work and seeing that it was still early, I thought of passing by to greet you guys. Is there anything wrong with that?"

"Oh no! Nothing wrong, but everything right," responded the curious ladies simultaneously.

"Did I not tell you that she would never forget us, Kgabalatsana or not Kgabalatsana, she is part of us?" said MamTshawe, beaming.

"By the way, *magogo*, before I forget." There was a sudden pause as if she had forgotten something; curious, MamTsamaye interrupted Nancy, as though knowing what she was about to say.

"Ha-ha! There it comes, proceed, for I know what it is." MamTshawe also sensed what her friend was referring to, and she answered Nancy's question before it was asked.

"He left, that foolish man of yours, Nancy," said MamTshawe, "and I have to confess that it is really better now that he is out of my sight. Out of sight, out of mind, as they say, because he was starting to bore me."

Nancy's facial expression changed rapidly, as she absorbed the news. This wasn't what she had expected – not at all. The two old ladies saw that she was shocked.

"*Hawu*! Why does it seem that you're disappointed?" asked MamTshawe. But Nancy couldn't reply. She murmured, blushed, and asked to be excused momentarily. Leaving the ladies, she went through the kitchen door towards TM's place. MamTshawe followed her, pressed keys into her hand, and returned to the house.

"He said he would be back, but did not tell us when," MamTshawe called over her shoulder. "Let us take him at his word."

Nancy opened the door slowly. She took a step backwards, hands to her mouth, as she took in the space. Dirty dishes were piled in untidy stacks on the table.

"Clearly, these have been unwashed for days," she muttered to herself. She opened a pot and worms spilled out of the rotting food. She threw the lid on the floor in disgust.

"I do not believe that he has been staying here like this since I left!"

Gladys' remarks at the bus stop were a sharp reminder to her that men could not be trusted. She took an apron hanging behind the door and started working through the mess. She attended quickly to the chores. She had been doing this, in the same house, for many years, so why not now? TM or no TM, as MamTshawe liked to say, she would do what she had to do to win him back. After hours of cleaning TM's mess, she collapsed wearily onto the crumpled bedding on the floor.

Nancy's mind meandered back to the day when they had first met. She had been an innocent young high school student but had grown to love the man. The events of their quarrels all came back to her mind. Thinking of TM, she fell asleep, awoken hours later by the alarm clock ringing on the table. She started, thinking that she was at home, and then realising that she was still at TM's.

Looking through the window, she saw that the sun had risen already and that neighbours were already making their way to work, or hanging up washing. Luckily, she had a day off. After washing and which she did in record time, she left the house, cursing: "Damn it, making a fool of myself again. What was I doing here and what are the neighbours going to think of me?"

Chapter 18

A Plan is Hatched

In Alex

It was early evening, and Alexandra Township was quiet, with the exception of the usual screeching of car tyres from the odd reckless driver.   Aunty Thando, Gladys and Nancy were seated close together on a sofa in Thando's house. Facing them was a television display cabinet, below which was a compartment in which stood a turn-table record player. Filtering through the speakers was the last part of a popular track.

Nancy stood up as the record stopped. It reminded her of TM, as it was his all-time favourite song, and she knew each and every part of it by heart. She put her head in her arms as Gladys pulled out a tissue and wiped her wet face. She had been crying a lot, lately, and both her aunt and Gladys could guess what was on her mind.

"Just stop behaving like a school girl who has lost her lover," her aunt would reprimand her, but to no avail.

"Tears and sorrow are not going to solve the situation that you are in, my dear," said Gladys to her friend. At that point, she had decided to play tough, hoping that this would scare and intimidate her, but the trick did not work.

"You are too hard on yourself. Believe me, he will come back, there is no way that he can survive village life, after all, there can't be any life for him there, not with you here, it's just a matter of days and you'll see him coming in. Dinokana is no longer a place for him. He just had a spell of nostalgia about some place that he once knew. Jozi is in his veins; we have been part of his life," said Aunt Noluthando, as she walked to the record player to change the record.

Nancy started sobbing like a child again. "Why is he then not even phoning? Why has he not even sent a telegram to say what you are saying? What have I done to TM that has made him suddenly walk away from me?"

Thando stood up and looked at her niece, recalling their tough discussions about the man.

"My niece has really become a child," she thought to herself, as she took a glass of water from a bucket that stood on the table.

She then took a pile of records and started sorting them one by one, looking for a record that she knew would remind Nancy of the good old days. A record that would bring back memories of her boyfriend during the jolly good times that seemed to have passed by.

She found the right one, wiping it gently on her blouse and then turning it around twice in her hands, before slotting it onto the turn-table. A Kippie Moeketsi tune came through the speakers. She took Nancy with both hands and swung her onto the floor and they started dancing, with Gladys watching them enviously, such good dancers were they.

The trick worked well, as Nancy's mood improved rapidly, and she became the Nancy of old within seconds. It was like a load had been lifted from her shoulders.

Then she slumped down again, as the music finished. "Why does it have to happen to me, but why me? Just a telegram from him would have helped."

"Come on, big girl," laughed Gladys, "you know the man better than us all, by now he has to drive hundreds of kilometres to the nearest shop, or perhaps to Zeerust, to make a telephone call. I would imagine that he has so much to do, seeing old family members, friends and trying to re-orient himself to a place he once knew."

"Relax and be at home, you are with a relative and a great friend here," said Thando. "Nancy, you know by now that I don't usually agree with this TM prattle and I'm aware that you had your back to the wall several times and you bounced back, but still, I gave you my support.

"Having said that, I fully support Gladys in saying that you need to relax and she has a point when she says you couldn't have been without better friends.

"Shall we say what TM did to you was an act of God, and I really mean it? One day when we meet again, he will have to explain and perhaps we'll find solace in his explanation. Gladys, my dear, shall we change the subject and let us enjoy ourselves and forget about TM?"

Gladys moved away from the two relatives and walked to the door, where she hung over the lower part, lost in thought.

"You are also such a confusing little thing, my Nancy. You know what real women do in times like these, and do not get me wrong, I am not for a moment suggesting that you do it; but to make a man angry and jealous, you fake an affair with another man and in most cases, this trick works for women - and you see the bugger running back to where he disappeared from.

"Oh, and there are also those two friends of his, one Sparks and Joseph; I wonder if I should not meet them, especially Sparks, because at least I know where he stays and that he is not far from here.

"Just leave everything to us and we'll make a plan. You know the old saying: '*n Boer maak 'n plan*' (a farmer makes a plan). And just recently a friend of mine taught me another one that Coloureds say, and that is: '*n boesman het 'n plan* (a Coloured person has a plan). Take it from me, I have a plan, too."

Nancy sniffed, wiping her eyes.

"What am I? And what would I be without you, aunty, and Gladys? You are such an inspiration in my life, more so in the last few days, you really fit the bill. Can you imagine my loneliness in the last two months without anything, just tossing and tossing in bed as if a mad dog, unable to sleep?

OK, you said that we should forget about this, so why then do I pester you? Let's just forget about everything."

"That's what I said long time ago!" said Aunty Thando, laughing.

Outside the house, a sparkling BMW drove into Noluthando's street, driving slowly and then stopping in front of the house, hooting twice. Nancy peered through the curtain. Aunty Thando and Gladys looked at each other, rather taken by surprise.

"Are you waiting for someone?" asked her aunt.

"Guys, I am sorry I have to leave, it's my transport."

She rushed into her room, took her jersey from the bed and walked out of the door, followed by her aunt and friend, who were curious to see the mysterious visitor. As they reached the car, Gladys remarked:

"I knew it would happen."

"What would happen?" asked Nancy. "Gladys, don't jump to conclusions, please."

Then, she introduced the driver.

"Manuel, these are my closest friends – the ones I have been telling you about."

Manuel greeted Aunt Thando and Gladys, speaking English in a strong Mozambican accent. The two responded courteously. Nancy stepped lightly into the passenger seat, waved goodbye and was off.

Manuel's car came to stop in front of a house at 2nd Avenue. He gave her a smile, expecting what he assumed would be a gift from heaven, something that he had tried but failed with many of the Jo'burg women whom he had met so far since arriving in Jo'burg from Mozambique. Again, he was proven wrong, for Nancy did not respond, but rather asked:

"But Manuel, this is not a cinema, whose place is this and why do we have to come here?"

"It belongs to my aunt who is on holiday in Maputo, I am looking after it."

"And so, what has that to do with me? Don't you think you are taking me for granted? We are not in love, Manuel, we are just friends."

"I did not mean it that way, Nancy."

"Please take me back home then; you have just spoiled my evening."

He obeyed the instruction without a word, fearing that he might spoil his future chances. Switching on the ignition, he skidded back towards Nancy's aunt's home.

Nancy got out of the car without a word, banged the door, and walked through the yard, not turning around once. He stared after her, speechless.

She found her aunt sitting alone.

"And what happened, I thought it was a date?"

"Men like to take advantage of us women and I am not that type, after all, he is not even my type, just imagine what my friends will think of me when they hear that TM's girlfriend is in love with a man like him?"

Outside, Manuel was still quite perplexed about what had just happened to him.

"Welcome to Jozi," he thought to himself. "You were warned to be cautious with Jozi women."

He pulled away, disheartened.

Inside her room, Nancy was shocked and disappointed with herself for having allowed the man to pick her up. She switched on the lights and took a glass of water that was on her dressing table, sipping it gently.

Slipping into her nightdress, she went to bed. Sprawled across the double mattress, she cast her eyes over the multi-coloured perfume brands littering the dressing table, the high mirror, and the big vase of flowers. Tears welled, and she ploughed her head into a big pillow.

"Damn, TM, why do this to me?"

Switching off the light, she went to sleep. Her rest was disturbed by another eventful dream. She was walking hand-in-hand with TM through central Johannesburg, entering the Carlton Centre to watch a late evening movie. As TM bent to kiss her, his face changed into Manuel's, and she refused to kiss him. Nancy woke up with a start.

***

In Zeerust

Kgabalatsana was on his first social outing since he had arrived back home and in his flashy Dodge sedan, cruised through the quiet streets, undisturbed by occasional cars passing by. Kgabalatsana was not courting the day-time recognition that he usually received, so he enjoyed driving at night now. Once bitten, twice shy – he had learned his lesson, thanks to the small-town white cop. Villagers hated loud music, and they were happy to tell him so.

The sky was patched with thousands of tiny stars, making a mockery of the street and shop lights on the main street of the small Western Transvaal town. Next to Kgabalatsana, sipping a juice with a long straw, was Nthabiseng.

"What a romantic evening. What a place!" murmured Kgabalatsana. "If it is not heaven, then I do not know. What else does a man want but a chick like you next to him?"

Nthabiseng responded with a satisfied smile.

"I did not know the romantic side of you, you've surprised me, and perhaps it was too soon for me, as I had long erased you from my mind, years ago when you disappeared. Do you still remember how I warned you about that city? Things you learn on the way as you grow hardly disappear from the subconscious mind – romanticism being one of them."

They came to a stop in front of the Zeerust Hotel as he opened the door on her side and led her out of the car. She was flattered by her newly-returned boyfriend's mannerisms and tender care.

"Men from the big cities are indeed more civilised than the rural lot; never have I been treated the way this man is treating me. But there is a lot that he has to explain," she thought. "I hope that this will lead to greater things."

They walked into a large, opulently-decorated and ritzy country town hotel reception room. Brightly lit, with chandeliers hanging from the high ceiling, there were oil paintings depicting the pride the owner had in this majestic place, and how much he valued his clients. He was predominantly patronised by the richest of farmers in the district and some urban visitors from the surrounding towns and Johannesburg. The local black population had no means with which to entertain themselves in such grand places. Some would take their chances by dressing in a manner that would give them an impression of not being locals. As a result of these factors: Kgabalatsana walked into the hotel and found, on comfortable sofas, two gentlemen, who, when they saw Kgabalatsana, jumped from their seats to greet him excitedly. These were the typical 'hang-about' locals, meeting or just talking to patrons from the cities and bigger towns.

They suspected that this black man was from *eGoli* (Johannesburg) and might open doors and connections for them. After all, he was clearly not from a village. This misperception was, at times, quite common in rural, small-town South Africa. Kgabalatsana knew this but relished being associated with such trivialities. He introduced Nthabiseng to the gentlemen, who seemed to know her, but who did not pay her much attention, as they viewed her as one of them.

"Welcome *bra* (brother), welcome *sis* (sister)," said the men in unison. Kgabalatsana acknowledged them politely, with a curt nod, but walked past and away from them to seats at the bar.

"What do you think of the place, my dear? Is it OK?"

"Well, it's the best in town and I have been here only once, during the day, when we had a work conference, but by and large, I have heard of it, and only good things. But it reminds me of the big hotels of Mafikeng where I worked for a short while after you deserted me."

A waiter came to take their orders.

"By the way, *rre* Kgabalatsana, do you know, or have they already told you, that I work at the same place as your sister-in-law in the village? You will perhaps know by now that in the small villages here, news spreads like wild fire. And most of the time, with no differentiation between fact and fiction.

"For example, my cousin yesterday told me that when they were at the river fetching water, she overheard two girls talking about a young Monare who had come back from the white men's city of Johannesburg and that this man left the village many years ago. I was horror-struck by this piece of information, though at the same time, must confess that it excited me that you were around. You know, we have so much to talk about, things about me, yourself and the little one."

Kgabalatsana looked at Nthabiseng thoughtfully for a few moments, and then seemed to lose focus, turning his eyes away from her. Finally, he spoke.

"There is a lot we need to talk about and I hope that this is just going to be the beginning of the long road to Jericho."

"I have been waiting for the start of this journey for some time now, *rra*, as Rethabiseng, our daughter, has a multitude of questions with no answers. But, of course, there are other elements in our relationship that I would not want to delve into right now – that which my parents asked me not to delve into, but I must.

"I do believe that you would know that Kgabalatsana Monare and Nthabiseng Rethabile are siblings and that is where we come in, and leading to that, these siblings have a child. This element within the jigsaw puzzle needs the two of us and nobody else. The big question, therefore, *rre* Kgabalatsana, is how we are going to solve this seemingly intricate dilemma? What does the Monare custom dictate in this regard?"

Kgabalatsana's face turned grey and beads of sweat appeared on his forehead. Nthabiseng realised that it was not possible for him to deal with the issue right now.

"All these questions need not be answered immediately, but in the very near future, *rra*."

She handed him a tissue and let the matter drop.

They remained at the hotel until late in the evening and retreated back to the village when they were satisfied that they had bonded enough and intermittently had reflected on some of the sticky issues. As grown-ups, they agreed that they would have to be discreet about being seen in public until they had come closer to resolving the problem confronting them.

It had been a long, emotionally-draining night, but Kgabalatsana was satisfied with the outcome.

Clearly, he did not know what to expect from Nthabiseng; after all, he was the one who had ditched her.

But, as he drove home, his mind wandered without direction through the decades that he had spent in Johannesburg. And he asked himself the question: "Was it worthwhile? Did I make the right decision by leaving the city? What does the future hold for me on this mother earth? Look what my elder brother has done for himself and his wife – he is now a teacher with a secure job, the wife working at the clinic. Nthabiseng is better off than when I left her.

"After all, human beings have a thousand unanswered questions; life is never complete until the end of one's being in this world." As Boysie and Dikeledi was preparing to sleep, realising that Kgabalatsana might not come back home, he thought to himself; 'My brother must have developed urban manners, how comforting it would have been if had spent his first night with the family,' as the wife extinguish the paraffin lamp next to their bed.

In the morning when Kgabalatsana arrived home, he parked the car in the yard, opened walked into the house to find Boysie, passing and his sister-in-law who was busy preparing breakfast. His brother was waiting for him.

"Kgabalatsana Johannes Monare, the youngest son of Japheth and Josephine Monare. Good morning little brother. Have a seat, breakfast is almost ready, your sister-in-law has been slowing down her pace and I suspect she has been waiting for you, otherwise by this time I would have long had my breakfast."

"Morning, *mme*." Kgabalatsana greeted his sister-in-law

"Morning, *rra*, your brother has been so talkative since your arrival, he has been eagerly waiting for you, I do not think he slept well."

"My brother takes life too seriously, *mme*," responded Boysie. The lady invited the brothers to the table, and proceeded to serve them their breakfast.

It was breakfast time in the Monare household and the two brothers continued the practices of their upbringing, as passed on from their parents: a developed understanding wherein all family members eat together, come rain or shine; and if one member has not indicated his or her absence from the table, the meal would not commence.

To Boysie, family was like a forest; from outside, it appears dense, but once inside, everybody can be seen to have his or her own singular position. He therefore understood why his wife had delayed breakfast; it was an adherence to this entrenched, time-honoured culture. All African families have their own beliefs, customs and ways of doing things – and this had been the Monare way.

Kgabalatsana, though, felt that he was coming apart at the seams. This happy family tableau made him feel like a fish out of water. He was happy to be served breakfast by his sister-in-law, but he still felt out of place.

"This reminds me so much of days gone by, when mama was still alive and when we used to fetch wood from the fields, water from the river, clean the hearth and fill the pots with water in order to ease things for the old lady before she started cooking meals," Boysie said.

Kgabalatsana remembered this fondly.

"Yes, cooking could only be done by her and nobody else. It looks like my sister-in-law has taken over that tradition."

True, thought Boysie, but the old days were gone.

"It was for this reason that I decided to take her place," said Dikeledi. "I used to watch her attentively from my first day of married life in this household. She would continue doing whatever she was doing without uttering a word – but if I dared disappear, she would ask, 'Where is Makoti (daughter-in-law)?'"

"Yes, indeed," replied Kgabalatsana. "I understand it all, we have talked about them since they left us for a world we do not know."

They continued eating in companionable silence. After clearing his plate, Kgabalatsana stretched and thanked Dikeledi.

"Good people, as you know, I have not been home for quite some time and I want to take a long walk around the place, reminding myself of my childhood days, when I played games with my peers, swam in the river and played sticks."

Boysie nodded. "That is understandable, little brother, you have all the time at your disposal."

He released his brother from the table, and Kgabalatsana set off to explore.

Chapter 19

There Was Gold After All!

In the centre of Zeerust, a taxi rank dominated, with dozens of cars carrying commuters to and fro, crisscrossing in all directions as they competed for passengers. A Johannesburg-registered taxi drove slowly into the parking lot of the taxi rank, negotiating passengers who were ignoring clearly marked white-and-black pedestrian crossing stripes. Hawkers sold an assortment of goods, such as fruit, sweets and wristwatches, shouting loudly for custom.

A shoeshine boy was busy polishing the shoes of a traveller, while a woman pushily offered her fruit wares to roaming customers. It was a truly African market, resplendent with a kaleidoscope of colours that beautified the rank-and-file ordinariness of a downtown weekday.

The Jo'burg taxi slowed to a halt. The driver hopped out, opening the door for a lady in a snow-white dress and matching shoes. She contrasted sharply with the women of Zeerust. Wearing a big, wide-brimmed straw hat, her glamour radiated. She looked in all directions, clearly a newcomer – and probably lost.

The driver handed her a suitcase as she paid his fare. She crossed the road, ignoring the wolf whistles and calls of the naughty young boys as they pounced on the sight of a new girl in town. Instead, she sought out another taxi – and a more mature man of whom to ask directions.

"Are these taxis by any chance going in the direction of the Zeerust Hotel?" she asked. "And are they the same ones going to the village of Dinokana?"

The man knew, instantly, that she was a new girl and definitely not from this part of the world.

"They go anywhere, my sister. You give me your destination and I fly you there. I run the best in town," he bragged.

The door was already flung open for the lady to hop in, and she did. After a few minutes' drive, the car stopped at the Zeerust Hotel. She was deposited on the verandah, where a porter took her luggage. Walking through to the hotel reception lounge, the lady approached an old man seated behind the counter. He stood up slowly as the porter rang the bell. Taking out his registry book, the man smiled a greeting and scrolled through the pages, looking for the lady's name.

"Good afternoon, madam Mabheka, welcome to the Zeerust Hotel – the jewel and pride of Zeerust."

"Good afternoon, sir," she responded.

"Oh, yes, Ms Mabheka from the Golden City. How I wish I were you, madam; I always envy people from the civilised world."

He scribbled in his book, took his payment and then called for a room key bearing Nancy's name and room number.

"Scott, please take Miss Mabheka to Room 202 on the Presidential floor."

"Yes, sir!" the porter responded, quick and efficient.

Nancy and her porter travelled by lift to floor number two.

When they reached the room, she found it lush and inviting. Candelabras dotted almost every surface, and the marble floor was covered in thick Persian rugs. The furniture was Indonesian wood and the walls adorned with paintings by George Pemba and Gerald Sekoto.

"Wow. It's a living heaven!" gasped Nancy.

"Yes, madam, this is our *crème de la crème* suite for top guests," gushed the porter, quite smitten by Nancy already. Her eyes swept over the luxurious, king-sized bed, puffed with soft, white silk bedding and dozens of plump continental pillows – enough to keep one wrapped up in bed all day.

"Through this door is the bathroom."

Scott the porter ushered her through, where she found gold taps, marbled sinks and tiles and the softest, most decadent towels. The bathroom was bigger than her bedroom in Alexandra.

Nancy thanked the porter, gave him a generous tip, and shut the door, turning immediately towards the bed. After relishing the womb-like comfort of the mattress and duvet, she briskly unpacked – and then settled down for a long afternoon nap.

***

At the same time, late in the evening Kgabalatsana's car cruised through the quiet streets of Zeerust, his second outing since he arrived in his hometown. He was dressed in a white suit, black shirt, red bowtie and white straw hat. On his feet were the signature brown-and-white Crocket & Jones shoes. Next to him was Nthabiseng in a soft, silken dress, white shoes and a light black jumper slung around her shoulders.

The two were quiet, occasionally glancing at each other. Nthabiseng wondered why Kgabalatsana wasn't saying much. What she didn't know was that his mind was elsewhere – in Johannesburg.

He kept a stiff upper lip all the while, trying to gain control of his thoughts and feelings. At that moment, she patted him on the right thigh, startling him.

"Gosh! You scared the hell out of me, girl," quipped Kgabalatsana. "What a beautiful evening, what an inspiring tranquility, no cars, no hawkers and beggars? Quality of life, my dear, that's what a man needs after such a long spell in the city."

"Women and the lot especially," retorted Nthabiseng teasingly, looking at him from the corner of her eye.

A short distance down the road, the neon lights heralded the majestic Zeerust Hotel. Kgabalatsana slowed down and swung the car into a side street.

"I thought that you had forgotten where you were going," laughed the lady, all smiles.

Kgabalatsana opened Nthabiseng's door and the couple walked towards the hotel entrance. They went straight to the dining area, pausing to look at the evening menu.

Unnoticed, an attractive woman in a wide-brimmed hat was seated almost behind the door. She couldn't be recognised, owing to the hat. Nancy was sipping her juice, in no hurry to go anywhere or talk to anyone. She had all the time in the world, and she knew what her mission was. As she lifted her eyes to look around the room, she saw the very man whom she had come so far to see. He was sitting with another woman. So! She had caught her fish without any effort. Gladys' words echoed: "It is a small place, and you should easily locate him."

The ease with which she had found him was rooted in her intimate knowledge of TM's character. Where else would a man of his nature entertain himself in a small, dusty town? He was not the type to hole himself up in the village, and it was for this reason that she had chosen the Zeerust Hotel as her first port of call, certain that this was where she would hook her fish. At her first glance, she became hot under the collar, but fought to keep her cool. And kept her fingers crossed.

Meanwhile, Kgabalatsana had his own suspicions too, but he didn't recognise her; not yet. Only her body seemed familiar: the way she held herself, the way she dressed. Nthabiseng followed his eyes, noticing the woman.

"She is definitely not from this part of the world," thought Nthabiseng. She patted Kgabalatsana on the back.

Kgabalatsana muttered to himself, "Beauty attracts men sooner than gold."

She overheard his remark, and they both laughed.

Nancy appeared to hear the laugh. She looked up and was annoyed. Perhaps they were laughing at her? Slowly, she put down her knife and fork, pulled up her hat slightly, with every intention of being recognised now, and called to the waiter to place an order.

"Make it a Nederburg merlot, sir," she said. Moments later, as the glass of wine was delivered, she took a sip, straightened her body-hugging dress, and got up to walk over to Kgabalatsana. His eyes bulged as he saw her coming towards them. His stomach lurched and heaved. Nthabiseng noticed his apparent distress and looked over to see Nancy. Kgabalatsana was beside himself with emotion and confusion.

The lady stretched out her hand to greet Nthabiseng. "Beautiful one, what is your name?"

"Nthabiseng, *mme*."

Nancy then turned to TM.

"*Dumela, rra*."

"*Dumela, mme*," TM replied.

Kgabalatsana's throat closed. He was out of breath. Nancy noticed the terrified look on his face and this pleased her. Seeing the once-wise man of Alex so flustered and intimidated by her presence was a triumph, particularly in front of his apparent girlfriend. What had happened to the Toppie Manoja mentality?

Or was this what rural towns did to the 'clever men' of the cities?

"Good evening, people, sorry to disturb your privacy," she said sweetly, not taking her eyes of TM. "My name is Stella and I'm from Cape Town. This is my first time in the beautiful town of Zeerust. I've just arrived this afternoon and I'm on my way to Lobatse in Botswana for a few days."

She stretched out her hand to TM, bending slightly as a mocking sign of respect. As their hands touched, she commented, "Your hand is sweating, *rra*. What is the matter? Would you guys mind if a stranger joined you, seeing that there is a spare chair? My table is rather secluded from the crowds."

"I see no harm," responded Nthabiseng innocently, kissing Kgabalatsana on the cheek.

"I hope you don't mind, *moratiwa* (darling)," Nancy said in a syrupy tone, but secretly irritated.

"Who is this girl who has become a thorn in my side?" she thought.

"You're ever so liberal with our precious time, my dear," said Kgabalatsana, as he lifted his eyes to look at her.

"She said her name was Stella, Stella from Cape Town," said Nthabiseng.

"There are still some private matters to be discussed and a third party might be privy to things she does not need to hear. We'll call you in due course. Don't worry, for the evening is still young and we will be here for some time."

"Please don't get me wrong, I did not mean to disrupt your precious privacy, and of course your romantic evening. I'll hear from you," said Nancy, as she turned and walked away, sashaying her behind and attracting the attention of every man in the room.

Nthabiseng sighed with relief after she left.

"Wow! What a brave doll. Out of the blue, straight to our table. Bang! But why did she choose us amongst all the guests?"

"Who knows?" Kgabalatsana was tongue-tied as he watched Nancy take her chair on the opposite side of the room.

"Does she not remind you of the dolls of Jozi?"

"As you heard her, she is from Cape Town and they are a different kettle of fish, typical Xhosa women, beautiful, brave, and daring," said Kgabalatsana, smiling at Nthabiseng. He had every intention of honouring his promise to call Nancy over once his private discussions with Nthabiseng were concluded.

True to his word, they later found themselves seated

on reception hall sofas with a number of other guests and patrons, though slightly apart from the rest. Nancy was cool as a cucumber, as though butter wouldn't melt in her mouth; Kgabalatsana had his head in the clouds and a vacant, worried expression, and Nthabiseng had metamorphosed into a social butterfly.

"You are in for it, Kgabalatsana, this is your day. And you have a lot to tell," Nancy thought to herself, as her eyes fixed on the rapscallion whom she loved.

Kgabalatsana called the waiter. "First things first, and what about the ladies tonight?"

Nancy gave him a wry smile, and responded, "My usual...."

"Which is?" asked Nthabiseng, jokingly, still at that stage not suspecting any connection between the two.

"Gin and tonic!" chirruped Nancy, not wanting to spoil the fun so early in the evening. "And I can guess that the *umnumzana* (gentleman) will have a brandy and coke."

Nthabiseng looked at Nancy and then at Kgabalatsana, puzzled.

"You know my stuff, lady," he said. "Well, any South African lady would have guessed what type of drink a guy of my stature drinks."

"What a stereotyping of South African men," said Nthabiseng. She turned to Nancy, curious to know who this brave and ultra-confident lady was.

"Well, stranger, can you tell us about yourself and life in the *Kaap,* the Cape?"

Nancy took a sip from her glass, ready for some fun. "Are you sure you want to know, madam?"

"Nthabiseng. You can call me Nthabiseng," she interjected.

"Well, Nthabiseng. It's a long story which I am not sure you want to hear, as it could take me the whole evening to relate. You see, my dear, I've been around. But seeing that you've already asked me, it would only be civil of me to respond."

She opened her hand bag and TM's eyes bulged, hoping that she was not going to do what he thought she was going to do.

Nancy took out her identity book and dropped it in front of Nthabiseng. An unexpected bombshell, Kgabalatsana thought to himself. His lips shivered and sweat dropped from his forehead; he took a gulp of his drink. Nthabiseng was surprised by the lady's action and as she was about to open the identity book, remarked:

"What a funny way of introducing oneself. Or is it Cape style?" She nevertheless, out of courtesy, rather than curiosity, opened the ID book, read it and then let it drop from her hands onto the table, as though it had burned her.

"So, this is it!" she shouted at Kgabalatsana. "Is it so? Am I right? Tell me, *rre* Kgabalatsana, that I'm wrong?"

Kgabalatsana was irritated by Nancy's prolonged gamesmanship. He remained quiet, not knowing where to start, for all hell had broken loose. Nancy took a sip from her glass, enjoying herself and smiling at her TM.

Nthabiseng pulled Nancy aside and whispered in her ear. "So, you lied to me about being from Cape Town and about your name, *nogal*?"

"Yes, I did, my dear. And there was a reason for that, if you care to know. I thought your 'honest' boyfriend was going to make use of the few minutes' grace when I left you in the dining hall and I thought that he was going to tell you the truth about me.

"True to his age-old tricks, he did not. Maybe he was too scared that you might leave him as he unceremoniously dumped me in Johannesburg. I was warned before of the likes of him, but I never heeded the warnings."

"Is it not strange that we women never learn?" Nthabiseng was, by this time, starting to realise what game the man had been up to, but she continued.

"For your information, stranger. He told me everything about you the very first time we met, and in one or two letters that he wrote to me while he was with you in Johannesburg," said Nthabiseng, the lies tripping off her tongue.

"Well, he always likes playing big in a small town. That has been his signature, but I hope he has learnt that there are things that he should learn from others," said Nancy, philosophically.

"Nthabiseng, our boyfriend left scars in that Johannesburg. He left women like me in a ditch. He served a two-year sentence in prison. I hope he has had the time to tell you all these things. I have been his life-time partner, with two abortions, but he had the audacity to just leave me in the lurch and disappear into thin air, Nthabiseng. I am black and blue because of this man of yours."

At that juncture, Kgabalatsana called a waitress. "Will you bring a glass of juice please?" Nthabiseng took the opportunity to try to clear up the mystery.

"You're gold, Nancy. You're an angel. You're beautiful and intelligent and have all the necessary qualities of a woman well brought up. Kgabalatsana needs a person like you; he needs a partner who can take him through the niceties and difficulties of life and I'm not sure if I can do that. You see, it is usually said that love can be blind and we have been in love for such a very long time, while on the other side we have been apart for that very long time. I think this has been the drawback, for love turned me blind; things that I could have seen were hidden from me by Cupid.

"I believe that you offer that hope for him, I would never have been in a position to deal with this matter the way you did. You've opened my mind; you've unravelled something in me which I've been trying to figure out since his arrival. I never knew what brought him back from Johannesburg after all these years. He never told me either, but again, let me at the same time give him the benefit of doubt."

She looked at Kgabalatsana said: "You see Nancy, you are *Ouboetie* Kgabalatsana's best hope. He needs you, but there are many things that he will have to learn, though I am not sure if he has not already been so taken over by city mentality that there is nothing that he thinks he can learn from we rural people. For your sake, Nancy.

"Let me tell you a secret and this might help you also in future, for you to internalise," She sipped her cooldrink, and smiled. "*Rre* Kgabalatsana is a victim of village intrigue, but I want to believe that he does not have a clue, as many in the village do not. I am not even sure how many people know the truth about his situation, except perhaps his brother.

"A few years ago, I used to work for a man in Mafikeng, who was in property development – a very rich and successful businessman with lots of connections in the region. I say so because he had lots of friends with lots of connections in the region. His house was frequented by councillors, chiefs, politicians, priests from all over the place. One afternoon, this rich man, my boss, who knew that I was from Dinokana, was fishing for information about land availability there."

"You see, Nancy, I don't know if your boyfriend ever told you about rumours going around regarding the wealth in the area of Dinokana. As a result of this rumour, there was a scramble by business people and investors. The Monare land became one of the targetted pieces of land, more so because it is near the river, where many people believe that there are alluvial diamonds.

"As I said, there was no doubt that my boss was always talking the hindleg off a donkey – and because of his wealth, he expected people to dance to his tune. He also did not see eye to eye with some rich people in Mafikeng. Thus, he created a lot of enemies who vowed that they would 'sort him out one day'.

"Indeed, this did happen, for he lost favour with none other than the Mayor of Zeerust. Apparently, the deal went sour at a critical stage when negotiations were about to be concluded. I later learnt that the Dinokana deal was never concluded, contrary to popular belief and contrary to rumours that the land of the Monares was sold and that uncle Boysie had got a lot of money out of that deal."

She looked at Kgabalatsana and wiped her eyes. Both Nancy and Kgabalatsana were stunned, to the point of being paralysed by the information that Nthabiseng was churning out.

"When you talk to some people in the village and in Zeerust, they believe that uncle Boysie stashed the money under the floor of the kraal and with some he built himself the house on part of the plot."

Kgabalatsana felt faint and sweaty. Nancy pulled a tissue out of her handbag and gave it to him.

"Furthermore, information went on to suggest that my boss had a contact in the village – one whom he used as his front man, as he could not buy land there by himself. The front man was going to register the land in his name, so as not to draw attention to my boss. The front man was rumoured to be close to our chief in Dinokana and the person who was going to register the land in his name was one of the councillors of the chief.

"The long and the short of it is that no contract was signed, and the matter dwindled, and nothing ever materialised. The businessman went to live in Kimberley and later died. And the interesting thing is that no one even amongst the elders wanted to touch this news for, putting a stamp on selling *ntate* Japhet's land would have been tantamount to backstabbing him, and this would have hurt every soul in the village for he was a revered man."

Nthabiseng looked at Kgabalatsana, weighing up how her news was affecting him. He rose to his feet, putting down the long empty beer bottle that was warm in his sweating hand, and began panting like a wild dog, and asked; "Why did you not tell me all this before, Nthabiseng?"

Her response was: "Who am I to delve into another family's matters? As I said, not even the elders wanted to touch this, so why should I have let the cat out of the bag? Would I or anybody who tried to unravel this not have exposed herself as a victim? I was taught by my late father never to volunteer information unnecessarily, for it might turn against you. Secondly, you never asked me about this although I am not sure whether I would have told you anyway."

"But why then are you telling us now?" he said, frustrated, relieved and offended.

Nthabiseng continued, in conclusion: "Even now at this hour, I am just helping a lame and ignorant dog over a stile in the hope that he will know how to handle the information, more so that the name of his brother is mentioned."

Kgabalatsana could not think of a word in reply

At this juncture, Nancy clasped Nthabiseng's hand, the women bonded by their stories. Suddenly, Nancy looked at her wristwatch and exclaimed: "It is time for me to go."

She opened her bag and took out a letter, getting up to hand it to Kgabalatsana, who was now seated a few steps away on the sofa with his daughter.

"Will you read this for the sake of Nthabiseng?" she asked him, sincerely and without anger.

Anybody observing the scene would have been struck by how mute, crestfallen and broken the man was, since the women had begun sharing their stories. Nonetheless, he nodded, and tore open the envelope.

The letter was from Aunty Thando and Gladys, telling him what had prompted their decision to allow Nancy to search for him in Zeerust.

"We are aware of the implications this might have for Nancy," they wrote. "But we encouraged her to take her chances."

Folding the letter carefully, he became aware that the ladies were standing, military-style, waiting to see what he would say or do. When he did not move, Nthabiseng spoke instead.

"*Rre* Kgabalatsana, this is the woman of your dreams, I never meant to take you away from Nancy. As things stand between us, there are other complications that still need to be resolved and maybe this gives us an opportunity to utilise the presence of Nancy to resolve those problems."

Nancy looked at Kgabalatsana in surprise.

Taking a deep breath, and with unconditional love so typical of her character, Nthabiseng continued solemnly.

"Take her, marry her and fulfill the dreams of years. She was meant for you and the rest of us were just filling the void in which you found yourself."

Nthabiseng took her jersey from the chair, took her bag and left the hotel, stepped outside and calling to a taxi as it pulled up. She climbed in, glancing once more at the surprised couple standing inside the hotel. Nthabiseng blew them a kiss and drove off.

"Please take me to Dinokana," Nthabiseng said to the driver.

The driver looked at the beautiful lady from his rear-view mirror, wondering where she came from and why Dinokana, for she did not fit the type that lives in village; she looked a typical city lady.

"Ugh! It is not for me to ask all these finicky questions; mine is to pick up and drop customers wherever they want to go and get my cash," he said to himself. But he was intrigued.

"You look tired sister, if I may say, you must be coming from afar."

He started a conversation, trying to break the ice.

"Not necessarily tired," responded Nthabiseng briefly, not in the mood to talk. The driver was disappointed, and remained quiet, much to her satisfaction, for the rest of the journey home. Shortly afterwards, he dropped her at her front gate.

***

The following morning, at a distance not far from the royal residence, all the Monare family in its entirety – Boysie, Kgabalatsana and Dikeledi - were standing on high ground near the river overlooking the beautiful land left by their father. They stood in a semi-circle, as if in a prayer meeting,holding hands in a human chain. About 50 meters away, was Nancy Mabheka, fashionably dressed in city clothes, and sticking out like a sore thumb. She was watching the Monare family assembly.

It was a day of receiving their lost child who had come back home, a lamb lost.

This was a ritual that Boysie always dreamt of, one of the ceremonies that he wished he could live to preside over. His parents missed that opportunity and unfortunately, Uncle Ntoa from Ramotswa, although he gave blessings to the event, could not come because of age and health

"So, this is the place where he was born," whispered Nancy to herself. "Now I understand his nostalgia about coming back home. It has its own beauty, in its own way. I never realised that rural villages in this part of the country were so beautiful, nor that people were so much attached to their ruralness.

"I also understand that I took him for granted, ignoring the old adage that 'you can take the man out of the village, but you cannot take the village out of the man.' He was so frustrated with life in that concrete city; the backdoor, makeshift rooms that he lived in; life in prison; losing girlfriends and always feeling hustled by Jozi life."

Though men and women would continue to flock to bigger cities, turning themselves into 'Jim Comes to Jo'burgs', when the chips were down, they would get tired of it all. And Kgabalatsana was one of those casualties, she believed.

With his hands folded on his chest, Kgabalatsana noticed Nancy standing at a distance. Dikeledi whispered to her brother-in-law and then to Boysie, and Kgabalatsana walked towards where Nancy was standing, and took her by her hand, bringing her into his human chain. Boysie smiled at his young sibling. Dikeledi ululated, the cocks crowd, sheep baaed.

"What a wonderful sight, what a spectacle; it's like an African Christmas, the house of Japheth resurrected," said Dikeledi.

"Indeed, my dear wife, this is the day I so dreamt of. Kgabalatsana told me this morning as he arrived at home, excited that his wife-to-be was in town, that the ancestors brought her home to be wedded in matrimony of her long-loved one. We talked about Nthabiseng, about Rethabiseng and his response was that Rethabiseng would always be part of the Monare family, as she is Nthabiseng's child, and that her mother has tended to her and nurtured her into the big girl she is today. That we will sort out in years to come."

They all joined hands and hugged.

Suddenly, they were disturbed by a noise in the distance. A woman dressed in white approached the Monare family, about 100 metres away, clapping hands and waving at them. It was as if she were an angel. Kgabalatsana fidgeted, trying to identify the woman. Then, he realised that it was Nthabiseng, and she had Rethabiseng beside her, holding her hand.

She noticed that the group had seen her. Smiling, she gently pulled Rethabiseng along, disappearing into the gathered crowds, as the Monare family formed a prayer circle. Nancy gripped Kgabalatsana's hand, saying, "This time I will not let you go. The mistake you committed by having left me in Hauteng is forgiven. You are mine and mine only, now, and forever, Amen."

"Yes indeed, I agree that I am yours and that you are also mine now and forever, Amen. Now I realise that there was gold in the City of Gold after all."

The bond that was built from that day between Kgabalatsana and Nancy Mabheka only strengthened. Their relationship was a passionate connection envied by all. Nancy's decision to follow Kgabalatsana back to Dinokana had been a blessing in disguise.

Together, they were united in land and love.